Something Desired
C.R. Misty

Also, by C.R. Misty

Simple Affair
Deeply Bound

Something Desired
C.R. Misty

Something Desired

C.R. Misty

Cover Design by Lady Maverick Publishing

Published by Lady Maverick Publishing

The International Boundaries Series | Book 3

Chapter 1
Nice Guys

Here we are you and me. My words on the page as you take them in, digest them and form your opinions. I am surprised and to be quite honest shocked but in another breath am thankful that you have been with me and taken the time to read a cheater's side of a story, my story. I needed to confide in you. I am a liar and an adulteress and don't deserve the life that I have. I admit that. What's the saying, nice guys always finish last? It seems that way. This world seems to be full of liars and the better you are at it; it seems the more successful you become.

Pretend, act and lie. I smile through my teeth to the onlookers, faking my supposed perfect life but I know that you see through it. All of that has gotten me everything that I have wanted, my marriage, my secret lover, my baby and my publishing deal which stemmed from a memoir of lies.

I sit here on the sofa and gaze out the window to see the light, cotton like snowflakes fall from the sky here at my home in Canada. It is weeks before Christmas and the baby is due to be born soon. I feel and look huge. My appointments with the doctor have been good. Everything is on track and they believe that this baby will come right on the scheduled time.

This past weekend my mom threw a baby shower for me. It wasn't a surprise; I knew that she would. With every woman's first born it seems to be the standard. My mom hosted the party at my new home which was great. My new place is large spacious and the bonus is I got to show everyone my new place. It was actually smart also because at the end of the day there was no need to pack up all the gifts into a car. I could just move everything up to the nursery which I was proud to show off to everyone. I invited the girls from work in addition to my mom and sister, Adrianne inviting my high school friends and the family and it was fantastic to be able to catch up with them.

Over the last bit of time, I have stayed home for the most part, taking care of myself, modeling the home to my liking, working on my writing and social media. I have been busy but life now is so much more different.

There is no need to be up before the sun rises in order to beat traffic on the way to work. There is no office politics that I need to endure. There are no pointless meetings, the kinds that senior management would have just to waste everyone's time in order to make them feel important. There is no running out of email space because you are receiving fifty a day with huge attachments. No fighting with the shredder and the office printer and no need to have to constantly defend your decisions.

I mean technically my publisher is my boss but the relationship is relaxed, everything is simple, automated. I write a book and the publisher takes care of the rest and the nice thing about my contract, is I am not bound to submit a certain quota of words or anything like that. Howard knows that writing is something that I love and he knows in time I will produce more and all I have had to do is make an appearance at a couple of events and that's it. It's perfect.

The girls from work ask me about my book and how the writing and how the promoting is going and I am honest with them, without throwing it at them that this writing career is a thousand times better than my old job with them.

Josh and I stood our ground in our decision to keep the surprise and we still don't know the sex of our child and that is okay for me because there are so little surprises in life anymore and this is one that can remain one.

The shower gifts are amazing. I received clothing which is mostly in whites' yellows and greens', neutral colors. I receive toys; supplies, gadgets and my mom got together with my sister and gave me a two in one stroller that has a built-in removable car seat.

I need to get up off the couch and walk around. Let's head to the kitchen. I need some water. Ice from the fridge dispenser clinks into my glass then I click the button to fill the glass with water, taking a seat at the island. I appreciate all that my family has done for me but to be honest, I have always hated attending baby showers and having my own thrown for me felt a little odd. I know you are thinking about the reasons why I don't like attending them but they are not for the reasons that you are thinking. Yes, I needed the help of Devon to conceive. I was never jealous or felt weird that my friends and other women in my family were having babies while I was struggling with the process and perhaps attending a baby shower was a reminder of my own failures to conceive, that's not why I hated going to them.

I always attended but the reason I hated them, was for one thing the organizer always seems to host them on a Sunday afternoon. I always wondered why not Saturday? Showers don't run into the evening they are usually hosted in the late morning and they often run no longer than 4:00pm. At least with it being on a Saturday, people can come and visit and the event won't interfere with any potential evening plans. The other thing is with having it on Sunday just sucks. I mentioned that already. It sucks because your final day off is wasted with going to someone's house and watching a pregnant person unwrap her gifts. I just want Sunday off to relax before the hustle and bustle of a new work week. Well, I don't have a typical work week anymore so I guess that doesn't matter now.

The other thing that I always hated at showers were the stupid games they would make us play like guess how big the stomach is of the soon to be mom, or guess the flavor of baby food or some sort of baby bingo. Yawn, so boring. I put my empty glass on the counter by the sink with the intent to use the glass again later.

Like I mentioned my shower wasn't a surprise and I asked to have some say in the matter. My mom and sister had organized it. I asked it to be simple, a get together of my friends and family and I asked for no stupid games and for it to be on a Saturday because I know that I can't be the only one in this world who hates doing stuff on Sunday. The other thing I asked for the party was I didn't want to be stuck un-wrapping gifts all day with everyone just watching. I wanted it arranged like a wedding, so if people brought gifts, they leave them on a table in the reception for the Bride and Groom to open on their own time. That's what I wanted, to visit with my friends and family and socialize instead of just being put to work in un-wrapping gifts.

My mom and sister came through for me and did exactly that and I think that even though this wasn't a typical baby shower, I think for everyone that attended, they enjoyed themselves

I had a catering service come in and they served all kinds of food, snacks and wine we had a gift table arranged at the entrance. Music played throughout the home and I got to catch up with everyone

As a thank you gift for everyone that attended is I had gift bags made that included my favorite scented lotions, lip gloss, eye shadows and in each bag, I gave a hundred gift card to be able to purchase books online. I wanted to add touch of me and maybe help my guests get into a great story or just simply discover a love for reading.

The evening comes to an end my mom, sister and friend Hailey stay behind after everyone has left and help me open the gifts, mark the names down of the gift givers and bring the gifts to the nursery and eventually my mom and sister head out with the caterers. I watch Adrianne and mom from my front door, get into my mom's blue sedan, circle around the drive way and watch the sedan's rear lights disappear into the woods, down the driveway that leads to the gates to the road. Not long after their departure it's just Hailey. Josh will be home in the next hour.

She admits to me, "I didn't want to say anything while everyone was here but I am pregnant!"

"Oh, congratulations" I give her a hug and I tear up, all of the estrogen that is going through me right now, I have been even more all over the place with keeping my emotions in check but that's okay because Hailey tears up also. I joke, "Why couldn't you get pregnant earlier so we could have been pregnant together."

She sighs and rolls her eyes, "Oh you know how it goes."

I do, all too well and have struggled to make this pregnancy happen and do things that I am not proud of. Trust me I don't regret doing what I did to get where I am today. What I regret is the lies and deceit that I had to do.

It is hard to explain. I love them but wish that my secrets could be more than secrets.

"How far along are you?" I ask while dabbing a happy tear from my cheek.

"Just a couple of months, it is still a little too early to announce it to everyone."

"Your secret is safe with me."

We settle in the living area for a few minutes and it's been on her mind. She asks, "So is Devon out of the picture?"

"I haven't seen him in over a month."

"That is good. How do you feel about it?"

I wonder why she asks the question and try to be as honest as possible, "I feel good. I'm focusing on the arrival of the baby." It's a half truth.

"Do you miss him?" She pries.

"I do but I know that the time apart is good." She says nothing and I feel compelled to elaborate, "Devon is a friend first and I miss the friendship. I miss talking to him every day. I miss sharing with him with all of the writing stuff."

She says, "You need to continue to keep the space from him."

"Is it wrong to miss a friend?"

"Jordan it's wrong to have feelings for another man when you are married." She gives me a disapproving glance through her blonde eyelashes.

Hailey knows me too well and I know that she is right. I have to humor her and let her believe that I am taking her advice to heart. I am, well sort of. I never told her anything else about Devon and the possibility of him being the father. Hailey doesn't need to know that or be burdened with that big of a secret. For the safety of this child, that secret will remain with me for as long as I can keep it.

With that I admit to her, "I know but it is what it is and all I can do is keep my distance and the times that I do see him I just need to keep it professional, that's all." There is no need to hash this out over and over again, you the reader have no need to hear it and you know that I live with this struggle. I change the subject, "So did you see any shower gifts that you would want me to pass over to you once mine has out grown the need for them?"

Hailey replies, "You have gotten some pretty cool things. I have kept some of Brittany's baby things so I am good for the most part. But sure, once they have outgrown things let me know and I will see if I need more when the time comes." Brittany is her little girl and this would be her second child on the way.

Our conversation is interrupted. Someone is ringing the doorbell vigorously. The only person that I know that does that is Josh. He often does that to announce his arrival and to be a goof and he does that especially when he knows that there is company over.

Hailey taps her hands in her lap as she gets up from the couch and says, "Well that's my queue I guess, that is Josh, right?"

I follow her lead and get up from my seat. I say, "I would be surprised if it was someone else. I recognize that ring." We both head to the entrance.

Chapter 2
Music

Just before Christmas is when it all happened. I don't want to get into the details of it all. It went well, Josh had taken some time off of work around my due date and it paid off. We went to the hospital together in the early hours of the morning before the morning traffic and just before lunch was when my baby girl came into this world.

She was seven and a half pounds of screaming pink little baby. Hearing her cry was music to my ears. She was healthy and strong and catching a glimpse of her before the nurse took her away, I could see that she had a full head of dark brown hair.

The nurses cleaned her up and handed her over to me after the doctor's had taken care of me and I took no hesitation, my instincts kicked in and I wasn't in the least bit worried about dropping her of anything like that. I get like that when holding other babies.

I look up at Josh who is next to me and white as a ghost. He will never admit that he was scared, nervous or worried about this entire ordeal. I look up at him as I hold her and the generally joking, confidant guy that Josh typically is, he is as quiet as can be as he looks down at the two of us.

She is no longer screaming any more. I am guessing that when she came out, she didn't find the fresh cool air of the room too appealing. I smile at the thought, she is her mother's daughter and I don't blame her, I hate the cold too. As soon as the nurses wrapped her up was when she settled down.

I have her facing Josh and she opens those newborn eyes of hers and looks up at him. I glance up at Josh for a second to see that he is still missing that color in his cheeks. Her eyes are blue. I smile down at her, I wonder, she is only moments old but it is like she is already trying to familiarize herself with us and for all those months that she could hear us while in my belly, she has this look on her face. Maybe I am imagining it but it's like she is thinking oh, so that's what you guys look like. I know it's just my imagination but that is the feeling I get with her.

Josh soon relaxes and the color comes back to him and I catch him smiling back at her as she watches him. I ask, "Do you want to hold her?"

"Maybe later" He replies in almost a whisper. A nurse in the room overhears us and she knows exactly what to do. She instructs Josh to sit down in the chair and she takes my baby girl and puts her into his cradling arms.

I lie back on the bed and watch him, nervous as can be but seeing him fall in love with her right before my eyes is something that can never be fully described. As I write this, it still brings a tear to my eye. It is like she has now become the most important thing in his life and its beautiful to see them together. She falls asleep in her daddy's arms. All that work with coming into this world has already tuckered her out.

That is okay because I could use the rest also. The last thing before I drift off is seeing Josh relaxing with her nestled in his protective arms.

Chapter 3
Fall in Love

By late afternoon my parents and Josh's parents stop in to see their grandchild and the little one is passed around for everyone to cuddle. They are quiet and the conversation is good, fun and light hearted.

My mom was so kind to stop by the home and bring some extra things. I packed one overnight bag thinking only of the baby but not really of Josh and me. My mom stopped in and brought me and Josh a change of clothes and stopped in at the drugstore to pick up some sanitary items for the both of us. She even brought me my cell phone and charger. I forgot mine in the rush to the hospital. Josh, thankfully remembered his. If it wasn't for him, our parents wouldn't have known of the birth. Sure, the hospital has phones we can use but they are of no use when you don't know the telephone numbers. That's the thing with cell phones you get used to having others contact information saved.

I watch everyone talk amongst themselves and not really paying attention to the conversation for my mind is already wondering. I want to tell Devon, send him an email or a text but I can't, not now with everyone here. Devon knows that it was going to happen at any time, well I will let him know at some point, he is my friend.

I don't mind the little one getting all of the attention that she is and I have to admit, I love seeing them all fall in love with her. The more I look at her I see myself in her and I am not sure that I see Devon in her. It is for the best, I guess. She could be Devon's daughter but the reality is that she could also be my donor's.

My dad says, "Jordan." It startles me from my day dreaming and he continues, "You are out in space kiddo. So, when are you going to decide on a name?"

I look at Josh and he gives me a shrug and I answer dad, "I have no idea what to name her."

My mom interrupts, "You guys need to decide on something before going home."

I say, "I don't think it matters if we don't name her right away."

"Well, the sooner you name her the sooner you can get her registered and covered for health." My mom knows and I hadn't really thought about the medical benefits and all of that wonderful stuff. I know that Josh and I will eventually decide on something but that something just hasn't been decided on. We had nine months and go figure we leave something like this till the last minute.

My dad says, "You're an author. You come up with character names pretty easily, there must be some that you like?"

I lean on my side while in the hospital bed, chuckle and roll my eyes at him, "Yes Dad but really all the names that I loved I have already used on my characters and now that she is here, I don't want to use my character names and then have her come back to me once she is grown, accusing me of naming her after one of my characters."

Josh's mother who is now holding our sleeping little girl suggests, "What about naming her Sara. I always loved that name and if Josh was a girl that is what I would have named him."

Josh makes a face at her, "Mom…"

She smirks knowing that she has embarrassed her son. She admits, "What, it's the truth. You would have been called Sara."

I try to not let my emotions show with that name. Sara, Devon's wife. The woman who hates me. I clear my throat trying to sound neutral, "I can't use that name, it's the name of a friend of ours."

Josh's mom says, "I am sure your friend would be flattered that you used her name."

Josh's mom has a personality that sometimes clashes with my own. Over the years I have had to work hard to build a good relationship with her because to be quite honest the only thing that we have in common is our love for Josh. I am not the only one that has struggled with her. I witnessed holiday family gatherings going wrong because of Josh's mom getting into some argument with other family members. The problem with her is that she takes no notice to reading people and if she does, she ignores it and she is one of those people that always has to be right and have the last word. Josh took that trait from her and it is one of the only things that I really hate about him.

I know her well enough to not feed into this conversation any further. My parents are here and I want their first meeting of my daughter to be a memorable one in a good way and not a family drama way. I just smile at her comment and Josh steps in.

"Jordan and I will decide later."

Josh's dad senses it and before his wife says anything more, he says, "That's a good plan. Jordan, I agree with your mom in the two of you deciding on something before you leave."

"We will. I mean I have a couple of ideas I just need to think about it some more."

Chapter 4
In the Whirlwind

Even though I have laid in my hospital bed as Josh's and my own parents have visited us, I still feel tired but I don't close my eyes. After they leave Josh and I finally get to work on naming our daughter. The nurses have taken her to the nursery and we chat in my now quiet hospital room.

I say, "You know that for the longest time I thought I was having a boy."

He shuffles in beside me on the hospital bed and asks, "Why did you think that?"

"All of that kicking, and feeling tired." I shrug.

He laughs, "Maybe she will be an athlete."

"Maybe" I reply.

Josh jumps right into it, "How about Jordana?"

"That's too close to my name. We already have enough names starting with the letters J and O. Josh, Jordan, it would be silly naming her that."

"I always liked the name."

"You always liked the name because that is the name of that actress that you have a crush on."

"Yes, yes" He rolls his eyes and continues, "So what were your thoughts about calling her Sara?"

"I do like the name, don't get me wrong but naming her the same name as Devon's wife doesn't feel right."

"She is a nice person."

Josh never found out the extent of what happened on the cruise between me and Sara. Sara never had the heart to tell him. I reply, "Yes, she is a nice person but right now with those photos that circulated I don't think she is very fond of me."

I wonder why he is hung up on that name. I think his mom has influence over him and I don't think that he was thinking about Devon's Sara but just acting on the basis that his mom as she was the one who suggested the name.

Josh says, "Okay I understand." He takes my hand into his.

I have to ask him, it has been in the back of my mind since seeing our little girl for the first time, "Josh, what you said a while back about the baby having brown eyes, did you really think that I would have crossed that line?"

We never really talked about it after that and we both sort of took the approach of getting through one day at a time until the baby's arrival. Things with us haven't been perfect since that last major fight. We just sort of let ourselves get lost in the whirlwind of our new lives. We never really settled it. Maybe because it just brought more pain, I'm not sure, maybe we both sort of wanted to forget that it happened even though the reality is it was haunting us both.

He says, "I was just tired I guess with all of the chatter at work. I mean every day you were in the newspaper for something and often it had something to do with Devon. The whisperings were getting to me at work and I guess that I was starting to believe them, that's all. I know that what you said with the timeline would not have made sense; I know that she isn't his. I just wasn't myself."

Again, I get away with keeping this secret. Maybe my donor's sperm worked and it isn't Devon's. I don't know and I am happy that Josh's doubts are ending here. I ask, "So are we okay?"

"Yes, I didn't mean to doubt you."

Hearing this from him makes me feel better about everything. I don't think that she is Devon's either. She looks like me.

Josh suggests, "I never told you about this name, how about Desiree?"

I tuck a strand of my straight brown hair behind my ear and ask, "Do you know anyone with that name?"

"No, I heard the name off of one of those crime shows that I like to watch and it's sort of stuck with me."

I like the name and ask, "How come you never told me about it for an option?"

"Jordan, come on. You know why I wouldn't have told you." He gives me a sideways glance.

"You thought I would use the name in one of my books?"

"Exactly, I know my wife way too well." He smirks and messes my hair a little.

"You got me." I comb my flyaway strands again, tucking them back behind my ears.

"So, what do you think?" Josh asks.

"I'm thinking." Desiree, it is pretty, I do like the name and say, "You know, you always surprise me."

He smiles and says, "I am not just for looks."

I chuckle, "Oh Josh, yes you are right."

"Are we decided yet?"

I ask, "Do you have any more options?"

He starts giggling and so do I. We are both beyond tired and finally he says, "That's the only suggestion I have."

"Well, I love the name."

"Me too, and you know what?"

I ask, "What?"

"The name also has a really nice meaning. It means desired."

I smile, "She was desired, and I wanted her for a long time." I say allowed, "Desiree Connor" There couldn't have been a better name for her, I had been waiting for her for a long time.

Josh smiles and says, "It sounds good. Her nickname would be Des."

We agree on it and finally I tell Josh, "You should go home and get some rest."

"What if I don't want to leave you?" He is still lying beside me in my hospital bed keeping me warm.

"Oh, don't be silly. I rather you go home and relax in a nice warm bed instead of that hospital chair and you can come visit us in the morning." I glance over at the outdated nineties pastel pink chair in the corner.

I twist his arm and finally he heads out. It is for the best. I rather one of us be fully rested than having the two of us being tired when we all get the okay to check out of the hospital.

It is getting to that time where I need to go feed her and before I head over to the nursery, I pick my phone up and message Devon to say, "She was born just before noon today. Her name is Desiree." I click send.

It is late when I get around to sending Devon the text and I don't expect a reply back from him to be received until tomorrow but just as I get out of bed and put on some pajama pants before heading down the nursery his reply flashes on my screen.

He writes, "Congratulations Jordan, that is wonderful news and you two picked a great name. How are you doing?"

I pause standing beside the hospital bed, picking up my phone again and replying, "I am good, sore, but having her here was totally worth it."

He sends me a smile face and writes, "I can't wait to see her. Well, I guess that you are about to head to bed soon given the time."

"Something like that; I had Josh and my parents over to visit earlier and Josh left for home to go get some rest and I am about to head to the nursery to feed her."

"Okay, I will leave you be. Have a good night and give her a kiss for me."

"I will good night, Devon."

Chapter 5
A Text to Devon

Today was alright, I did the usual, a bit of work, a bit of writing and a bit of helping Sara with her honey do list at the end of the day.

It's late in the evening and I find myself on the couch relaxing beside Sara as she is totally wrapped up in her medical series show. Things have not been the greatest between us but today has been decent. I'm not really into her show but I watch it with her because it seems to make her happy.

Every day seems to get a little better with her. I glance at her while she watches her show and get the feeling of how things were before the cruise. Sara seems like she is okay. I mean she seems a little less pissed off at me. I hope we can get back to that point. I know it will take a while.

My phone vibrates in my pocket and I just know it has to be Jordan. I haven't heard from her all day. I glance over at Sara who has not taken notice to the vibrating noise of my phone. I decide that it is safe and I get up from my spot.

Sara asks, "Are you heading upstairs?"

I say, "Yes, I need to go to the bathroom then get a drink. I'll be back down in a few."

She regards me for a moment, as though she is trying to scan me with her eyes to see if I am being honest with her but that look to her leaves her eyes as mine meets hers. It is like she is consciously trying to hide her doubts from me. I don't react to it. Her efforts to try to keep her doubts concealed, I take as a sign that she wants this good streak that we are on to last.

She asks, "Can you bring me down a light beer?"

I nod and head upstairs, taking my phone out of my pocket once I am at the top of the stairs and out of sight. I glance at the screen, it is Jordan, just as I had thought and my momentum of walking to the restroom comes to a grinding halt as I process the message on the screen. She has had the baby. I knew it was going to happen soon but without warning it has happened, she is here, her little girl. A picture of the newborn flashes up on my screen.

She is beautiful, wow I don't know what to say except some congratulations message to her, I press send but know that it doesn't truly convey how I feel without actually being there. Our conversation is short as I know Jordan is tired and messaged me as a courtesy. We say goodbye and I just forgot what I was doing. Oh yah, ugh, washroom and Sara wants a beer.

I return to my spot next to Sara with her beer in hand. She takes the bottle, glances at it then back at me.

I ask, "What?"

"You brought be down one of your beers."

"I'm sorry, your right. You wanted a light beer."

She says, "It is okay I can drink yours if you don't mind."

I get up again and extend my arm to offer to take the beer back, "It's okay, I don't mind, it's my fault, I can go get a light one for you."

She hands the beer and I head upstairs.

Chapter 6
Into the Cool Winter Air

The next day after lunch hour Desiree and I get the approval from the doctor to go home. Josh meets us promptly with the SUV at the front door of the hospital ready to go.

It is a nice surprise that there is no one from the media to meet us on the front steps. Nobody tipped them off and these last couple of months I have remained out of the public and the nice thing is that the media has lost interest in the supposed scandals and have moved on to other gossip. I don't mean to sound conceded but with other celebrity gossip the media usually follows births but who knows maybe this attention is all going to my head and I am not as popular as I had thought. Anyway, I am just happy that there is no media here.

I place her in the car seat and sit with her in the back of our SUV. The drive home felt like the longest drive in the world. I glance at the land marks to gauge how far away we are from home. I think Josh is driving slower than he normally goes. I won't ask, I understand why but, in another breath, I am anxious to show Desiree her home, her room, her things. I know it doesn't make sense and I know she will never remember this day but I will and I can't wait to have her home safe and sound where she belongs.

Before the fame and the riches, we had purchased this SUV so it is still pretty new. We have started to enjoy the money coming in but we have also been smart with our spending. We needed the new home, mainly for the security and for the privacy but as for our cars we have yet to upgrade them. They are not extravagant; they are just modern nice cars and to be honest I love my SUV.

Desiree is just a little sweetheart. I catch her looking at me as we drive and I let her grip my finger and it's not long after, her eyes close and she is fast asleep.

I can tell that Josh is nervous because he isn't speeding so much and is very gentle with pressing too suddenly on the brakes. He glances into the rear-view mirror at me and asks, "How is she?"

I speak to his reflected eyes in the mirror and say, "Asleep again."

He says, "I wish I could fall asleep that easily."

I laugh at him and say, "You do."

"No, I don't!"

"Yes, you do, your head hits the pillow and you are snoring within moments."

He looks into the rear-view mirror back at me and sees my smile and replies "Sure Jordan" making sure that I see his reflection rolling his eyes at me.

It is true Josh sleeps like a baby while I toss and turn, struggling to fall asleep. Well, I can't say that I struggle as much anymore. Since I quit my job, I stress less and do sleep easier although sometimes social media keeps me distracted in the later hours of the night, but looking at social media is a choice when struggling with stress wasn't.

We pull into our snowy drive and Josh keys in the security code for our gait and we move forward with the sound of the SUV's tires making crunching sounds as they roll over the crisp snow.

This home of ours is just starting to feel like home and not just some super fancy hotel that we have been staying at and having Desiree here with us just makes that feeling stronger that this is where I belong, here and with her and Josh.

She starts to cry as we emerge from the car into the cool winter air and we are quick to get into the home. We have already gotten snow and this year will be a white Christmas.

"Ah baby girl it's okay, I know I hate the cold too." I set her carrier down on the tiled floor and quickly remove my coat and Josh does the same.

He asks, "Why do you think she is crying?"

"I'm not sure? Could be the cold or a diaper changing or feeding."

I pick her up and know. "It's her diaper."

I say to her, "Baby girl you are as stinky as your daddy."

Josh snaps back, "Hey, I think she takes after her mom in that department."

I take her up to the nursery and get her cleaned up on the change table. To my surprise Josh comes up to watch and I ask him, "Do you want to help?"

He shakes his head, "I think that you have it all under control." I roll my eyes at him.

I have changed diapers before when I was a teenager but I am out of practice and the tricky thing is keeping the heels of her tiny feet out of the mess. I put her into a fresh new sleeper.

The Christmas tree is lit up in our living room and I just sink into one of our recliners with Desiree in my arms. Josh does the same.

He asks, "So, what now?"

I laugh at him and say, "Oh I don't know." These last couple of days have been something else and now it's like everything is about Desiree and that is okay. I had things on my mind but with this new little girl around I had forgotten and now they are just popping up again.

I say to Josh, "I wanted to ask you something for a while but I kept forgetting. I just want you to know that I am not trying to start an argument it's just conversation, that's all."

"So go ahead." He says, still relaxing in the recliner.

"Well, I am happy that you stopped working your part time job but what about your day job? I know it is good money but really you no longer need to work."

He sighs, "I know but it's not something I am ready to give up yet."

"Why?"

"Oh, I don't know, I guess that I like the people I work with and the work that I do."

"When you head back to work you will miss out on Desiree."

He sighs again and I know that he doesn't want to talk about it. I continue, "Hey you know what? This isn't something that you need to decide on right now, it's up to you but maybe if you don't want to let go of your job just yet you can take like a leave without pay or something and that way you don't need to head back to work in February."

I see him relax a bit. I know that he likes his job and he says, "Yes that is an option. I can find out more and see if that is something my boss will let me do."

I smile that's the most I can ask of him. I know I can't push too much with rebuilding our marriage.

I ask, "So changing subjects did we get all of our Christmas shopping done?"

He starts laughing, "You are kidding right? We still have our parents, each other and my niece."

I sigh, "We should get something for them soon. What were your thoughts?"

"You know, my mom probably wants some gift card to a clothing store, my dad likely has a specific tool in mind as for our niece, I think she wanted some brand name items."

"For my parents I have no idea. Well actually that's not true. I know it is the middle of winter but I was thinking of combining their gift and getting them a screened gazebo for their camper."

Josh smiles, "That is good."

"I know we talked about it before and we will keep the gifts reasonable to not up show anyone but I was thinking of maybe giving everyone an invitation to come vacation with us in Fiji in March?" I know that this doesn't make complete sense and I am totally contradicting my statement of not up showing anyone with the gift exchange but in my head giving an invitation versus actually giving a gift is different.

"Who would you invite?" Josh asks.

"Both of our parents my brother and sister and your sister and her family. I figure we could do a formal invitation at Christmas and that gives them time to get their passports ready if they aren't already."

"I think that's a good plan. What about Howard Stem?"

"Oh, he already knows that March is for me. He doesn't seem to have any events going on until the end of April anyway and even that I can decline if I needed to."

"Well, you are the boss." He speaks.

I chuckle, "Wow I don't think that I have ever heard you admit to that."

"Oh, don't get used to it." He smirks.

"So, when do we get their gifts?"

"Well, you have already forgotten. The nurses said to take it easy for the next month so tomorrow I can go and get it done while you stay home. I just need a list."

"Okay well, your siblings are done and so is my sister. Our niece, get a gift card to that store she likes.

There is no sense in picking something out for her only to have her return it. Your mom does the same, she likes to shop, so pick up a gift card to her favorite department store. Your dad, get him a nice power tool and my parents pick up a gazebo. Maybe try to do beige to avoid the fading of the sun and try to go with a 12 foot one."

"Do you need wrapping paper and cards and stuff?"

"Yes, actually I haven't seen our crafts stuff since we moved. Pick up some rolls of wrapping paper, tape and Christmas cards."

He asks me, "Should we get each other a gift?"

I smile and say, "Sure but what I had in mind I think that you wouldn't want it to be a surprise."

Josh asks, "You are getting us a 4-wheeler, aren't you?"

"You will need to wait and see."

"So do I get something for you to open?"

"No, what I am getting will be a gift to the both of us and besides you are on board with going to Fiji and that makes me happy." Josh prefers to be a home body.

Desiree starts to nudge and fuss and I know that it is time to feed.

Chapter 7
Go From There

In the seven years that I have been married to Josh and have owned a home, this is the first year that we are actually hosting Christmas. Well sort of my mom and mother-in-law have taken care of organizing Christmas dinner at our home. In the days leading up to the big day Josh and I have decorated our home in the spirit of the holidays, white lights, vanilla candles. Stuffed snowmen, a nativity scene. A Christmas tree in the living room and wreath on the front door of our home. Josh even made a special trip to the hardware store to buy extra decorations because our home is much larger than our other home.

I am starting to get my strength back and enjoy the activity and Desiree is a good little baby and is often not far, just lying in her baby rocker either watching us or sleeping.

Truth be told I haven't talked to Devon since the brief text when I told him the Desiree was born. I don't even know what his plans are for Christmas. For all I know he could be visiting his brother and his family in upstate New York, which would mean that he is just a few hours away of driving from me. I curl up on our new plush corduroy couch and decide to send him some texts.

As a matter of fact, I can't believe how awful I have been in that I didn't event show him a picture of Desiree. I send him a message, "Hey Mister, wishing you and your family happy holidays and I meant to share with you earlier but I guess you know how it goes with being a new parent."

The next text is a picture of Desiree, just that cute little chubby cheeked girl, with her dark brown straight hair and those blue eyes that are barely open. I send it to him and see something in her that I hadn't noticed before, the shape of her eyes aren't mine but the color is. I don't know if my donor had a different shape then my own but the shape of her eyes look like Devon's, well a mix of our eyes.

He responds within seconds with a smiley face then he types, "Ain't she something. Wow she is beautiful Jordan."

"Thank you."

He continues to write, "I can't get over how much she looks like my brother's kids when they were that age."

He is convinced and I don't know if I am yet to be honest. I say to him, "Do you see yourself in her?"

There is a moment of pause before the response comes in, "It's hard to tell. She is still a newborn but I'm not going to lie she does look identical of my brother's children when they were newborns."

"She is such a good little baby Devon. I meant to message you sooner but life sort of got in the way."

He says, "That's okay, I rather you take all the time that you need to take care of that little angel."

I send him a smile and say, "So, what are your plans for the holidays?"

"Well, Sara wanted to visit her family near New Jersey and I am actually texting you from my brother's home in upstate New York."

"You are so close. You know, if you wanted to come a little further and visit you are more than welcome and Sara is invited too." Sara never really forgave me and I don't blame her. She seems to be working towards forgiveness with Devon and that's okay and her and Josh continue to get along good. Just because I and her clash doesn't mean that I will deny her from visiting with Devon and getting to catch up with Josh.

"Let me see what I can do. Sara is in New Jersey for a few weeks so it would just be me if I did go. Let me get back to you on that."

"Sure, I just want to say that I meant to share with you sooner and don't feel like you need an invitation. Whenever you want to just send a message to me and we can go from there."

"Thanks Jordan, I really appreciate that and wow she is a beautiful little thing. Well, I have to go for now and we can talk later."

"Okay bye Devon."

Chapter 8
The World is Quiet

Christmas morning is something that I never pictured quite like this. I had always wanted a child and with the struggle to have Desiree the focus for me in that time was basically to save money for the procedure, track my cycle and relax. During that time, I never visualized a Christmas morning with a baby or even with a newborn for that matter.

Josh and I tend to normally wake at an early hour and to keep things as simple as possible I had been keeping Desiree in our bed at night just because it was so easy just to breast feed her and she seems to sleep better next to a warm body. So just after 7:00 AM Josh is the first to wake and I wake to his bustling around in the master bathroom, the lights of the bathroom reflect onto the floor of our bedroom. I slowly open my eyes to adjust to the light and my little girl is awake and just relaxing next to me. She watches me with her eyes watching my expressions and I smile at my little sweetheart.

Josh comes out of the washroom and notices that I am up. He whispers, "Is she awake?"

"Yes, she is just waiting for mummy to get up." I give her a cuddle and play with her tiny hand. He climbs back into bed which he rarely ever does after getting up and nuzzles up to give her a cuddle too.

She doesn't really do much at this stage just looks and focuses on us as we smile at her.

Josh lays back for a second and says, "This is a nice feeling."

I laugh at him and Desiree looks my way to detect the noise and I say to Josh, "You must be over tired."

"Maybe I am, but we couldn't have it be more perfect. Look at her, look at our lives and all of this. I may be sleep deprived but what we have now I would be satisfied with for my entire life."

"What did you do with my husband?" I say to him playfully. It is nice to have him be in good spirits.

He rolls his eyes and replies, "You are a nut."

"Well, if I am a nut, should I take back the gift that I got you that is hidden in the barn?"

He is surprised, "You got me something?"

"I did and don't act surprised. We already talked about it."

"That's funny because I was just in the barn two days ago."

"Were you snooping around?"

"Maybe." He grins.

I admit, "While you were out yesterday was when I had it brought in."

"What is it?"

"Ah ah, you have to go see for yourself."

He huffs, "Whatever" He pretends that the surprise isn't killing him in anticipation but I know him too well and know that he is excited. I watch him get up; he is in nothing but boxer briefs. He walks over to his dresser, takes out a sweater, some pajama pants and socks and dresses.

I pick up Desiree, give her a smell and she seems good, no diaper change needed and follow Josh's lead with putting on some clothes.

The windows in our living area give us a view of the snow-covered fields and empty paddocks and barn. The previous owners had horses and the barn was one of those kinds of buildings where they had made half the section for the horses and the other half was more like a garage to keep, a lawn tractor, maybe a couple of cars and a 4-wheeler.

I hold Desiree and day dream for the moment, visualizing us out back with a couple of horses. Maybe in the spring I will look for a horse for my own, I don't know, I'll have to see if I can manage it.

I thought Josh may have come down to the family room first but he isn't here and I follow the noise of him moving around, down our hallway and find myself at the front door entrance.

I ask, "Are you going to see your gift?"

He rolls his eyes, it's all an act and says, "Well, you aren't going to tell me?"

I laugh and roll my own eyes at him, "It's a surprise. Wait a few minutes, I want to come with you. Help me with Desiree?"

We stuff her into her cream, teddy bear eared snowsuit and I through on some snow pants and a winter coat because I have no idea how long this will take. Josh hands me a hat, mitts and a scarf and I wrap the little scarf around the hood of Desiree's coat.

The air is crisp and the world is quiet. In the winter you don't get the singing of birds with their morning songs. Usually there is a breeze but this morning all is still. I am sure that if we shouted out, the sound would be clear and it feels like the world is listening.

We walk around the back to the barn and each step we take is accompanied by the snow crunching beneath our boots.

In we go and I have Desiree in one of those things that allow her to rest on my stomach but allows my hands to be free and I open the barn door.

His gift is in the center of the garage portion, purposely parked on an angle so that all of the curves and edges can be seen well sort of, I had the deliverers drape a huge white tarp over it and stick a big red bow on it.

Josh skips over and there is no hesitation. He just pulls the tarp off to reveal a two-seater, black Arctic cat all-terrain vehicle.

He glances back at me to share in his excitement. There is no more rolling of the eyes theatrics he gushes, "Jordan, I can't believe you!" He circles the machine and says, "This is the very model that I wanted. I can't believe that you remembered!"

I chuckle, "Babes, I am not just for looks."

"No, you're not. Thanks so much!" He comes over and gives me a kiss and asks while holding me in his arms with Desiree nestled between us, "Did you buy yourself one?"

"No, I figured I would buy the two-seater so that I could ride along with you. Maybe when Desiree is old enough to ride, we can look at getting a second one."

"That makes sense." He is not disappointed.

"Why don't you start it up?" I walk over to the door and press the button that opens the garage door than hand him a key."

"Want to get on back?"

I shake my head, "Go ahead I'll watch."

He smiles and says, "I'll go easy, don't worry about Desiree, I'll drive nice and slow."

I chuckle "No, I have seen how you drive."

He doesn't take it for an answer and picks us both up and puts us in the back seat.

He says, "We can go up the driveway and check the mail."

"Okay." I let out a forced sigh but truthfully, I am just as excited as he is to go on the first ride.

He gets on in front and starts up the four-wheeler. It's got a smooth deep hum of a new toy that needs to be broken in. The seats are comfortable but the cushions are stiff and new but it's okay for this ride because I do have my snow pants on.

Josh asks, "Are you two ready?"

"Yes"

He goes slowly down the driveway and through the path of trees that leads to our home. Our driveway is long and the house can't be seen from the road with the privacy of the evergreen trees. It bends to the left slightly and leads to our gaited entrance. Josh needs to put the machine in park for a moment to hop off and hit the key code and the black iron gate swings open.

The machine glides to the road and he takes a left down the street. The machine speeds up but it's not so fast that it would make me tap his shoulder to slow down and I tilt my chin down and Desiree's little eyes are observing all of the movement as we go.

The paved country road has a couple other homes like our own where the driveway is gated. Some homes you can see from the road and others you can't. The ones you can see are magnificent, brick homes some looking simply traditional but grand other are dynamic looking with the different layers and shapes. I haven't really seen any of our neighbors we have only been here for a short time and besides having the baby and having the cold whether keeps people inside. The only opportunity I think that Josh or I would have would be meeting them at the mailboxes at the end of the street which Josh takes us to and he puts his toy in park.

He fishes into his coat pocket to take out his keys and checks our mailbox, thankfully there are no bills. I know that thought sounds weird coming me but some things never change, whether you have lots of money of not, getting a bill is never a good feeling.

Josh pulls out three Christmas cards and tucks them in an inside pocket of his jacket and hops back on.

"Are you to ready to head back."

"Yes"

Desiree's first Christmas and first four-wheeler ride. I wonder if she will come to love going out on the ATV as much as Josh does or maybe come to love some of the things that I do, like writing or horses. Anyway, that is my mind wondering.

Soon enough we are back at the entrance gate and driving back up to the house. Josh lets us off before driving his Christmas gift back to the barn.

Coming back into the home I hear the phone ringing and answer immediately, "Hello?"

"Jordan?"

"Hey it's dad, Merry Christmas"

"Merry Christmas. What time are you and Mom coming over?"

"We are aiming for 11:00 AM. Your mom has the turkey all ready to go. Make sure you have your oven ready to go." I hear my mom's voice saying something in the background and dad pauses a moment to listen and then speaks to me, "She wants to know if you need her to bring any platters and she made a double chocolate cheese cake and is asking if you have a cake tray?"

"I have dishes but tell her to bring just in case because Josh's mom is also bringing a few things so I'm not sure where we are at for dishes."

"Okay see you later." Dad says.

"Okay bye Dad."

Josh comes into the house and looks surprised, "You two don't even have your jackets off yet."

"No, my dad just called and said that he and mom should be here for 11:00 AM. When are your parents coming?"

Before Josh has a chance to answer, the telephone rings again. This time Josh answers, "Hello?"

I listen as I get Desiree and myself out of our winter attire.

Josh speaks to the person on the other end, "Yes, yes Desiree is up. No, I didn't give her my gift yet. No, neither Desiree. I'll show you when you get here. What? Okay, I'll buzz you in. Is the gait opening? Okay see you in a moment."

He puts the phone down while I eagerly wait for his response, "My parents are here now."

It's only just before 9am, and we are all still in our pajamas. I know they are anxious to see Desiree and get things ready for today but wow I wish I had just a bit more time alone with my husband and daughter before everyone else arrives.

I say, "okay"

"Stay inside. I'll go meet them and direct them where to park." Josh still has his jacket on.

"Wait"

"What?" He asks.

"Pass me the mail in your jacket."

He hands me the 3 Christmas cards and I return to the living area to have a look and give Desiree a quick breast feeding.

The first card is from Hailey and her family. She has a family portrait of her husband, daughter and herself in front of the fireplace at their home. The card is wishing us season's greetings from her family to ours.

The second is a store-bought card with a winter landscape scene and I open it and reveals that it is from my mom and dad wishing Desiree a happy first Christmas and seasons greeting to all 3 of us. The last car of the 3, I don't recognize the hand writing but know right away who it's from by the return address. The card reads from our family to yours have a very Merry Christmas Desiree, Josh and Jordan and all the best in the new year, love Sara and Devon.

I am kind of surprised that Sara sent us the card. It's her handwriting. I would have recognized Devon's.

I have my phone in my pajama pocket and send a quick thank you to Hailey, and I will see my mom and dad soon to thank them and as for Devon and Sara, I am not even sure that Devon knew Sara had sent the card out.

I send a friendly text to Devon, "Hi I just wanted to say Merry Christmas and thank you for the Christmas card, we received it this morning."

Devon responds within a moment, "Merry Christmas and you are welcome. Sara is in the habit of sending out Christmas cards."

"I thought Sara hated me?"

"She was angry at the both of us but she is getting better with me and I think this is her way of getting passed it. She isn't about to be your friend but the truth is that she isn't going to turn her back on Josh and she knows that you and I have careers where we will meet fairly regularly."

"I understand. So, any updates on if you will be making the trip over?"

"The plans are still up in the air. I want to but just have to see."

"Okay well have a Merry Christmas and thinking about you."

"Yes, you too. Bye babe."

I put my phone away just as the door opens and our company comes trudging through. My mother-in-law with a dish of food in hand and my father-in-law and husband carrying wrapped gifts."

She yells with her booming voice, "Jordan? Where is my grandchild?"

"We are just in the living room having a feeding." My raised voice upsets Desiree and she fuses a bit. I carefully put her on my second breast. She settles down again as I rub her bottom while she feeds.

My mother-in-law shouts again, "Where do you want the potatoes and carrots stored?" I sigh,

sometimes she just doesn't catch on that shouting isn't always the best. I try to wave her over to not startle Desiree. Josh sees that I'm busy when he comes into the room to lay the gifts under the tree.

I whisper to him, "I can't really get up can you help her out?"

He nods and goes back to the entrance and I hear him say, "Mom give me those."

She fuses "Well if we are having any for lunch they should be left out on the counter."

"Mom just go away. I got it."

"Josh!"

"Mom there are some more gift at the entrance. Go put them under the tree."

His mom makes my heart race at times. She is like a horse with its blinkers on and only focuses on what's immediately ahead of her and paying attention to nothing else or no one else.

His dad comes to the living area and I have a blanket draped over myself and Desiree. He says, "Good morning and Merry Christmas. We can hug later." He sits on a recliner adjacent from us and Josh's mom walks in fussing on where to place the gifts."

"Sheila, what are you doing?" Josh's dad asks.

Sheila, kneels down in front of the tree but instead of adding the new gifts under the tree, she is taking the gifts that are already placed under the tree and pulling them out from under it, undoing my own efforts from earlier.

She answers him, "We had a couple of Josh's gifts piled together and I wanted to spread them out evenly."

He rolls his eyes, "Honey, just place the gifts down. Who cares?"

Still kneeling in front of the tree she turns to face him and replies, "I do Ted!" Sheila refocuses on her gift placement as Ted gives up on her and says to me, "So I gather that Josh has seen his gift already?"

I smile and answer, "Yes that was what we did this morning." I had told Josh's father, Ted at some point that Josh was getting a 4-wheeler.

"How does it run?"

"Great, he took Desiree and Me for a little ride this morning to the mailbox at the end of the road. It's a comfortable ride."

He nods and says, "That's great so how did the little on like her first four-wheeler ride?"

I glance down at her for a moment, smile and say, "Oh she didn't mind. I think she was trying to focus on all the things in her vision. She was a good little girl and didn't fuss one bit."

Sheila suddenly tunes in to our discussion, "You guys took my grand baby out 4 wheeling?"

"Yes, just up the street Grandma." I answer.

"Did you put a helmet on her?"

Josh comes in from having been in the kitchen, "Mom what is your deal today? Yes, we went for a ride and no we didn't have helmets. I was careful and drove slow and she was in one of those carriers that strap around Jordan's body."

"Oh Josh!"

"Don't oh Josh me, oh mother, just settle down its Christmas morning."

I bit my lip. Ted whispers to me while mother and son are arguing, "You know Sheila. When she doesn't get enough sleep, she gets like this."

I whisper back, "Yes I am used to it. Well, if she needs to take a nap later on in the day we will understand."

Ted murmurs, "I let her know subtly and make it seem as though it was her idea. You know how much she likes being told what to do." He winks at me and I smirk.

Desiree has finished feeding and I gently burp her and take a smell, no diaper change yet but soon enough I'll have to give her one.

Sheila comes over and sits next to me and says to Desiree, "Ah come here baby girl." Taking her from me. As much as my mother-in-law can be at times very difficult to be around with her odd habits of worrying about the littlest things there is one thing that she excels in and that is her unconditional love for her son and now her grandchild. She is wonderful with babies and within moments Desiree falls back to sleep in Sheila's arms. I guess that the fresh air and feeding has tuckered her out for now.

Ted, Sheila, Josh and I talk all morning and catch up and Josh eventually gives me my present. "Josh, you didn't have to. You gave me that gorgeous ring on the cruise I don't need anything else."

He smiles, "Don't be silly, I wanted to."

He hands me a wrapped box. It is a little over a foot in size I have a look at it, hesitating, he says, "go on."

I carefully remove the shiny red wrapping paper and know instantly what it is, the lap top that I had been wanting to get myself for a long time. I wanted it even before the publishing contract. The thing is that compared to its competitors it was priced a couple thousand dollars more and because of that I put it off and now with the publishing contract and having a baby the thought of getting it had taken a back seat.

Josh asks, "Do you like it?"

"I love it! Oh my god thank you!"

"I thought that you would. It's the most reliable system out there and all of your components are built in. You can work on your writing, do photo editing, video chat for when you are away from home and store everything that you need."

"Thank you!" I give him a hug and kiss and ask the important question, "Have you set it up yet?"

He admits, "Remember when I was out yesterday and you had my four-wheeler delivered?"

I giggle, "Yes, I remember."

"Well, I picked it up while I was out and while you were being sneaky."

"Yes dear." I hug him again.

I glance at the box and Josh says, "I can help you set it up later if you want."

"That's would be great thanks."

"That's what I do." He winks at me with those flirty blue eyes of his. Right now, he is reminding me of when we first started dating because he has that happy care free look to him.

Ted asks, "So are you going to unwrap the rest of those gifts?"

Josh says, "Do you want us to do that now or later tonight?"

Ted shrugs, "Now is good."

Chapter 9
Open My Card

After the morning gift exchange with Josh's parents the phone rings and the gait to the driveway is opened with the press of a button from here inside our home, to let my mom and dad in.

I say to Sheila as she still has Desiree in her arms, "She must be ready for a diaper change."

Sheila smiles and says to Desiree with a baby talk voice, "Did you pee pee on grandma?" Sheila answers me, "I can change her. Go see your mom and dad."

"Thanks" I lift myself from the comfy couch.

My parents come in without a knock they just open the door with dishes of food in hand. Josh puts a jacket and boots on to help my dad bring in more stuff from the car and Ted joins them with the intent that his son will bring him to the barn to show him the new four-wheeler after helping bring in all their stuff.

My mom says while leaning in to hug me, "Merry Christmas sweetie. Where is Desiree?"

"In the nursery with Grandma Sheila getting a diaper change."

Dad comes in with the turkey and hands it off to me before going back out to the car and Josh and Ted come in and leave some boxes and a guitar case at the door.

I set the turkey on the counter alongside some of Sheila's dishes. Mom follows and adds her chips, salsa, a cheese ball and box of chocolates to the remaining space on the counter.

Once I have my hands free of food dishes I say, "Mom, Josh and I purchased snacks the fact that you brought the turkey was more than enough."

She knew I would comment and just shrugs it off, saying, "Whatever we don't eat, we will take home. It's better to have more than not enough."

"True" We are going to have so many leftovers.

Sheila joins us in the kitchen with Desiree in hand and my mom goes to greet them with arms open to scoop up her grandchild. Sheila passes Desiree off to my mom.

Sheila asks me, "Where are the boys?"

I reply, "Oh just outside. I think Josh is showing them his Christmas gift."

The phone rings again and I buzz my sister, Adrianne and her boyfriend through the front gate. As the rest of the day passes, more arrive. My brother, Ethan and his girlfriend and Josh's sister, Emma and her family. This is nice and surprisingly easy.

I don't know why Josh and I never volunteered to do Christmas before now. Besides being in a bigger home this year our old home would have been just fine to accommodate the crowed. It's sort of like a Christmas potluck with all the guests arriving with food to eat and the perk is we don't have to drive anywhere on Christmas Day.

I'm not going to bore you much more with the day. I mean it's a typical Christmas Day with plenty of company, conversation, a wonderful Christmas dinner and the rest of the gifts that the family brought are exchanged.

After everyone has settled and the gifts are exchanged, I give Josh the nod and he returns with cards that I had put together for everyone. Josh, loudly and obnoxiously clears his throat, what a goof but it gets everyone's attention and the room gets quiet. Josh explains, "Jordan and I have these cards for you and I ask that you open them now."

My dad teases, "What if I want to open my card later?" Giggles erupt in the room.

I say to Dad, "We want you all to open the cards at the same time because it's all the same."

Adrianne asks, "Is this a gift?"

I say, "You will see."

Josh gives a card to everyone and says, "Open them!"

The room goes quiet with the exception of envelopes opening and then the first to say something is Josh's mom, "Guys, you don't need to do this."

Josh explains, "We wanted to. I know not all of you like to travel but Jordan has always wanted to and with being on the cruise earlier this year with others that we knew we wanted to have you all come."

I say, "I had a blast on the cruise and would love to have my family come. The experience is far better with people that you know. The trip is still a few months away so if you want to come, you have time to get your passports and yourselves travel ready."

My mom is grinning from ear to ear as she glances at my dad. The two of them rarely travel because of family and my dad is not keen on the actual travel part, but the look that she is giving him and his reaction looks as though they will accept the invitation."

My brother asks, "So, this isn't a joke, right?"

I chuckle, "Nope, you are all invited to come to Fiji with us."

My dad says to him, "The joke is that she is inviting you so that she has you as a babysitter."

I say, "Yes that is exactly it. You can watch Desiree while I sun tan on the beach." I chuckle.

The invite seems to be taken well and the conversation in the room is now all about everyone planning it out with booking time off and who is driving with who to the airport for when the time comes, what vaccines we need, how long the flight is and overall, the general consensus is everyone is going to try their best to attend.

Soon enough Christmas is over for another year and eventually everyone heads home. Josh is holding Desiree after taking her from his mom's arms and we finally lock up.

I say, "She looks so much smaller in Daddy's arms."

"She is a little sleeping machine"

"Does she need to be changed?"

"No, my mom changed her when you were cleaning up in the kitchen."

The house is as clean as it's going to get tonight. The left overs are put away, the dishwasher is running, the gifts that have been un-wrapped are neatly tucked under the tree waiting to be put away in the morning and I am zonked and so is Josh.

Josh asks, "Do you want to try and have her sleep in the nursery tonight? I mean if she wakes in the night, you can bring her back to our bed. You know we'll just have her start to get comfortable with sleeping in her bed?"

To be honest it has been so much easier just having her sleep next to me but tonight I feel like Josh needs this time and I reluctantly tuck her in her own bed.

It's been a few weeks since having her and things are still pretty sore. I know I am healing because every day I feel better but I guess with the change in pace of caring for a newborn the energy level is low.

We crawl into our bed and cuddle. Between the two of us, I am usually the one asking for it but I guess with just over three weeks, Josh is getting eager, so much so that he cuddles and kisses and makes it known by poking me in the leg that he is standing tall.

I giggle, "That isn't subtle."

"He needs some love." He smiles with those determined blue eyes of his.

I know that I'm not ready or interested in being touched where I am still tender so instead, I direct him to lie back and feel his length with my lips and tongue. He is swollen hard and swollen tall and he is warm to the touch. I kiss his tip and lick and slowly take him in and go after his balls grabbing and squeezing them gently. I drool over his shaft and jerk him firmly with my hand. I play with him hard and have to slow down because his breathing tells me that he is close and we have only just begun.

His hands try to reach for my sex, while my back is to him and I am resting against his side as I go down on him. I carefully try to lead his hands away but he manages to grab me there touch me, he feels my wetness and says, "Are you sure you don't want to, you are soaked."

"This is just about you tonight." I take him back in my mouth knowing full well he is ready to explode and it makes me horny, makes me want to and shows me that my drive is still very much alive. This is the first time that I wanted it since having Desiree.

He says, "Let me up."

I take his order by surprise and ask him, "Don't you want to come?"

"I do and I will let me up."

He takes me firm in his grasp and lays me down. I crave it but know that it will hurt. All he does is give me the look and I lay on my back so he gets on top, pins me down. He is careful of me but greedy too and as I lie between his legs, he jerks off over me. His breathing is controlled and heavy, then he closes his eyes and it pulses out, hot warm white lava, onto my chest and stomach.

I smile seeing my man's satisfaction and his body relaxes as it is all emptied out. I touch his cream with my fingers and lick them clean. He grins then dismounts and goes to put his briefs on and climbs into bed for the night.

Chapter 10
Food and Comfort

Boxing Day arrives and it's a quiet day at our home, well sort of quiet in that there is no dinner scheduled or anything except for mine and Josh's parents stopping in to visit.

Josh takes some time today to set up my new laptop and walks me through how it works. I love it. I love the fact that it's so secure. I like the fact that the design is sleek and I like how fast it is and how it is compatible with my phone.

Our office is very cool, I haven't really explained the layout. The room faces the back of our property overlooking the field and the barn. The room sort of has the feel of sitting high in a loft and also has the feel of a spacious room because the ceiling is raised and all of the windows that line the round shape of it give the open feeling because of the panoramic view of the property. In reality it is a cozier space and has enough room to fully accommodate an office for one. There is a large table top that serves as desk space that is built into the outer wall of the room so Josh and I are able to share the generous desk space. I think the previous owners may have done some sort of artistic design because the room has so much natural light and plenty of desk space to create. Along the interior wall is the door to the office and on that same wall there is built in floor to ceiling book shelves which is great for me mostly. It may have been an artist's office at one time but for an Author it is the perfect office space and creative escape.

There is a point in the day where Josh decides to go tinker with his four-wheeler and Desiree is asleep so from the office, I start up my laptop and send a message to Devon, "Hey, how are things going today?"

I wait a few minutes as I look through the rest of my social media feeds and organize my folders. After I am done, he still hasn't replied. I know, he is on holiday, give the man a break, but the thing is that knowing how Devon is he always has his phone on him and I know my message has already alerted him. It's likely that he either can't right now or there is a slim chance but he may be away from his phone. I send another message and write, "I was wondering what the plan was or if there were any updates." I click send and on queue like she knew, Desiree starts crying. Her cries come in loud and clear from the baby monitor I had set on the desk. I logout of the social media. Devon never responded and Desiree needs either a diaper change, a boob or both, so I walk down the hall to her room.

I peek over the railing of her crib and say, "Ah baby girl, you have some lungs on you." I scoop her up into my arms and know immediately what the problem is. She peed but for some reason, maybe the diaper wasn't fastened properly but up the back of her sleeper is wet with pee.

"Oh, it's okay. We will get you cleaned up sweetheart." Poor little thing. I remove her sleeper and diaper and her skin is pink from her being upset I wrap her in a blanket, pick her up and walk down the hall to the main bathroom. I start to run a bath for her in the tub. She needs it anyway and hope that the warmth calms her down as she is still screaming.

I dip her in and go to work lathering her body with soap and shampoo and wow had I thought she was screaming before she is really screaming now, her little face is a shade of purple.

"Baby girl, I thought you loved baths? Maybe you are not so much like mommy because I love them." I emphasize my last three words as though I could persuade her. The bath is short and quick, she is clean and I scoop her into a towel and bring her back to the nursery. She is warm now clean and dry and still upset and I lay her on the table, message some lotion on her delicate skin and get her into a new diaper and sleeper. Still, no break, my ears are starting to hurt and I decide that she must be hungry. I get comfy in my bed this time. I know that it is the middle of the day but my gut is telling me to lie down with her, relax and maybe all she needs is some food and comfort from her mom.

I cuddle her up next to me and learn that it was hunger after all and soon enough she is dozing again and I close my eyes too for a little nap.

Chapter 11
Here to See

I have no idea what time it is but am startled awake with the sound of Josh calling my name. For god's sake he should know better. Desiree is still asleep and I'm not about to answer back and wake her.

After the longest minute of him calling for me, he figures it out and stops hollering for us and finds his way to our room.

His lips move to form the word, "Sorry" without making a sound.

I whisper to him. "It's okay she is still asleep."

He joins us in the bed. The fresh winter air must have tired him out and I close my eyes again with my husband and daughter next to me and wonder off to sleep.

It was like only a blink of an eye but I feel my body jolt and am startled awake with the sound of the telephone ringing. I blink a couple of times and glance down at Desiree cuddled beside me on the bed. She seems to have been awake for a little while. Her legs and arms wiggle and her eyes try to follow her own twitches. She is just content as can be with her mom and dad nestled up next to her. She seems to be looking for the source of the noise with her dark blue eyes. I try to reach over her and Josh to the night stand table next to Josh but he beats me to it and in a groggy voice answers, "Hello?" He pauses as the caller talks to him. He answers in a raspy voice, "Yes, yes, I was awake earlier today. Okay bye." He puts down the phone.

I ask, "Who was that?"

He rolls onto his back and replies, "My mom and dad. They are here."

"Oh shit, I completely forgot." I close my eyes for a moment, scolding myself internally for forgetting.

He lets out a yawn and says, "Tell me about it. Aren't your parents coming over to visit too?"

I sigh and say, "Yes."

I get out of bed and slip into some simple black yoga pants and a comfy sweater and pick Desiree up off the bed because let's face it, the grandparents are here to see her.

Chapter 12
Even, Really, Feel

The Christmas and New Year holiday were nice. There was a steady stream of visitors throughout the week. You already know that Josh's and my parents visited and they even came a couple more times after Boxing Day. Hailey and her family stopped in as well along with my other girlfriends and come New Year's Eve Josh and I decided to stay in and do a movie night. We have been pretty tired and it was a nice relaxing night with a fire lit up in our family room fireplace, popcorn to snack on, soft drinks and a perfectly content little baby.

The second week of February Josh's paternity leave comes to an end and that morning I am up with him to see him off. This will be my first day on my own.

We had talked about it before him going back, well it is more like argued about it. Josh knows that he doesn't have to go back to work and I have encouraged him to quit, and give him the okay to let go of his career since my author career provides more than enough income to support our family.

He said no. You know that because we wouldn't be at this point of him returning to work today but it was the way he said it. I made the argument that he has the chance of a lifetime to be home, enjoy every day with me and our little girl.

His argument was that he will see us every day and that he needed his job to have a routine, keep sharp and maintain a sense of a normal life. I don't know, I really don't get it. I mean he can find activities at home that he can engage himself in and he has the opportunity to focus on his own hobbies.

Anyway, I see him off and it's just us two girls today. As you can take a guess Devon didn't visit. He did eventually respond to me asking and offering him to come visit. Devon explained that he couldn't make it out because Sara went along with him on his trip up to his brother's home and that he couldn't get away from Sara to visit me. I have not really talked to him since he had explained his reasons for not visiting.

I know that Devon and I talked about it before. We talked about if he was able to get me with child, that he would stay out and leave everything to me and Josh to raise and care for them. Devon and I agreed to keep things simple and allow for Josh and me to have a family. He wanted the unborn child to have a mother and father and not the complications of anything more than that. Devon explained that he was just happy to have the chance to be able to help. That was then and now the things that go through my head is that I love Devon and I do want to keep things the way they are but another side of me wonders why he isn't running here to see her? I think I am just being over sensitive, I guess. I mean, I look at her and Devon has said so too, she looks like his brother's children when they were Desiree's age but then again, most babies sort of look the same as newborns. I glance at her and the telling thing is she has my eyes, blue. Perhaps Devon has his own doubts that it isn't his?

I always keep Desiree near and this morning I decide to set us both up in the office. For my baby shower I had received this cute baby rocker chair that all I need to do is secure Desiree in and turn it on and it does all the work for me with gently rocking her.

There is actually enough room on the desk to place her and I set her up in front of me so that I can smile and talk to her as I work on my writing.

The panoramic window gives us the scene that you would see off a season's greetings card. The landscape is draped in a blanket of white. There is no breeze because the tree branches are also lined with snow and the world seems quiet as the chunky flakes hit the landscape floor.

I don't even really feel like writing. I mean, I knew that having Desiree would change my world but I never thought I could be so deeply in love with her so quickly that it consumes me.

It almost appears as though she is smiling as she watches me and I smile back and play with my little girl's hand. She is absolutely beautiful and as each day passes, she looks a little more unique with her changing from newborn to infant and I notice something new about her all the time, a facial expression or when she is alert and content, she likes to tap her right leg, just silly little things.

"Baby girl, how can Mommy write when all she thinks about is you?" I rest my head on my crossed arms that are resting on the desk as I stare up at her for a moment. I then look back out on that landscape and it makes me feel like Desiree and I are the only two people in the world.

My new laptop has loaded moments ago and I finally take notice and open up my last document to see where I had left off. It has been so long and I will probably have to do a bit of reading to figure out where I had ended in the story.

I have social media opened and I browse the news feeds but nothing is interesting. To be honest I am not sure that I want to even be social today because I am kind of out of my groove.

At that thought the telephone rings on the desk and I pick it up, "Hello?"

"Jordan?" It is a man's voice.

"This is"

"Jordan, it is Howard Stem. I just wanted to give you a call and catch up. How was your Christmas and New Year?"

I smile, funny how life is sometimes, guess it was intended for me to be social today, "It was good. The family visited and got a lot of help with Desiree. It was nice. How was it for you?"

"Congratulations by the way. Oh, I had Christmas in upstate New York at my daughter's home with her husband and two boys. Was fun, her boys are six and four so they are busy bodies and a couple of days before the New Year I flew out to Japan to work on a new endeavor for you and Devon. It is actually part of the reason for me calling."

I should be thankful that I have such an amazing publisher working hard to make me successful but something in the pit of my stomach just hopes that it is nothing and that I can have my time with my girl.

I try to ignore the thought and say, "Go on."

"Japan has a population that you can't bat and eye at. It is a vibrant country and full of culture, creativity and is cutting edge. They are trend setters to the world."

"Okay."

He continues, "I have been in talks to get both yours and Devon's books translated. Well, the translation is complete and the work has been sent to be printed and I want you to come out to Japan for a few days. Actually, take the week and we can tap into this new market."

Desiree dribbles a bit and I reach over for a tissue and dab her little lips and chin dry before answering, "Howard, thank you for doing all of that for me. I had no idea you were releasing it in another language. I thought we were just working on promoting the English version?"

"No problem Jordan. Sorry you were kept out of the loop. I would have told you but it was around that time when you were having your baby."

"How long is a flight to Japan?"

"Tokyo is a little over thirteen hours by flight."

My feelings that I was trying to ignore surface, "Howard as much as the opportunity is amazing, I don't think I could bring Desiree. That's such a long time to have a baby in an airplane and I can't leave her behind."

"Bring Josh and he can care for her."

"Howard, I don't even have a passport for her. I only just applied for one for our trip to Fiji in the spring."

He clears his throat, "I want you to do what you feel is right. This is an amazing opportunity to make a great impression out there and you know that I can't make you do something that you won't or can't do. All I ask is that when Josh gets home. Talk to him, lay out all of your options and whatever you decide is best give me a call in the morning and I will leave it at that."

I stand and pace the office, "Howard, I don't want to come off as being ungrateful but it is just not as easy for me to just pack up and leave."

"I understand, well talk to Josh and we will discuss in the morning. Good bye." The line goes to a dial tone.

Chapter 13
You Must Be Josh

Leaving this morning was easy. I just kissed my two girls goodbye and left. Driving down the highway alone was calming. This is what I have always known, my entire life. It's a constant, normal and I feel like myself. I stop in at the drive thru and pick myself up an iced cappuccino even though it's winter. It's my favorite drink.

The girl running the drive through window asks, "Anything else?"

"Yes, can I get a box of assorted donuts?"

The damp coldness and the fact that the sun has not fully risen in the winter sky, it's just breaking over the horizon. Her cheery voice seems out of place coming through loudly on the frosted metal speaker. She says, "Sure, drive on up to the window."

I pay and it's another fifteen minutes of driving before pulling into work.

The parking lot and office building is the same as I remembered it before having left on paternity leave. It's the same salt-stained cars, the people locking their car doors and walking to the building with briefcases and some have a coffee shop cup of coffee in hand and there are those same morning smokers having their disgusting breakfast habit outside the main entrance.

I park the car in my usual spot near the trees in front of the cafeteria windows and step out into the brisk air.

I run into Paul, a software tester on the team I work on. He's steps ahead of me, turns and holds the glass door for me and says, "Hey buddy!"

A gust of warm air hits my face as I step through the door. I reply, "Hey Paul, what's happening?"

We walk a few paces and wait together for the elevator to arrive. Paul explains, "They moved our group, so you have a new cubicle."

"Where?"

"Same floor but you're closer to the kitchen."

The elevator dings at its arrival, the doors open and we both step inside. Paul presses the button and the doors close. I say, "Oh wow that seems good."

"You would think." Paul chuckles and I know that it's not good.

The elevator dings at the arrival to our floor and the doors open. Paul explains, "Listen, congratulations by the way on the addition to you family."

We both step out into the hall. I reply, "Thanks"

I spot a new person in the hall. She approaches us with a folder clutched in her arms. My guess is she may have been on her way to the copier.

She approaches, her black high heels taping lightly on the tiles in front of the elevator. She shuffles her folder in her arm, mindful to not allow the papers within to slide out. She smiles, quickly wipes her hand on her black dress at her thigh and extends her hand to me.

In a childlike voice she says, "Hi I'm Mandy. You must be Josh. We work on the same team and they have been telling me all about you."

At the corner of my eye Paul waves and mouths, "I'll talk to you later", while Mandy's back is turned to Paul.

I shake Mandy's hand replying, "Hopefully good things."

She giggles, "Gosh, you're funny. Yes, it has been all good things."

There is a moment where we both laugh and go silent. I ask, "How long have you been working here?"

"I started when you went on paternity leave. I have been filling in your position." She runs her free hand through her shinny blond hair and continues, "Today's not my last day."

I smile and ask, "Will you be starting in a new position?"

She says, "Gosh no. I'm staying put."

I'm a little confused. It's always been only me in the position. I ask, "Do you know if I'll be starting in a new position?"

Mandy shakes her head, "No sweetie. We are working together." She approaches and touches her free hand on my back. "Come with me. They moved us to a new spot and I'll get you caught up. I'm really looking forward to working with you."

Chapter 14
Sara's Morning

My eyes feel like sandpaper as I blink them into focus lying here in bed. Being old does that. I roll over to see that Devon is already gone, probably downstairs. I smell the faint smell of a breakfast blend brewing.

I flip the sheet off of me and swing my sore legs over and slip my feet into the slippers next to the bed. I hate how he sneaks out of bed every morning and never bothers to wake me. I like to sleep in but sometimes I like to rise early. It's irritating how he always does that.

I peek through the sheer down into our yard. The pool looks inviting, I'll have my coffee by the pool this morning and maybe take my phone down with me and talk to my online friends.

Where is my phone? I glance back at the unmade bed and spot it on the nightstand.

I step towards the bed but nearly trip over the cat, "Fuck!"

He meows and purrs and continues to rub against my legs.

I glance down at the persistent fur ball and say to him "Some days I think you are secretly plotting to kill Mommy." The cat decides to plop its body where the sun is hitting the floor at my feet.

I grumble under my breath, "Stupid cat" I don't bother to pick him up and instead grab my phone and head downstairs.

Just as I suspected, the coffee is made and I pour myself a cup. Devon is at the table sipping on his own cup while looking at his smart phone. He startles to the sound of my mug clicking on the granite countertop.

He looks up and says, "Good morning"

I reply with a simple, "Good morning" These days there isn't much to say. I still hate him for what he did and I hate him even more in knowing that he pretends to love me. None of this is real. Us being civil with each other, us pretending to enjoy the others' company, this home with its family portraits of him and I on the wall and framed with sayings of love. None of this is real.

I take my coffee black today. It is fitting seeing that I am bitter right now. I watch him pick his phone up and he starts typing something. I don't even care to know who the message is for or what it's about. He has already betrayed me and yes, I'm a fucking hypocrite to go along with all of this, our fake fucking life.

I could have left him and put up a fight. I could have sued his sorry ass for a chunk of his worth. I could have rid any memory of him and started over. I could have done anything but this.

I loved him with all of my heart. Loved his ambition, his personality, that boyish carefree fun that he used to be. I loved how he played with our grand kids, and loved how he was my world and protector.

Who are we kidding? I still love him and I fucking hate myself for it. I want to believe him, his plea for me to stay and his promise that his heart is still mine. I'm weak and I hate it.

I top off my cup again and ask, "Do you need a top off?"

Devon glances up and says, "Sure". I pour some coffee into his mug. He has some sugar on the table and puts in one spoonful, then stirs gently, with his eyes still on his phone.

I return the pot of coffee to its spot on the machine and decide to not bother. He's pre-occupied. I grab a bran muffin, lifting the glass cover from the decorative tray on the counter and walk towards the French doors that open to the poolside.

Devon glances up when door clicks open. He says, "Babes, come sit with me."

"Naw, you look busy."

"I'm done. Please come sit. There is butter here for your bran muffin."

I close the door and take a seat across from him at the kitchen table and look into those never-ending brown eyes of his. A girl can get lost in them. I hate how beautiful they are.

I remove my phone from my pocket and place it on the table next to my muffin and reach for the butter. He wants my company then he needs to start off the conversation because I have nothing to say to him.

He patiently watches me cut my muffin and spread butter on each half. As I take a bite I glance up.

He says, "This morning I was talking to Howard. You met him on the cruise."

I say, "Yes, I remember Howard."

Devon continues, "Howard had my latest novel translated and he set up a trip for me to go to Tokyo to attend some book signings and such to promote the book."

I stare at him. I should be happy for him. I should be smiling right now and reaching over to give him a congratulations kiss but I don't move. I don't say anything. I just glance into those eyes of his. He needs to fight for me. I see he is trying but it's not enough and I just think, fucking Howard. I bet Howard also invited that little home wrecker since they work with the same publisher.

Devon acknowledges the silence, "Look babes, this is good news. I was expecting you to be a little happy for me."

I look down for a second, the cat must have followed me down to the kitchen because he is now at my feet, rubbing against my leg and I shoe him off for the moment. I huff, "How is this good? You're doing just fine selling English copies."

He leans back in his chair and replies, "Yes but this is a new market and a chance to make more."

"We have enough." I lean back, crossing my arms.

Devon says, "I have been nothing but polite and courteous to you this morning. What is this about now?"

"You're not even trying. Every opportunity you get, you jump in and go. Jet across the country and now over an ocean. You run away." I gesture with my hands making air quotes when saying the word opportunity, like it will make the point I am trying make come off that much stronger.

I see that hurt him. He frowns and raises his voice in defense, "I'm here for you. I am here, now trying to have a normal conversation with my wife and despite you trying to turn this conversation into a fight. I still try."

I spit back, "You don't" The cat meows at my feet.

"Sara, you need to see that I am trying and meet me halfway. If this is too hard for you than what's the point of all of this?"

I blink a tear away. I'm not going to cry. I wish we could go back in time to the way it was. This is hell and every time I look at him, he reminds me of the love we had and then the affair he had and it hits me all at once. Love and hate. I so want to punch him, then fall into his arms and be held by him. I'm a mess and he has made his point.

I say, "This is hard."

He sighs, "I know but please see me here and know that I'm here because I want us to work."

I need to know and ask, "Is she going to Tokyo?"

"I don't know. Howard didn't say and I didn't ask."

I nod and he continues, "Look, I want you to come with me." I look down watching the cat persistently weave through my legs then his. Devon says, "It will be fun and a chance for us to rebuild. We had a good time when visiting my brother recently, can't we continue on that same positivity?"

He is so convincing and I want to agree and go but my heart is still screaming don't. I'm still hurt and I'm not at the same point of acceptance as he is in being ready to work on this completely.

I mutter, "I can't."

"Why?"

I shake my head and admit, "I'm not ready." This time he looks down at our cat who I am sure believes that we are talking to him. I continue, "Look, I want to, I just need more time to regroup. Besides, I don't want to be a downer. This trip seems important."

He shakes his head, "Sara you're not a downer. I want you to come."

"I'll stay behind this time. I promise I'll go to your next thing."

Chapter 15
Chance It

The driveway gate beeped on the home security system notifying me that Josh was pulling up to the house. I walk down the hallway and wait for him inside our front door to let him in. I open the door to let him inside and can tell that he is tired and when he starts to feel that way usually it means the crankiness soon follows.

I try my best to keep upbeat and I have no idea how I am going to tell him about Japan. I am not even sure if I want to go. I mean, I should go and when someone gives you an opportunity like that, I should take it.

He steps in the threshold, looking down and being careful that he stays on the entrance mat with his snowy, salt-stained boots.

I ask, "How was your first day back?"

He smiles and sighs, "Oh you know, some things never change."

"What happened?"

He wipes this boots on the mat to rid the snow and says, "Same old office politics that's all. I guess while I was away, they decided to move my desk to another cubicle. I actually have absolutely no privacy."

I take his lunch bag and brief case from him and tuck the brief case under a small table at the entrance and I continue to hold his lunch bag for him. I ask, "Are you on a new team or something?"

"No, it is the same team; they just decided to move us to another spot on the same floor."

"That's stupid."

He hangs up his jacket and answers, "Yes I know."

"So how is everyone? How are your friends?"

We walk to the kitchen, "Everyone is good. They got me all caught up on everything and well they asked about you and Desiree."

"Did you take any pictures of her to work with you?"

"I had some saved on my phone. I should print one out to pin up in my cubicle."

"We have some picture frames you know." Without being conscious of it I follow his lead around our kitchen, keeping in step with him as we converse.

He stops and turns to me to ask, "Jordan, would you mind doing that for me?"

I abruptly stop and look up into those tired but a little less cranky looking eyes and say, "Not at all, it gives me something to do when you are not around. Say, I fried up a package of bacon earlier today. Would you like me to make a double decker Bacon, lettuce and tomato sandwich?"

"Sure, thanks dear."

"No problem." It's a relief to see him start to relax and open up to me on how his day went and I want to keep this momentum going.

Before he had arrived, I had sort of been tidying up in the kitchen and Desiree is all set up in her little rocking chair, content as can be. She is such a good little baby and just watches us talk to each other. Josh goes over to see her and he makes some silly noises to her. She isn't quite smiling yet but she looks happy that he is playing with her. He looks over his shoulder back at me and asks, "How was this little munchkin?"

"She was great. She only cried a little after she pooped herself but other than that it was a good day; she ate, slept and kept me company while I worked on some writing in the office earlier today."

"How is the story coming along?" He asks as he takes a seat at our kitchen island. I noticed that he loosened his tie and unbuttoned the top buttons of his dress shirt in an effort to get comfortable.

I bring our sandwiches to the island and sit with him to eat. I admit, "It was alright. I mean I haven't written in a while so it was kind of hard to find that groove again. I did a lot of reading to figure out where I had left off and sort of went from there."

He nods and then pops a chip in his mouth then asks, "Did anyone call?"

Do I chance it? He seems to be in a better mood than I had thought. Might as well get it out now. I clear my throat and he tilts his head to the side and asks, "Is something wrong?"

I take a breath and answer, "Nothing is wrong, really. I did receive a call and was going to talk to you about it but I didn't want to bother you with it, if I thought you were too tired."

He puts his sandwich down on the plate and gives me a gentle look and says, "I am tired, but you may as well tell me now."

"Okay well, I have mixed feelings about it but know that I should. I received a call from Howard Stem and long story short he wants me to fly out to Japan next week to promote my book."

Josh ponders it for a long moment that I squirm in my seat and try to not hold my breath and then he provides me a response that I didn't expect, "You are going to go then, right?" He picks his sandwich back up like he is surprised that he put it down in the first place and takes a generous bite.

Surprised I answer, "Yes, I think I need to. They translated my book and I would be attending some book signings out there. The only thing that is making me reluctant to go is Desiree."

He shrugs, "Maybe we could all go together?"

"That's what Howard suggested but Josh, Desiree doesn't have a passport yet so I can't bring her."

Josh brushes the chip crumbs from his goatee with his right hand and says, "Oh that sucks. Okay well if I stay back, I will probably just end up working. I can ask my mom to come over and care for her during the day. I am sure she would be happy to."

Josh's mom is retired so it's likely a sure bet that she would say yes in a heartbeat.

I am kind of in disbelief. I really thought he would argue with me to stay home. I ask, "You are not mad that I would be gone for a week?"

Josh shakes his head, "I mean, I'm not happy about it but let's face it if these events are what makes up your work duties. We know that they don't happen often. I mean when was that trip to New York? That was last fall so this is really only your second event in a few months. Your publishing contract is what has given us this life and you should keep your boss happy. That is my motto."

I take the last bite of my own sandwich and say, "Thanks babes, I really needed to hear your approval. I just don't know, a week without seeing her I am going to just die."

"There is video chat. I will make sure you get to see her." He smiles and takes both of our plates to the sink to rinse and put in the dishwasher.

"Don't let me forget to pack my breast pump, god could you imagine if I left that behind."

He closes the door to the loaded dishwasher, turns on a wash cycle and turns his head to say, "Jordan you think about the weirdest things."

"Well, it's true. She misses a feeding and they leek."

"Please, let me at least digest my dinner." He complains and I give him a kiss on the forehead.

Chapter 16
From Frosting Over

The winter season is in swing and Josh's first week back at work ran smoothly. I thought that it would be hard to care for Desiree on my own but to be honest it has been wonderful. Even when she cries it's never for long and it's just an excuse for me to pick her up and soothe her and take a break from whatever it is that I am doing.

I packed my things for the trip to Japan and really have no idea what to expect. I have no idea what Japanese culture is like. I have no clue how this book signing will go. I mean it's a pretty simple process with greeting fans with a handshake, making small talk with them and signing books. Besides the event its Japan, I don't know a single word of the language. Maybe Howard will provide me with a translator at the signing, who knows?

Josh's mom, Sheila, agreed to come over and help out with caring for Desiree and I spent some time practicing pumping my milk so that I know how to do it while I am away. It also gave me the opportunity to have Desiree practice taking a bottle.

Over the course of the week, I have slowly warmed up to the thought of being away. It will be a nice break from routine and allow myself a change in scenery. Speaking of which, I have no idea if I should bring a winter jacket to Japan or a spring coat? I have no clue what the weather is like out there. Searching for these answers is a job for my phone. I will need to look that up before I go.

The thing now that makes me a bit nervous is seeing Devon again. He has sort of kept his distance but I am equal to blame. I have not really tried to reach out to him other than over the holidays and those plans fell through.

My gut feeling is that Devon is no longer interested in me and that his only focus is on Sara. I don't think he even really wants to meet Desiree, which kind of pisses me off. I know what the rules are but I can't help but feel that little twinge of anger at that fact. Anger and hurt. I have exploded on people in the past in getting cross with them. I have lost friendships because of that but as it stands right now, whatever Devon wishes to do or not do I need to respect him for it even if I don't agree. After all, whether Desiree is actually his or not, he did provide me a chance.

I sigh as I think about it. We are likely staying in the same hotel. I wonder if Sara will be there.

Sunday night Josh drives me to the airport I will be departing to Japan just before 8pm. There is one stop in Vancouver to refuel and I should arrive in Japan for 10am Monday. Tonight, the winter air is crisp and the SUVs defrost is blasting warm air on the windshield to keep it from frosting over as Josh decides to drive up to the airport's drop off spot. He has to work in the morning so there is no point of him waiting around for me to leave and besides, Desiree is strapped into her car seat in the back. I would rather Josh bring her back home sooner than carry her around the airport.

Josh assures, "This is just a moment in time, before you know it you will be back home."

I sigh and rest my head on the seat while looking back at him, "I already miss you and Desiree."

He laughs, "You miss me too?"

I giggle, "Yes, of course."

He says, "Well, I will miss you too. Come here, give me a hug and a kiss."

I lean in and wrap my arms around him and give him a goodbye kiss and to be silly I hold onto him a few seconds longer than a hug should be and he says, "Um Jordan you are going to have to let me go."

"I know, I just need to have my fill that's all. I love you." I close my eyes for a moment and enjoy his embrace.

"I love you too. Have fun and get out and enjoy your time there. Desiree and I will be just fine. It will be dad and daughter time."

I smile and give him one more kiss on the cheek and a promise, "I will call you once I arrive."

I glance back and she is fast asleep. I simply touch my finger to my lips to kiss it and touch my finger to her head lightly. My eyes tear up at the thought of being without her but urge myself to open the door and step out into the cold.

I take my large rolling suitcase out of the back of our SUV. I stack my carry-on bag on top, wrap the shoulder strap around the handle, roll it to the side walk and blow a final kiss goodbye to my man.

Oh, I feel terrible. I mean I did nothing wrong and Josh did agree and encourage me to do this. I sigh and raise my face to the star lit sky so that those tears absorb right back into my eyes instead of trickling down my face and making my cheeks cold. I pull my luggage behind me, getting out of the winter air and into the airport. The sliding door entrance blasts warm air at me like the end of a touchless car wash. It feels so nice that I want to just stand in the entrance for a little longer to warm up but I don't.

I glance around. There are not many flights departing at this time so it is easy to spot the check-in. It sounds silly and I am not sure why I would expect anything different, considering that I am going to Japan but the lineup is full of people of Japanese descent and I am one of a few Caucasians embarking on this particular flight.

As I stand patiently in line, I receive a tap on the shoulder and turn to see a beautiful young Japanese woman. I say, "Yes?"

"You are Jordan Connor, right?" Her straight dark bangs end just above her inquisitive cat like eyes, it catches my attention. She also has a touch of black liner on the outer corners.

I smile shyly because I intended to sleep on this flight and didn't put on any makeup, "Yes that's me."

She smiles and says, "I know who you are. I haven't purchased your book but I have seen articles in the news about you."

I put on a brave face, being recognized by strangers is still new to me. This conversation can go either way and the hairs on the back of my neck are standing on end. I answer, "I am flattered; well don't believe everything you hear in the media."

We inch closer to the counter, shuffling our bags alongside. She waves or something, I see the movement in the corner of my eye and glance back at her. She says, "Why don't you just end your relationship with your husband and start a life with Devon Chambers?"

Jordan, you have a thirteen-hour flight ahead of you. No need to make enemies now. I simply respond, "One of life's mysteries. Well enjoy your flight." I turn and face the counter. In the minutes that I have spoken to her I have already sensed that if I answered in a way that she didn't agree with, I believe that she would argue her point and possibly cause a scene.

I proceed to the counter. It is my turn to check in and the young woman behind me continues to say, "I heard your book is translated to Japanese. I will purchase it."

I turn out of courtesy to face her and answer with a thank you and focus my attention back to the woman working at the airline counter.

My bag is weighed; she collects my information and gives me direction to the terminal.

I pass the indoor waterfall and go up the escalator to the next level. I don't feel like doing anything really. The little store shops aren't appealing to me or the airport lounge; I just want to sit and wait to board the plane and maybe close my eyes for the night.

I go through security quickly and soon find myself sitting in one of those uncomfortable airport waiting chairs with a view of the runway though there is not much to see other than the faint glow of blue lights that line it. The plane is already at the window so it shouldn't be long.

Just as the lineup downstairs the waiting area is full of Japanese people waiting to board the flight. I don't recognize anyone and no one seems to take notice of me. It makes sense because if all of these people are on return flights back to Japan than they have likely not heard of my book. Soon they will but at least I have the luxury of being just another average person waiting to board their plane.

That young woman that was talking to me in the lineup strolls on by, spots me and without any hesitation decides to sit directly across from where I am sitting. A cold chill goes up my spine and I shiver.

She rests a posh little pink carry-on bag with chunky black straps on her lap. I think she is about to pull out a phone or an e-Reader to stay busy while waiting but I am mistaken. Her skinny pale hands rest on top of the bag and like she has no filter, she states, "You know I have read many articles about you and Devon Chambers. You would make a nice couple."

I don't even know what to say to her. I smile, seconds go by and I don't think she even blinks. Her cat like eyes are eager for me to acknowledge and I give in. I ask her, "Are you a fan of his work?"

Her eyes light up as she smiles and says, "Yes, I love thrillers. Your boyfriend is talented."

I decide there is no point in reiterating that Devon isn't my boyfriend and instead focus on the topic, "Yes, Devon has a gift for storytelling. Do you write?"

She has this obnoxious laugh that sounds kind of like loud hiccups, "Oh no Mrs. Connor I am a student who loves to read and loves her gossip columns and seeing your reactions. I know the gossip is true about you and Devon. You don't need to say it, I know."

I know best then to start an argument with this stranger. God, some people just irritate the hell out of me. The annoying thing is I really can't get up and leave. I have nowhere to go. I decide it's time to look busy and I take out my phone.

She sits forward in her chair, trying to catch a glimpse of my screen. She asks, "Are you calling D. Chambers?"

I look up at her, just amazed that she isn't taking this as a sign to leave me alone. I reply, "No, excuse me."

Taking the opportunity, I quickly get up and take my bag and walk away to a clearing that is still in view of the window where the airplane is parked. I won't be a distraction to others and also to not let those over hear my conversation, not that it is a private conversation I just rather keep to myself.

I really want to talk to is Devon. That chatty woman's instincts of me are right but quite honestly that is none of her business. The thing is Devon seems to enjoy the challenge that the public presents us and I know he would get a kick out of putting this woman in her place.

I want to confide in Devon and ask his advice on how to deal with this woman who feels she knows everything about my personal life. Right now, I can't though because I know that Devon is being distant. I know that every time he feels that he is getting too close in desiring me for more than just the fun and games, he pulls away. Over this passed month after the birth of Desiree, I think he took one look at the photo of her and is pulling away because he has fallen in love with her and wants to take over for Josh.

I know that Devon does this and it's not the first time either. Before we even met and were talking and video chatting online, Sara had sensed something in Devon, a change and I know it was him falling for me and the moment she asked him about an affair he cut me off, broke up with me so to speak, but it didn't last long. He came back because I am his desire and for some strange reason, he still chooses to hold on to something that is already lost with Sara even after the incident on the cruise ship.

I am not sure if he does it out of respect for me and my family. I have no clue because if I wasn't tangled in this with him. If I was just some random person weighing in on his own relationship with Sara, I would not wish that upon anyone. She fails as a spouse to love Devon and desire him and make him feel like he is her world. She doesn't seem to trust him anymore, so he is constantly walking on eggshells when he is around her. She is insecure, she smokes like a chimney and she is quick to judge and feisty. I can still feel the sting on my cheek from her hand and no matter what everything is always her way.

It's sad to see my Devon in this life that he has fallen into but that is the life he chose and he feels some weird need to stand by his decision even though I know that he isn't truly happy.

He hurts, I know it and maybe talking to me, I, the one who loves this man for who he is and he knows it, I think that I make him happy in one breath because he can see a better life with me and at the same time feel sad in another breath because he feels like I am not a possibility to him.

It's a hard thing to watch someone that you love struggle with and I know you the reader are pinning this on me, but really this isn't my fault. It's no ones and you can't train your heart who to love, it chooses for you.

I know Devon is struggling but rather than be pissed at him for ignoring me, I accept this reality and remain open to him. For anyone else I would just give up and waste no more time and let them work it out on their end. I give him the space that he needs and when Devon is ready to talk again, I'll welcome him with open arms. It is better this way than to hold a grudge. Devon really is a great guy when he isn't being tied down by these silly rules that he has set for himself.

Anyway, enough of my Devon anxiety, I guess that is me just being nervous because I will see him at some point in the next thirteen hours. The person that I should want to call right now is my publisher, Howard Stem. I dial and he picks up in two rings.

"Hello Jordan, did you board your flight yet?"

I murmur into my phone, "I am just waiting to board. It shouldn't be much longer."

"That's good. Are you comfortable flying alone? I really didn't mean for you to travel solo. You know, if I was not already in Japan, I would have booked our flight together."

He already answered my question without me having to ask. I was curious if Devon would be making this flight or connecting with me at the stop in Vancouver.

I say, "That's okay Howard. I will be sleeping most of the time anyway."

"That's good. Well, I will be meeting you when you land and we will get you checked into the hotel and go for a bite to eat to catch up."

I glance at the flight staff at the counter. They are getting ready to turn on the mic to start calling people up. I reply to Howard, "Okay sounds good. Well, see you soon."

"Okay Jordan, have a safe flight and we can catch up soon."

I tuck my phone in a pocket and glance at the waiting area. There is a seat that is closer to the window and I make sure to take a spot where the rest of the seats are occupied so that woman doesn't follow and relocate next to me again. I pay attention to the people before deciding to sit with them, making sure that they are absorbed in their own things and they appear to be. I walk over but just as I am about to get settled, the attendant announces that they are boarding first class. I jump for joy internally I just want to get settled and relax for the night.

Chapter 17
Strip of Pavement

Initially, I was dreading the thought of a twelve-to-thirteen-hour flight. The longest flight I had been on prior to this one was a flight from Ottawa to Victoria but riding first class and sleeping the entire way was a breeze.

I woke up when the plane made a fuel stop in Vancouver and while the service crew pumped fuel into the tank of the plane, I pumped my breasts under the blanket that was handed to me when I first took my seat. I woke up sore. I would have fed Desiree by now and the pumping feels weird but it is a much-needed task.

When the plane took off from Vancouver, I slept straight on thru until landing in Tokyo. I think in this passed month, don't get me wrong I love my baby girl but I had totally forgotten what a full night's rest felt like.

I wake up at the sound of the flight attendant's friendly voice asking me to put up my seat and buckle up. A glance outside the window reveals that the plane is making its circle around the runway. The view is just nuts. I have no idea how pilots can land these planes and the fact that this runway is just a strip of pavement in the ocean just boggles my mind.

People often complain about long flights but I have to say that these overnight ones are the way to go. I can get used to flying first class with the hum of the jets and the sound of wind passing by the body of this carrier makes for great white noise. It allows me to block out distractions and allow for sleep.

Anyway, enough of my talk about sleep, there is something about looking out the window as a plane descends to earth that absolutely amazes me. I peek out the window and we are coming in for our landing. The runway sticks out like it is some massive dock only it's a solid runway lined with twinkling lights. My heart jumps at the anticipation of the landing. The water is getting nearer. The moonlight sparkles like tiny gems on the water's surface. Boats and even the people on them quickly come into view. They zoom by as we fall to earth and the faint screech of the tires touching down on the pavement marks the pilot's accomplishment as the plane slows and then taxis in to the airport.

Chapter 18
A Translator

The pilot announces the time. It is 11pm Monday night, just as expected. One thing that I learned about Japanese culture is that being on time is very important, so much so that I have heard that if their subway trains happen to be late, passengers can request a ticket from the conductor to present to their boss to explain being tardy for work.

It's nice to get up and start walking again. I feel good, calm and relaxed and it is not hard to spot Howard Stem when I enter the airport. He stands out with his thin tall build and silver hair in a sea of Japanese people.

"Hello Jordan, welcome to Tokyo!" He shakes my hand like a politician with one hand firm around mine and the other hand holding my left elbow.

Seeing a familiar face is comforting. I say, "Hi Howard, thanks for meeting me. I don't speak a sliver of Japanese so I am not sure if I would have found my way to the hotel."

He chuckles, "It is my pleasure and you would be surprised how much you could do without knowing the language."

I shrug, "That is true I guess." I glance around. I was expecting to see Devon here but I guess that was me just being foolish. Why would he show up now? He didn't even want to see the little girl he helped me create.

I continue on another thought, "Shall we get going to the hotel?"

"Yes, soon. It's just there is one other person that we are waiting for?" His words trail off as he glances passed me in trying to spot the other one.

"Who?" My heart starts to race and I follow the direction of Howard's glance. I wonder if he means Devon.

Before he answers he looks beyond me to wave someone over and I look in the direction. Oh my God it can't be her. Howard explains to me while he watches her approach, "I flew you in a translator."

God it's totally her. She smiles and walks with a spring in her step with her carry-on bag, hanging on her shoulder. I say to Howard while watching her approach, "How come you didn't tell me we would be sharing a flight and no offense but why couldn't you find a translator here?"

Howard does not even notice the twinge of annoyance in my voice. He explains, "I didn't have time to tell you. It was too short of notice and I picked her because she is a friend of mine from New York. She was able to bus over the boarder to make the flight in time. She missed the New York departure." He changes his attention to the young woman, "Miss Saito, so happy that you made it on such short notice."

"It is my pleasure Mr. Stem." She greets him with a slight bow of her head, making her dark bangs move.

Howard takes a step back in a gesture to include me. He glances at me then says to her, "You two ended up on the same flight. Well, the client I was explaining over the phone is this woman and her name is Jordan Connor." I smile for the introduction but only to hide my disappointment.

Miss Saito smiles, "Yes, we met briefly at the airport in Ottawa." She glances at me, bowing her head slightly and I feel inclined and return the gesture.

Her demeanor is completely different. She is formal instead of the prying gossip fan personality that I had first encountered and tried to get away from before the flight.

I ask, "Miss Saito, I thought you had said that you were a student?"

"I am a student but do this also. It is good money and a little of this work every once in a while, goes a long way and allows for me to focus more time on school."

I simply say, "Good for you." I try my best to remain polite to this young woman with flawless skin, cat like eyes and slender but healthy body. She is apparently here to help me. I can't believe it, of all the people on this planet and Howard has to pick this chick.

We gather our luggage and take a taxi to the hotel. My annoyance with the fact that I am stuck with Miss Saito for the week is forgotten for a bit. Let me be clear, I'm still annoyed it's just that now I am distracted by the sites as we drive on route to the hotel. It is a cool day but not cold, jacket weather with the temperature at about 3 degrees Celsius which is about 37 degrees in Fahrenheit. It reminds me of early spring back home. The first thing that I notice is that the sidewalks are double the size that I am used to seeing back at home and there are a lot of people walking about even for this late into the evening. The buildings are all sorts of shapes and sizes in a lot of shades of beige, grey, and white and to add everything looks new. I don't see a trace of litter; everything is clean and taken care of.

Miss Saito and Howard talk amongst themselves for a few moments as I distract myself in the architecture of the city.

I eventually tune back in when I hear Miss Saito's voice say Devon's name.

She says, "I was convinced I would be a translator for Mr. Chambers." I know when she says convinced, she really means hoped.

Howard explains, "You will be working with the two of them tomorrow for the book signing at the library, but your focus will be mainly with Jordan. This is her first time here while Devon is a little more accustomed to the culture."

I join in on their conversation and say, "Devon never told me that he had been here before."

Howard clears his throat, "He has been here a couple of times with me in the past few weeks, basically seeing through the translation of his and your books. He did a few back-and-forth trips."

Devon never even mentioned this to me and although this shouldn't come off as being a big deal, I can't help but feel hurt that he never shared any of this with me in the brief conversations that we had.

Miss Saito blurts out, "I think I know where we are going. We are getting close to Roppongi Hills. Is that where our hotel is?"

Howard nods and she smiles and explains, "It is a good spot."

I ask, "So, how did you two meet?"

Howard explains, "Tail Fin Publishing likes to hire University students to give them a chance to gain some experience. I met Miss Saito last summer. She worked for Tail Fin full time over the summer break. She started off with assisting in editing and we soon discovered that she was fluent in Japanese. Yours and Devon's books are not the first we have had translated and while in talks with Japanese book retailers last year for other books, we found her most helpful in the discussions."

She beams as a result of Howard's praise and adds, "My major is in English. I understand that you have no education?"

I nearly choke. What a bitch of her to say something like that and it's not so much the words she said but how she said it and the conviction in her articulation is just so slight that Howard is oblivious, but I hear it. It was meant for me. I take a breath and remain as composed as can be, "You are mistaken Miss Saito. I do have an education. I have graduated High School and also hold a college diploma in Computer Science."

She nods, while her chin is raised slightly and those dark brown eyes look back at me, "Forgive me. What I meant was you have no education in English."

Bullshit, that's what she meant. Oh boy, this is going to be a long week. I explain, "I am really just a good story teller and those nitty gritty editing jobs are left to the people who can't come up with interesting material. They are like janitors of the publishing world and clean up the authors mess, so to speak."

Her annoying hiccup sort of laugh erupts as one of her hands rest on her chest and she says, "So true!" She winks at me as she says it.

Howard does not even catch it and I try my best to be good. Howard points the massive hotel to me. The first floors are a square structure of white concrete and glass and about twenty floors up the square shape graduates to a cylinder-shaped tower. The additions to the building don't have as many floors but hold ballrooms and restaurant lounges.

Tokyo so far has impressed me. I have never had the desire to travel here but now I am happy that I have made the choice to come and experience it and maybe when Desiree is a little older, I could bring her and Josh.

The building is impressive. It sort of reminds me of the grandness of the hotels in Los Vegas but this one has the wealth, quality and care that went into the design of this structure.

I bet this place is beautiful at nighttime.

The taxi drops us off at the entrance and walking into this place feels as though you are walking into a palace. The lobby is vast, clean, and open. There is a line of green bamboo trees in massive vases down the center of the room and sitting areas. There are dark leather couch arrangements for small social gatherings, which are thoughtfully placed in this large area. Along one side is a wall lined with wall sconces and are filled with tall sunflowers that leads to the reception desk. Along the end of the room is a hall that leads to the elevators and that hall is marked my two massive statue heads.

Across from the reception are a couple of escalators that lead up to shops and restaurants. Everything in this massive room is done up in whites, browns and the odd splash of yellow and gold.

I am not sure what I was expecting but the receptionist speaks fluent English and I am able to check into my room with ease and without the help of Miss. Saito.

Once I am ready to go up to my room Howard says, "Miss. Saito and I will let you get settled. Did you want to meet us back in the lobby in about one hour?"

Miss Saito explains, "Actually Howard, give me about thirty minutes, I need to freshen up and we can go through the agenda before Jordan returns in an hour."

Howard nods.

I reply, "Sure" I need to shower and get changed into some clean clothes anyway and give Josh a call to let him know that I made it okay.

Chapter 19
Just a Man

The hotel suite is really nice. It's not like when I was on the cruise ship in terms of style and the fact that you felt like you were on a ship. This suite is elegant and simple, just as the lobby, the room has a white, beige and brown color palate. It's clean and what's different about this suite is it does not feel like a hotel suite. It feels like you are stepping into someone's home. It's calming and relaxed which is just what I need.

Coming in through the door I find myself in a living room, with a large beige L shaped couch in its center and it's situated in front of a wall unit with a flat screen television. There is a brown coffee table and a couple of side tables. If I continue passed the couch the bedroom entrance is on the left and opens to a giant king size bed and continuing passed the bed is a large washroom with a white basin sink. The sink looks like a bowl on the counter. There is a glass door shower, white toilet and there is an abundance of white fluffy towels and a couple of white bath robes.

The Japanese sure know how to accommodate their guests and I have to remind myself that I am in a hotel and not someone's posh condo.

I drag my suitcase into the bedroom and I crawl up onto the bed for a moment with my smart phone in hand and send a text to Josh. "Hey babes, I am just sending you a text to let you know that I made it okay." I click send and reach into my carry-on bag for my pump and work on myself with my phone in reach, waiting for Josh's reply.

When I finish with the pump and I am about to jump into the shower there is still nothing from Josh. Wow that is weird. It is around midnight here, so he is thirteen hours behind me, which would mean that it is maybe just after 11am Monday back home? Oh, this time difference stuff really messes with me. I know that he is at work right now so he could be in a meeting or something.

I need a shower now and to think I have a book signing to attend in the morning and now I am wide awake from having the sleep of my life on that flight. Jeepers I should have tried to stay awake on the flight. What the hell was I thinking?

Slipping into the shower, I feel like a queen who is being pampered. I was expecting my bare feet on the light beige tiled floor to be cold, but to my discovery the tiles are heated. I open the glass door and turn on the water and let it run down my back. It's soothing and refreshing and it wakes me up even more.

I should try to sleep, try to read or do something calming so that I am ready for tomorrow's events, and then there is Devon. I don't think that I want to see Devon and chances are that he may be meeting us in the hour and if not, I will for sure see him at the signing.

Well, whatever, I should grow up and just get over these games that we play. I step out of the shower unsure of what to wear. I know I said that I should stop playing these games but if he is there, I want to look good and kind of give him a little payback to show him what he has been ignoring for this time.

I stand naked in front of the fogged-up mirror and take one of the white towels and wipe the condensation from the mirror. My body isn't what it was. I am still frumpy looking; my breasts are huge which I have never said before being pregnant with Desiree but that's about the only thing going for me. I still have a bit of a tummy that I need to work on.

What to wear. I go to my suitcase in the bedroom and take a high wasted dress out. It is a navy blue with gold paisley and the dress ruffles out and ends just above the knee. It is perfect and will conceal this post baby body.

I blow out my hair and put a bit of makeup on, take a breath to let it out. Don't be a chicken, Jordan. He is just a man.

Chapter 20
A Degree in English

Tokyo is a city that does not seem to sleep and as I ride the escalator down to the main level lobby, I glimpse at a couple of small groups of people who are socializing on the couches in the center. There are a couple of receptionists at the main desk and both are on the phone.

I glance around for Howard, Miss Saito or Devon but no one is here. I glance around. Behind the reception desk is a clock that tells me that I am about fifteen minutes early. That explains it.

I look around, well there is no sense in me waiting around like a lump I take a glance at the escalators that go up and decide that the lounge on the second level is a sure bet.

I haven't had a drink since Desiree's birth because of the breast feeding but this week my milk is just going down the drain so I may as well indulge.

The lounge is like any typical lounge with its layout, dim lights and the style is modern, with a Japanese flavor to it. I take a seat at the bar and the bartender dressed in a white shirt, black vest and black pant smiles approaches.

He says in French, "Good evening, Miss"

I reply in French, "Good evening, do speak English?"

He answers in English, "I speak English also. You looked French. You dress like most French women."

I take it as a compliment, "Thank you."

He nods and asks, "Can I get you something to drink?"

"A glass of red wine please. Do you have a Malbec?"

"I do, let me pour you a glass."

As he serves my drink, I take out my phone and send a message to Howard to let him know where I am and it's not long after I have a hand touch my back.

I glance up and say, "Hi, Howard, you changed your clothes." He is wearing a dark denim with white collar shirt and grey blazer.

"I wanted to get into some evening wear. Jordan, you look great. I would not have thought you just had a baby."

"Thanks" I beam.

He takes a seat on the bar stool next to mine and explains, "Devon and Miss Saito have already got a table for us over on the restaurant side."

The bartender overhears our conversation and says, "Miss, if you want to take your drink you can go meet your friends on the other side."

I answer, "Thank you" Howard and I stand to go and I leave money for the bartender and head over to the restaurant side.

I lead the way with my glass in hand and I spot the two of them almost immediately. Miss Saito's back is towards me and across from her is Devon. They are laughing and that look Devon has. He has given me that endearing look before and jealousy sinks in. What a fucker. He knew I was here and he didn't even send me a text, not even a simple hello.

He has already moved on to Miss Saito. I guess I am not fun to him anymore.

I try my best to remain calm and pretend that his presence doesn't irk me and I make sure to approach with confidence in knowing that I am worth way more than this little university translator.

I catch his eye as Howard and I near the table and he does a double take, like he is surprised by my presence. I'm not falling for it.

From behind me Howard says, "Devon, I see that you two are getting acquainted."

He stands to greet the both of us and gives Howard's hand a shake first. "We are. How are you doing Howard?"

Howard shrugs his slender shoulders, "Oh you know, a lot of organizing and by the way, everything is on schedule and we are ready for tomorrow."

Devon answers, "That is great to hear."

Howard takes a seat beside Miss Saito and Devon steps closer to me. I extend my hand for a formal shake and he grasps it gently with his two warm and gentle hands. He gives me a quick kiss on the cheek and whispers, "It's great to see you again. You look beautiful as always." Those warm brown eyes of his appear sincere. Jordan don't fall for it.

He is smooth as always and I know that this is just a polite hello and that is all, I say, "Thanks, it is good to see you also." It's hard for me to keep my real feelings internal but somehow, I manage.

He is holding back and on what I have no clue but so am I. I want to tell him how much of a jerk move it was to cut me out and not visit. I want to tell him to grow up, be an adult. Our biological exchange was exactly that and it shouldn't mean that we can't continue on, and be friends. I force a smile and have no choice but to take a seat next to him.

Like the gentleman that I fell in love with, Devon pulls out the chair next to his and gestures me to take a seat.

The silly thing about the restaurant dining experience is that I thought Japan would entail having to eat

Japanese food all of the time but this restaurant in the hotel has a menu that serves French food. I guess, like home you can get your variety of restaurants and it's a pleasant surprise that there are so many food options.

Howard asks Devon and Miss Saito, "So what were you two talking about before we crashed the party?"

Miss Saito answers, "Oh just our educations. I learned that the famous D. Chambers has a Degree in English and I am working towards one. We have something in common." Her little almond eyes meet mine for a moment to confirm that I heard her and her perfect teeth are as fake as that fake little smile she is making.

Yes, bitch just suck up to him. I ask her, "Do you plan to write books?"

She nods, "Yes of course but not the kind that you write." She looks down the bridge of her tiny flat nose almost daring me to a match.

I take the last sip of wine in my glass and ask, "What kind?"

She glances across the table at Devon who returns his gorgeous smile. Miss Saito continues, "Inspirational, books that people gain something from reading them, not like yours."

I can't believe that neither Howard nor Devon is picking up on any of her jabs.

I glance at her and know exactly what she is doing. I may as well ask since we are going down this route and I say to her, "Miss Saito how would you know that my readers would not have gained something from reading my book? At the Ottawa terminal you had mentioned that you had not read it but planned to purchase."

Before she speaks a word Devon interjects, "Jordan did you see this menu?" He slides it slowly toward me so that it's an inch away from where my wine glass is.

I glance down at the menu and in a breathy response I say, "No I haven't but you know what, I think I am going to leave you three for the night." I start to slide my chair out.

Howard says, "That is a shame, Jordan. We have not even reviewed tomorrow's events. Is something wrong?" His concern is sincere which is frustrating to me.

I am so pissed off but I haven't been pushed to the point of saying what's really bothering me and instead just say, "I just got a sudden cramp in my side. I am heading back to my room. You can email me whatever you all decide, have a good night, guys." I tuck the chair back to the table and head out of the restaurant as fast as I can without running.

I head down the escalator to the lobby and dry a tear from my eye with my clammy hand. Fuck this shit you couldn't pay me enough to deal with that little snot, Miss Saito, along with the man who absolutely crushed my heart.

I walk by the reception towards the exit. The worker behind the reception desk takes notice and asks in English, "Is everything alright?"

Like that I'm brought to my senses and dab away another escaped tear and step towards the desk, "Could I have a tissue?"

He hands me one to dry my face and I calm down. He asks with a heavy and almost robotic sounding accent, "Is there anyone that I could call for you?"

I chuckle the only person here that I would want him to call is socializing with Miss Saito and Devon. I explain in a sigh, "I am okay. I was just in some bad company that is all."

He nods and I continue, "Is there somewhere I could go to relax?"

"Are you staying here?" He asks politely.

"Yes, I am under the Howard Stem reservation. My name is Jordan Connor."

"Ah yes, the author." He says it with a polite smile and continues, "We have some relaxation saunas and hot baths on the third floor. There is also a meditation garden about a two-minute walk, out the door and east down the corridor."

I'm decided and say, "I will visit the garden. You have been a great help, thank you."

He nods and I return the gesture and with that I walk in the direction of the garden. My brand new heals click along the marble floor as I exit and head to the garden.

Chapter 21
Wish You Were Here

The garden is not hard to find as it is just sparkling with lights. The grass is emerald green the pond is a twinkle of light. There are all sorts of small, groomed trees, and flowering plants that are in full bloom. To be honest when the receptionist mentioned garden, I had pictured one of the groomed gardens back in Ottawa, the kinds that only consist of plants and not twinkling lights. There is no mistake that this garden is well groomed but the lights make this place look magical, like it's some enchanted forest full of fairies.

I take a seat on a rock next to the water.

There are a few others here and don't have the area to myself but I am left alone to think things through.

I can't sink to Miss Saito's level. She does not have the million-dollar contract and I do. I have to start greeting Devon like a business acquaintance because that is all he is now. My thoughts turn to Josh, he may be back at his desk. I poke into my purse and pull out my phone and finally feel like something is starting to go my way. Josh my love that I have taken for granted sent me a text, he is my constant. The text from him reads, "Great to hear that you made it okay and wow that is a beautiful room and hope everything is well." I had sent him some pictures of the room in my message from earlier.

He sent is reply about five minutes ago when I had been at the reception desk. I need a friend right now. I put my purse down by the rock so that I can use both hands to reply.

I write to him, "Things are good but I wish they were better. Long story short, Howard got me a translator for the books signing. You would think that's a good thing but honestly, she is a total bitch. I was supposed to be having a late-night meal at the restaurant with the translator, Howard and Devon but I just walked out on all of them. I couldn't handle it."

My video messaging alert comes up on my phone's screen. I guess I am still connected to the hotel's Wi-Fi.

The screen goes black for a moment and then Josh appears. "Hey babes. I had to see you."

"Thanks, I appreciate this." My heart calms down at the sight of my husband.

"Are you outside?" He asks.

"Yes, I am just in the hotel's garden." A tear escapes down my cheek and he sees it.

"Ah Jordan, you should be having fun right now. You can't let others get you all worked up like that."

I look away from the screen for a moment because hearing Josh's voice makes me want to cry more. I miss him and Desiree and it's not only Miss Saito's presence, it is Devon too that is making me upset but I leave that out and just sniffle. I look back at my screen and admit to Josh, "I know, I think I am just tired and not thinking straight. I really wish you were here right now." A couple more tears run down my face.

He sighs, "I can see that. What happened at the dinner to get you so upset?"

I steady my breathing and explain, "She basically insulted me, said my book was not good and she was implying that she was more educated than me."

Josh tries to regard it with a straight face but as I recap it to him, I see where this is starting to sound funny and a smile flashes across my lips because of the goofy expression on his face. He smiles back and acknowledging my smile says, "There you go. See how ridiculous you sound. You know not everyone will like your book and how high of an education does she have?"

I say, "She is going to school for an English university degree."

Josh asks, "Does she have the degree yet?"

"No" I reply. My voice sounds a little more certain as I talk to him.

"There you go. She isn't more educated than you but once she gets that degree, I would say that she will be only then, and you are upset about this?"

A sigh escapes my lips as I reply, "Josh, it's not really about what was said. It was how she said it. It was like she was trying to insult me on purpose despite the fact that she has been hired to help me."

"Jordan, whether your instincts are right or not, you need to drop it. You have a big day tomorrow, get some rest. I hope you go back to your hotel after this call."

"I will but I need to get something to eat first."

"Well, my advice is leave Howard and them to their meal. You need to cool off. Are there any fast-food places or vending machines?"

I glance up instinctively but quickly realize that I am still sitting in this enchanted garden and look back to the screen at Josh and say, "Not that I saw but I'll just ask the reception if they would bring some food up to the room."

"There you go. Babes I should get back to work. That smile looks good on you. Just keep your head up and remember these things are just trivial. I love you." He smiles and I smile back.

"I love you too. Give a kiss to Desiree for me."

"I will, good night."

"Bye"

Chapter 22
Bear Hugs

The door clicks open and I enter my hotel room. Earlier the receptionist explained that there was a food basket on one of the tables and a small fridge equipped with water, juice and beverages that I never noticed until now.

I immediately walk to the basket and go for the chocolate bar and grab some water out of the fridge and take a seat, sinking into the fluffy couch.

The conceited side of me in the back of my mind thought that Devon would try to get away from his dinner with Howard and Miss Saito and come find me and we would get to catch up, settle whatever it is and fuck each other like two long lost lovers. The truth is he is likely still in the restaurant socializing, well more like flirting with Miss Saito. If I were to guess, they will probably hook up at some point this week and well the only thing stopping them from getting to that point now is Howard. He is still with them according to his schedule he had outlined in an email.

I check my phone in hopes that maybe I am wrong but nope, there are not texts from Devon. He has moved on and I wish I knew why.

I take the last bite of the chocolate bar and wash it down with water. It is approaching 2 AM and now fatigue is starting to set in. This comfy couch is tempting but I urge myself up and into bed.

Sleep comes fast but the morning comes faster.

When I wake the following morning I meet the party down in the lobby, Devon, Howard and Miss Saito. They are all dressed to impress. Despite my ill feelings for Miss Saito, she is looking quite good in a slim fit violet pencil skirt, grey shrug and nude color pump. Howard is dressed in a beige blazer, dark denim pant, with a rose shirt and tie and the father of the most beautiful little girl in the world who I want to hate but can't is looking sharp in a dark grey toned plaid blazer, dark blue top and light grey pant.

I decided to wear a black, high waste dress that flows to the knee a thin gold belt and a floral print blazer.

It's cool in Tokyo this time of year, jacket weather but with us spending time inside for the most part I decide that my floral print blazer is enough to leave like this.

My eyes meet Devon's. I want to look away but it's already too late. He says, "You look beautiful Jordan." He makes it known that he has looked me up and down. I bite my bottom lip and wonder perhaps Miss Saito was not good in bed because there is space between Devon and Miss Saito. Howard is standing between the two of them.

Starting to get lost in those warm brown eyes, I answer, "Thanks Devon. You all look great. Were you guys up long after I left last night?" Josh's advice to head back to my hotel room and cool off last night helped. I'm able to push those ill feelings of Miss Saito and Devon aside.

Miss Saito rolls her eyes and Howard says, "Oh we were there for about an hour longer. It is too bad you couldn't stay." There is a tiny glint of caution in Howard's voice. He must have sensed something last night in my abrupt exit. He is unsure whether or not to pry deeper.

I say, "I wanted to but when you have a pain in your side it is hard to ignore." I look right at her and give the slightest glare, making sure she is the only one to see it. Those almond eyes see me and she looks away, like she is uninterested.

Howard says, "Shall we head out?" Howard made his choice not to pry. We all walk to the hotel's main entrance to meet a cab parked just outside the doors.

I take a seat next to Howard and across from Miss. Saito and Devon. The conversation in the car isn't good enough to mention and besides I tuned out anyway. I just observe the interactions. Miss Saito and Devon seem to be keeping more at a distance despite them sitting next to each other. Something happened last night. I can feel it. Part of me wants to know and part of me doesn't and Howard as usual is playing absent minded.

We pull up to the white two-story library. Its parameter is surrounded by a gaited wall with a hedge. Tokyo is an interesting place and this library almost seems like it's in some sort of private compound. We step out and walk up the brick path that leads through the gates to the building. I glance around and this library is surrounded by land, lots of gardens, paths leading to ponds and people walking about enjoying the nature.

There is no crowd to greet us however when we walk through the doors and enter the library, we see that it is in full use. People are at the counters doing computer searches. At the far end of the library, I see what looks like a book club meeting underway. There are people walking up and down the aisles browsing. There are people tucked away in corners, completely absorbed in a story. It is a similar feeling to how some of the more popular bookstores feel like back home in Canada.

I spot our table on the other side of the room with our names printed first in Japanese then underneath printed in English on folded paper place holders. Our books are on the table. This is the first time that I see my book printed in another language. Everything is different and the only way I can tell that it is my book is because my name place holder is next to the stack on the table.

A thin short gentleman in a three-piece suit greets us in Japanese. His words are accompanied with a bow and we all greet him with a bow as well.

He speaks to us with the help of Miss Saito. She is the bridge in between, communicating his words to us and our words to him.

Basically, the setup is exactly how we see it. There will be a short reading of each of our books in Japanese by the library staff. He has library staff picked out for the reading and after that there is a simple meet and greet with having Devon and I sign books.

The man in the three-piece suit starts to converse with Howard and I decide that it's okay to look around. I approach the table on my own leaving my party behind. Curiosity has overcome me and I want to get a closer look and see what my book looks like in the Japanese version. As I approach the table I see the cover, it is completely different. It is done in a Japanese Animation image of a man and woman looking into each other's eyes and even though it is done in cartoon form, there are features on them to make it look similar to me and Devon. I'm not sure that I even like it. It looks weird and to top it off the title looks like the writing is from another world. There is no relation to the western world's alphabet. I pick up a copy and instantly see that the spine is on the right side. Was this printed wrong? I open the book to what feels like the back, I see a title page, what looks to be some sort of copyright page and then the opening chapters only the text inside the book is written vertically. I am so confused, is it supposed to look like this?

"It looks weird to you, doesn't it?" The words are spoken within steps of me. I glance and it's Devon who has come to join me.

I murmur, "Yes, is the book supposed to be printed like this, backwards and vertically?" I feel embraced to ask the question to Howard since I should have paid more attention to the entire translation process, but then again Howard sort of left me out of the process since it was all done around the time of Desiree's arrival. I decide it's safe to ask Devon.

He chuckles, "Yes, this is the way that their books are written. Do you like the cover?"

I look at him and shake my head no, smiling with my lips closed. I don't know whether to laugh or cry at this revelation but decide to stay quiet since Howard put a ton of work into making all of this happen.

Devon replies in a low voice, leaning closer to me, "Don't worry I will keep that between you and me." Like always, in his own way, he shows that he cares. He is my protector.

I flip through more pages of my book, close it to look at the cover once more and then put it back down on the top of the pile. I sigh, "Devon, what happened to us? Why do things have to be weird like this?"

He looks away from me, down at the table and he picks up on of his books, pretending to inspect the cover. He says, "Jordan you know how I feel about you but you know that things were going sour at home. I needed to take a step back that's all."

My gaze is still on him. I say, "Devon, I just don't get it? Sara figured it all out and knows that Desiree is yours. How does cutting us out entirely help matters?"

He places the book back down on the table, returning it to the stack of copies and looks back at me this time. "You know why. You know that I want to switch places with Josh and I know that feeling is wrong and besides it is disrespectful to both Sara and Josh. I needed space to focus back on her and it doesn't mean that I ever stopped loving you. Know that."

"I don't understand why there can't be balance? Why, is a simple hello so difficult and you flirting with Miss Saito last night, I saw that. How will that help things with Sara? You slept with her."

He steps back, "What? No, that's not me. I went to my room alone last night. I am not a perfect man but you have to let me get back on track and that way is the only way that I know."

I look at him for truth, "You didn't sleep with that little bitch?"

He sighs, "How many times do I need to explain things, I stand by what I said and that is a no. I have no interest in her. You know where my heart lies and I just need to get back on track."

A sadness appears in his brown eyes. He is living the same nightmare as me in loving more than one. I believe him. Maybe my instincts are wrong, they probably are but I believe him.

I look up into his big brown eyes and apologize, "I'm sorry, I just feel so lost at times and we used to be so close and when I saw you laughing and kidding with Miss Saito, I felt like it was a sign of interest in her."

"That is where you are wrong. We should talk privately and catch up." He speaks.

I feel myself flush when Devon defends himself. I remove my floral print blazer in reaction to feeling warm, revealing my black dress. I fold the blazer over my arm, run my fingers through my hair and reply, "Yes we should. Did you want to meet discuss things back in my room?" I know it is a bold move to invite him to my room but he did say that he wanted to discuss things privately.

"Yes, we can chat later." To my surprise he accepts the invitation but it is clear to me that this is a peace offering at friendship because just as Devon agrees he walks back over to Howard. I hesitate but then follow a moment later to join our group.

Miss Saito approaches us with the librarian organizer at her side. He speaks and Miss Saito translates for us, "He is asking you two if you like your book designs? He contributed to the design."

You really have to lie in situations like this. It would be horrible to insult someone after the fact. I don't like it, the animated look just doesn't do it for me, but I do realize that anime is a fairly big deal here and that cover was picked in order to appeal to popular demand. Both Devon and I smile and explain that we like the look of our translated books. Miss Saito translates our approval to him and then explains, "The readings will be done in a few moments. He asked for you to take your seats and, in a moment, you will hear his voice in Japanese followed by mine in English calling attention for those in the library to attend. Do you have any questions?"

I ask, "Where is Howard?" I didn't notice when he left.

"He had to step out for a call to Tail Fin."

Miss Saito asks again, "Anything else?" Both Devon and I shake our head no.

People fill the area where Devon and I are situated. The readings are spoken and I have to say that it is a strange experience to hear your book read in a foreign tongue. I know my book off by heart and know the passage that was picked to read. I could tell by the body language and the expressions on the audiences faces at what points the speaker was at but not a word they spoke was recognizable. It was like, without having seen the audience soak up the story, I would have had no clue what was being read.

There is a short question period and Miss Saito helps Devon and me out with answering the questions and soon the book signing commences.

This isn't quite as large as when we were in New York or even quite as big as when I was still nobody and it was only Devon that was the household name, that time when I attended his book signing at the Ottawa book store. It was packed with Devon's fans. For this event, there may have been fifty or so that attended. This is small scale for us but a good introduction into how to handle language barriers and such.

People approach the table and it is pretty even in the amount of people who wish to meet Devon and me.

I eagerly sign books for my new fans. They are so polite with their bows and Miss Saito helps me speak to them.

Most don't know much about the tabloids Devon and I face in North America although some do and comments are said as well as questions translated.

One little old woman approaches the table coming to meet me first. We say our polite greetings to each other and her question is translated to me. Miss Saito explains, "She wants to know how you get along with two storytellers in the home?"

I smile at the old woman who is waiting for my response to be translated through Miss Saito. I glance up at Miss Saito and say, "Tell her there is only one storyteller in my home and that my husband is at home caring for our baby right now."

Miss Saito proceeds to talk to the woman and I notice her eyes dash from me to Devon and then down like she is embarrassed. The reaction isn't fitting and something doesn't feel right.

"Miss Saito, what did you say to her?"

"I told her what you said." She smiles at me but something in her eyes makes me doubt her.

I ask, "Why was she embarrassed?"

She shrugs, "I'm not sure."

She is lying, and I feel it yet there is no one else here to translate for me. I make a knee jerk move and say, "I can manage from here."

She giggles, "What?"

"I don't need you any longer. I will just say my hellos and sign." I force a smile as I say it as I wish not to cause a scene. She regards me for a moment and Devon glances over and asks, "Is something wrong?"

I speak over Miss Saito before she can get a peep out, "Nothing is wrong Miss Saito is just going to step out and find Howard." She gives me a glare and I smile and wave bye to her. She said something different to that woman and I wish that I knew what it was.

I work through the rest of the book signing and the happy faces help me forget Miss Saito for the time which is good. The line dwindles down to the final people.

I glance over at Devon and he seems to be managing as well as I am.

Howard and Miss Saito return after the final people have come up to the table. She looks like a little teenage snot who knows she has been caught but maintains the, "what are you going to do about it stance". I won't trouble Howard about it since she is a descent translator. Howard isn't one for strife and frankly I don't want to be raising issues with the man who has transformed me into a best-selling author.

Howard looks pleased, "Your book piles have depleted. That's great."

Devon says, "A lot of people walked away with more than one copy so that helped. It was a smaller signing but it was good, right Jordan?"

"Yes, I think we did well."

Miss Saito says nothing and I don't care to raise it with Howard. Howard says, "Well this has been a great day. If you two would like to have a Japanese version of your book as a keep sake you can take one and leave the rest. The library staff will take care of cleaning up."

I jump on the opportunity, despite not liking the cover. I am still proud of the fact that my book is now translated.

Howard and Miss Saito guide us out with our goodbyes to the library staff and at the last minute I explain to Howard, "I think I am going to stay out a little longer and enjoy the sights."

Howard says, "Sure thing Jordan. I wanted all of us to meet for dinner again back at the hotel. You know, to catch up on things." He lingers on the last sentence.

"Sure, I just need to get out for a bit. We have been cooped up inside."

He smiles, "I don't blame you."

"Okay see you tonight everyone."

Devon asks, "Can I tag along with you?"

I do a double take. He is serious. I reply, "Sure"

He grins the same way he did the day we first met and I can't help but smile back. He says to Howard and Miss Saito, "I will see you guys this evening also."

The library is situated within a gorgeous park and my initial plan was to walk along the pathways and enjoy the beauty. It's cool here about nine degrees right now but in comparison to back home in Ottawa with the minus twenty-degree weather, this temperature is a treat.

I button my floral jacket and he takes my hand and puts it in the inside of his arm as though he was guiding me. We walk in silence for a few moments. When we are far enough away and no longer see Miss Saito or Howard, Devon finally asks, "What happened today between Miss Saito and you?"

"She lied to my face." I'm annoyed again just thinking about it.

Like the flow of a river Devon is steady and calm. He says, "Explain"

Something about him holding my hand is calming and I open up, "She was translating for me to an older woman and she said something to her that made the woman look embarrassed. The older woman left the table in a rush and when I asked Miss Saito about it, she blew me off."

Devon's pace slows a bit while he asks, "You don't know what she said?"

"No, but for someone to leave the table like that is not good and I could just tell that she had lied to my face. Like, who does she think she is? I don't get how Howard doesn't see it?"

He sighs, "Nobody is perfect."

We walk up a wooded trail in the park and pass a couple of other tourists. I wait for them to be out of earshot even though they probably don't understand English then say, "I know but still, you would think Howard would eventually catch something like that. Anyway, it's done, hopefully the damage stays just at that and I know how I feel and will tell Howard that I will pick my own translators if I am fortunate to have my book translated again. Anyway, enough about me. Do you think you will keep her as a translator?"

He looks up into the tree canopy and sighs, "Is this a loaded question?"

"No, I get you are acting like that because of what I thought had happened last night. I can tell you are being truthful. I'm just asking." I feel foolish about thinking that there was something more between Miss Saito and him.

"Honestly, I have not had any problems with her like you have. Well, I have had a small problem which I was going to explain to you this evening but since we are here and I can tell you now."

I say nothing and he explains, "Yes, your instincts were right she was flirting with me and I don't know what she wanted. She was asking casually about us, Sara, and Josh. She was more interested in our personal lives as opposed to helping us translate our communications with our books. I kept repeating the same stuff over again, which was, to not believe the tabloids and eventually she seemed to take it as an opportunity to move in on me." I glare at him, he says, "Jordan for god's sake, you asked me to always be honest with you and I am, hear me out, I declined her advances and she got the message, that I am dedicated to Sara. I am not even sure if Miss Saito was genuinely interested in me which doesn't matter because I'm not interested in her. I have a feeling that she was just flirting with me to find out information on us or to get us in trouble or something. It was like she had another agenda or something."

Our footsteps make weak hollow sounds as we walk over a wooden bridge where there is a pond below. There are some plants and shrubs growing but it's a little too cold for flowers.

I say, "I believe you but that just doesn't explain why you wouldn't just use another translator."

He shrugs, "It is water under the bridge."

I smirk, "Are you trying to be funny?"

He chuckles and then bear hugs me, "Oh girl, you have to smile sometimes. Sure, Miss Saito is a bit of a rotten apple but it's nothing that I can't manage. It's done, she has been put in her place and I didn't seem to have any issues at the signing. You my dear there is a bit more to it and trust me I am not trying to throw it in your face. I support everything you do and I think for your circumstance what you are doing is appropriate but for me a stern warning seemed to clear it up and if something else happens than I will deal with it."

We exit the gates of the park and find ourselves walking down the side walk. He asks, "Do you want to get a cab? There is this amazing mall not far from here and it looks like it has a roller coaster on the outside. Did you want to grab a bite to eat and maybe shop?"

"Okay"

Chapter 23
Dressed in Padding

The day rolls by at a good pace. I catch up with Devon, my friend and for the first time in a while I don't feel the slightest bit of animosity towards him. We eat, go on that roller coaster and he actually accompanied me on the ride, unlike Josh who always stays back. Josh prefers that his feet remain planted on the ground.

After a day of catching up as old friends we eventually retire back to our hotel rooms and he shows me the gentleman side to him and walks me back to my room.

We are at the door to my room and my heart flutters at the thought that this friendship may soon move up a level. He says, "This was nice Jordan, I needed this." He gives me a hug, just a friend hug, nothing more and pulls back for a moment and whispers, "You know you're a mother when."

I look up into those mysterious brown eyes of his and say, "What?"

He clears his voice and then leans down close to me and says in my ear, "You need to milk those puppies."

I look down, "Oh my god. Devon why didn't you say anything earlier?" I scold him. I have two small wet spots showing on my black dress where my breasts are from my milk.

He puts his hands up and says, "I just noticed now, honestly! You did have your jacket on so I am sure that I was the only one that saw and your secret is safe with me." He smiles but I can see he is still staring at my puppies.

I grumble, "Yes, well thanks for telling me and yes, I better milk my puppies before dinner. Will I see you in an hour?"

"Yes, I have to make a call to Sara anyway. See you tonight."

After saying goodbye to Devon, cleaning myself up and dealing with my boobs I decide that now is a good time to message Josh. He is usually up early for work and I send him a little hello. "Good morning, I am about to head down for dinner in a bit I just wanted to say good morning to you and hope that you have a wonderful day."

He is up because instantly I receive a reply from him, "Hey babes, what time is it there?"

"It is just approaching 6pm here."

"I just got up. It is a few minutes before 5am."

"I figured as much. How has Desiree been? How have you been?"

"Oh, you know same old. Desiree is doing just great with her grandma. My mom should be coming over in the next hour to spend the day with her. I think they plan on doing a grocery today and run some errands while I am at work. Did you have your signing already? How did it go?"

I sink into the comfy couch in the main area of my room, anticipating that messaging Josh will take a few minutes. I write, "Oh it was overall good. Had a bit of a blip with Miss Saito but I am going to tell Howard that I will get my own translator for any other signings."

"Did something happen?"

"Yes, but it is all water under the bridge now, don't worry about me I managed it and thanks for making yourself available last night to chat. I needed that."

"Glad to hear that things are going better. Well, I better start getting ready and your little girl says hello, although right now she is sleeping."

I miss her so much. It surprises me how much I could miss this new little person in my life but I do. "Josh, could you get away with snapping a picture of her and sending it to me or do you think you will end up waking her?"

"You miss her, eh? Yes, I think I can get away with not waking her. Give me a moment."

While I am waiting on Josh to send me a picture of our sleeping little girl I receive a text from Devon, "Hey there, we are just waiting in the lobby right now. You would be happy to know that your friend won't be accompanying us tonight."

"Hey Devon, I'll be down in a few moments, just lost track of time and P.S. I think that is the best news I have heard all day!"

Josh replies with a picture of our sleeping baby girl. Wow she is just so precious. I touch the screen with my finger, like I am touching her cheek. I reply, "Thanks love. Wow, I so want to jump on the next plane and head back."

"Enjoy your time out. You need a break from this mommy stuff and winter. I do hope that you take the time to enjoy yourself."

"I will, I promise. When she wakes up give her a kiss for me."

"I will, I love you and have a great night."

"I love you Josh, have a great day."

I get up from the couch, place my phone in my purse and head down to the lobby.

As usual Devon looks amazing. He is dressed more for the evening, wearing a dark denim with a brown leather belt and black print shirt with some grey design hoody and a dark blue corduroy jacket over top.

I do a double take at him. I am so used to seeing him dressed a certain way like for his book signings and this is just completely different. Devon of course catches me checking him out and I blush for being caught. Howard is on the phone and waves at me as I make my way down the escalator into the lobby. I decided to wear a dress I purchased in the afternoon. It's a navy print dress and I sport some grey leggings and grey fur boots with a camel-colored coat over top.

Devon says, "Well hello, that dress looks great on you."

"Thank you." My cheeks still feel warm.

"You look so different."

I ask, "Good different?

"Yes, I'm not used to seeing you dress like this."

"Should I change into something different?"

"Naw Jordan you look just fine to me."

My cowboy is a gentleman as always. Slowly my body is coming back to what it was before the baby. I feel better about my appearance a little bit more every day.

Howard gets off the phone and we head out to the cab that whisks us away to a restaurant. At some point there had been a change in plans on the restaurant and we venture out. It is a good change I don't need the memory of last night at the restaurant in the hotel.

Tokyo is for sure an experience all its own and if you don't have Tokyo on your bucket list of places to travel to you should for sure reconsider and add it.

We decided on a new sushi restaurant in the heart of the city. We step into the establishment and it reminds me of walking into some night club. Wow, they know how to make spaces beautiful here. The ceiling is layered in dark sand wood paneling. The walls are lined in wood and glass tile finishes. The floor is a combination of dark stained woods and ivory tiles. The tables and corner walls have lights reflecting up from the floor. The bar and chefs' tables have blue lights on them which just adds that touch of color to this interesting place.

The aroma in the air is fresh. I can smell the mild vapor in the air of fresh vegetables, rice, different sea foods and the tables are occupied with upscale looking people enjoying a night out. I glance around, some look to be businessmen who are out on the town, doing deals outside of the office. Others look to be out on dates. There doesn't seem to be any touristy type people. Everyone is dressed well and it's a mix of all sorts of people, old and young enjoying the night out.

The host greets us with a bow and in English he asks, "Do you have a reservation?"

Howard answers, "Yes, under Howard Stem."

The host quickly checks for Howard's name on his list and with a slight nod confirms that the reservation is there. He then extends one arm he replies, "Please follow me right this way."

I whisper to Howard, "How did he know to speak to us in English?"

He chuckles, "Jordan you look like a North American, that is why, and we are closer to the business district so there are a lot of English-speaking people in this area."

I whisper. "I understand."

We take a seat at the table and the host gives us each a menu before he departs. Devon and Howard start talking shop and I do what comes naturally and have a look at the menu while tuning them out for a few moments. This book stuff can get a little boring at times with always talking business, strategies, what to check out, what to read, where to go, which book signings to participate in. I let the men talk while I pretend to be listening as I read through the menu but really, I don't care right now. I am missing home even though it's the dead of winter.

I feel like I have fulfilled my author stuff for this trip and to be honest I am also content with clearing the air with Devon. I am happy that our friendship remains intact. This has been a good trip and about Miss Saito, I don't even care to know where she is or why she couldn't make it out to the restaurant this evening. There is no sense in even bringing up her name.

I glance down at the menu. Sushi really isn't my thing and to be honest the only sushi I have ever had didn't even come from a traditional Japanese restaurant. I tried one of those deli sushi platters that the local grocery store does up. It is sort of like a fast-food thing for people like me who don't like to cook but want a meal that isn't the typical fast-food burger and fries.

I consider this my first real time in trying authentic sushi. Devon and Howard continue to talk and I look through the menu. Thankfully it is translated to English and also has images of the food. I am decided on what I want. I am going with the crab sushi and oh I suppose I could have a drink since my breast milk isn't being consumed this week. I know exactly what I want. Something different, well not that different. I do love my wine and instead of doing the typical glass of red I feel like a glass of white, Chardonnay.

I close the menu and tune back into the discussion between Devon and Howard. They are actually not talking about books for once but it's a conversation that is of no interest to me. It's about the results of their precious Super Bowl from the beginning of February. American's, they get so worked up about a sport that I just don't get. Football to me is a bunch of men dressed in padding that clobber each other to get a weird shaped ball across the playing field. All the hype around it is just nuts. The commercials, the half time shows, the passionate fans, the countless number of parties that happen and all to watch a game. I find it fascinating the appeal that it has but it's just something that I can't get into. I know my place and these two are deep into talking about it even though it's all done for this year.

I listen as the two discuss play by plays and what they would have had the players do and to my relief the waiter comes to the table.

"Hello, what can I get you to drink?"

Howard speaks for all of us, "He and I will have your best pale lager beer and she will have a glass of your Malbec."

I speak up and say, "Howard, actually I would like something different." I ask the waiter, "Could I have a glass of your Chardonnay?"

The waiter says, "Certainly" bows and leaves the table.

Devon takes a break from the football discussion with Howard and asks me, "Choosing something different?"

I perk up, "Yes, felt like having a white wine tonight."

"Got yah." Devon knows that I usually go for a Malbec. His smile is so alluring and sitting next to Howard and across from Devon, I have a front row seat to a handsome man that completely distracts me at times.

Howard brings up more book talk, "While you two were doing the book signing earlier. I got in touch with the people who manage one of the larger book store chains in Tokyo." I have mixed feelings about this. I want to do the signing but I rather not have to dive into the conversation so soon with telling Howard in nicer words that I am no longer using his stupid translator. Howard continues, "Tomorrow I have arranged a quick photo shoot. It's more for press, then I have organized for you to do another meet and greet and I promise I have nothing else planned so you are free for the rest of your stay."

Devon says, "That's great that you managed that, Howard."

He smiles, "I thought so. It is just such a long journey to make for one event and I am trying to squeeze us in where I can."

I say, "This was a much different experience than New York was with the language barrier and all." Why did I just admit that?

Howard says, "I agree, and it's a good thing that we had Miss Saito here to help."

Her name startles me like a rude smell that makes me need to hold my breath. I want to let him know but the waiter interrupts the chain of thought.

"Your drinks." He places them at our settings then asks, "Madame, can I take your order?"

"Yes, can I have you crab sushi dish?"

His eyes close shut for a second as he nods and answers, "Of course."

The waiter takes the next order, casting his attention to Devon. "For you Sir?"

Devon replies, "I will have the sukiyaki." The waiter nods and then looks at Howard who says, "I'll have your assorted sushi platter."

The waiter departs and I have my chance to get it off my chest. "Howard?"

"Yes" His calming gaze has my attention.

I clear my throat and say, "For tomorrow I am just fine without a translator."

He sips his beer then says, "It is always good to have one."

"I'm not disagreeing with you, it's just." I am trying to leave out the emotion.

He tilts his head to the side, obviously completely confused and I can't do it. I can't say what I want to say and bring on the slightest cause of negativity. Miss Saito is his handpicked translator and to decline her would be like declining his personal recommendation.

I say, "Oh I know that she is working hard for us. It's just with yesterday's signing I felt like I got along well even with the language barrier."

He chuckles, "That's why I hired her. She is a hard worker and it's always good to have a translator, just in case."

I nod and I catch a glimpse of a concerned glance from Devon. He knows what I was trying to do and his eyes say, just hang in there. One more day of her, not even, just a couple of hours of having to endure her at most.

Our dinner comes and I discover another food that I end up liking. Back home, I never understood the hype around sushi, like I said before I have had those dishes made at the grocery store counter and I could say that they were not bad, but sushi was a dish I would never crave. I compare sushi to shepherd's pie, good, hits the spot and satisfies the hunger but not something I would go out of my way to have often. This real sushi I totally get now how people come to love this stuff. It's much different in taste and in a good way.

Dinner is nice tonight; the company is good and before long I am saying good bye to Howard and Devon.

My room is clean when I return. There is a new basket of assortments, clean towels in the washroom and the bed is neatly made. I step out of my heels and remove a load of bobby pins from my hair to let it flow freely. I take out my phone and send Josh a text to let him know how the evening went and say goodnight although he is thirteen hours behind me and it is late morning for him.

My state of mind is okay, just going with the flow of things and content with the second half of the day that seemed to set my world back in place.

I decide to put off my shower until the morning and instead get into some comfy pajamas and settle on the couch and hope that there is something in English that I can watch.

I click the remote, channel surfing for a few moments. My phone is on the table in front of me and the screen lights up. I lean over, thinking that it was Josh lighting up my screen but nope it's Devon.

The text reads, "Hey, I didn't want to make it obvious but could I come to your room?"

Before I have the chance to reply he writes, "This Japanese television sucks and I would rather spend my downtime with a friend."

I reply, "Hey, sure come on over."

Within ten minutes a light tap at the door signals his arrival. I open the door and he gives me a look up and down and smirks. He is a flirt but I know he had said I was a friend in his last text.

I shrug, "I wasn't expecting company." I think this is the first time he has seen me looking homely in my pajamas instead of my usual routine of dressing up for him. My hair is all wavy from letting my hair down.

He smiles while walking across the threshold, "It's quite alright and no matter what you wear you are a hottie in my books."

I chuckle walking passed him and over to the new basket. I glance over my shoulder back at him and say, "You are too kind. So, let's say you and I dip into this treat basket and watch some show that we don't have a clue what they are saying."

His eyes have a glow to them as he relaxes onto the couch and I bring the basket over. He says, "Girl, you know how to make crappy activities sound fun."

"You know it sexy!" Oh, I didn't mean to let my old nickname of him slip but decide not to apologize for it. He knows it was probably a slip. I continue, "Hey you know what? They have your favorite snack here?"

"What's that?" Our eyes meet for a second and I am the first to let my glance go to the basket to search for it.

I reply, "Those little peanut butter and jelly crackers." I lean closer to the basket and reach in, pulling them out of the center of the arrangement.

"Boohaah, give those here!" Our fingers touch as I hand the crackers over and I can't bring myself to look at him because I know I will blush.

I settle with a package of fudge cookies and I get up and walk over to the mini fridge and offer, "I am having a chocolate milk, want one?"

"I would love one." Devon replies looking back at me.

I bring our drinks over and sink into the couch next to him and hand over the remote while I munch on my cookies. A few moments go bye in silence as we just eat and stare at the shows passing by on the screen and you know what, we are comfortable without the need for conversation.

I finish my pack of cookies and I am not sure if I want to dip into something else. I glance over and his cracker wrapper, which is already on the coffee table.

He asks, "What were you going for next?"

"I don't know? I was thinking something salty but the fact that we just had dinner I don't understand why I have the munchies." I lick my lips, self-conscious that I may have chocolate fudge cookie crumbs on them and Devon keeps looking at me in a way that is causing my heart to thump.

He casually says "Maybe you are pregnant?"

I give him a playful shove, "Ha ha ha, ya right. You know, since Desiree has been born, Josh and I haven't had any. We came close last week but I was still a little sore."

He replies, "That is understandable. When my ex had our son, I think it was four months before she came around."

"It's not the fact that I don't want to, it's more the toll it takes. When we have time, I am tired and not to mention I was sore when the opportunity presented. I sound like an old person."

"You sound like a mom."

"Thanks" I'm not sure if he meant that as a compliment or a jab.

He replies, "No problem. How about we split that bag of kettle chips?"

After a few moments of being distracted by Devon's channel surfing and the combination of being tired after a day out and about, I forget that he was making me nervous and I snuggle up to him on the couch. We share the bag of chips, my teddy bear. Devon actually manages to find some action movie being played in English.

As we watch a text from Josh comes in, "Hey, did you want to meet up after work?"

I reply, "Josh? I am still in Tokyo. Did you mean to send that to a friend?"

Devon glances down and I explain, "I just got a text from Josh about meeting up after work. He probably meant to send that to a work friend."

He regards me, "Is everything okay between you two?"

"As far as I know it is. He seems to understand that the tabloids are not real."

I ask Devon, "Have you talked to Sara today? Is she okay?"

I feel the rise and fall of his sigh as I am all comfy next to him. "We are as good as good can be. She has been through the ringer but has chosen to stay."

I don't look up at him and continue to relax as he wraps and arm around me. I keep my eyes on the movie as I reply, "I know that is what you want."

I see my phone light up as a text comes in from Josh. He writes, "Sorry, yes I meant to send that to a buddy here at work. We were going to shoot a bit of pool before my mom leaves for the evening." I'm comfortable reading the messages from Josh in front of Devon and don't move from my spot on the couch with him.

I reply to Josh's message, "Gotcha, well I am off to bed have a great rest of the day. Love you."

Devon glances over understanding that I need a moment to text a reply to Josh and he waits for me to click send before he answers, "As it is now, yes."

His answer is confusing because I am not sure if he is alluding to us being together this evening or the fact that he has managed to keep a lover and a wife. I no longer challenge him in trying to decipher his weird comments. It always turns into conversations that I rather not have. I know that he will make it clear to me if he wants to play.

We continue watching our movie and soon enough my boobs start to hurt. Without thinking I touch them; they aren't leaking yet but they are sore enough that I can't put it off any longer. I was warm and relaxed snuggled up next to Devon. There is no need to make him leave. It won't take long to go to the bedroom to find the pump. As I get up off the couch, I take off my t-shirt and expose myself. I need to pump my girls.

Devon is a deer in the headlights. He swallows then asks as I'm about to leave to the bedroom, "What are you doing?"

I start to laugh only because I am tired and just the combination of us relaxing, for a moment I felt like I was home. I didn't forget that I was with Devon but for a moment in time I forgot that he is a guest in my suite and not my spouse. I say, "My god, I must be tired. I'm not trying anything I swear. Geez I'm embarrassed but then again you have seen them already. I have to take care of my girls; they are starting to leak." I fumble through my words but give up and walk quickly into the room and close the door so that I can take care of matters. I'm sure he's going to leave now since I just made this entire evening awkward. Devon was staring and the last thing I want to do is distract him since he has made it clear that he is working on his relationship with Sara. I love him but respect his wishes to focus on his own relationship.

A few moments passed and as I predicted, Devon taps on the bedroom door. Before I can say anything, he slowly opens it as I try to cover myself under the covers. I see the fire in his eyes as he approaches the bed. Now I am the deer in the headlights. I say nothing, I know his mind is already made and I feel myself ignite with a hunger of wanting him again.

He loosens his belt and it drops to the floor along with his pants. He removes his shirt and then pulls his briefs down, exposing his swollen member. I want him and he knows it but the silly thing is the distraction of my girls. Wow they hurt so much and the thing is I don't know if I should let the pump do its thing, stop for a bit to allow Devon to give himself to me or what?

He climbs in beside me and having the experience of being a father he takes the machine and turns it off for the moment and puts it on the table next to the bed. I rub my girls; oh, they are sore.

He murmurs, "From the moment I saw you I wanted to suck those puppies of yours. Wow they are massive."

His eyes are hungry and he holds them gently and then places his lips to my nipple for a taste. I lie back and let him, my kinky man and the longer I allow it the harder he sucks and it feels painful and as a relief all at once.

He is making me wet as I feel his own blush poke me and he takes his hand and slowly traces a path to my sex. It is like he is giving me the time to say no, but the thing is I want it and allow it. He continues down passed my hips and slowly down to the top of my lips. I sigh, he has stopped there and he bites harder on my breast. I gasp but don't pull away. I tilt my pelvis up to his fingers and he knows that I want it and he proceeds to that right spot that turns my body to jelly. He makes my pussy wet like a submarine with screen doors and brings me to the edge. I sigh again in frustration. He stops for a moment and looks into my own hungry eyes with that grin of his. I'm not sure why he has stopped and I look to him for an answer.

He asks, "You want me?"

"Yes, I want that big dick of yours massaging my insides and coating me with your juices." I pant back to him.

He smiles and says, "I want you to get on top."

He lies down and I slowly take his massive erection. I am still tender but manage to handle him and besides it's been a month now. It feels different like my muscles are tired down there but needless to say his size fills me up and it still feels like there is a massive dick inside me. I slowly rock my hips and he brings me down to him so that my girls are in his face. He focuses his attention on one and bites down and then sinks his face between my girls while I continue to move up and down slowly along his shaft.

It is a bit of a struggle to get the muscles working. I am so close but at the same time it's like I have forgotten how to get my release.

I sigh and with that Devon takes his last suck, emptying my other girl with a milk drip on his lips. He says "You have sugar milk in them puppies' girl. You're having trouble, aren't you?"

I sigh in frustration but not slowing I gasp "I'm just so close."

He takes his hands, placing them on my curvy hips and presses firmly so that the weight of his hands brings his length further into me. He says, "You like that, I can tell."

"I do." I close my eyes and let a smile cross my pouty lips.

With that he takes control, dominating me even though I am the one on top and he makes my kitty purr and I moan to the beat of my throbs.

"That a girl." He chuckles at the surprise on my face. Wow that was good.

He keeps me on top and presses himself into me watching my expressions from the pleasure. I notice the muscles in his arms and chest flex and relax with each move. He speeds up his motions and brings himself to his edge but doesn't release, instead he pulls out and I know what he wants.

I place my warm lips on him and within seconds he gives me his own sugar.

We relax together in the bed. It is an unspoken truth. We know that we don't need to remind each other. This, what just happened, it is what it is and as long as it is kept between us the world will continue to function as it should.

He regards me for a moment and I look up at him. He says, "If it could be like this all of the time, I would be in heaven."

I sigh and say, "I wasn't picturing heaven in a country where I didn't understand the language."

"Jordan, you are such a dork." He chuckles and tickles me.

"Hey, stop it."

"What I'm not doing anything." He's still tickling me.

I try to squirm free, "Devon, you're going to make me pee in bed and I'm not joking!"

"Okay, okay." He smiles, "Should we shower?"

"Only if it means we will sleep after this." I explain.

"I tuckered you out, have I?" He touches my arm lightly as he asks.

"You have and it was absolutely amazing. I needed that but I have to admit my muscles are completely out of whack down there." I was embarrassed to admit that to myself but with him I feel like I can be honest. I am healing and all of this no longer feels the same.

"You still felt good to me." His is gentle and honest and it makes me feel better about the post baby situation and I give him a hug.

Chapter 24
Front Page News

Wednesday morning, I wake alone in my empty hotel suite. Devon returned to his room after we showered. It was for the best. Tokyo is a new market and there is no need to start the tabloids here with the entire affair bit.

Today there is going to be a short photo shoot at the book store for marketing purposes and I decide to not rely on myself for hair and makeup and book an appointment with the hotel's hair salon. These are the perks to staying at a hotel that caters to business. You have easy access to professionals that specialize in making people look great. It is just amazing.

I pick out my clothes today and decide on a black dress pant and blouse with the button open just down to my chest and I accessorize it with gold earrings, necklace bangles, and belt, finishing the look with flat shoes. I feel great inside and out and the worry that I tend to have about hair and makeup is all but nothing since the professionals have that bit covered.

I head down to the lobby for the morning and the salon is just along the corridor on the second level of the lobby atrium. I should have booked hair and makeup yesterday with my book signing but the thought had just escaped me then because there was so much to do.

It is clear that I am still not really used to the life that my books have given me. The opportunity to live, I mean I can now afford my own personal assistant to help me out with this event stuff. I could hire someone to look after booking hair and makeup and coordinating my schedule around the events but then again Howard hasn't called on me much because of the birth. I am rambling, just trying to rationalize it. I guess that I really don't need a personal assistant since I am really not doing many events and besides Howard has helped thus far in that department with planning the events.

The salon is clean and the decor is all in white. The girl at the main counter checks me in. She has a heavy accent but is fluent in English. "Jordan Connor?"

"Yes"

"Aki will be your stylist for today please follow me."

I'm not sure if I mentioned this but being on time is a very important part of the culture here and when your appointment is at a specific time, you need to expect that it is exactly that. I check my watch and I am thankfully on time. If I was late, it would have been considered very disrespectful.

I sit down and Aki greats me with a smile, "Nice to meet you. So, you wish for hair and makeup."

"Yes, I have a photo shoot today." I smile at her waiting for her instruction.

"How exciting." She approaches closer and plays with my hair and continues, "I can feel that your hair was just washed and there is no product in your hair."

"That is right." She gestures me to take a seat in a salon chair that's in front of a mirror.

I watch her reflection as she continues to tassel my hair in her slender hands for a moment, thinking what to do and wasting no time. She asks, "You are wearing the outfit that you have on now for the photo shoot?" I nod and she explains while still playing with my hair, "I will do a messy side bun and give you some volume before it is pinned in place so that it doesn't look flat and what I will do is give you an edgy side bang to frame your face." Her red lips beam a smile to me in the mirror.

I smile, "Sounds great"

She works quickly with her fingers working through my brown silky hair and while she moves my strands in place, she says, "A lot of our clients are celebrities but I have never worked with a celebrity that is front page news."

I chuckle, "You are being way too kind. I have met success as an author but I am definitely not front-page news. Authors don't get that sort of press."

She shakes her head, "I speak the truth you are front page news." She pauses and while still holding my hair in place with her other hand, she reaches for a newspaper on the counter in front of my chair and hands it to me.

The tabloids are all in Japanese text and in the center is a collage of pictures of Devon and me, at the book signing, getting into cars, walking in the park, shopping at the mall. I also recognize the older woman from the signing in one of the pictures. Miss Saito had said something to her and I have the sinking suspicion that it is written here.

"Aki, I didn't know that this was in the newspaper. Could you tell me what it says?"

She leans closer to me to read and explains, "It is saying that you are here to introduce your book to the Japanese market and it also says that you are spending time with your lover D. Chambers, while your husband and child are home in Canada."

I touch my hand to my head. I can tell from the pictures that the old woman was the one who fed that to the media and her source was my fucking translator.

Aki sees I am clearly upset and she continues, "Tokyo sees articles like this all the time. Any advertising is good even if it is not true. Don't worry Jordan, I will make you look beautiful today and this will be all forgotten by tomorrow."

"Thank you" I sigh.

As Aki pins my hair in place, I wonder if Howard saw this and if he could connect the dots? Well, whatever it's done. Why would Miss Saito do that to us? It is all too familiar and I just don't understand.

By the time Aki is finished with my hair and makeup, I glance into the mirror, I actually look like a celebrity.

"Thank you, Aki."

"You are welcome. I wish you good luck."

I leave a large tip as a thank you. Aki doesn't know but I left her more than I was planning to because she shared the information from the newspaper. I head back down to the lobby and meet Howard and Devon.

I catch Devon's subtle glance and know that he approves of my appearance and I smile back as I approach them.

"Howard, did you see the newspaper?"

His voice doesn't waiver when he replies, "I had. It seems like it was some very imaginative fan of yours."

"Howard, it wasn't that old woman's fault. Miss Saito had said that to her. The lady was asking questions and Miss Saito said something to her that made her leave the table in an odd state." I had to say it. I mean I tried to the night before at dinner but now the words just fall out of my mouth.

Howard doesn't seem surprised but more like disappointed. "Jordan, if you wish not to use her services, I will completely understand. There is no way of knowing for sure who said what so it is not something I can't act openly on."

"I understand."

As we walk to the cab Devon murmurs to me, "I think she was bought off."

I whisper, "Steven Peach?"

"Yes"

I shake my head at the mention of his name. What is that guy's problem? He got his revenge and Devon and I still managed to overcome the collateral damage.

When we arrive for the photoshoot and there are paparazzi to greet us. My instincts are to hide and run as fast as I can into the building but Howard reminds us to breathe, smile and take it in stride. Devon doesn't need the pep talk; he is in his element. Howard's advice is more for me. This is too much. I don't like this; my palms are sweaty and I can feel my chest flush.

Thankfully there is security at the doors to keep them out and it's like a sigh of relief once inside.

Devon whispers, "Are you good?"

I nod. He gently rubs the side of my back. He knows that I am flustered. The photo shoot is nothing to write home about, it is just a part of the job and the hired photographers get the shots that they need of Devon and me with our books. I eventually relax and even have a little fun with it and the book signing afterwards is easier. We are soon done our work for the day.

While back in the cab Howard asks, "What do you have planned for the rest of the day?"

I sigh, "I think I am going to retire back to the hotel and try to get in touch with Josh. I may go out later once the paparazzi give up."

"Yes, it is probably for the best. Well, you guys are officially here now on your own time and of course Tail Fin will pick up the tab. You two are free."

I want to go home at this point, get back to Desiree and Josh and I think I may have some more damage control to do if the news from Japan has reached North America.

Chapter 25
Good for Him Good for Me

I step into my hotel suite and shortly after Devon taps on my door. I recognize his three light taps.

I open the door to confirm that it is him. I back up and he steps in, careful to let the door close behind him with a gentle click. He will always be my cowboy, wow he just does it for me, so handsome and focused like I am the only one for him.

Before I have the chance to do anything he takes me in his arms and kisses is me. "I wanted to do that all day Jordan. Damn you are beautiful girl."

I say nothing and lean close to him, biting that sexy bottom lip of his. He grins at my persistence and bits back while stepping forward so that I step back further into the room.

He growls and says, "Girl you drive me nuts."

I feel for his pants and unzip and let him out. He doesn't disappoint and I am hungry for him, I go down on my knees and put my lips to his swollen length. He sighs and I can feel he is absolutely loving it and it is driving me wild. His scent, his man standing tall for me, he is pre coming in my mouth and I lap him up. He is mine and I can't shove him in any further as I suck his shaft hoping for him to glaze my throat.

I stop for a moment and watch his eyes open and I say to him. "We are taking this to the couch and I want you to give me all of your hot lava."

"Damn girl, I am okay with that."

I love giving him head, love to see him so relaxed that he can't do a single thing but remain rock solid and explode on my queue. His sighs and thrusts into my mouth as he tries to seek more pleasure, his eyes rolling in the back of his head as I lick and suck and move up and down and taste the tip of his head. It makes me so wet that I am nearly coming on myself. I tease and play and he says in a breath, "I'm going to come." With that I draw him in further. He throbs out his warm liquid happiness for me to taste.

"Girl you are good and I am not done yet. I want to fuck you so bad."

He sits up and he struggles to remove my gold belt. I help him and get out of my clothes. He pulls me onto his lap and I take a seat on his hardness.

He pumps into me and presses up against the weight and I moan at the feeling of him messaging my insides. Each breath of his hitches and the smell of him makes my body quiver. I never desired a mate as much as him. He is taking it slow for me, controlled and I kiss his warm lips.

Even though I initiate the kiss he takes control and he tastes me with his tongue like I am some sweet savory dessert. His tongue is warm, gentle and in control and desire takes control and all I know right now is Devon, my desire, love and man.

He whispers to me, "I want you to get yours."

Again, it's a struggle, my muscles are still gaining strength but Devon makes me sopping wet. He slows his pace to slide in deep and allows me to feel all of him. He knows that I am hungry and want to climax and he takes his hand and reaches behind pressing into my other opening with a finger. Touching the nerves that quickly send me moaning to the edge.

"Oh, you are yummy, squirt all over me." He whispers in my ear.

My heartbeat is racing and I moan and explode. "Mmm you are my everything cowboy."

He smiles, "You are mine in this moment."

I say to him, "I know you have another in you."

"I do. I know you are having some trouble. I can hold off."

I pout, "I want you to get another."

He looks at me unsure and I slide off of his length for a moment and then slide back down onto him with my other opening. It's a tight fit but he slides in. My hot lube has covered the area.

He sighs closing his eyes.

"Does that feel nice?" I whisper to him while rocking gently.

He whispers, "Wooha, you are so tight."

I slide up and down his length and he does not object. He is quickly on the edge, not used to the feeling of a tight, slick and juicy, voluptuous ass pleasing him. His hands soon take control making me move to the rhythm of his own desire he slows me down so that he can last.

"Oh Jordan, ah Jordan, you make me so fucking hard I am about to explode."

I whisper, "I want your white-hot loving. Give it to me."

His final thrusts are strong and he plows me hard knowing that I can handle it like this and lets out a sigh of relief as he releases his love deep inside me.

I smile knowing full well that it was good for him, good for me. It is nice to get to sleep with your friend.

Chapter 26
Natural Disasters

While watching the evening news, I learn without having to understand the language, the motive for Miss Saito to go rogue on us and make up a bunch of crap to feed to the press. There is a short report of Devon and me. We sit down on the couch in my suite and learn the details. We have no clue what is being said but I can take a guess by the images being provided on the screen. The television crew try desperately to question Miss Saito in a video clip. It looks like she is headed back to the United States seeing that she is outside the airport and there we both see from the news footage that she is traveling with the thorn in Devon and my side, Steven Peach.

I glance at Devon for his reaction and say, "He paid her more?"

He sighs, "That's the only reasonable explanation. What a fucker."

"How long is he going to bother us?"

"I don't know. All I know is that he holds grudges and since he can't ride our coat tails with the profits coming in on our book sales, he will try to hurt us by other means and that is with our relationships."

"If Josh sees this, it isn't going to drive a wedge between him and I. Josh has a good understanding of the media and trusts me."

Devon looks at me, "Are you sure about that?"

"Yes, why are you questioning it?" I stop watching the television and glance at Devon.

"Jordan, I thought Sara was tough as nails when it came to that sort of stuff, but eventually you know the rest. She started to have her doubts and then things led to her finding the truth."

I shake my head, "Josh isn't like that. Besides, he isn't even in tune with me like Sara is with you. Steven will never make Josh doubt me."

His chest rises and falls and he picks up his beer that he had been nursing from the coffee table and says, "For both our sakes I hope that you are right. If Sara catches wind of this latest news, I am sure that it will be the end and Steven will win his match." He takes a sip of his beer.

I say, "This won't get to North America. Think about it, with the news that we do see, hardly anything ever comes from this side of the world to our television screens back home. It only ever seems to be natural disasters or war not who is sleeping with who."

He nods, "I suppose that you are right. Well, I better get back to my own room. I need to do some work before bed. See you tomorrow?" He picks up his empty bottle with intent to drop it in the trash near the door before departing.

"Yes" I follow Devon to the door.

I hug him and he gives me a kiss on the forehead. Devon whispers, "You have to let me go."

"I know just give me a second." He chuckles because of my extended hug that I am inflicting on him. Eventually I let him go and I soon find myself alone to retire for the night. After sending Josh a quick little hello. I won't bother going online to look at the media. I know I'll be up all night if I allow myself to pay attention to it.

Chapter 27
Miss Saito's Purse

I step off the plane and into the airport with my little pink carryon bag with chunky black straps on my shoulder. This trip was worth it and for the money I made I would do it again. It was exciting and I felt like I was a part of something and at the end of it I have the extra money that I can use as I see fit.

I pick a second bag up at the luggage pick up and then continue thru the airport. Some of my friends in the USA ask if I feel bad for doing what I did to Jordan and Devon and I tell them that I don't. How can I feel bad for doing something that gets me ahead? Honestly what happened will eventually be forgotten those two aren't that famous. Besides, those two make so much money that this won't put them out. I pause outside of LaGuardia Airport Terminal and spot the next available taxi in the lineup and proceed towards it.

They should have expected it since they have cheated, its karma. I can tell a liar from far away and those two are doing a poor job at hiding the truth from the public.

Those two need to quit their crying and get over themselves. If Steven Peach asks me again for help, I'll accept. He pays well and the job is easy and fun like a game. I feel like I am a sneaky character in a game that has accomplished her mission and getting her reward.

The cab driver pops his trunk and I put my luggage inside and step into the car. I give the cab driver my address and we are on route. The money has already been deposited into my account and that makes me so happy.

I'm already making more than my friends and with such little effort.

Chapter 28
Mount Nango

This day is for myself and to be honest I need to get out of this hotel and the city, see some sites before heading back to Canada. I decide on a pair of black leggings, grey loose cowl neck sweater and a light grey wool jacket with a brown knee-high leather boot. I don't think I will ever get tired of having the luxury of shopping. I love my new clothes. Before I became a well-known author I had money, mind you I always remained on a tight budget, and only ever purchased when the best deals were on, clear out prices and such and now when I see something I like I can simply get it and that is exactly what I did with Devon the other day.

It's just after 9:00am and have an idea of what I want to do. I plan to jump on a train to one of the nearby mountains, mount Nango. It will allow me to clear my head and maybe refocus myself.

Before leaving I check my phone and there is a message from Josh. He says, "Hey I got your message earlier and I am worried about you, I caught wind of what hit the media. You know you could have told me. Hope you are okay."

God Jordan you are stupid at times. Of course, he is googling the news on me and of course he would see. Well, his reaction is good, at least he doesn't believe it. I text back, "Hey, I am okay, it was Miss Saito that fed into the lies. Anyway, she was a no show at the photo session yesterday and I am almost certain that Steven Peach was behind it. Anyway, I was hoping that you wouldn't see it just because it was a bunch of bullshit that ultimately had no effect on the outcome of our trip. I am taking today to see some of the sites since there is no book related work scheduled and this evening, I'll be jumping on my flight home. I can't wait to wrap my arms around you, bye lovey."

I think it is okay. Josh is a facts kind of guy and well even with the media it's a "they said" situation and the photos don't show anything other then what they were.

I should message Howard and Devon so that they aren't left wondering on where I am if they stop by my room and I am gone.

"Good morning, Howard, I am just stepping out early to see some of the sites. If we don't cross paths today, I just want to say thank you again for the opportunity. I will be back at the hotel this evening to pack up and check out. I hope to thank you in person and if not, you know where to find me." I add an emoticon with a wink face and send it.

My last message is to Devon, "Hey I am just heading out on my own this morning to be a tourist. If we don't see each other before my flight departs, I want you to know that the best part of this trip was getting to see you. Anyway, have a safe flight."

I click send and then head down to the lobby.

The early morning brings a lot of activity at the reception desk and that is okay because I am not ready to go now, I plan on taking the late flight out tonight to sleep and not be caught with the feeling of wasting a day in flight.

"Jordan?" A voice hollers and an echo of my name repeats in the hallway.

I turn to see him, "Oh hey cowboy." I give him a hug and ask, "Are you flying out this morning?"

"Actually, no I have another day like you." He smiles and I already know where this is going. I feel a date card coming on. Devon continues, "You know I was thinking, all of our meeting up can't always be about you know. If you will have me, I would like to spend the day with you. Would you like that?"

I can't contain my smile; he is so cute. I admit, "It's always nicer to share the experience with a friend. I didn't want to ask you to come and have you be bored to death. I really picked an activity for myself to relax and such."

Devon nods, "If you need your alone time, I can take no for an answer."

I shake my head, "No, that's not what I am saying. Well, I don't know what I am saying." I chuckle, "Devon, I would love you to come with me but I warn you that you may be bored.

"Try me. What did you have in mind?"

"Well, I had my heart set on getting out and seeing nature, and the skyline. I was planning to go to mount Nango, mount Maku, and mount Shiro, it is about an hour train ride to get there."

"Wow that is quite the trek to become one with nature and see the skyline. Could I maybe make a suggestion?"

"Sure" I am pretty easy going when making plans, as long as I am out doing something new and different, I am open to suggestion.

He continues, "I know you mentioned that you want to head out and see the nature in the area. I actually heard of this really nice temple in the city and it's actually not a tourist trap. It's not as busy as some of the other temples in Tokyo. The place is called, Zojoji Temple. Apparently, it is enormous and built in the 1300's." He glances at me to see if I am approving of his destination suggestion. He continues, "Anyway, you said nature and the place has a beautiful garden. Apparently, there is a market just a short train ride away that we could grab lunch there."

I say, "Okay I am with you so far but what about getting a view of the skyline? That was another reason I was thinking about doing the mountain hike."

"Oh, don't you worry about that I have got you covered." A spark of mystery resonates from those brown eyes of his.

"What do you mean?" My curiosity has his full attention. I am no longer aware of busyness of the hotel lobby we are standing in.

He leans closer, "Have you heard of Tokyo Tower?"

"I have."

"It kind of looks like the Eiffel Tower in Paris, only this one is smaller and it is painted orange. I have seen reviews that the view from the Tower is great. So, can I twist your arm and have you change your plans?" He has that confidant grin of his. The cowboy smile that makes you wonder if he is being a bad boy. He is, with making a girl change her plans but I have to admit that his plans seem much more interesting than mine.

"There you go changing my mind cowboy. It seems like great plans, actually sounds much better than the plan I had made."

Like a gentleman he answers, "Your plan was good but this old cowboy wouldn't last with hiking up a mountain."

I roll my eyes, "Devon you say the silliest things sometimes."

He gives me his arm and leads the way. The shopping the other day was good, fun and different with being able to shop in another city but having a day to do this before the flight back makes it feel like this was a sort of mini vacation.

The paparazzi don't bother us today. There are no articles in the paper or anything like that. The press has moved on to their next story and without really knowing I am guessing that Miss Saito is not popping in anytime soon. I am confident that she did indeed return to the United States based on what we saw on that news feature last night.

Zojoji Temple is just as Devon had described. We walk the grounds in the crisp cool air. It feels like a Canadian spring day. The only thing that is odd about the grounds and gardens is they are lined with rows upon rows of these little statues that resemble children. They are even dressed in clothing.

I ask, "What do you suppose this is all about?" I point at the little statues.

He shrugs, "I have no idea, but it is pretty interesting."

We continue walking along the rows of these statues and he asks, "You know that you and I will always be best friends, right?"

I say, "Of course. I was only upset because it felt like you were turning your back to me. I know we are both busy but I do expect for us to connect and talk every so often."

"I know. You know I only did what I thought was best. You have a new addition to your family and I don't need to be someone looking in from the outside."

"You are not intruding and I wish you would just be normal." I look up at him, seeing concern on his clean-shaven face.

He chuckles, "Jordan you know none of this is normal but I do get what you are saying. I will always be here for you. I won't make that mistake again." He wraps his arm around me as we continue along the gardens. Something has changed in him from the night before, it is small but it's almost like some weight has been lifted. I guess it is Miss Saito now being out of our hair and these book signings are out of the way.

I sigh, "My cowboy."

He chuckles, "What?"

"Oh nothing. I just like these moments we share. Can I tell you something?"

"What's that?"

I take his hand, stopping him mid step, lean up to his ear and whisper, "Your dick feels amazing."

He replies, "Boohaah!" It's a little louder than what is normal for the temple and a few people nearby turn their heads in our direction. I giggle and he continues to say in a whisper this time, "If you ever wanted, just ask and I can give you another child."

I smile, "Thanks that means a lot. Desiree means more to me than I would have ever imagined. I actually wanted to leave Japan shortly after arriving but Josh encouraged me to stay and enjoy myself."

"That was nice of him and think about it, you will see your family very soon."

I take a few pictures of the child like statues. Devon offers and takes some pictures with my phone of me with the statues so that I can send a picture of myself to Josh. I send my best photo over to Josh through text after Devon hands back my phone.

I ask, "Do you want me to take some of you to send to Sara?"

"Naw that's okay."

I chide, "Devon, she probably misses you."

He is reluctant and my only guess is because of the fighting between them but I know that if he puts some effort into sharing what's going on over here it could help. Well minus the encounters he has had with me. Finally, he gives in and hands his phone over to me.

I tease him, "Devon what kind of smile is that?" He shrugs and I continue, "Smile like I am showing you, my boobs." I start giggling.

He chuckles and grins and I take some good pictures of him.

We go into the temple it's beautiful, colorful, well taken care of for such an old structure. We probably spend an hour wondering around and eventually make are way to the train and end up in the market feasting on fresh sushi for lunch.

I check my phone to see if I receive a message from Josh he writes, "Wow neat pictures. Desiree and I will meet you at the airport. Do you know what time you are landing at?"

I struggle with time. Hmm I would arrive the next morning late morning, I text him, "I should be there around 11:00 am your time." Home is thirteen hours behind but the flight itself is about 13 hours so it will be like picking up where I had left off whereas when I had gone to Tokyo, I lost a day in travel. I think that's how the time difference works?

Afterword, Devon and I walk the market together and talk about everything and anything. I catch a glimpse of him and he seems like he is holding back on something even though we have been talking none stop. I ask, "What's eating you up?"

"Oh, just dreading going back home to Sara. That's all. I know that it sounds bad but it is my life and I need to deal with it."

"You will make it right. She probably liked those photos from the temple that you sent to her."

I can tell that he doesn't like talking about her to me and I just leave it at that because I see the look in his eye, sadness and I don't want our last day in Tokyo together to be sad. I say, "Well Josh saw my pictures I sent him earlier from the temple he thought they were neat."

He says, "Follow me."

I follow him through the busy streets full of stands and shops and into a clothing shop with so many racks full of apparel, it is so crammed that you can hardly move. He pulls me into one of the racks and I know what he needs.

His hands are busy moving down my body to my sweet spot. He rubs and I pull my pant down and bend my ass to him. I am already wet for him and need my own release.

He pulls out his length from his pant and slaps it on the top of my rump before tracing it down my moon and down to my wet opening. He shoves it in slowly but with a dominance that I have no choice but to take him. He is in control of this and he presses and pushes deep. I have to bite my lip to keep from moaning and he moves more to his own rhythm, steady.

We are in such a high traffic area that it's not long when I see the clothes hangers on the rack that is concealing us start to move as someone is browsing.

I want to stop Devon for the moment and hide so that we can't be heard but I know that he won't have it. He continues taking no notice of our company. I try to hold my breath and I watch some hangers being removed off the rack and they seem to take no notice of us.

He reaches around and messages my clit and like a good lover I explode all over his shaft and fingers.

I don't see but know that he has licked his fingers and his hand is back on my hip as he drives himself into me and gets his. His breathing tells me and I wait for him to pull out and quickly go down and lick his still hard shaft dry. He is sensitive and sighs when I do and I stand up to face him. Devon is nothing but smiles as he takes me in for a hungry kiss.

"I always wanted to do that with you." He whispers.

I whisper back, "Glad I could please you cowboy."

We sneak out of the clothes rack. One of the shop keepers takes notice and starts to shout.

We look at each other and laugh as we rush out of the shop like kids.

After we are down the street I admit to him, "Only with you cowboy could I ever do that. You know I wanted to stop."

"Oh, I know." He puts his arm around me as we walk together.

"How did you know?"

"Your body tensed up."

"I knew you would not have let me." He chuckles and says nothing and we continue to walk along the shops.

I pick up a couple of little outfits that Desiree will grow into and Josh is always a sucker for treats. I pick up a couple of sweet candy for him.

Later in the day just before sunset we find ourselves at Tokyo Tower to see the skyline and do the silly things that tourists do. We walked out on a glass bottom and took some fun pictures and then got suckered into paying the extra money for the ride up to the highest platform.

The sky was all sorts of colors we had missed the sunset on our way up but the view was still great and we got a few more tourist type pictures.

I say to Devon, "You know what?"

"What?"

I admit, "I like what we have. We did well you and I and to think it all started with a friendly hello over social media."

He laughs, "Yes, I remember those days."

We stare out into the horizon and I wonder aloud, "So you and I, when we first met were still trying to reach those dreams of becoming successful authors and now, we have reached our dreams. What is next for you?" I look up at him.

He shrugs, "I will keep writing more books I suppose. Maybe do a bit of traveling once the promoting dies down for this novel and maybe buy another home."

I say, "Another home? Didn't you and Sara just move into that gated community?"

He sighs, "Well you know what they say. Real estate is always a good investment."

"Well not always but I get what you are saying. I'm happy with the home we just bought but you know, I would like a summer home and live maybe closer to you, somewhere in Texas. I always wanted horses. I mean the place we have now comes with a paddock and barn but you can't do much during the winter."

He glances back at the horizon and I follow his gaze. He says, "Yes I hear what you are saying. That would be cool. Say what about that Tropical Island and helicopter you were wanting to get?"

I roll my eyes, "I realize, yes I have money now but not enough for that sort of thing. Maybe later on. I think that I need to write more."

I ponder to myself how it's funny that the press picks and chooses what is important because no one takes notice of us here. We are just two average looking tourists amongst a sea of them.

Devon grabs my hand and steals a kiss with the Tokyo skyline as our back drop.

We head back to the hotel for our final checkout. I take a quick shower to freshen up and it's back to my family and the frigid cold winter that we get in Canada for February.

I meet Devon and Howard back in the lobby for a final goodbye until our next book related meet.

Howard, like a professional, shakes my hand, "We did good Jordan. No rush but I am happy to say with gaining this new market you are winning over more fans. I can't wait to get your next book out on the market." He winks at me and continues, "Don't worry for now and just take your time. Be a mom and when you are ready, I will be here. Besides we can always break through to other markets in the time being with translation of your current novel."

"That sounds great. You made my dreams come true."

Howard says, "Have a safe trip Jordan and we will talk again soon."

I look at Devon, "You are heading to catch your flight now too?"

"I am."

"Want to taxi together?"

Chapter 29
First Person

The trip back is a good one. I say goodbye to Devon at the airport. Before we go our separate ways, he says, "Oh Jordan, where does my mind go sometimes. I have something for you. Well actually it is for Desiree."

He hands me over a little bag. I peek inside, there is a little stuffed teddy bear doll wearing a traditional Japanese dress.

I smile, "Ah that is so cute. When did you get that?"

He winks at me, "Picked it up when we were at the market earlier today."

"Is that so, I didn't even see."

"It's because I am that good."

"Well thank you."

"You are welcome and I want you to know that just because we don't get to talk every day that you know it is not because I am ignoring. I think about you every day, but I know that this is your family and I need to stay at a distance to keep from interfering. Please know that and one day you will understand and appreciate why I did what I have. You know that I have been through a divorce once before and no matter what, I would not wish that on my enemy. I want to keep that from happening to you."

"I get it and you and I are good."

"Good" He gives me one final kiss and we part ways once more. Devon's plane flight is to the United States while mine is a flight to Canada with one short touchdown in Vancouver for fuel.

I sleep the rest of the way home and just before landing I wake to check my accounts and such and I have a nice new lump sum of money from Tail Fin and I wonder if Josh saw it too.

The flight attendant approaches, "We are landing please buckle your seat belt."

The seatbelt light comes on and I glance out the window to see thin black lines. The roads below and the city is draped in a blanket of snow.

I swear when I walk out of the terminal, Desiree is the first person that I see. She has grown, "Ah come here baby girl."

Josh lets me take her and I just kiss her sweet little cheeks over again, "Mommy missed you so much."

Josh gives me a kiss on the cheek while I kiss our baby girl and he takes the handle of my suite case as I hold our daughter. He asks, "How was the flight?"

"It was good. I slept pretty well the entire way and it is nice coming home the jet lag is not as bad as going there and losing an entire day."

He nods, "Makes sense."

Winter is still in full swing even more so then when I had left. The snow banks are higher, our dark blue car is nearly white with all of the road salt.

I forget for a moment that we live in a new home and coming up to the gait at our entrance is a reminder that I am returning to a life of new wealth.

The driveway has just been cleared of snow as the tracks still look fresh.

I ask, "Did you hire a snow removal service?"

He makes a noise, "Pshh, who do you take me for. I am still the same man. No, I actually purchased and accessary for the ATV and did it myself."

"Oh, very cool. Well, you know if it ever becomes too much to do, we can always hire someone." He smirks. Josh prefers doing things himself.

The house is clean and tidy when I come in. "Wow Josh, was this you or your mom's doing?"

"A little of both." He appreciates that I noticed.

Desiree drifted off to sleep on the drive home and I lay her in her crib for the rest of her nap. This place is starting to feel like home and everything is in a way too perfect.

We head over to the kitchen. I need a bite to eat and heat up some pizza left overs, the telltale sign that a man has been on his own. I smile to myself well, it's a welcomed sign and hey who doesn't love left over pizza?

I join Josh on the couch with a slice of pizza in hand. We have the television turned down low in order to not wake Desiree and at the same time be able to hear the baby monitor when she wakes.

Josh's demeanor changes and I look at him for some sort of answer. He says, "Jordan we need to talk."

Chapter 30
Lies or Confess

Sara had crossed the line. I never thought she would especially after all the time that had passed since the boat cruise. I thought that she would stay out and well she needed someone to confide in while Devon was away so what better person to reach out to then Josh, my husband.

The house is quiet, with only the hum of the television on, the aroma of the pizza in the air and it is just Josh and I alone and siting on the same couch.

Josh repositions himself so that he is angled towards me instead of the television. He explains, "Sara is convinced that you and Devon are having an affair and I want to believe you but there is something and I can't pin point what it is but I feel that something more is going on."

Josh is concerned but calm when he says what is on his mind. I don't know how to respond. If I should just continue on with the lies or confess.

"What did she say?" The words escape me and I already feel guiltier for trying to buy more time.

Josh explains, "It was the Japanese press. Sara says that she sees it in her husband's eyes from the photos. She is convinced that you two are in a relationship and that she wanted me to know. Are you in a relationship with Devon? Don't bullshit me. I deserve honesty."

I didn't think that Sara would do that. Devon even reassured at one point that she would keep out.

I sigh and explain, "Josh, I admit Devon is a handsome guy. We are friends. We have a lot in common in terms of writing, but you are my husband and my love."

He gives me a good long look searching for truth and I say nothing more. I don't want to be caught in a lie but something doesn't feel right. I mean he seems to accept my reassurance but it's like he is holding back as though he is harboring hidden doubt. He asks, "You love me?"

"I do. Do you still love me?" I turn the question back to him.

"I do." He assures but I can already see that Sara has done her damage. There is doubt in him. I feel it and there isn't a thing I can do but continue to lie. Well, I don't even know the next time Devon and I will meet so that will give me time to prove to Josh that he is my man. Should I have confessed?

Chapter 31
My Own Game

After a couple of weeks, I start to find my routine again as a stay-at-home mom with my baby. My days usually consist of waking up and relaxing with my baby girl while Josh works. By the afternoon we usually head out, do some shopping together and stop in to visit the grandparents and by 4:00pm I am usually back home to put dinner together for our little family.

One day in the late morning I find myself folding some clothes and deep in imagination working on plots and such as I go through the motion of chores. Half paying attention as I am deep into a plot idea, I pick up a thong from the laundry and am about to toss it into the small pile of my other underwear but stop and glance at it for a second. This isn't mine. Everything soon becomes real very quickly. There is not a chance in this world that this is my mother-in-law's under garments. I take a seat on the bed next to the pile of clean clothes and think. What do I do? Do I confront him? Do I even ask? I should have trusted my gut. I mean that text when I had messaged Josh from Japan. It felt strange and I should have known something was odd. Things start to make more sense, Josh's long work days when we don't need the money and fuck, also the fact that he hasn't quit his job even though we are now set for life.

It all makes sense now. I wondered why he didn't want to quit. He is seeing someone and work is his freedom to make that happen.

That night when we had pizza and he confronted me about what Sara had said. He was giving me an out and I didn't take it.

This is karma and I completely deserve this. The thong escapes my grasp and falls to the floor and I let myself sink off the bed and to the ground. I sit and just look down at the kinky little butt lace lying there next to me.

This doesn't feel good. Now I know how it feels. He is playing my own game of lies and you know what, I don't blame him. We have become sort of checked out of our own relationship. As I sit there on the floor, I am at a loss of what to do and just like that the phone rings. I jump at the sound and get up after two rings and grab the phone. It is too late, I hear Desiree crying in the background, woken up from her nap.

"Hello?"

"Hey honey, how are things?" It is Josh.

"Oh, things are okay, I am just doing some laundry but Desiree has woken up."

"Oh, sorry dear. Was it me?"

"Yes, but it's okay she would have woken up not long after your call. Don't worry about it."

"Is everything alright? You seem down."

I know I can't bring it up now, not a chance. I answer, "I am okay. I am just working on a scene and running into a bit of trouble that is all."

"Okay well I called to let you know that I will likely be an hour late. There is a meeting scheduled towards the end of the day and I can't get out of it." I completely get it now and know what he is doing. He asks, "Jordan can you hear me, okay? I said that I would be running late."

I force myself to answer, "Yes, okay got it. I guess the phone is dying or something."

"Alright see you tonight." The line goes silent and I am at a loss for words.

Desiree's cries are coming in on the baby monitor. She snaps me out of it and I pick the thong up from the floor and toss it in the trash.

Chapter 32
Playing Chicken

This is it; my family is made up of all lies. I have had an affair, and Josh seems to have done the same. A few weeks have passed since I found the thong in the laundry. I have chosen not to confront Josh because I know that there is no reasonable explanation for it and you know what, I don't blame him for what he did. I did the same and I have been doing a lot of thinking and observing. Devon and I still talk but there have been no extra activities since Japan and our talks for the most part have been really tame. Then there are my confirmed suspicions of Josh on the other hand, I think whatever he did, I think the relationship that he has with his mistress is at a minimum.

To be honest it is hard to read Josh. Some days he seems like he is dedicated to his family while others, he makes the choice to "work longer hours". The question now is, are we both playing chicken? Does he love me? Do I love him? Do either one of us have the guts to confront the other and perhaps put this marriage to bed? I love Josh but it's not the same anymore. We have grown apart. Is he brave enough to get a divorce? Am I?

We are mid-March and the weather is becoming milder. It is late morning when I decide to take the stroller out and take Desiree for a walk. I have had a lot of time to think about this entire Josh thing and my sham of a marriage. He must love me enough to not want to end it. I push the stroller down our long, treed driveway. I walk up to the security gate and press the keypad for it to open. I push the stroller through a thin layer of slush, walking down the road to the street's community mailbox.

Normally I share everything with Devon but this, I can't. Divorce is a sensitive topic for Devon. I know that he is working on salvaging his own. Hell, what Josh had shared with me from the conversation Josh had with Sara made me curious. I wanted to ask Devon about what Josh learned from Sara but my gut is telling me to leave it alone and let Devon share when he is ready.

I arrive at the mailbox and find that Desiree's passport is here. I recognize the Government's return address on the beige envelope. That puts a smile on my face for the moment. Everything for our trip to Fiji in April is ready.

My smart phone vibrates in the pocket of my winter coat and I take it out to see. It is my good old friend Hailey she writes, "Hey girl, how are things? My belly is growing by the day. I hope that you and Josh are doing okay. I saw some more bad press on you from Japan."

Hailey, I love her, she is a sweetheart but sometimes she just isn't on top of things which is okay I suppose because she is often pre-occupied with her own little girl.

I write back, "Things are good. I just got Desiree's passport in the mail this morning so we are all ready for Fiji. Yah the press in Japan can be a little cruel. They will make up anything to get people to read."

"So, you and Josh are, okay?" Her text is received seconds after having sent my reply.

"Yes" I push Desiree's stroller closer to the melting snowbank on the shoulder as a slow-moving car passes. The driver is a neighbor, they wave and I return the gesture as they pass.

I wait for Hailey's reply to come up on my screen. She replies, "That's good well I ran into Josh downtown yesterday during the lunch hour. He was having lunch with some woman."

Oh boy, well I see that all of this is creating doubt even amongst my friends. I shrug it off as nothing even though I know that it's not and text back, "Oh yah, that's just his co-worker they are close friends. She is really nice." I pretend to act like I know Josh's mistress, though I have no clue who she is. Good thing Hailey isn't actually here with me because she would be able to read me like a book. My lies are becoming so much that I not only lie for myself but now I lie to keep my husband's affair secret.

Hailey writes, "Oh okay, I didn't know he was close with his work friends?" That's a weird thing for Hailey to say. I know what she is hinting at but I refuse to feed into her suspicions of Josh.

I write back, "Yes, she even visits from time to time." That's a truth though Josh's mistress doesn't visit while I am around but that is none of Hailey's business.

"Okay well, I will talk to you later then." Hailey finally drops it.

I reply back, "Okay bye."

Well, that was weird. Desiree starts to make noise, it's just murmurs of sounds right now and I tilt around so she can see me, "Hi Des, Mummy has your passport, yes she does." I smile at her and she smiles back. Okay time to walk back.

Aside from the trip planning for next month which is coming up fairly quickly and the writing I try my best to keep my mind wondering about Josh. If we both love each other he will figure it out and eventually he will leave the mistress just like I chose to stay with him over Devon. I am too tired and busy for that matter to confront the issue and instead continue to keep my head in the sand. Winter is coming to an end and with the warm weather around the corner I have started to look for a horse as well as start to look for a summer home in the United States with property that is close to Devon.

I leave Desire's stroller outside the front entrance and scoop her up into my arms and enter back into the house.

Devon and I have sort of been talking on and off about me getting a summer home whenever we are not talking about writing. He has been sending me links to some prime real estate and I think this afternoon he has found me "The Home". After sitting Desire in her baby rocker next to me, I sink into my office chair and scroll through the images of the home's interior as well as the images of the property.

I enlarge a picture of the outside of the home. It is perfect. The driveway isn't as private as the one here in Canada but it is a long one and the front property is wooded with some sort of pine. The property even has this log fence that boarders the property. I think it is there more for appearance then anything. It has an interlocking brick driveway right up to the home.

The home itself is a reddish-brown brick two story structure. It has gorgeous porch that wraps around three sides of the home and includes a corner gazebo. The garage is a separate building that is situated passed the home. Towards the backyard there seems to be some outdoor kennels, under more pines. I spot some chain link fence in one of the photos, it is all neat and tidy. Perhaps the owners breed show dogs? Beyond the garage the property opens up to a couple of large paddocks with a six-stall horse barn.

I review the details and view the photos. This is great and the price seems reasonable although we could always try to offer a little less and see if the seller is willing to negotiate. Devon knows me too well. My winter escape dream home is right on my screen.

I send a text to Devon, "Wow just saw the home you sent to me this morning. I like it! I am going to talk to Josh and see if he wants to make an offer. I see the address of the home. How far away is it from you?"

He responds, "I thought you would like it. That one is about twenty minutes from me. You are not in a gated community but the area is very private. It is mostly horse and cattle ranches out there."

"Thanks for sharing, I am going to mention it to Josh tonight. I wanted to ask how you have been doing."

"Oh, I'm good, just busy with work and stuff."

"Yah apart from this summer home and horse shopping it is the same old. Desiree is doing well; Josh is still busy at work and when I have a moment I sneak in a bit of writing."

I know that we are both lying to one another. If I do a search on "D. Chamber's", the media has him going through a divorce and with what Josh had mentioned from talking to Sara, I believe it.

I have to wonder if Devon believes the lie, I'm feeding him, that I'm fine. I can't keep doing this. "Devon, could we talk or video chat or something? I really need a friend right now and it is not something I can talk to my girlfriends about."

Five minutes roll by and not a peep from Devon. I am about to give up on him. He's got to be preoccupied or something but then the phone lights up. "I am here. I can't video chat right now but you can give me a call and we can chat for a few minutes."

"Okay" I give him a call as quickly as I can.

He answers within a ring, "Hey Jordan, are you okay?"

I blurt, "Josh is having an affair with someone from his office." I can hear him take a breath and I continue before he speaks, "I know this for a fact. It has been going on for a little while and before I had just ignored the signs but this morning, I found a thong while folding the clean clothes and it isn't mine."

He speaks carefully, "Jordan, you know that I am here for you with whatever you decide." I know that he only means that at the friendship level as he has made it clear that he is trying to mend his relationship with Sara.

"I know, thanks. I just don't know? I haven't confronted him and I don't know if I will. I mean, I love Josh but I sort of deserve this."

He interrupts, "Jordan don't say that. Things happened for other reasons. Do what you feel is right and no matter what I will be here for you."

I feel like a small weight has been lifted off of my chest even though nothing has been fixed. I just needed a friend to confide in and Devon offers that. I say, "Thanks. I wanted to ask because of the media. Are you and Sara, okay?"

"We are okay. It's just a rough patch that's all." He isn't ready to talk and I know not to cross the line. He says, "Well my beautiful friend I should get back to work. I am just cleaning up the yard. Focus on the things that make you happy and one step at a time."

"Okay, I will, thanks."

"Give Desiree a kiss for me."

"I will, bye."

"Bye Jordan"

Sometimes I wonder if I value my friendship with Devon more than he does because I just opened up to him with sharing a suspicion that I had been feeling for months and a secret I don't plan on sharing with anyone else and Devon isn't willing to confide in me with the things that are going on in his life. The media is all over it and hell even Josh had talked to me about it.

Chapter 33
You and Not We

I took a nap with Desiree in the late afternoon so that I am awake for when Josh finally comes home. Just before our security system beeped advising that the front gate to the driveway was opening, I removed the skillet from the hot element on the stove and walked over to the front entrance to meet Josh. I had made him a bacon, tomato and cheese omelet.

"Hey dear, how was your day?"

He hangs his coat in the closet and says, "Oh you know how it is. Just happy to be home." Now that I know his secret, I pick up the scent of her perfume on him. It's a faint jasmine scent.

I say, "I put together an omelet for you."

"Thanks honey. Why do I feel like you have some news?"

I laugh because I know that I am kind of hovering. It is the first real laugh I had all day and admit, "I have some news and I wanted to tell you before doing anything further." I choose to focus on the positive and ignore addressing the thong I found earlier.

I walk with him to the kitchen and join him at the kitchen island after bringing him the omelet I made. I already had my lap top open and ready to go for him to see the pictures of the home.

I position the laptop a little closer to him and angle the laptop screen for him to see and say, "Isn't it gorgeous. It would be a great winter escape, it's private. We would have space, land, and a garage for you, and a barn for me. Should I go ahead and make the offer?"

Between mouthfuls he asks, "So this is closer to Devon?"

I gulp and tell the truth, "We would be about twenty minutes from Sara and Devon." I hold my breath wondering if this is the talk.

"Go ahead make the offer." He says with a mouthful of food. It's too easy. I can almost breathe but have to assure.

"Are you sure? I mean normally you say something about money?"

He stops eating for a moment and explains, "Jordan, I saw the deposit from the Japan sales. You can afford it. I trust you." I notice that he said you and not we.

I had prepared for some debate and it's like Josh is totally indifferent. I say, "Okay, I'll call the real estate agent. Do you want to come with me if I fly down this week?"

"No, it's okay." My heart breaks a little. I know I no longer have his heart and Josh is probably already making a mental note to spend time with his mistress while I am away. This is totally karma. I deserve it.

He doesn't see the disappointment on my face for the fact that he doesn't even care what I do. I pretend, that the thong, the scent of jasmine on his shirt collar or his indifference doesn't bother me. I burry my emotion and continue pretending like life is fine, that I am fine. I say in a breath, "Oh I forgot to say, Desiree's passport came in the mail today. I can bring her with me, do you mind?"

"No that's fine. I won't have to call my mom on short notice." I knew it. I made it too easy for him. No wife, no baby and he is all set. I wonder how long we will continue like this. We are both cowards for not coming clean.

I say, "Okay then it's settled." I smile but feel uneasy it was too easy and really, I know what will happen while I am gone. He will have her over.

I sit in my office later on in the evening. It is just before 8:00pm when I make the phone call to the real estate agent, expecting for the call to go to voicemail. I am surprised when she picks up and in a cheery southern accent she answers, "Sheila M. here. How can I help you?"

"Hi Sheila, I was expecting to leave a voicemail for you."

She giggles, "No Mam every call is an opportunity. What can I do for ya this evening?"

"Well, my name is Jordan Connor and I was recommended a property listing of yours that you had for sale. I like what I see from the website and would like to see it." It feels weird to be doing this on my own. I have always had Josh with me when shopping for a home and not having him here in the office as I make this arrangement feels lonely.

"You are that famous author, right?"

I laugh, "I am an author yes."

"I think I know the property that you are talking about." She continues to read the listing number to me and she is absolutely correct.

I ask, "How did you know?"

"Dear, you just seem like the type. Well, I see that you're calling from out of town. Where exactly are you right now?" I wonder if Devon mentioned to Sheila to hold the listing for me or something.

I answer Sheila's question and say, "I am actually in Canada but I am serious with having a look and considering this place as a winter escape. I would be willing to fly out there as soon as tomorrow."

"Then I will hold it for you my dear and I could meet you at the airport."

"Oh no, that's okay really."

She laughs, "You Canadian's sure are cute. Don't be silly, it is my job and besides I can show you the town on the way up and such."

"Thank you, I will email you my flight time. I will have my baby girl with me tomorrow."

"How old is she?"

"Two months."

"A little sweet pea. In that case I will bring my SUV. Okay dear talk to you tomorrow and when you can, send me you flight detail."

"Bye Sheila."

"Goodbye Jordan."

Chapter 34
Knowing What You Want

The next morning Desiree and I land in Austin, meet Sheila and are on route to the home. She is a chatty woman, very friendly and talkative. She is the kind of person that can strike up a conversation about anything. She is like a breath of fresh air. It's nice to have new company to converse with.

Austin is warm and different from my home town. As we pass through the city, it has beautiful high-rise buildings with intricate designs, we pass over a water way and I even spot the odd statue of a cowboy as we move along route. Everything seems new here.

Pretty soon we are moving along a highway out of Austin and she says, "The nice thing about the city is everything is here, all in one place and if you need an escape from the city, it's just a short drive." She smiles and tassels her golden shoulder length locks behind her ears. She continues, "Your future home has the privacy that I think you are seeking as well as you are a short drive from a quaint little town and you are less than an hour from Austin. Also, you know from the posting that it isn't in a gated community which to me is a bonus. I find personally I prefer normal communities; they are just perfect and besides there is no sense in putting up a wall and blocking out the landscape, but that is just me."

"Oh, I completely agree. I mean for me I have not lived this way for long and am still getting used to what is available in this price range. I see the appeal to a gated community but if you can get away with not having to live in one, I think it would be a bonus."

"You are a cutie pie." She glances my way for a second then her eyes are back on the road. She asks, "So your home in Canada, you just purchased it right?"

"Yes, it hasn't been a year yet. It is a larger home, out of town, you can't see the house from the road and has a security gate and a bit of a driveway. On the property there is the house and then a second building that is half a horse barn and half a garage and there are a few paddocks in the back. Come to think about it, it is similar to this place."

Sheila glances at me, lifting her oversized sunglasses from her nose, revealing her dark brown eyes. She says, "There is nothing wrong with knowing what you want. Well, your place back home sounds lovely and I think this one will speak to you the same way as your Canadian home did."

We pass through the little town that she was talking about earlier. Sheila points out the gas station, grocery store, hair salon, a few clothing and specialty shops and a little park and before we know it, we are on country road again.

We start to slow and she mentions, "The turn off is coming up right here." You can hear the gravel crunch as the tires of her SUV roll over top and the land is wooded and every few minutes it opens to rolling grassy hills lined with brown wood fence. She explains, "These are the neighboring properties, other ranches, this property belongs to another home. There are a couple more neighbors and you can see that the homes here are nicely spaced out. There all far enough away to have privacy but close enough that you don't feel alone out here. There is a couple of cattle ranches passed your soon to be second home we are looking at today and this road is actually a dead end which means less traffic."

I like that Sheila is confident in her listing because it makes me feel good about making time to take this trip to see it. I say, "This looks great." Desiree starts to fuss. The sound of the tires rolling over the gravel must have woken her up.

Sheila says, "Look at that, just in time." She turns into the driveway lined with trees and it opens up to the scenes that I have looked at from my laptop the day before.

She explains, "The previous owners are at work right now which is perfect for showing."

I ask, "Do you know why they are selling?"

"It's a career move. They are moving to the Dallas area." She reaches for her leather notebook behind the passenger seat and tucking it under her arm then opens her door, swinging her legs together, she is wearing a below the knee pencil skirt and steps out of her SUV.

I smile and nod and unbuckle my seatbelt, stepping out into the country air. I open the back door and scoop Desiree up in my arms and put her into a baby carrier, fastening her to my front so that I can rub her back periodically. She seems content with being held.

Sheila says, "Isn't this nice." She gestures with her arms for me to take it all in. She turns and glances around at the property and says, "What shall we start with first?"

"The house is fine." Sheila's outward excitement makes me smile. I feel good about this place and with just standing here I am already ready to say yes.

We walk up the porch steps and I notice in the corner gazebo that there is a hanging swing and she catches me taking a glance.

"What a nice added touch."

"It is" I can see myself relaxing there with my laptop and writing.

We step in through a single door entrance that is flanked with two side windows. The flooring is large terra-cotta tiles, with light beige walls and the ceiling is lined with aged planks of wood which makes the home feel rustic.

The home is grand but the way the rooms are designed it gives you an intimate feeling and it feels like home here. Sheila guides me through the rooms and the beautiful views of the property and I know that I am already sold. The basement even comes with a wine cellar.

After seeing the inside of the home, we step back outside and walk the grounds. I spot the owners horses grazing in the open field. The trees by the home leading up to the garage are mature pine type trees and the garage is an oversized double one with a visitor suite on the second level. The horse barn beyond is simple, clean and well-kept with full size box stalls for the horses.

I can see myself living here even more so than the home back in Canada. I can see Desiree growing up and attending school here. I can see my parents making the trip down and staying here on holiday. This is my home it already feels like home.

Sheila interrupts my day dreaming but does it in a way that is gentle and asks, "I have a feeling that this is it, isn't it?"

I smile, "Normally I would try to not get attached but yes and the weird thing is I think that I have dreamed of this place. I can see Desiree growing up here."

Sheila smiles and explains, "There are some great schools and programs for children here and lots of opportunity. This is what I love about my job. That moment when you know that your client has found the house of their dreams."

I am humbled. I can't believe I am here at the home of my dreams, literally. I say in an excited and wavering breath, "So how do we make this happen?"

"We come up with a fair offer and wait for them to play ball and we go from there. Will you be staying in town tonight?"

Oh, good question I didn't even think to purchase my return flight because I wasn't sure on the time it would take. I respond, "My plans haven't been made yet. I can if you need me to."

She says, "I can start everything moving along right now with an offer. Is there anything that you wanted to do in Austin today?"

I rub Desiree's back while I think for a moment. I say, "Well, I have a friend that I can call besides that I may need a rental car."

She nods and we walk back to the car. I notice Sheila making a few notes as we approach the SUV. Sheila says, "Let's head back to my office and you can go ahead and call your friend."

The silly thing is with the short time frame that it took for me to travel here to Austin I didn't even tell Devon that I was coming. I send him a quick text while Sheila drives us back to her office in the city. I text, "Hey cowboy, that home that you forwarded to me, I actually looked at it today and am here in Austin. Maybe we can meet up later today." I click send but try not to get my hopes up in seeing him because I know that this is likely too short of notice for a visit and besides Sara hates my guts and there is probably no way he can get away.

We are now on the gravel road heading toward the main road and Devon's text is received, "So did you buy it?"

I text back, "Trying to. The realtor is going to work her magic."

Devon writes back, "That house just screams you."

"Tell me about it. Wow, I like it more than the stunning house I have back home in Canada."

He says, "Well, I can meet you in about an hour or so. I am actually just running some errands. How about you send me the coordinates of the real estate office and I will come pick you up."

Chapter 35
It's Done

I do as the real estate agent instructs and I take the afternoon and try to relax as much as I can. Buying a home is nerve wracking but in a good way and especially if you have your heart set on the property.

Devon picks Desiree and me up as promised from the realtor's office and he drives us to his home. Devon's new home is nothing short of breathtaking and I can already see that Sara has started putting the effort into making the home their own. What is a little surprising is that she isn't here and when I had asked Devon about it, he just shrugged and said that she was visiting family this week up in New York.

We are sitting by the pool side. Devon holds Desiree in his arms while gently swinging on his cushioned outdoor swing. I take notice that her little fuzz of hair on her head is an exact match in color to his brown hair and I see his features in her. There is no mistake that Devon is her dad. My donor was a blond and my own brown hair is a lighter shade.

While he glances down and her sleepy face, I ask him, "I am not intruding, am I?"

He doesn't even look up at me and is completely fixed on trying to make Desiree smile. "No, not at all. It is actually good that you are doing this now and not next week. Sara should be back by then."

I come out and ask, "Devon I see the media and I start to question it. Are you and Sara getting a divorce?"

He looks up, a bit startled and sighs, "The water is still muddy between us. Right now, honestly, I have no idea. One day we are okay and the next day I have no idea. Part of the reasons for her leaving was because of me."

"Sorry" I wrap my arms around my waist.

"Don't be. Whatever happens it was meant to be."

"Yes, I suppose. Should I leave?"

Again, he looks up at me and this time reaches for my hand, "What? No silly, stay and complete your purchase. It's nice to have you two here." He changes topic, "She certainly is growing."

"Yes" My phone rings and before I can speak a voice on the call says, "Hello Jordan?"

My heart starts to beat a little faster. I answer, "Hi Sheila" My heart thumps in anticipation.

Sheila cheers, "You got it!"

I stand up and raise my voice, "Shut up!" I notice my daughter startle in Devon's arms and he rubs her back to calm her. I can't help but smile, her surprise is adorable. It looks like she is about ready for a nap though because her eyes blink closed as Devon snuggles her up close to him.

Sheila explains over the phone, "It's done! They accepted and the closing date is all set for you to take over for May 1st."

I gasp a sigh of relief and say, "Thank you that was too easy. Thank you so much!"

"I was happy to help, I will need you to return to the office to sign everything."

Chapter 36
Candy Game

Weeks before the trip to Fiji, Josh's parents were at their home relaxing in the evening, during the middle of a work week. The two of them are retired but often get asked by their neighbors for a helping hand. It can be anything like helping clean fish to landscaping to going over to their neighbors' place for drinks and helping them with baking. They live in a retired community so it's common for neighbors to help neighbors and both of Josh's parents had spent the afternoon at a friend's place lending a helping hand and now they are home and it is after dinner.

The two of them in the past year have gotten into using social media and going online to look up information where before they may have had the local news station on. Josh's parents are both in their living room. Ted is on his laptop, sitting on his leather recliner and Sheila is sitting on their flower print couch with her tablet in hand. They both love playing this candy game and while Ted is still concentrating on getting a level up in his candy game, Sheila has jumped onto her social media newsfeed.

While she scrolls down the newsfeed, swishing down with her index finger, she chats to Ted, letting him know who posted what and what is going on in other people lives. She describes what she sees to him, the cute photos that people shared, inspirational quotes and interesting videos. Ted isn't much of a social butterfly. He enjoys the company of his family and close friends but doesn't feed into the gossip that this social media site brings.

As she makes it a point to inform him about the stuff in her news feed, he provides her with, "yes", "right", "good for them", "that's good" and "neat".

She is so absorbed in what is on her tablet that she doesn't even take notice to the lack of attention that her husband is committing to her, which is a good thing because if she had noticed there may have been an argument about him not giving her his full attention.

She notices a message in her social media inbox and the pop-up indicator is too hard to ignore.

"Dear, someone just sent me a message."

Ted replies without looking away from his game, "What does it say?"

"It is a message from a Steven Peach, do you know him?"

Her husband tunes in a bit more as her question can't be answered with a simple reply. He says, "The name rings a bell. What does it say?" Even though he gave her more than a two-word response, he hasn't looked away from his laptop.

She stops swishing her finger on the screen, pushes her reading glasses up a touch on her nose, concentrates on the screen then replies, "He just says that he is sharing some news of Jordan while she promoted her book in Japan." She glances at the message. She isn't used to receiving messages and takes a moment to learn that she needs to tap the hyperlink. When she taps it with her index finger, it directs her to one of the popular gossip columns. She reads the article.

Last week in Tokyo, famed authors Jordan Connor and D. Chambers were promoting their latest book releases that were both recently translated Japanese. The two of them were spotted signing their works at a couple of public events which were a success.

It is speculated that the two have re-sparked some romance between the two and were spotted at various tourist spots holding hands and appearing to be on a date. This is not the first time that the two have been speculated to have been an item. Both are currently married but for how long is the question.

She scrolls down the page to view pictures that have both Devon and Jordan together. One seems to be from one of the signings, a candid where the two are captured talking to each other and Jordan seems to be laughing at something that Devon had said. Another photo seems to be of them at a restaurant together but the picture also has Howard Stem in it and a third one seems to have been taken at the Hotel lobby in Tokyo where Jordan and Devon are having a conversation.

These photos are innocent and the picture that is being painted for her makes her certain that there is more to it. Josh's mom studies the photos over and over then says to her husband.

"I think Jordan is in love with someone else."

Josh's dad doesn't hear her words the first time. Still into his game he doesn't look up but asks, "What?"

"I said, I think Jordan is in love with someone else."

This time he glances up at her. He sees that whatever it was that she has read has upset her because her tablet is resting on her lap and she is now looking straight into his eyes. He asks, "Have you been reading those trash columns?"

She is insulted by his comment and her voice raises an octave, "Yes dear, maybe I have. It's not the column, it is the photos, see look."

She passes her tablet over to him and with his tired eyes he peers down at them through his glasses, giving his eyes a moment to adjust.

She continues, "Look at the way Jordan is looking at that man. That is the same way she looks at Josh."

He rests the tablet down on his lap and sighs, "Honey, I think that you are making something out of nothing. You can see that Jordan is at a signing and with people that she works with."

Sheila is offended by his regard for what she thinks, "Dear, I am saying what I think. It's not the article, it is the pictures, I think there is something more Dear." The annoyance in her voice has raised her tone.

Ted folds down his laptop screen and says, "And what are you going to do about it?"

A bit taken back she says, "I think that I am going to call my son and tell him what I think."

He shakes his head and huffs, "No you're not. Do you think Josh is completely oblivious to the tabloids? Chances are he has seen them already and chances are good that the two of them are working it out. He doesn't need his mother budding in."

"I am not budding in!"

"Yes, you are and you need to leave it alone."

She raises her voice, "If I see that my son is in trouble, I have every right to say something. As a matter of fact, I am going to call him right now."

He reaches for the phone on the side table before she can stand up and get it. She demands, "Give me the phone!"

"Give it a rest." He holds the phone out of her reach.

"Give me the phone. I am allowed to talk to my son."

"No, this is where you need to bud out and mind your business. That stuff that you read, that garbage you call news is something that Josh and Jordan need to work out on their own."

She stops trying to reach for the phone and rests her hands on her hips and spits back, "Well, I don't think it is right."

Ted tucks the phone under his arm and replies, "Yes and that is something that you need to keep to yourself and only if Josh asks for your opinions, only then do you provide."

"I just want to help him."

He grumbles, "He doesn't need your help. This is exactly the stuff that I mean. People don't like it when you bud into their personal lives. Leave it alone."

She is fuming at Ted for not letting her get her way but even more so because she knows that he is right. Sheila knows that she is outspoken and often regarded in a harsher way by others because of it.

She shuts her tablet off and leaves her husband in the living room.

He hears her footsteps fade towards their front door and as a result hollers, "Where are you going?"

"I am going for a drive." She yells.

Still in his recliner he continues in a raised voice, "Remember what I said."

"Yes, whatever Dear." She slams the door behind her.

Chapter 37
From Going South

Josh's mom gets into her car and drives down the road to the edge of their neighborhood and pulls over to the shoulder. She doesn't care what her husband said. Her emotions have taken over and instead of taking a moment to regard what Ted said, she does a knee jerk move and calls her son.

Josh answers, "Hello?"

"Josh?"

"Yes."

"It is your mother." She isn't good at hiding her emotions and Josh knows something's up but doesn't want to make a deal of it because he knows what will come.

He asks, "Are you home?"

"No dear, just in the car."

"Where are you headed?"

"Oh, just coming back from the store. Listen I need to talk to you."

"Sure, what's up?"

"Do you know what Jordan was doing in Tokyo?"

He sighs, "Yes Mom, she was promoting her books."

She says, "Listen I think she was..."

"Mom, I need you to stop. I know you have been seeing things on the internet and I need you to realize that people like to make things up to make money."

"Josh that is not why I am calling." Josh is just like his father and it bugs her that both her husband and son don't see things the way she does.

There is a moment of silence on the line then Josh says in a calmer tone, "What were you going to say."

"I just think Jordan is getting a little close with that D. Chambers guy."

Josh is trying really hard to keep this conversation from going south and he sighs again, "Okay Mom, there's my point. You can't believe everything that you read."

"I am not dear." Her reply is clipped.

"Yes mom. Well, I better let you go, besides you're on your way home and I am sure that Dad misses you." Josh loves his mom but can't stand when she gets like this and he rather end the call as soon as possible.

She sighs, "Yes Dear, I love you."

Josh quickly replies, "Love you too, bye." She stays on the line as it goes silent with his abrupt click.

She stares ahead at the road. Her conversation with her son Josh was just as her husband predicted and it makes her even more annoyed in the fact that she knows that her spouse was right. She wishes that people would just see things the way that she does and take her advice.

Chapter 38
That Tropical Island

The next morning everything is done in Austin and Desiree and I are on our way back home to Josh.

He meets us at the airport and we both ignore the underlying signs of what is going on and he welcomes me with a polite hello.

As he opens the trunk for me to put mine and Desiree's bags inside, he says, "Well, I guess congratulations are in order for the two of us?"

I smile, "May 1st we will have a home near Austin." He closes the trunk and we both check Desiree who is already buckled in her seat before getting into the SUV.

He takes the driver's seat and I am in the passenger and we slowly pull out of the Ottawa Airport. Josh teases, "Whatever happened to that tropical island?"

I smile and roll my eyes saying, "In time. This place is just gorgeous and I know you will like it."

He shrugs, "I am sure it is nice but you know that I was never a fan of living in the United States. I rather stay in Canada year-round."

I roll my eyes again, "Yes dear, well just give it a chance for me?" I know Josh is a home body and what he doesn't get is that this second home, if he gives it a chance will feel like a home for him and not just some vacation spot like he thinks.

"I will. Oh, I forgot to mention your mother called yesterday?"

"Did you tell her where I was?"

"I just said that you were at a friend's place. You can tell her the news."

Chapter 39
Headache and Heartache

From this point leading to our trip to Fiji in April is pretty uneventful. Life is a routine. I meet up with Hailey a couple of times, once at her place and once at mine and we catch up with all of the things that are going on with our lives. I leave out the Devon stuff and me knowing that Josh is having his own thing going on with another woman.

I do the shopping, go to our Mommy and Me swimming lessons that I signed up for recently and when I am not being a mom, I sneak a bit of writing in. Although I am finding that I often just stare at the screen. I am really struggling with a story and maybe I just need to take a break from it.

April comes and Fiji is here, a vacation with the family.

The nice thing about having family vacationing together is that you are never alone and the bad thing about vacationing with family is that you are never alone.

My dad has always been a little anxious when it comes to getting on a plane to go anywhere and it sometimes feels like I am pulling out teeth with him. At one point he wanted to cancel the vacation giving me the excuse that he didn't have the money and I had to remind him that the vacation was already paid for. With the help of my mom, we managed to get him to suck it up and go.

Josh's parents on the other hand are a whole other can of worms. Josh's dad is a pretty easy-going guy and as long as there is a plan, he is usually for it but Josh's mother is something else, a ball of stress. I had to deal with her worrying of the baby catching some sickness while in Fiji, having her get worked up on being able to see her son and planning out the day's events right down to the minute and the list goes on. At least I don't need to see his mom every day. I do admit that she drives me up the wall.

Things work out, well sort of. Just days before the departure Josh says to me one night, while we are both in bed, "Jordan I hate to do this to you because of all the planning and involving the family but I won't be able to go."

I roll over to face him while under the sheets. "Josh, I have been planning this trip for months and your family is coming."

He gazes up at the ceiling and sighs, "I know, it's just we have finished testing at work and the software launch is the week of Fiji."

"You booked the time off. I don't understand."

His voice is starting to give me a headache, "I can talk to them and see what can happen."

I know it is all lies and he is taking it further each time and I so want to just scream at him and tell him that I know but where would that get me? A fight, then a divorce and a headache and heartache of dividing everything and going our separate ways. I don't think that I want that but maybe I do. Maybe it is like ripping off a band aid really fast and maybe we will both be better off after the fact.

I think about Desiree. Would it be better for her if we went our own ways or if we stay together and pretend? I mean Josh and I don't really fight but I think she would eventually catch on as she grows older. Wow, I can't think about this now.

"Jordan? Jordan?"

"What?" When I glance at him, I see that I have his full attention.

"Wow you were out in la la land. Does that seem okay?"

"What?"

"I said that I would talk to my boss and see if I can get out of it. No promises and it may result in me arriving a day or two later but that is better than nothing, right?"

"Yes, I guess."

"Why are you rolling your eyes at me?"

"Sorry, I didn't mean to. I guess I am just tired that's all. Whatever you can do, it would be great. I just had my heart set on you coming."

He brings me into his arms and it's the first time in a while, "I will try."

All I can do is accept this peace offering and leave this as water under the bridge. His touch feels so foreign to me. We still haven't since Desiree.

He holds me close and I already know that something in him as changed. Deep down I am pissed about his affair but there is this other side of me that wants to reclaim my territory. It's fucked up but I want him to be mine again.

I turn to face him inside his arms and it's like my confirmation that I need him has ignited him and his eyes are desiring more. I just forget everything and kiss him. My tongue tasting his and reclaiming my man. I feel his stiffness and I want him, want to please him and move my lips down to his tall one and lick it like a juicy lollypop. He doesn't disappoint and I am half hungry and half angry that he was intimate with another woman and the desire is there to bring him back to lusting for me.

I suck his tip with my hot wet juicy lips and tongue. Licking and sucking until he is so hard that he is leaking on my tongue. He presses up into my throat and I allow him in further. I stroke his shaft that is coated in my saliva, sliding my silky warm hand up and down his length. He sighs and I feel his hand on my back pushing me down so that I swallow him whole, smelling his scent and making me slick. This is the first time that I have truly wanted him since having a baby and the first time I crave him deep in me.

I throw my slimed panties to the floor and straddle him, pinning him down and rocking to my own rhythm. I don't care about his right now I want to get mine. I sit up and reach behind me grabbing his testicles and rubbing them and feeling them rest up against the crack of my ass. He thrusts up, knowing full well what sets me off and I whimper at how deep he goes. The feeling is coming back and I am re-learning my body. Quicker, deeper and harder and then I get mine, squirting all over him but he doesn't mind. His veiny hard shaft is giving me pleasure and I know that I don't feel the same to him, not now but I want this to be good for him, so that he second guesses going to another for affections.

I pull him out and I can smell my sweet tangy scent all over him and slide him into a tighter place. He gasps this time and I know he likes it. My slickness has dripped back and is making everything warm, wet and smooth. He feels massive and my slow thrusts make him want more.

He whispers, "Let me up." He makes me kneel on the bed and he takes me from behind pressing hard and holding me in place with his strong hands. I reach behind and touch his sack that is slapping up against me and I start to touch my own opening. Rubbing and playing with myself as he enjoys my rump. He sees what I am doing, takes his hand and presses his finger into my sex, using his palm to massage. I squirt all over him again.

He rubs my juice into my ass cheek and within moments I know I have set him off. He explodes like a fire cracker. I feel him pulsate deep into me and his motions slow. He says nothing and I look over my shoulder to see a clearly satisfied husband.

I ask, "Shower?"

He answers in a played-out voice, "Sure"

Chapter 40
Cowards

Sometimes I wonder what this life has come to, why we do the things that we do or don't do. I am a coward; Josh is a coward and Devon is a coward. All of us playing these wicked games of lies. Lies to ourselves, each other, our friends and family. Sometimes I want to just lay my cards out and come out clean, get it over with and either mend or move on.

Sleeping with Josh post baby is good and I know that men need to feel desired in that way. A woman once told me that, husbands need to feel wanted, lusted for and they crave to please their spouse. They need to know that the woman they married desires them intimately.

I have not been good to Josh for a few months and only now fulfilling what I think is making him come back to me. I'm not stupid and know that his work affair has still not ended. To be honest I am not quite sure where his relationship is at with her. He seems to be coming home on time more regularly and I suspect the flame is growing cold with the other woman but then again, he has still held firm with not being able to make it out to Fiji at the same time as the rest of the family.

So, what do I do with the news? I want to scream at the top of my lungs but all I really do is nothing and instead since Josh's plane seat is already purchased and his accommodation paid for what do I do? I call my girlfriend Hailey and ask her to join me.

I actually had to twist her arm to come. Hailey can be silly at times. Her excuse for not wanting to come was her baby belly showing in a swim suit and I had a long conversation with her explaining that having a baby belly shouldn't make her want to hide it and besides she would be on the other side of the world. Who else would she run into other than my family? Oh, as I tell you this, I shake my head at how silly she is. Hailey is coming and her spouse decided to stay back with their daughter saying that Hailey needs girlfriend time and a break before the next one arrives and that was the ultimate push she needed to justify going. I'll have to thank her spouse later but for now the time has come yet again to pack up and depart for the airport, Fiji bound.

Josh is a good spouse and picks up Hailey and then drives me, Hailey and Desiree to the airport. His mom as usual is a nervous mess before the departure and gives us a call while on the drive in. I can't stand his mom when she is like this and I just shake my head in embarrassment for Hailey having to hear her on the hands free in our SUV.

Her raspy voice from years of smoking, drinking and hard work comes in loud and clear like a shouting old hag into the speaker, "Josh?"

"Good morning, Mom."

"Are you on your way to the airport?" Her voice hurts my ears and she makes Desiree start to wine. I just think, yes Desiree that is how I feel too.

"Yes mom, we are on our way now."

"You're going away?"

"No, we are on our way to the airport." Josh shouts into the mic overhead.

She replies, "You don't have to shout, I was just asking. Your dad and I are in the car also." Desiree starts to full out cry. I am in the back seat with her while Hailey is sitting in the front passenger side next to Josh. Josh glances back for a moment to see that I am trying the best that I can to sooth her. I rub her hand and play with her dark brown peach fuzz hair to let her know that I am close. I try to distract her but she is upset now and I think she just needs to cry it out, hell I want to cry too.

His mother says, "Oh is that Desiree in the car? Hi baby!" Desiree starts to scream and I hear a giggle escape Hailey's lips but she shushes herself quickly by covering her lips with a hand.

Josh now annoyed with the call and the screaming says, "Yes Mom, Desiree is here, she is going to Fiji too. Was there something you needed?"

"Dear, do you mind sitting with me and your dad on the flight there? We just miss you and I wanted to catch up a bit."

Josh exhales and says, "Mom, remember I mentioned that I wouldn't be departing today. I have something that I need to finish up at work."

"Oh Josh, can't you get out of it?" You can taste the disappointment in her voice as she says the words.

"No, I can't for the hundredth time. If I get the chance to visit it won't be until later in the week and that is only if I can get out of it."

"Well try to get out of it."

I know he is rolling his eyes in the front seat and he says, "Yes Mom. Is there anything else? I am trying to drive here with a fussy baby in the back."

"No dear."

"Okay bye Mom."

"Okay bye dear." There are a few seconds of silence and she says, "Love you dear."

He answers quickly, "Love you Mom."

"Bye" She always needs to say the last word and at this point I resort to taking Desiree out of her baby seat and breast feed. She is one angry baby. The feeding seems to do the trick and sooth her.

It is days like this that I question having invited the extended family, what was I thinking and this is going to be nuts.

Just then my phone vibrates with a text. It's my mom this time, "Dad and I are just heading to the airport. See you soon."

I smile to myself, a simple text, if only Josh's mom would learn how to text, interactions would be so much smoother.

We drive up to the Ottawa Airport drop off and Desiree and I get a quick kiss from Josh. Hailey gets a polite wave goodbye from my husband.

The airport is a buzz today with people. Hailey walks alongside me and I carry Desiree in the car seat. We find our airline counter and wait in line to be processed. Soon enough, I spot my mom, dad, brother and sister to my relief. Having Josh's mom here first would have been hell on earth. Especially trying to explain that Josh just dropped us off and couldn't come in to say hello because he needed to sneak off to work when really, he is making time to fool around with his office friend.

Chapter 41
A Familiar Sight

All I can really say in nice words is the flight to Fiji was colorful. As predicted Josh's mother asked about her son and complained and fussed. Even in the airplane she was finding things to fuss about, her seat, the air pressure, and that her drink was watered down. Sometimes I feel sorry for Josh's dad having to put up with her. I said a polite hello to her in the airport waiting area before boarding and made small chat but when it came time to boarding the plane, I stuck with my girlfriend Hailey and my brother and sister. Josh's sister, Emma will be attending but she had to take a later flight. We should see her either this evening or by the next day.

Ethan and Adrianne are in the seat ahead. Hailey and I are behind while my mom and dad are behind us. Josh's parents are behind my parents. I am thankful that my own mom and dad are a buffer from Josh's parents. My mom is a bit of a quiet person and her personality doesn't match that of Josh's mom so she kind of reacts like me towards her, polite and formal and that's about it. My dad on the other hand is an outgoing guy. He does pick and choose who he befriends. With them he keeps it light hearted and courteous but also keeps it polite as he knows the Josh's Mom's personality type.

The plane lands in sunny Fiji and the energy of our group is electric. Sheila has had a few to drink on flight and she is all laughs and joking when we come off the plane and step into a bus to take a short ride to the resort.

I sure have to give myself a pat on the back for picking this place. I had always wanted to visit Fiji and this resort isn't your typical large hotel type resort. The rooms are little huts done up in wood plank, wicker furniture and trimmed in white fabrics throughout the room. There is the odd accent of green plants in the space. It doesn't feel like a resort at all and instead more like staying at someone's posh tropical cabin.

Hailey and I bring our luggage into the cabin. The resort did offer to bring our luggage to the huts but both of us figured we could manage. If Josh does show up later in the week, which I doubt he will, I will just reserve another cabin for Hailey.

I purchased the sweetest little bikini for Desiree and that is my first item on the agenda, to get beach ready and grab some food at one of the little beach side restaurants.

Hailey closes the door to the hut with her back. I hear it click shut and she utters, "Oh my god your mother-in-law is something else!"

I roll my eyes, "Yes, tell me about it."

She smirks at me, approaches the bed, rolling her suitcase behind, then places it on the bed, opens it and starts to transfer her clothing from her suite case to one of the dresser drawers while saying, "I mean everyone has a story about their mother-in-law. When Brittany was born and I just wanted my alone time with my baby, my mother-in-law just wouldn't leave. I mean she would but only when I would give up on giving her hints and just go to bed. That first week after Matt and I brought Brittany home, my mother-in-law was always around from early in the morning and she wouldn't leave until after supper. Matt wouldn't say anything to his mom. I mean, why would he?" Hailey pauses for a moment then picks another drawer to tuck her swim wear in and continues, "It is his mom after all, but wow I feel your pain with your own mother-in-law."

My stuff is already tucked away in an adjacent dresser and now I am just trying to get Desiree into this cute little baby bikini. I say, "I don't mind having family around, it's just her personality. It seems to clash with everyone and that loud, obnoxious voice of hers."

Hailey chuckles, "Yes I heard it."

I have Desiree dressed, "Ah isn't she something and this baby sunscreen the smell wow, I just want to eat her up."

Hailey is already changed. I convinced her to go in a bikini too since it's kind of awkward to sport a maternity swim suit and I put on my own bikini. I am still a little frumpy but whatever. The nice thing about this is that this is a private resort and the trip has been a well-kept secret.

Hailey and I are not the first to the beach, my brother and sister have already beat us. My parents must be settling in and it seems like Josh's parents have as well. We walk up to the little restaurant on the beach and grab some ham and cheese sandwiches. We spot Josh's sister at the breezy beach side restaurant.

Emma says, "Oh my goodness look at Desiree, all ready for the beach!"

I hold Desiree in my arms and say, "Yep, we are just going to get some food in us and find one of those big umbrellas to relax under all day."

Emma says, "Oh I heard from Josh. He wanted me to let you know in case you had not received his text. He asked the boss and should have an answer soon."

I nod, look down at my flip flop for a second, slipping it on and off my foot as I think of something positive then say, "Oh that's better than not being able to come at all. Did you tell your mom?"

Emma rolls her eyes and touches my arm, replying, "Are you kidding me? I will leave it to Josh, I'm not going get involved with that!" She chuckles.

Hailey and I finish our sandwiches and make it down to the beach. Emma eventually joins the rest of the family. The afternoon is spent relaxing and I couldn't ask for a better-behaved little girl. The only time she fussed was when she needed to be changed and when she was hungry."

At one point I am lying on my stomach looking out at the turquoise water when I spot a familiar sight. Devon?

Chapter 42
Nothing Means Something

I stare, either that's his look alike of that's him, alone walking where the waves roll up onto the sand.

Adrianne is relaxing beside me on a beach towel, takes notice of me, looks up from her magazine and asks, "What are you doing?"

I startle, "Oh nothing, just adjusting to the light."

Adrianne follows my gaze and sees that I was staring at someone. She asks, "Do you know him?" She can tell that I recognize something.

I look back in his direction and admit, "He looks familiar, but I am not sure. Anyway, if it is him, he is too far to chase now."

Without looking down, she earmarks her spot in the magazine, closes and sets it down beside her, half on her towel and half in the sand. She is curious now too and offers, "Do you want to see? You can leave Desiree here."

"Umm" I stare out longingly towards the figure that is getting smaller in the distance along the shore.

She grumbles, "Jordan don't be shy, go!"

I get up lazily and jog for a couple of minutes through the sand to catch up. I pass him at a jog but break into a walk so that I can catch my breath. I look back over my shoulder and see his face and then stop and turn to face him, "Devon? What are you doing here?"

He shrugs and smiles like he knew I would find him, "You told me you were coming and well it seemed like a good escape. I needed a break."

I am still panting a little when I ask, "A break from what?" A wave scurries up getting both our bare feet wet to our ankles.

He shrugs and looks shyly into my eyes, "Oh nothing, I just needed to see you and do something nice for once." Nothing always means something, and I know that it will eventually get revealed but here on the beach is not the place.

The breeze is a little stronger by the water and I brush a few loose strands of my hair out of my eyes and decide to change topics and ask, "Do you want to meet my family? My friend Hailey is also here. You had met her way back when at the waterpark." Devon is being a little funny. It seems like he is being shy which isn't like him at all and before he says otherwise, I am leading him by his hand back to the group.

As we walk up. Hailey lifts her oversized sunglasses away from her eyes. She recognizes him, "Devon, Jordan never said that you would be here?" Her smile is contagious and Adrianne smiles too.

He chuckles looking down at the sand for a second before lifting his gaze back at them. Devon explains, "Naw, this was a last-minute decision."

I introduce him to everyone else and it's not long before he says goodbye to the group of family at the beach. He politely explains that he has a call that he needs to be on soon. I touch his arm as he steps away from the group and he pauses, giving his attention to me. I whisper in his ear what hut we are in to meet up again later.

Chapter 43
One More Time

I have dinner with my family and close friends. Something that I thought I would never see, my mother-in-law and mother getting along with each other. It is not that they didn't like each other, it is just that they don't see one another often and they are complete opposites. My mom is an easy-going soft-spoken woman while my mother-in-law is a rough around the edges loud mouthed lady. Lady is a generous word to describe her. The bond they have is the wine and the two of them are sitting next to each other and are all laughs while enjoying their drinks.

Hailey and I are sitting next to each other further down the table. Hailey casually asks, "So did you not invite Devon to dinner?" Her voice raises slightly emphasizing "dinner".

"I haven't seen him since the beach. I mean I could have sent him a text but I think as much as he is on some sort of vacation his work has sort of followed him here."

"How do you do it?"

"Do what?"

Hailey shrugs her shoulders and elaborates, "Be an Author and a mother at the same time and not get all caught up in the work?"

I glance up at the ceiling made of dried palms for a second "Oh, I just set a boundary that's all."

She gives me a long glance then murmurs to me, "Be honest with me, are you seeing Devon?"

I startle subbing my toe on the table leg and wince while replying, "Hailey, no, he is just a friend and a fellow author and nothing more."

She gives me a good long look and I just want to be out with it, come clean and tell someone, anyone that I am in love with Devon without the judgment but I can't. I polish off my glass of wine and say to Hailey, "I need to excuse myself."

She looks up at me, "Is it something I said?"

I tuck my chair in and tell her, "No, I just need to freshen up. Could you keep an eye on the munchkin?"

"Sure" She glances down.

I walk out of the restaurant and once out of eyesight I race back to my hut. I can't deal with the questions not now and just as I click the key to my room I hear a whisper, "Jordan?"

I startle and turn to find him behind me. "Geez Devon don't do that."

"I was going to come see if you were back from dinner and invite you to my hut." His eyes are beautiful even in the moonlight.

I whisper to him, "Devon, we are just having dinner now I just needed a breather."

He smiles and it is hard to ignore his inviting lips. He replies, "I hear yah, well me too. What do you say, spend ten minutes with me?"

I look into those endless brown eyes of his that are hungry for some. I can't do this in knowing that Hailey seems to be on to me.

"I can't." The words slip through and I just want to so bad but in the same breath I don't. I don't know what I want.

He tucks a strand of loose hair behind my ear and whispers to me, "I see the look in your eye, trust me."

He leads me down a cobble stone path to his hut that's actually only steps away. I had no idea how close he was. I expect that he is going to invite me in to his hut to chat and maybe explain the real reason for being here, but he leads us around the side and to the back of his hut. It has a balcony with comfy furniture that faces the ocean. He leads me up the steps and I am drawn to look out on the water as the moon reflects off of the water and lights up our world.

He comes up behind me as I lean over the railing and stare at the water.

He whispers in my ear while resting a hand on the small of my back, "I know we both want the same thing right now." He runs his fingers gently over my shoulder then down my arm and takes my hand in his and I look up at him, "What is it that I want?"

"You want this." He presses himself up against me so that I can feel his stiffness. I smirk because he is right and he knows it. Devon lifts the back of my dress and presses himself in. I sigh as his massive erection fills me, his scent, his sighs and grunts make me forget whatever it was I was worrying about earlier. I look out at the moonlit ocean and know that this is what I want and have no other care but my own greedy thoughts.

I stand there tilting myself up so that he slips in deeper with each thrust. I forget where I am and he is quick he presses harder with each thrust, commanding his dominance, making my legs turn to jelly as I leak down my own legs with the pleasure. I am close and he knows and gives no signs of easing up. He is taking it from me. I explode and moan loud into the night air, with each explosive pulse as I vibrate with pleasure that is given from his massive erection.

He is so incredibly hard right now and I sigh with the feeling of being given total bliss.

He takes me from the railing and sits us both in the chair on the balcony with me on his lap pulling me back onto his erection. I am still sensitive but he forces me down hard and fast.

He whispers, "Bounce" Oh, my cowboy wants to be ridden. I feel more in control although he is steering me with his hands on my hips for the moment but they slowly run up my chest feeling under my bra. He pinches hard and I gasp and lean back into him and tilt to the side so that I can steal a kiss from him. His warm tongue, God that tongue is something, I bite it and that sexy bottom lip of his. He runs his fingers through my hair then holds me in place as he continues to kiss and nibble down the length of my throat. His thrusts are slow for a moment and he reaches over and touches my clit.

I whisper to him, "Get yours, I should head back."

"One more time." He demands. I should just let him because he is good. He never disappoints, hard, loving, and passionate and I feel like I am his entire world when he has me. I come within seconds and as my kitty purrs, he shoves in deep, thrusting hard, and controlling his own release. His touch and scent make me soaked for him and I know, his own pulses and sighs give it away.

I feel his body tremble. I know that he needed it and I guess I did too.

Chapter 44
Lots of Stuff

I slip my dress back down. I wasn't wanting any but wow I feel better now and Hailey's questions are forgotten.

I linger for the moment not sure on if I should ask or wait. He smiles at me and asks, "So I guess you are going to head back to your family?"

I lean back on the railing, my back to the ocean and say, "I can stay for a few minutes. Desiree is being looked after."

"No, you should return to them." His hands gently rest on my shoulders and his thumbs lightly rub my warm skin.

"Devon it is okay. Really, it looks like you can use the company." I see the warm brown color of his eyes in the moonlight.

He briefly smiles at me, the way a person does when they don't really feel happiness, that same sort of moment like when Cinderella knew her time had a limit, "Jordan, having this little bit of time with you has made my entire night. Go on back to your family. I am going to relax tonight. There are some things that I need to take care of anyway."

I hold him in my arms, resting my head on his chest for the moment and ask, "What kind of stuff?"

"Lots of stuff." He tickles my arms, and I know that he has made his choice. He continues, "We will see each other tomorrow. Enjoy the rest of your night and you are lucky to have your family here, truly enjoy these opportunities, okay?"

I fake a sigh while smiling up at him, "Okay, well you made my night too." I stand on my tippy toes and give him a peck on the cheek and walk back.

He is different, I just don't know, he lights up when we are together but there is something else and I wonder. I mean it's normal for him to leave Sara behind. I mean he has been doing it for the last year with all of the events he has had to attend and Sara also seems to do her own thing. I don't know maybe I just fear the worst.

Chapter 45
Glass in the Air

When I arrive back to our table Hailey tries to warn me something is up, I see her frantic look but her warning is not quick enough. Josh's mom has had too much to drink and she is running her mouth to everyone who will listen. It is hard to ignore her and she spots me return to my seat.

She says in a loud raspy drunk voice, "That girl there is my daughter in law and I love her but those tabloids are true!"

I catch my own mom glance down and my dad look to Josh's dad to do something.

Ted says, "That's enough!"

She slurs her words saying, "No, don't shush me, I do love Jordan but she is cheating on my son with that D. Chambers Author and did you see him. He is here. My daughter in law is a cheater! Can't keep those legs of hers closed!" She is now standing at the table with her wine glass in the air like she is making a toast to the entire table only now others seated around are now watching her theatrics.

My heart stops and I can feel my cheeks flush. She takes notice of me and doesn't let up. She just gets louder, "Jordan, I love you but you can't keep that little cunt of yours in check. I bet that baby is his, she looks like D. Chambers."

Josh's dad yells at her, "Would you shut the fuck up?" Ted stands up and shoves his chair to the table.

She sets her wine glass down and huffs, "No, I have a right to speak." Sheila is about to take a seat again but her husband grabs hold of her arm.

Ted scolds, "No actually you don't, come on. You're a fucking embarrassment to this family."

He pushes her out of the restaurant with her grumbling her right to stay but it is already too late and the mood has changed.

My dad leaves his seat, coming around the table to where I am seated and asks, "Are you okay kiddo?"

I am so mad that my hands are shaking. I tuck them in my lap to hide the trembling and reply, "Yes" Having Dad here helps calm me a touch. He doesn't ask about the accusations; he knows that it's not the time.

He offers, "If you want, your mom and I can take Desiree and you can take the night off."

I glance up into his blue eyes, shake my head and say, "No, it's okay Dad, really."

"Jordan, it is fine besides we don't get to see our granddaughter enough."

I smirk, he is trying to make me smile given the situation and it works. I say, "That's funny because you and Mom are at my home every other week."

He rolls his eyes, "You know what I mean. Just let us help you out is all that I ask."

I give in, "Okay"

Josh's sister is the only one left of her side of the family and she says some polite goodbyes to my parents, brother, sister and my friend Hailey. Before she departs for her room, she approaches me last, gives me a hug and whispers in my ear, "You know that we all love you. Mom gets ideas in her head and doesn't know what she is saying half the time."

I know that this is Emma's way of making a peace offering. I say, "I know, well hopefully tomorrow will be better."

"See you tomorrow Jordan." She pulls me in for one final hug. I smell the flowery scent of her expensive department store perfume on her tanned skin and then she retires for the night back to her resort hut.

Ethan gives me a quick hug and kiss goodbye. I wonder, him and I are very alike when it has come to relationships. He is a fairly private person but I know that he has dated more than one girl at the same time and I know that if this was to ever come out, that I think that he would understand. He keeps everything simple and I know that no matter what he is my brother and will always love me. Adrianne on the other hand, she looks at me as if questioning my very existence like suddenly I am this person that she doesn't know. Clearly what Sheila had said tonight had an effect on her.

She comes over and says, "Well I am going back to my room. Jordan, what she said isn't true, right?" She glances at me with those same blue eyes like our father only hers are framed in long dark lashes.

I can't hold her gaze and instead look down and my dad steps in saying to her, "Just drop it."

I hand over Desiree to my mom and head back with Hailey to the hut. Not much is said on the way back as we walk the sandy paths in the warm night air. The sand making that ruffling sound beneath our sandals with each step.

The air is a bit warmer in the hut as we enter. I guess it's the lack of the ocean breeze even though we have the windows open. The breeze is a gentle whisper tonight.

After the door clicks closed, she asks, "Are you okay?"

I sigh, "Yes, I should be used to her being an old bitch but she always seems to catch me off guard. Like, how did it even get to that point?" I fall back on one of the beds and stare up at the wicker ceiling fan.

She shrugs, taking a seat on the bed beside me, "I think Josh's dad was trying to get her to take a break but it didn't stop her." She pauses for a moment and asks, "When you left, where did you go?"

I tilt my head up to look at her and reply, "I came back here to freshen up."

Her head tilts to the side as she replies, "Jordan, I checked on you and you weren't here."

"Oh, after the washroom I just did a walk around all of the huts, took a walk down the beach and made my way back. I just needed to stretch my legs." Deny and refuse to admit some more is all that I ever do now. After a while lies become natural, so much so that you start to believe them yourself. This is what I have become.

Chapter 46
My Kangaroo Baby

As each day passes by, sneaking around becomes easier. The group sort of spreads out with their activities, each becoming more comfortable with the resort and picking activities that they enjoy doing. For me it's Devon. It isn't always about getting some love from him. It is more just to catch up and just to connect with my friend.

I shouldn't feel like it is sneaking around, we are friends and fellow authors that work for the same publisher, but with Josh's mom uttering crap in her drunken mess has made me feel like meeting up with Devon is wrong.

Despite the attention, it doesn't stop me and this morning I have Desiree back from having spent the night with my parents. I decide to strap her onto me and carry her in front like she is a baby kangaroo. I meet Devon for breakfast at one of the ocean side restaurants.

I spot him already seated at a table by the railing that overlooks the ocean. I take a seat at his table, across from him with my kangaroo baby still strapped on but now she is sitting in my lap. He glances up through reading glasses, pausing from reading a newspaper and says, "Well good morning! You look lovely today."

"Thank you." I fidget with Desiree's baby carrier straps and loosen them a bit to free my shoulders.

Devon folds the newspaper, tucking it behind the salt and pepper and leans in, talking more to Desiree then me, "I see you have that beautiful to daughter of yours."

"I do, she had a sleep over with grandma and grandpa. Not sure how they did it but apparently, she slept the entire night for them. She has yet to do that with me."

"Soon enough I suppose. What was she doing at their place?"

"Long story, basically it was just my mother-in-law being a shit disturber and causing a bit of a scene last night. Anyway, my dad thought it best that they take care of Desiree and give me the night off to cool down."

He tilts his head, "Oh that doesn't sound good, is everything okay?"

"Yah, well whatever." My eyes wander from him down to the fork and knife at my place setting. I catch myself and glance back up at him explaining, "People see Sheila for what she is, I could have sunk to her level but it is her own embarrassment." He sips his coffee; I know that he doesn't like seeing me like this so I drop it.

The waitress comes by with breakfast and I force a smile at the sight and ask, "How did you know that I like my eggs scrambled?"

He chuckles, "Jordan, you have told me everything about you, silly."

I giggle, "Yes I guess that I have. How is it that I am always the one asking you questions?"

He smirks, "Could be that you like to talk and I like to listen."

"Are you saying I am motor mouth?"

"No, I just let you talk. I like the sound of your voice."

We eat and I forget for the moment, the crap that happened the night before. "So how are things? How are you?"

He spreads some jelly on a piece of toast then scoops some scrambled eggs over top and says, "Oh you know, being successful isn't all roses. The book sales are still going well and the Japanese market is giving me that much more. The tabloids are still annoying as ever. I am sure that you are dealing with the same especially with your mother-in-law." I nod. The thought of my mother-in-law makes me want to throw up.

I turn the conversation back on him and ask, "How is Sara?"

"She is okay."

He counters, "What about Josh, is he here?"

I knew Devon would eventually ask about him. I answer, "No, he is coming later in the week. He needed to stay in town to finish off some launch at work or something." I can't even begin to think about Josh right now, but I am. I wonder how I will confront him about his mom or hell just think about what he is even doing right now and whether he is alone or in the company of the other woman.

I think Devon sees my unease and tries to make light of it saying, "Well, that's good that he is making the effort to come."

I sip my glass of chocolate milk then ask, "You are here alone? Your son or brother couldn't make it out?"

"Like I said, this was sort of a last-minute thing, I didn't even ask them. I needed time and space from everything."

I scoop some scrambled eggs onto a piece of toast but pause and glance saying, "Not everything."

"No, not everything. I needed to see you."

"Well, I am happy you are here."

He changes topics, "So what are you doing today?"

"Not sure yet. I may do some snorkeling and just relax at the beach. You?"

"I think that I may find a hammock, relax and drink a few ice-cold beers." He finishes his toast and moves on to tackling the strips of bacon on his plate.

"That sounds nice I may join you later."

He glances over my shoulder and my mother and father-in-law are approaching.

Josh's father says, "Good morning"

Josh's mom seems embarrassed and angered at the same time. I know what Sheila is thinking and I try to squash the thought of what's on her mind. I am not going to feel guilty for having breakfast with a friend. "Good morning, guys. This is my friend Devon Chambers and he is an author too. We are published by the same publisher. Devon this is Josh's mom, Sheila and dad, Ted." Ted looks a little worn out and I just hope that Sheila just leaves all the junk that is in the tabloids alone.

There is an awkward pause. Last night she couldn't shut up and this morning not a peep. Devon combats the silence and says to them, "Hello, nice to meet you. Your son is a great guy. I enjoyed his company on the cruise last fall."

Josh's dad says, "Yes that's right. That would have been the time that Jordan signed on with her publisher."

Devon nods, points his finger and replies, "Yes, that was the cruise."

The expression on Sheila's face softens. My guess is that she may be starting to factor in other things besides tabloids. She says, "Hello nice to meet you. We are going to go grab a seat, bye." I know that she doesn't like Devon, the mention of him or me socializing with him for that matter. Whatever, I have the right to surround myself with the people who make me happy.

Devon murmurs as the two of them take a seat at a table at the other end, "Tough crowd."

"Oh, she is rough around the edges. A fucking delight to be around."

"Ah be nice Jordan."

I smirk, "I am nice. I paid their way here."

"Have you gotten any writing done since you have arrived?"

"A bit, yesterday while at the beach but other than that no."

"You know it's good to have a break from it. Besides with a character as unique as your mother-in-law you could possibly make her a character in your work."

"I could" I'm not sure if I would ever do that. If I did, there is that possibility of me hating my novels.

The waitress picks up our empty plates. We are at an all-inclusive so it's a weird feeling whenever we sit at these beach side restaurants because it always feels like we are dining and dashing. Devon leaves a tip as there are no bills and says, "You should. I see the resentment in your eyes when she is around. It would be good to translate that to words."

"I hear what you are saying and will think about it."

"Well, my dear, I should let you get back to your family. Thank you for having breakfast with me."

"It is nice to know that you are near, thank you."

I give him a hug and a kiss on the cheek goodbye. As we are in embrace, I look over his shoulder and see her glare. I close my eyes, deciding to ignore it.

Chapter 47
Plantation Island

This morning Ethan had planned for a day spent on a catamaran, where we would get to see the islands, do some snorkeling and have lunch on Plantation Island. Hailey, Adrianne and I were the only ones from our family that got reservations for this excursion and that is okay with me. I really hadn't the chance to spend some quality time with my siblings.

Emma had offered to take Desiree for the day but I insisted on bringing her to get some nice photos of her on her very first vacation.

I strap Desiree over my shoulders and bring a beach bag full of the essentials, my camera and head out to meet Ethan at the pier.

Hailey and I walk down the pathway that leads to the beach.

Hailey asks, "So are you going to tell me?"

I glance at her, "Tell you what?"

"How was breakfast?"

"Oh, it was good. Nice to catch up with him. He is spending time to himself today to catch up on some rest and relaxation."

She blurts out, "You know the tabloids are saying that him and Sara are getting a divorce."

"I know but I didn't pry. I mean I asked him, sort of but I made it like I was just asking in general. I know something is up, but I don't want to push him to share if he isn't ready."

She looks ahead as we start to walk through the white sand, "I understand. What do you think about all of it?"

I adjust the brim of my baseball cap so that the sun isn't glaring in my eyes as we continue to walk. I sigh and explain, "Oh I don't know. I mean I am surprised that Devon is here of all the places in the world to go to but I know the media likes to stretch the truth. I am sure there is some truth to it but I am thinking at most, maybe it was just a fight. Devon is a dedicated man. He wouldn't just give up on Sara like the media is making look like happened. Oh, there's my brother waving us over." Hailey and I pause our conversation and we wave back.

The view of the pier is what you would see in a gorgeous photo. The water is calm this morning and a clear turquoise. The pier is built of weathered wood planks and at the end is an impressive, large white catamaran.

There's a crew of two young men, I am guessing late twenties or early thirties at most. They are doing their final preparations of the boat before we head out. The two men are talking and calling out instructions to one another as Hailey and I approach Ethan.

Ethan greets us with a warm smile and a hug. He is funny, he spreads his arms out as far as they go so that he can hug both me and Desiree. He then gives Hailey a polite hug.

"Long time no see!" He speaks.

I say, "So true, well this should be fun. I always like the events you plan."

He nods, "I try."

Hailey says, "Wow it has got to be years since Jordan, you and I have done anything."

He nods, "I think the last time was at Jordan and Josh's wedding."

Hailey giggles, "You are probably right. How are things?"

"Good, I have never been on one of these kinds of boats."

Hailey smiles, "That makes two of us."

I answer, "Actually, four of us, this is mine and Desiree's first catamaran ride."

Adrianne quietly approaches looking not too awake. She murmurs, "Good morning"

I say, "Holy moly its mid-morning and your still tired?"

She yawns, "I went out after dinner to one of the night clubs."

I ask, "Alone?"

"No, our brother was with me and so was Josh's sister. I just had a hard time getting to sleep after."

One of the men holler from the boat in a loud booming voice, "Good morning, everyone! I see that your party is all here."

My brother, Ethan hollers up to him, "Good morning! Yes, we are all here and ready to do this!"

The man walks to the back of the boat and it is the first time that I notice the steps on the end of the pontoon. He says, "My name is John, my friend over there is Rick. We will be your guides. Come on board and watch your step."

Ethan is the first then me. John looks at Desiree and says, "Why hello there!" He explains to me, "There are some comfortable seats under the canopy for you and your little one."

I smile, "Thank you." And step up onto the pontoon.

Hailey and my sister, Adrianne board and are greeted with the same warm welcomes.

Adrianne immediately goes to the front of the catamaran where there is a spot to sun tan on a net where the bottom looks down into the water. Ethan takes a seat across from me and Hailey.

Rick offers us some cool refreshments while John explains the schedule.

"For today, we are touring the waters. The water is calm so you are free to move about the boat once we are at a cruise. Find a spot, enjoy the ride and we will make various stops along the way and stop for lunch on Plantation Island. Does that sound good?"

We all give him our approval and he says, "Great, you guys are going to have a blast!"

I hear the sound of the boat motor start at a hum and the sound of the water being pushed through the propeller and the gurgle of the engine being lowered into the water. We back out and I watch the shore as we get further away from the pier and out into the turquoise oasis.

Ethan says to Hailey and me, "You know I have been looking forward to doing this for a while. I had read up on this boat tour before traveling and all the reviews were great. They have these sand dunes that are just out in the middle of the ocean."

Rick overhears and confirms, "We are stopping at one of the dunes this morning."

Ethan says, "Right on!"

Rick says, "Wait until you see. More beautiful in person than in any picture."

"I am sure of it."

Desiree's gaze is fixed just a couple of feet ahead where the mesh starts. I ask, "Are you looking at the water baby girl?" She hums and makes some bubbles with her saliva. "Silly girl." I wipe her lips with my hand.

Ethan is not one for gossip and makes no mention of last night's events regarding my mother-in-law and instead our conversation is of the sights, the weather, things going on in his life and Hailey's.

Ethan is planning on taking some summer school after he finishes the semester just so that he can get a course out of the way and to also lighten his course load for his next year of university in the fall. Adrianne is listening but her eyes are closed, catching up on some rest from her sleepless night. I can't really add to Ethan's conversation because I have never attended university so I can't truly relate but I listen and ask questions and Hailey chimes in with her own University experience and gives my brother some pointers.

The engine is shut off, the sails are let opened by Rick and the jolt caused by the wind filling up the sail with the warm tropical breeze brings smiles of excitement to each of our faces. There isn't much of a breeze either but you couldn't tell that to the sails as they carry us along like the boat is light as a feather.

John sits next to me and asks, "You want to go sit on the net?"

"I do but I'm worried about her." My eyes glance down at the little bit of soft brown hair on her head.

John nods and replies, "Ah no worries I can hold her until she needs her mom." I am a little reluctant but he encourages, "Go on I love babies." He holds his arms out gesturing me to hand her over.

I look at Hailey and can tell that she approves by the look in her eyes and then I glance back to John. I smile and decide, "Okay. Is there a trick to getting onto it?" I free myself of Desiree's baby carrier and help John into the straps so that Desiree is secured to him.

John chuckles, "You may want to crawl on in case of a wave. You will see."

I crouch down at the netting and crawl onto the mesh and start to laugh. John says, "See, that's what I like, people having a good time on our boat." He bounces

Desiree and she giggles though I wonder if it's me that she is giggling at.

Adrianne opens her eyes to see that I am crawling towards her. She asks while yawning, "Hey what are you doing?"

"What do you think I am doing? You have to wake up you wouldn't believe what you are missing."

I knew the wind was moving us along but looking down through the mesh to see that we are zooming over is very cool. We are high enough and the water is calm enough that only the odd splash touches us. Ethan and then Hailey joins us.

I look back at John, who has Desiree looking like she will nod off soon. She is resting on his ripped chest and her eyes are fighting to stay opened. He startles her by hollering to us, "You guys look great. Do you have any cameras for photos?" These boat tour guides seem to remember everything.

I answer, "Yes, just in the main compartment in the bag at your feet."

John pulls out my little point and shoot and starts taking pictures of us. Adrianne opens her eyes and smiles and John clearly looking at my display screen gives his approval, "You will like these great photos."

It is not long before Rick brings down the sails and drops anchor at a sand dune. There are a few other catamarans with tourists here also. It is literally a swimming party in the middle of the turquoise ocean.

Desiree is alert again because of John but isn't fussy. She laughs and I call out to her saying, "Are you laughing?" I look up at Hailey, Ethan and Adrianne and say, "I think that was her first real belly laugh. All the other times I would get smiles and sort of a giggle noise but that's a laugh."

Her laughs sort of turn to noises as she glances at her surroundings, people swimming nearby from the other catamarans and everyone getting ready to get into the water.

Our guide, John explains to us. "It is shallow here. If you stay towards the middle of the boats, it is pretty well waist deep." He points at an opening between the boats furthest from us, "Over there it drops off to about 15 meters so if you are not a good swimmer or have a child please stay within the circle of boats."

Before heading into the water, I lather Desiree and myself in sunscreen. Wow I just love the smell of her sun tan lotion and put some floats around her arms and we all take the plunge into the ocean.

Ethan and Adrianne decide to play fight in the water not far from us and Hailey and I take it easy with Desiree. She is definitely my daughter, not that I had any doubts it's just she is one happy girl in the water. I love to swim and I think she does too.

I say to Hailey, "This is the life!"

"Sure is, if you had me take a guess in high school what we would be doing in our thirties, Fiji would have never crossed my lips." She wades in the water, then explains a little more, "I mean, I would have expected to travel with Maggie but us? Not a chance. I mean I pictured us married, with kids and successful but not to this level."

I agree, "That makes two of us. Say, if the roles were reversed and you had an extra ticket of your own chosen vacation." I smirk at her and continue, "Would you have invited me on your extra ticket?" I look down my nose at her making her smirk.

She laughs, "Of course I would ask you."

I say, "Where would your vacation be?"

"Honestly, I have no idea. I think, probably some ranch type retreat in the United States. Like see the canyons on horseback and relax at a nice private resort."

"Wow that is good!"

"Really, you think? I just think wow, when I hear of your recent travels, all of these exotic places and all I can come up with is a trip to the United States."

"I totally think seeing something like the Grand Canyon would be an amazing vacation and experience. Maybe one day we could. You know that I recently purchased a summer home down in Texas, right?"

"What? Jordan, holy shit you are always full of secrets."

I shrug, "It all happened pretty fast, I figured why not. I hate winter and I always wanted horses. I haven't done much at all with it so there isn't much to talk about. I flew down earlier and toured the house. I liked what I saw and made the offer. The truth is I likely won't visit that home until the late fall."

"Wow, congratulations!" Hailey replies and then dips her head back into the water so that when she brings her head back up her hair is slicked back.

I say, "Thanks but I want you to come down and visit me. Bring the entire family. Josh isn't big on the idea of living outside of Canada for long amounts of time and maybe this is the bitch in me but secretly I am hoping that he quits his job and enjoys life. I mean he really doesn't need to work."

She nods, "I am totally there. I promise."

"Good!"

Hailey speaks to what I had said about Josh. She says, "That is so weird about his job. Have you asked him why he doesn't quit?"

"I have and I don't know. I think he does it to feel wanted or needed or something?" I lie to her. I know it's because of an affair.

"I am sure that he feels that when he is home with you and Desiree."

"Oh, I make sure to show him my love and appreciation. I think I need to just give him time to get used to all of this. I think that he thinks that he will one day wake up and this will only be just a dream."

"I get that."

We glance over and Ethan and Adrianne who seem to have settled down with the play fighting and have changed pace and are now having a normal conversation. They swim over and Ethan takes Desiree.

He says in a squeaky voice to her, "You're a little fishy!"

I tease, "You will scare her with that voice." He gives me a face and Desiree makes some mumbling noises; she is happy. I ask him, "This is the first time holding her?"

"Yes, well I don't like holding them as newborns. At least she has some more meat to her." He changes subject asking, "So what are you guys talking about?"

I say, "Oh you know just this and that."

The rest of the morning with them is amazing and I think we all feel like kids and Desiree is the coolest little girl. She gives us the odd fuss here and there but otherwise I could not ask for more.

Our catamaran docks at Plantation Island and we enjoy some fresh food, live music and the perfect weather at the beach. Our guides have been so great and I think what an amazing life these tour guides have in being able to enjoy all of this while at the same time, consider this work. It must not feel like that for them. I don't think any of us felt like tourists on their boat. The experience they gave us made us feel more like guests and friends. After we are done eating the pace sort of relaxes even more. We along with parties from the other catamarans are at the Island. Some go sun tanning, others are reading in the shade, some are in the water keeping cool. Our two guides are tossing a Frisbee with Ethan. Hailey, Adrianne, Desiree and I are still at the table grazing on the last evidence of our food.

A familiar voice says, "Jordan, you must be enjoying a nice vacation." She is such a fake.

I recognize that slender figure approach wearing a little black bikini, oversized beige sun hat and a white chiffon cover up. Pretending to sound interested I reply, "Miss Saito, out of all the places I would run into someone, what are you doing here?"

She smiles, "Oh I got a nice little bonus from someone you know and he sent me here for some rest and relaxation." She winks.

"Good for you, I suppose it pays to create lies."

She forces a laugh, "You are so funny! Well, you for one knows it does with your storytelling. By the way I have read your book and have to say it wasn't bad but to be honest I enjoyed the gossip columns more."

I need to know and don't bother that Adrianne or Hailey are listening in at this point, I ask, "Why did you do that to me in Tokyo?"

Her fake smile grows larger and she says, "I knew you were holding a grudge. You are famous, popular, I knew you without reading your books. I did it simply because someone offered me more money." She shrugs.

"Steven Peach?"

She smiles, "My client wishes to remain unknown. Well, it looks like my boat is about to depart. Goodbye!"

Miss Saito leaves as quickly as she appeared and Adrianne and Hailey have the, "what the hell just happened" look.

I explain, "That woman was my translator in Tokyo and she caused a world of hurt. I caught her feeding lies to fans at my signing and the next morning everything she fed to them was made public and then she was gone."

Adrianne shakes her head, "How is she even here? Of all the places in the world."

I sigh, "She had to have found out about my whereabouts from Tail Fin. My guess is that she never got let go and she probably is on call to translate for them."

Adrianne asks, "What about Devon? Could he have said something to her?"

"Devon doesn't like her either. I know at some point I told him that I was vacationing here but he would not have shared my vacation plans with Miss Saito."

Adrianne glances at me, "It is just weird." She sighs, "All this stuff that surrounds you, I know it's the fame but I don't know, sometimes I just expect things to be like they were before all of this."

Hailey listens quietly while we talk. I explain, "It's not all bad. This trip would never have happened without fame."

"I know but seriously even on a remote island and you are still running into people."

I shrug, "It's been pretty good actually and it's only people that I have known and no crazed fans."

She's asks, "Do you ever think that it is the people that know you that feed the media?"

"Oh, I totally do but that's something that is out of my control. I have to trust them and hope that the ones that I know and love give me that respect. It's hard not to suspect people that we are close with but so far I don't believe it to be friends and family intentionally tipping off media."

I know that she worries for me. I worry about my family being safe. I glance around at the people. It is the same casual laid back scene you could imagine for a beach. People are sun tanning, some are playing in the surf, and some are having drinks. No one here seems to be out of place. No paparazzi hiding, spying, whatever you want to call it but now since we have talked about it, I feel as though I am being watched.

Chapter 48
No Knock

After returning from the morning and afternoon of swimming and touring the area we retire back to our huts to get settled. Hailey and Adrianne will meet back up with me later. It is the point in the afternoon where everyone is sort of at rest.

Hailey mentions that she is going to the cafeteria at the resort to grab a snack so it's just me and Desiree in our hut.

I change her clothes into something a little more suited for the evening. A sound makes me look towards the door. I see a letter on the floor.

That's weird, no knock nothing.

I race over to the door to see if I can catch a glimpse of who the sender may have been. Opening up the door and looking in all directions I spot a couple strolling down one of the paths and that's it, I know it could not have been them. Perhaps Miss Saito, who knows, at this point I don't even care. Well, that's a lie. My fear that it is Devon saying a goodbye for good is a possibility. I know that he tries to keep our lives separate and I know that he still is in love with Sara.

I rip the letter open and read.

Mrs., Jordan Connor,

From the time that we first met, the ambition and promise in you was special, electrifying and infectious. I wanted to be a part of your world desperately and I sure hoped that you were going to let me in.

I made the effort to make it a reality and the fact that you rejected me so abruptly and harshly shows me your true colors.

You are a blood sucking little bitch. You and Devon both.

Did you think I would just go away, after the cruise, with my tail in between my legs? No Jordan, that's not me and you of all people should know that when I go down, it is with a fight.

It is unfortunate that we couldn't be business partners. As a result of you walking away from a chance in a lifetime, I have made the effort to tarnish your image. If you are wondering about the tabloids and Miss Saito, know that I was behind all of that.

It wasn't just the effort of ruining your image. I wanted to make your life the living hell that mine is. I have had to work hard and fight to get noticed while you and Devon skate by with little to no effort and with mediocre novels. I came close once with my trader partner Devon and you know that he betrayed me. You did too in partnering with him and his publisher. I have lost my chance at fame, fortune, my marriage, everything.

Since we are on the thought of shitty lives, do you know the real reason why Devon is in Fiji?

I have to say that your mother-in-law is a very impressionable woman. That took little to no effort. I chuckle as I write this because all I did was message her on social media and provide tabloid links to your activities.

Oh, Jordan sometimes I want to pity you because you just don't know what is coming and maybe Devon will tell you?

Every writer likes to take credit for their work and Jordan, after it is all said and done and you are left wondering how, perhaps we can sit down for coffee and chat about it.

Anyway, that is it for now.

Yours truly,

Steven Peach

Chapter 49
It Pissed Devon Off

Days before Devon even knew that he would be taking a trip to Fiji he was at home on his computer, working on his writing. It was a quiet day in his world. Sara had been tinkering around the house. Devon and Sara's relationship had been to hell and back. Nobody's worlds are perfect but if you were to ask him on this day, he would have given a more positive outlook on it.

Devon had taken a moment to wonder off in his head. Gazing out the window at the sky with its fluffy white clouds rolling by and thinking that perhaps he could take a shot at writing romance novels instead of thrillers, hell Jordan seems to be fairing out well in that genre and there seems to be less fact checking and research because they are plain and simple, love stories. On the topic of Jordan, he ponders for a moment what she is up to. His mind often goes there, wanting to be with her, making her smile, holding her close and be the man that she wishes him to be. He has thought about it many of times. He can't just leave behind fifteen years of a life he made with Sara and besides he had gone through a divorce once before. That in itself is hell. He sighs at the thought; I am better to just continue to live this life with a woman that I do love but am not happy with.

He grabs a pencil on his desk and flips it round and round with his fingers. At one point when the relationship with Jordan was fairly new, he knew that if she had said the words, I want you, he would have given everything to run to her and bring her back to the United States. He even suggested it at one point. It was too early for her to decide on something so drastic. Truth be told, he had scared her and she gave him a diplomatic response of putting Josh and Sara first before the lust and also explained to him that she had a good career that was hard to come by and she wasn't prepared to let that go. It was a knee jerk reaction on her part and Devon sensed it but at the same time her reaction had forced him to take a step back and think with his head.

His affections for Jordan even scared him and the military side of him forced some ground rules for the both of them to follow. As he sat back in his chair continuing to flip his pencil around in his hand, he realized how stupid it was to restrict them like that. He never had to do that with any of his other friends, why her? He knew the answer and it just pissed him off the effect she had on him. He stares back at his computer, wanting to send her a message but he refrains and just opens up a saved image of her.

Chapter 50
Sara's Habit

Just before Devon left for Fiji he was back at his home in Texas. Sara was out relaxing by her oversized in ground pool. She had done an amazing job in such a short period of time with making this home their own. It had been her first-time hiring designers to help her plan the designs and looks of each of the spaces in her home as well as putting together some top-notch landscaping of their property and she did it all while Devon was traveling and out promoting his work.

Sara, like all of us in this story had not come from money; she didn't know what it was like to live in a gated community and initially had her doubts when Devon had suggested it when his fame was bringing some overly passionate fans to their doorstep back at their previous home in Austin. At the time she saw the need for a more secure place to live and in the end, she was happy that they had decided on this home. Her initial thought was that a gated community would feel like living in a cage but truth be told, the only thing that was different was at the end of the street there was a security gate to pass through with the car, so the home itself felt like a home and not some sort of caged in compound.

In this moment she was out sitting by a little side table near her pool, relaxing. She was having a cigarette after taking the morning to pull some of the weeds from her garden next to the pool. She was tired from the mornings gardening and knew that if she wanted, she could hire gardeners to do the work for her but sitting there after the work was all done gave her a feeling of accomplishment and satisfaction that paying for a gardener would not have given her.

She looked up at the sky for a moment as she blew out a puff of smoke and thought how pretty the sky was with all of those fluffy white clouds rolling by. Sara had picked up the habit of smoking from her daddy. From as far back as she could remember she had always remembered her dad smoking a cigarette after a chore was completed and at a young age, she got into the habit herself, picking the same brand of cigarettes that he smoked.

Every time she lit one up, the smell would take her back to her years as a child and remind her of her father. That smooth menthol smell was comforting to her. Funny but good as she thought to herself that her kids never picked up on the habit like she had and silly to think of how much of an opposite she was in that sense to Devon.

Devon never cared for her habit and wasn't afraid to tell her. Maybe it was that stubborn Italian blood in her, she wasn't sure herself but she never wanted to quit and never would. If she was to do anything it would never be for Devon. It would only be for herself. Nobody would ever be allowed to tell her what to do.

She taps the ashes into an ash tray and takes another inhale and exhale. Devon's last trip was to Tokyo. He had been home with her ever since and he adjusted his focus to coming out with his next novel. Sara was secretly happy for this, well to be honest, initially she was happy about it but never let Devon know it. She still had ill feelings of him after the cruise. She loved him but in the same breath wanted him to suffer the way she had with figuring everything out.

Sara thought that with Devon being home after the Tokyo trip it would be different. She knew that he was fighting to win back her affections and she wanted him to fight a little more. What she thought was that they would be doing more together now that they had some time together, but her reality was what it was now. No matter what she found herself doing around this humongous mansion she was often doing it alone. They were rarely in the same room together.

She had read the translated stories of what had happened in Tokyo and in retrospect they had been pretty tame from the reality she knew. The truth is that her husband fathered a baby for another woman. She knew that the Tokyo tabloids were just digging for gossip and she knew how bad the truth actually was so when Devon had returned home the feistiness that she normally would have had remained focused on Devon's previous actions, on what Sara had learned while on that cruise. Sara was constantly making him suffer and the result she was getting from him was the result of her own actions and she knew it. Deep down Sara knew that eventually he would stop trying. Sara hated herself for being the way that she was but was even too stubborn for her own good and hated herself for the person that she had become.

Devon never really knew it. Perhaps he guessed it but Sara had opened up to her closest friends. Her friends' opinions were always the same, divorce him, sue him, Sara you have got nothing to lose and you will feel better about it once it is water under the bridge.

She had thought about going through with a divorce a lot during the time that she had stayed away after the cruise. The thing that makes her hesitant is the fact that she had been with Devon for fifteen years. The saying, opposites attract, that would describe their relationship fully. Sure, some people didn't get it. Devon was so much younger than she was and her kids had ill feelings towards her and Devon in maintaining their relationship. They didn't hate Devon for the person that he was; they hated their mother for sleeping with a man that was around their age. Sara didn't care what her kids thought or anyone else for that matter, but now, things were changing and that stubborn Italian blood in her maybe brought under control. She may just listen to her friends' opinions.

She knows it in her heart what she needs to do but also just has hope that maybe if she could stop punishing him for something that has already happened that things would change for the good. The question is this, can she stop punishing him? She doesn't even know the answer. Sara knows that if Devon didn't love her anymore then he wouldn't be trying, but for some reason, knowing that should be enough but the sad thing is it's not.

She snuffs her butt out in the ash tray and the cordless phone rings, "Hello?"

"Sara?"

"Yes, this is she."

"Sara, we received a parcel for you at the gate. I just left it on your door step for you." She recognizes the security guard's voice.

"Okay, but why didn't you just let the courier through like you normally do?"

"It wasn't a courier, mam. It was a man that left it with us here. The letter is safe, we have checked. He said he was just an old friend and that he had come unannounced and didn't want to disturb you so he asked for us to make sure that you receive it."

Sara already doesn't like the sound of this but is too stubborn and curious to let it go, "Who was he?"

"Oh, I don't know, he didn't give a name, just said he was an old friend."

She gets up from the chair with the cordless still at her ear and at this point she hears a click on the line and says, "Oh Devon, I got the phone."

"Okay just checking." The second click on the line tells her that Devon has hung up the phone.

She continues to ask the guard as she walks through her home towards the front door, "What did this man look like?"

"Tall, thin, middle aged."

The description isn't helping her much and she decides to give up on it as she opens her front door, "Okay, well thanks for leaving it at the door. Enjoy the rest of your day."

She clicks the cordless phone off and slowly reaches down with her old sore body. Her limbs are already starting to stiffen from this morning's work as she picks up the envelope.

For once she has something addressed to her and not Devon but what worries her is it simply reads, Sara Chambers.

She walks to the grand staircase and she eases her body down, taking a seat on the second step. She thinks, wow I'm being an idiot to be all worked up over some letter, just get it over with. She closes her eyes for a second, gains her composure and quickly tears open the envelope like it was some sort of band aid she was ripping from her skin.

She pulls out a hand written letter and with it, some pictures fall onto the tiled floor.

She picks them up first and knows. A tear drips down her face as she holds her other hand over her sun chapped lips to stifle her own sobs. The pictures are of Jordan in Devon's at Tokyo Tower. What hurts even more is that she sees the happiness in his eyes when he is with her and this confirms that he no longer loves her like that. Another photo looks to be taken moments before or after. Their lips are locked in a passionate kiss and a third one shows them walking. Devon appears to be leading

Jordan through some busy market with her arm hooked into his. Sara allows herself to gaze at them for a moment but then she stops, by coaxing herself to snap out of it. She wipes her tear-soaked face with her shirt and tucks the photos back into the envelope. She is not going to let her emotions take over and she is determined. She needs to see this letter which she folds open and reads.

My dearest Sara,

I know that you have had the chance to see the photos and are reading this to find out why. I don't have those answers for you but at least you know now that what he said was over, is not. These were taken in Tokyo. The market place and Tokyo tower, you can look it all up on the internet to see for yourself as proof that these were taken recently.

I know that you are likely feeling betrayed by him. Trust me, a long time ago I felt those same feelings. Sara we may not be friends any longer but at one time I enjoyed your company at the dinners and functions that you would attend to support him and I hate to see someone that I know turn a blind eye to what is really happening here.

People like Devon are greedy and selfish. For him to keep a wife and a lover at the same time and it go on for so long without any consequence is painful to watch and I would like to consider this letter as a friend sending a friend a message. Now you know that his affair is far from over.

I don't remember you ever being weak. You're a strong level headed woman and I know that you needed to see and now you have.

I hope that one day we could be friends like we were way back in the day and you can now understand why I left the letter with the security guard.

If you would like to catch up, you know where to reach me.

Best of luck,

Steven Peach

Sara crumples up the letter and a sob escapes her. Steven is an asshole for doing this and she isn't stupid. She knows Steven's motive for this letter and the sad thing is she knows that his letter worked. The pictures are real. The emotions on Devon's face are real and she knows that he no longer feels that for her.

Her sobs go unheard in this massive home of theirs. Her sadness soon turns into anger. Anger at herself for hoping that it would all go away. She was so naïve and it soon turns to resentment at Devon for fooling her for all of this time. The forgiveness he had been seeking from her, the gifts, jewelry, flowers, praise and affections had all been an act, all of it.

Her anger abruptly brings her to her feet. The stiffness in her body is forgotten and she marches up the stairs with the photos and crumpled up letter in hand.

Chapter 51
Sara's Crumpled Letter

The door to Devon's office is closed like it often is. Sara doesn't care and barges in to find him sitting at his desk.

She flings the photos one after the other at him. They spin in the air. Some of them land on his desk and a few manage to hit him in the chest and fall in his lap. Sara shouts, "Did you think I would not figure it out? Explain to me what the fuck these are?"

He's shaken up and frozen, looking up at her. She screams at him with her New York-Italian accent making its appearance, "Don't you dare stall this. You don't need to think of some bullshit excuse. You have wasted enough of my time. Pick them up and look at them."

He is quiet and not even trying to calm her temper like he naturally tries to do whenever she gets worked up about something. He picks the photos up and looks at one after the other. There is sadness and disappointment in his expression. Sara can't even tell after fifteen years if his emotions are for the fact that Devon knows he was caught or the fact that he realizes that his relationship with Sara is now over.

Her fists are clenched at her sides and the crumpled-up letter is tight within one fist. She screams, "What do you have to say for yourself?"

He shakes his head and his gaze falls somewhere around her feet.

"Answer me you poor excuse of a man."

He has nothing to say. There is no strength left in him to fight for them, their relationship, her. Sara knows and her temper escalates.

She approaches him, "How dare you! How dare you let this happen! How dare you lie to me, cheat, pretend that it's over with that slut and lead me to believe that you actually love me. Well, I have news for you Devon Chambers, it's over!" She slaps him hard across the face and his cheek instantly turns red. He doesn't look up at her and it disgusts Sara even more. She walks towards the door and turns to yell some more, "Fuck you and to think you could get away with fooling me for so long." She is about to slam his office door but decides that she has more and storms back in, "To think, that I thought highly of you. I thought you were an honorable man to me as your wife, hell even as an army veteran but really Devon you are none of that. You're not honorable or brave. You are nothing but a lying, cheating coward." She waves a finger in his face and finally his brown eyes look into her own brown Italian-American eyes. She continues this time lowering her voice from the yelling, "You know what else Devon. You mean nothing to me." She pulls away and marches out of his office, before she passes through the doorway, she chucks the crumpled-up letter and it hits a painting of the U.S army helicopter that he used to fly during the gulf war. The letter bounces off the painting and to the floor just in front of his desk.

Chapter 52
Sara's Lost Cause

Sara knew that this was it. She gave Devon chance after chance and his heart no longer belonged to her. It wasn't just the lies and the cheating Sara was upset about, it was the fact that she knew the spark between them was gone and she was feeling hurt from having lost a love that her man used to feel for her. She knew that Devon had tried to fall back in love with her. She knew it but also knew that some things are just lost causes.

It pissed her off, all of it. All of those years with him and he can't bring himself to love her the way that she had loved him.

It was no longer about trying to make it work. Even before Jordan came into the picture, Sara and Devon had a couple of times where they had separated but they always came back to one another but this time wasn't the same. He was no longer fighting for her affections, his motions, actions, whatever you want to call it was empty.

Sara moved about the house in a rushed fashion, getting her things together and packing. She tossed a large suitcase on their king-sized bed and started throwing things into it without really looking at what she was packing and stuffing it all in. She went into the safe in their walk-in closet and took out her passport. She knew that she didn't want to leave the country at this point but it was just something that she didn't want to leave behind only to have to collect later. There are photos of Devon and her that she hung around the room when they had first moved in but Sara left them there even though she desperately wanted to pull them off the hooks and smash them against the walls.

"Who are we fucking kidding" Sara murmured to herself as she zipped up her suitcase. Those photos of them were taunting her and she grabbed them from the wall and pitched them as hard as she could to the floor with the glass shattering. She took some frames off of her bed side table and threw them hard. With the sound of the glass breaking, it made her feel a tiny bit better.

Devon comes into the room slowly, from the sound of all of the noise. He watches her without saying a thing and she screams at him while pointing down at the destroyed picture frames.

"All of this was fake. All of it!" She takes another photo and slams it to the floor. "I knew, but I gave you a chance. I knew that you didn't love me anymore. I could feel it in my bones, but your assurances made me stay. Devon why?"

He whispers, "I don't know."

"That's not good enough. Why did you waste my time?"

"I wasn't trying to."

"Fuck Devon, I am not a character in one of your books that you can do whatever you feel. It would have been easier to have ended it when you knew the love for me was gone."

He looks down at the floor because he can't look her in the eyes and it is another affirmation that she is right and that this is it. She pushes her clothes down into the suitcase, zips it closed and then rolls it down the hall and drags it down the stairs.

Devon doesn't offer to help like he normally would. He knows his offer would be rejected. He follows her at a distance. When Sara has reached the bottom of the stairs, he is at the top, slowly taking the steps down. When she gets to the front door he asks, "Where are you going?" He still cares for her.

"To the airport." She huffs. He doesn't push any further he somehow just knows that her plans have not been made and if he dips into it further it will set her off that much more.

She gives him one final stare. She gazes into his empty eyes and when he gives himself permission to look at her, she slaps him hard across the face.

"I loved you and you threw it all away." She spits the words out like they are bitter on her tongue.

Sara slams the door behind her.

Chapter 53
Sometimes Rocks Crumble

Devon answers the door and stands in the entryway to his hut, "Hey, I would have come see you if I knew you were back. I was just giving you time to hang out with your family because I understand that this trip meant a lot to you."

I shake my head, "No, that's not why I am here." Devon steps back opening the door and I walk on into his hut with the letter in hand.

"Jordan, what's wrong?"

I hold out the letter, "Devon this was slipped under my door."

He takes it cautiously from my hand. Desiree is asleep in my arm. She is tuckered out from the events earlier. I watch his eyes read the letter. He speeds through quickly and then reads it again. I know this because of the look of disbelief.

"Devon, do you want to tell me what this is all about? He wants to make my life a living hell, what does that mean? Is he planning to kidnap my baby?"

"Jordan, I don't know." Usually, Devon has some sign of assurance or determination or a sense of purpose when obstacles like receiving this letter occur and right now all I see is an emptiness.

I persist, "Apparently you do. Why are you really here?"

He sighs and I ask, "Devon please explain to me what the hell is going on. Is my family in any danger?"

"I don't think it is like that."

"Then you need to explain."

"I am here because Sara is divorcing me." He is like a deer caught in the headlights. I stare back into those brown eyes of his and he explains more, "After the cruise, I couldn't mend it. I did everything a man could do to win her back. I showed my stick in the sand that I was committed to her but her mind was already made up. I guess once that trust is broken it can't be mended.

Everything is underway to separate the assets, the homes, our belongings and our lives. It's hard to stay and watch your own life fall to pieces and the only other things that bring light to my world is you and your daughter. I didn't know where else to go so I figured I would come here. I hope to not interfere too much with your family vacation. I just needed to take a break from what's going on at home to regain my footing."

I am like a dear in the headlights now. My Devon, the man that I have always admired for having control of his life. Now all I see is a man before me who has revealed what he had been carrying on his own for so long. He is just a man who has been doing his very best and that is all he is, vulnerable just like me. I hesitate but then slowly take his hand in mine, "I saw the tabloids but I didn't think it was true. You could have told me."

He chuckles nervously and I think I catch him holding back a tear, "I didn't want to burden you with my problems."

"Devon don't be ridiculous. You are the sweetest most generous friend a person could ever ask for and sometimes rocks crumble and that is okay."

He nodes, appreciating my concern and explains, "That letter in your hand, a similar one was given to Sara the day we separated. That is why I am here. Steven won and Sara has left for good."

Chapter 54
The Gravel Path

Josh arrives in the evening on Wednesday and by Thursday morning we have some time to ourselves just him and I. His parents are taking care of Desiree for the day. We decide to spend the day climbing Mount Tomanivi. It is an extinct volcano and its peak is thirteen hundred and twenty-five meters which is forty-three hundred and forty-one feet. It will take the day. We are not out of shape or anything but in the same breath we haven't trained to climb mountains so today we anticipate that we will be out for a good chunk of the day.

To be honest when I initially told Josh about the climb, I had only mentioned that it would be one hour or two. I don't know why I had said that to him. Well actually I do, Josh is a very hard person to convince to try new things. He is a creature of habit and when I finally won over his interest with doing a hike up an extinct volcano, I knew that making the most of this time with him was a must.

We are up early, 5:00 am and quietly get dressed, pack a backpack with a change of clothes, sunscreen and we head over to one of the resorts restaurants for a hearty breakfast.

The restaurant is quiet, there are only a couple of other occupied tables and none of which are from our party of guests, which is completely fine with me because these last few days have been hard and confusing, especially with Devon nearby.

"So, what do you think of the resort?"

He looks around with his tired but neutral face. Even when he really likes something he tries to conceal it, the same way that you would if you were at a car dealership and really liked a car but didn't want to let the salesperson know in hopes to negotiate a good deal.

He answers, "It's nice."

I prod, "Nice as in, it's just okay or nice as in wow?"

"Jordan don't get weird. It's nice, you picked a good destination."

I smile, "How is your food?"

"Good, how's yours?"

"It is good."

Sometimes talking to Josh feels the same as making chat with a stranger. Just then the waitress comes by and asks if everything is alright. We tell her that it's great and I ask her if they have any bottled water and wrapped snacks and explain that it's because we are climbing the mountain today. She helps us fill our bag and we are soon on our way up the dirt trail.

It's a warm foggy morning and the conversation is light, friendly. I am not quite sure what is on Josh's mind but whatever it is I don't want to pry it out of him. The last thing that I want is to turn this into a fight. I want this to be the kind of day that I had planned which was a happy one.

I ask, "How are you doing?"

"Good"

I glance down as I walk along the gravel path and say, "I know that the muggy whether can get to you. If you need to stop just let me know."

"I know Jordan."

I glance at him and he gives me a smirk. He is a man of a few words this morning and I wonder if he's being this way on purpose now just to bug me but decide to not ask. We approach a junction on the path and examine the signs. There are faded chipped away painted arrows with lettering that is hard to make out. To be honest I am not even sure if the sign is written in English.

I look up at the sign and then back at Josh and ask, "What do you think?"

He chuckles, "I can't make it out."

I stare back up at it and think aloud, "Well, that one seems to point to some alternate route, while this one seems to be measuring a distance. This route must be the way up the mountain."

"Okay then we choose the second one."

There doesn't seem to be a difference in the paths at this junction both seem to be muddy trails and we proceed up the second one. It's just like my life, whether I choose a life with Josh or a life with Devon, the path will be similar.

We take our time maneuvering the route and when we think we are alone we discover that we are not the only ones making the climb. As we break for water other hikers pass us. Each one with a smile and a happy hello as they continue along.

Minutes soon become hours and the trail becomes thicker with vegetation and the incline becomes steeper. I look back and Josh is no good with the heat, his eyes are fixed a couple of paces ahead of him on the ground and he is just glistening in sweat. I say, "I need a drink." I do it more for him then for me. If I had asked him if he needed a drink he may have declined.

He turns around for me so that I can open up the bag on his back and pull out a protein bar for us to split and a couple of bottles of water.

He is clearly tired and grumbles, "I thought this was only supposed to be a couple of hours?"

I shrug, "That's what I thought."

"Sure, sure." He rolls his eyes and takes a good long, much needed sip.

I ask, "Well regardless of how long this hike is are you having a good time?"

He gives me a tired smile, "Of course. I am with the woman that I love."

It sends a shiver up my spine. I wish I that I felt that same love for him that he does for me. Well, I am not so sure he loves me the same anymore. I never confronted Josh on his on indiscretions. It could have been just a lapse in judgement on his part. I hope that whatever it was or is hasn't become emotional. I guess that means that I do still want Josh. I smile at my own realization of knowing that I still love him and maybe there is hope. I give him a simple kiss on those salty lips of his. "Shall we continue?"

We go deeper into the forest. The path gets more over grown with vegetation. A few other groups pass us on the way up. Some are older hikers with ski polls to support themselves, some are young couples and some are families with pre-adolescent teens.

I don't mind. It is not a race. I just want to get us both to the top without rolling an ankle or obtaining a clumsy injury.

"Do you hear that?" I ask him.

"Sounds like water." Within moments we come to this great opening in the jungle. Other hikers have stopped along the rock pools, some even filling their canteens with water pouring down from the falls.

We stop to take in the site, smell the freshness of the misty clean tropical air. This wasn't something I was expecting and we take a couple of selfies together. This adventure has already rewarded us.

Soon enough we are on our way up further and even come across a couple of rock faces, where we need to maneuverer the rock by using the cracks in the rock as footholds. It is tiring, scary, exciting and I can't remember the last time that we had worked together as a team without arguing of any sort. It is nice and I start to feel one with him again.

Eventually as we walk, we catch the odd glimpse of the ocean that gives us an idea of just how high we are. It becomes harder to tell. The jungle is so thick and we have now been walking for hours.

"Josh, would you look at that?"

He glances over his shoulder and says, "If you are happy with going this high, I am okay with that and we can head back if you want."

"Josh, really? We are getting close to the summit. Do you really want to tell people when we get back that we only walked part way up the mountain?"

He shrugs, "We don't need to tell them the truth."

I glance at him and there is a twinkle in those tired blue eyes of his. I say, "Well, we have made it this far. I want to see the top and say that we climbed a mountain in Fiji."

"Oh alright."

We continue up and after a while of walking through thick bush, we eventually get a bit of a break and the ground starts to clear of brush and turn more to grass and moss as we make our way up above the tree line.

It is quiet up here. You can see the ocean and the waves hitting the shore but you can't hear it from here. There are no birds or crickets or anything that is making noise. The only sounds are our footsteps, heartbeats and lungs breathing in and out.

As we walk up closer to the peak, I start to see the other groups that had passed us along the way. Some are sitting in the grass and enjoying a picnic, others are walking the parameter of the peak taking in the three-hundred-and-sixty-degree view.

As I walk towards them, I can feel a slight temperature change, it is cooler here in the open then it was while trekking through the dense vegetation. The breeze is light, clean and the view is nothing short but amazing. I am always amazed by these views. You often see them in pictures or even in movies but to see it firsthand makes you realize how tiny you actually are in comparison to this world.

We approach this rickety old sign; it is in exactly the same state as the sign back at the junction. The wood has been weathered, the paint, faded and chipping away and the sign itself looks to be starting to collapse but we walk up to it and touch it.

He looks at me with those blue eyes of his and whispers, "Don't ever tell me that I do nothing for you. Today I climbed a mountain for you." Josh pretends to be hard on me even though I know that it is just his way of kidding and his way of saying that he loves me without actually saying the words.

I give him a good long hug. I don't care that he is covered head to toe in sweat. I am just happy that he is here to share this with me. I whisper to him, "Thanks baby. It means the world that you are here."

As usual I hold onto the hug longer than usual, you know that awkward type of hug that has gone on for too long. Josh peels me off of him, "Okay, okay, I am hungry and thirsty let's eat."

Josh and I don't need to be constantly making conversation with one another to make the atmosphere between us comfortable, there are a few times where we fell silent on the top of the mountain and that was okay. We were enjoying our food, the company and our view and that was meant the world for the both of us. As we sit together, I think, maybe this is what I needed, time alone with my husband, away from life, social media, work, and all of the gossip that goes with it. I do love this man and I think that I can fall back in love with him. Maybe Devon was right when he made the effort to at least try to mend things with Sara.

As we sit there, I steal glances like a school girl checking Josh out. Josh is handsome and I am still attracted to him even after being married to him for years. Those strong, confidant blue eyes, his five o'clock shadow, the definition in his shoulders and arms and his toned legs; he is strong, masculine and has the personality to go along with it.

I get caught. He spots my glances and even today he still makes me blush. He sighs and says, "God Jordan, sometimes you are just so incredibly weird."

I laugh, "I am allowed to check out my husband."

He rolls his eyes, "You don't need to be so creepy about it. It is like you are undressing me with your eyes."

"What if I am?"

"Don't be ridiculous, not now."

"Ah you are no fun!" That is where Josh and Devon are different. Devon would have crept off into the woods with me to have a nice little fuck before going back down the mountain. The thrill of that would have excited Devon but with Josh, he is a private sort of man, who enjoys the comforts of a comfy bed to roll around in and enjoy himself.

I don't pursue Josh about it. Whenever Josh says no to something, I can rarely convince him to change his mind. Soon enough we make our way back down.

It is strange how our bodies work. For me, the climb up was easier, my calves are good and I didn't mind the climb and even though I am not used to climbing mountains my stamina was pretty good while Josh struggled at times. On the descent it was like the roles were reversed, he led the way while I struggled down. Maybe it was the height and having to look down that slowed my pace or the fact that my muscles were starting to tire or a combination of the two and with each step that I took or stumble, Josh was there to steady me.

The climb down proved to be just as challenging and took just as long and along the way we made a few friends. Of all places in the world, we met two Americans. They were men in their late thirties, early forties who chirped up as they heard us talking.

The taller man asks, "Hey how did you like the summit?"

I answer, "It was beautiful. Did you two enjoy the hike up?"

The shorter one with the greying hair says, "It was good. I was expecting the paths to be better marked and groomed. It isn't like the mountain ranges back near home but all in all it was a good experience."

Josh asks, "Where are you from?"

They both answer in unison, "New Jersey."

The shorter one asks, "What about you two."

I say, "Ontario, Canada" I should have known that they were from New Jersey with their distinct accents. I heard it just a touch but now with their confirmation, it stands out that much more.

The taller man says, "So I take it that you like hockey?"

I chuckle and admit, "I know this sounds weird but we actually don't follow the sport that much. We are terrible fans."

The tall one gives me a smirk and says, "Well this is a first, a Canadian who doesn't like hockey. Isn't hockey your national sport and your only sport?"

I start to giggle, "Yes, it's a pretty big deal where we are from and no there are other sports too. So, New Jersey, you guys were hit by that terrible storm a few years back. Is everything back to the way it was?"

"No, there are still a lot of homes that are in need of repair. Our mayor is full of promises but the job is still not complete."

Without thinking I say, "I think all politicians are like that."

He says, "Yes you have a point. I mean, it wasn't our worst storm the state has seen."

"Really, I mean I saw on the news all of those trees torn up from the ground and the Jersey Shore, the roller coaster was all crumpled up into the ocean."

"Oh, it was bad, no mistake, I guess it will just take time to get it all back."

I look down at my feet, deciding where to put them as I make my way down a rock face. I ask, "So you said that for this hike that you were expecting a different type of hike. What have you done that is closer to your home?"

The tall one explains as he follows and uses the same foot holds behind me and Josh, "We have done the forty-six in Lake Placid and are now branching out to other countries and such. Mount Tomanivi is another Mountain I can add to my book."

I smile at him. That is cool. It sounds like he has some sort of bucket list of things that he sets out to accomplish. I have meant to create my own bucket list but have never gotten around to it.

The shorter one asks, "Speaking of books, you look very familiar. Are you Jordan Connor?"

I blush, "Yes I am."

The shorter one looks to his friend and says, "See, what I said?"

The tall one answers, "Yes you were right. The tall one introduces himself; my name is Bob and my friends name is Pete."

"Nice to meet you both. This is my husband Josh."

The men exchange handshakes as we make are way closer to the start of the trail.

The shorter one isn't afraid to say and I already know that they have seen things in the media, with the slightest look they gave to one another as I had introduced Josh. He comments, "Those tabloids are terrible. It is clear that they aren't true. I can see that with the two of you here."

I look down and back up at him, "It is just a part of our lives now, I guess. I won't lie it is hard at times to deal with. We are humans. That is partly the reason for our vacation."

"Yes, I don't blame you. It is good to get away sometimes just to regroup. It is good for anybody."

The talk with these two is refreshing and a nice distraction from the task at hand. My muscles are starting to cramp and I am sure that Josh is likely hurting too. I have to admit that towards the end it was getting hard. As we make our way to the end of the trail to the parking lot, we part ways with these two friendly strangers and continue back to our rented car in the parking lot.

I forgot to pack some pain killers in our back pack and at this point Josh's leg muscles are starting to tense up. He slows his pace and I remain by his side. I am sore also and tell him, "There are some meds in the car and in about twenty minutes you will feel better."

He says, "I hope so."

Just then a skinny, toned, young blond woman jogs passed us accompanied by whom I believe to be her boyfriend, who is tall, lean and fit. I don't doubt for a second that these two likely jogged up and down the mountain that we just did. As she passes us with a bounce to her step, she hollers back to her partner, "Honey, I think that was our best time so far!"

Josh whispers in a long low pained and tired voice, "Fuck you!"

I giggle, "My god baby are you jealous that she is jogging and you are limping?"

He gives me that tired smile, the twinkle in his eyes, shows me that it is just his dry sense of humor, "Dam right I am jealous." He grumbles to himself and I watch that young woman hop away as though she had just started her jog. I don't think that I even saw a drip of sweat on her. I am envious too.

Chapter 55
Much As Ever

Back at our hut we arrive back by late afternoon and the pain that we feel in our muscles is eased with some pain killers and an Epsom salt bath. After that we are calm, relaxed and well I haven't been with my husband in some time and we make the most of the time that we have alone.

We lie together on the bed and it is funny because it is not your typical love making romantic scene that romance novels often produce.

I murmur to him, "I am so horny for you but man I am so tired."

We both start laughing uncontrollably and finally he says, "Me too, I don't even know if I can get it up, I am so tired."

I tilt back my head and start laughing like I am being tickled. Silly how our bodies sometimes fail us, finally I ask, "What do you want to do?"

He lays there for a moment, "I don't know. I want to but wow I could use a nap. What do you want to do?"

"I am with you but tonight we have Desiree. We can be quick, then take a nap and go to dinner?"

He doesn't say anything and slowly puts his arm around me to snuggle his chest against my back and he reaches down to my opening and touches that warm little spot. I try to reach back to touch his and he whispers, "No, let me." I stop struggling with him and let him because I know that he won't allow me to win the struggle. he messages lightly at first and I want more and tilt myself toward his commanding fingers and then he presses and I tilt back slightly. It is sensitive and with that motion, I feel his swell against my back side.

Instinctively I want to reach back to touch or even turn around to suck him but I know that I can't and he continues circling my girl, pressing and inserting, rubbing and making me drip. My girl throbs within moments, and I shiver with the pleasure that he has given.

I lean back and he kisses me and says, "My turn."

He turns me on my stomach and he presses himself into my swollen, sensitive opening, sliding in with ease because I am so slippery. His size always surprises and he knows how to get exactly what he wants with me. He reaches around with a hand, lifting my hips slightly and he slides that much further in, making me gasp and his finger grasps my spot in the front and within a moment I am coming again and with that he thrusts hard into my throbs and he pumps his loving deep into me. I feel that tired body of his tremble and I love the fact that he is still able to enjoy me just as much as ever.

Chapter 56
Loose Canon

What a day, climbed a mountain and made love to my husband all in a day's work. I am tired but feel good. I have this sense that I don't need to end it with Josh. Whatever it was he was doing with another woman, I was more than guilty of the same indiscretions too. I can accept that it is okay because none of us are perfect and I can forgive him and myself. All I know is that this is where I am supposed to be, not away from my family in Tokyo and not trying to win Devon's affections. I am to remain here with my husband and child and become the strong family that we were meant to be.

I need to still be a friend to Devon because that is who he is, a friend who gave me my ultimate wish but I need to face our realities and clean up and make right the mess. I can do it.

"Jordan?" Josh startles me.

"What's up?"

"You were somewhere far away. Is everything okay?" I smile and look into Josh's loving gaze. "Yes, couldn't be better. Are you anxious to see our baby girl?"

"Always, are you ready?"

"Yes"

We walk over to one of the resorts many restaurants for dinner. Tonight, we picked the Italian one and we meet up with everyone. Josh is met with a warm welcome from everyone and his mom gives him such a loving hug that he has to ask her to let go. Even though his mom bothers me at times I have to admit it is cute of how fond she is of him. She picks up Desiree and Josh scoops her into his arms. He sits down with his parents and my parents ask me to sit with them.

Mom asks, "How was the climb?"

"It was hard but fantastic. I am glad that we did that."

"Did Josh have fun?"

"Yes, we are both exhausted but all in all we had a blast. It was a challenge, adventure and the reward in the end was spectacular."

My dad says, "That is great kiddo, we are happy that you got to catch up with him." He pauses for a moment then continues in a lower voice, "Listen Jordan, your mother and I don't want to upset or worry you but your mother-in-law, all she could talk about were those tabloids today."

I say, "You know that they are not true."

My dad sighs, "I trust that we have raised you to do the right thing. I know that Devon played a hand to helping you reach your goals and that you work with him. Your mother and I get that. Your mother-in-law on the other hand is convinced that what she believes is truth."

"Dad, where are you going with this?"

He looks me in the eye and murmurs so that his voice doesn't carry across the table. "We think it is best, to ask Devon to leave and allow the family and your mother-in-law to enjoy the rest of the vacation."

"Dad, he has every right to be here as does anyone else."

"Please don't question us. All we want you to do is just ask him. As it is right now, she is a loose cannon and your mom and I know that you and Josh are working things out. You don't need more trouble. We aren't saying your mother-in-law is going to lash out. We just think it is best that Devon leaves so that she can stop dwelling on it."

I sigh and dad says, "Just do it."

"Okay but now?"

"Jordan, maybe after dinner would be best. I can go with you, if you would like?" My dad offers.

"No, that's okay, I can walk over on my own and ask. What did she say?"

"It's not important, I have told you the gist of it."

A waiter fills my wine glass with red, "Thank you." I immediately take a sip. This is just annoying and she is with Josh right now and if she hasn't done so already, she is probably pushing her own opinions on him and today's day of re-connecting with my man will be all just a waste.

Hailey takes a seat at the table next to me.

"Hi Jordan, how was the hike?"

"It was good. How is your new hut? Is it different from the one we were in?"

"That's good to hear. The new hut is the same size and is just a slightly different layout. Your sister and I spent the day on the beach. It was nice to relax. This pregnancy is different from my first one, some days I am full of energy and other days I just want to sleep all day, this was one of those days."

"Well, your tan looks good on you."

"Thanks"

Dinner is served, my parents must have ordered for the table and three pizzas are placed in the table's center, a vegetarian, a meat lover's pizza and the traditional pepperoni pizza. There is just something about the smell of hot melted cheese that makes you mouth water and we all forget our manors and dig in. I think everyone at our table took at least two slices.

Hailey says between bites, "You know, my little girl loves vegetarian pizza."

"Yah right, really?" I glance sideways at Hailey trying to figure out if she is joking.

She chuckles, "Yes, really."

"I thought kids hated vegetables."

"So did I, but I'm not complaining. Sometimes she picks them out of the cheese, matches the colors up and then eats each pile one color at a time."

"You know I think I remember when I played with my food as a kid. Just thinking about the concept of kids playing with their food, it is really weird that they do that."

"What do you mean?" Hailey asks.

"Well, just the idea of getting your hands all sticky and dirty. It's funny how that doesn't seem to bother them but that feeling bothers us as adults. Even taking baths; I think there was a time when I hated taking a bath."

My mom buds in, "Yes, that is true. I used to scream at you to come in from playing outside with that friend of yours from the yard across from ours. You would always yell, fifteen more minutes' mom. I would wait and you would still ask for more time, just to stay out late and play."

Hailey says, "That's another thing my little girl likes. She loves the bath. Mind you she has a ton of water toys to play with so that helps."

"Are you missing her?" I ask.

"Always, I called Matt earlier today to remind him to pick me up from the airport and I got to speak to her today. Made me miss her that much more."

"I know the feeling. Going to Tokyo was a ruff week. Being away from Desiree, Josh and in a country where the language is nothing close to English."

I glance back at Josh and he sends me a wave he has settled in a spot between his mom and sister. I wonder, well wonder is a light word, it is more like worry that his mom will stir up crap.

Things seem to be going well and that is probably because she hasn't yet started to drink like a fish.

Oh, she drives me nuts, just looking at her makes my skin crawl and the sad thing is that she hasn't even apologized. She doesn't even think she is in the wrong. That is what pisses me off the most.

Well, all I hope is that as Desiree grows and starts to remember things, my wish is for her to never see her grandma drink and bitch and complain to everyone.

My mom nudges me, "Jordan?"

I startle, "Yes?"

"Don't dwell on it." I must have been staring in their direction because my mom seems to know exactly what I am thinking about.

I sigh, "I know."

Ethan and Adrianne lead the rest of the discussion at our table for the rest of the dinner and it is to my relief. They joke and kid and I forget for a bit about what was bothering me until I finish my last bite of pizza and my dad whispers over to me, "You should step away now. They seem to take their time with dessert so you can slip away and come back."

"Okay, thanks for the advice." I quietly excuse myself and sure enough Josh and his family at the other table don't even take notice. The good thing is that it appears to be going well since Josh has arrived. They all seem content and my baby girl is doing well with her daddy.

Down the path I go to Devon's hut. I don't even know why I am doing this because chances are that Devon is out at one of the restaurants now having some dinner also. Well, whatever, even as a grown woman my parents still have that influence over me and I am doing this more for their peace of mind than my own.

I tap gently at the door. His hut is quiet, he's probably out. I wait there for a moment just to please my parents and be able to go back and assure them that I tried. I fidget with my feet, tapping my toes over the door mat. This is stupid and just as I walk away the door slowly opens.

His voice is quiet, "Hey Jordan."

I turn and take a step forward, asking, "Hey, can I come in?"

"Of course."

I close the door behind me and then wrap myself in his arms. He laughs and hugs me back, "Ah Jordan, what's wrong?"

"My mother-in-law."

He throws his head back and laughs again, "Oh girl, you know just about everyone's mother in laws are problems."

I mumble into his chest, "I know, I just hate her so much sometimes."

"I hear ya. Well, you haven't really explained why you are not with your family right now."

I hold his hand in mine and lead him to the bed to sit. "I was with them. My mom and dad actually asked for me to stop in to see you."

He tilts his head to the side, "I'm not following."

"Look, I feel like a bitch for even suggesting this to you but I think it's best for you to leave Fiji, well if you can. The only reason that I ask is because my mother-in-law is a psycho and she has been running her mouth regarding all the tabloids of you and me and the thing is that I am trying to improve things between Josh and I and with her here she is undoing all my efforts with her outspoken bullshit."

He takes my face gently into his warm hands and says, "Say no more I get it."

"Really?" I ask.

"Really, I am heading out tomorrow evening anyway, something has come up at home and I need to return."

"Sara?"

"Yes."

I gain some sense of relief that it's not ultimately my fault for him having to go. I say, "Okay well thank you, for doing nothing outside of your planned plan." I smirk and he grabs me for a tickle, "Jordan, you are just so silly sometimes. I would have done as you asked. Tomorrow evening works for you?"

"Yes"

"Okay, well I will lay low tomorrow maybe hang out at the opposite end of the resort to give that pesky mother-in-law of yours some space."

I roll my eyes, "I wish she didn't have this sort of power over everything."

He says, "It's okay, really." I give him a hug and kiss on the cheek and return back to the family.

There is a chocolate fudge brownie with a scoop of ice cream that is dribbled with chocolate sauce over top. It looks like the options were that or an apple cinnamon swirl with vanilla ice cream.

Hailey says as I take my seat, "I ordered for you."

I smile, "Thanks, that's what I would have picked."

"That is why I picked it for you." She winks at me and I flash a smirk.

I take a glance over at Josh's table and the mother-in-law seems to be behaving. I don't think that I will ever organize a family trip like this again. Maybe minus her but in reality, I can't not invite one and have the rest.

By the end of the night after some wine, pizza and chocolate fudge brownie, I walk back with my tired man and sleeping baby girl.

Josh asks, "Why didn't you sit with us?"

I shrug, "Hailey saved me a spot at the table and besides we spent the entire day together."

"I still think we could have sat together as a family."

I shrug, "I am sorry. There is always tomorrow night."

He takes my hand and brings us to a stop along the path and in a whisper, he asks, "Do you like my parents?"

I say in a hushed voice, "Of course."

"Well, my family doesn't feel that way and quite frankly I can see how they think that."

This is likely his mother's doing. She had to have said something. I reply, "Josh, you don't even know the extent of what I have had to endure over these last few days and really we shouldn't be talking about this out here." I release myself from his grasp and at a brisk walk head back to our hut. He is on my tail the entire time with Desiree asleep, thankfully, in his arms.

Whenever there are any issues that are raised between me and his family, he always sides with them and it always disappoints me that the one who is supposed to be my partner in life is not so much so when it comes to his family.

He lays the baby in the crib and we move to the living room area to carry on this discussion which is more like an argument.

He says, "My mother feels like she is not welcome here."

I sigh, "Josh, it was my idea to invite everyone. I was a good host and when someone is constantly at you, there is only so much you can take. Hell, why don't you talk to my family, Josh? Ask them what your mother did the other night at dinner. It is very hard to deal with her but you never see that side of her."

He shakes his head, "Jordan, she told me what she saw."

"That is a fact of our life now. We will always have someone trying to bring us down. She needs to look away from it."

He regards me, "Be honest with me and think before you answer. Tell me, is Devon here in Fiji?"

I look down at my hands for a second and back into those concerned eyes, "Yes, but not because I invited him."

"What is that supposed to mean?" He spits the words out like they are bitter on his tongue.

I go on the defense, "Josh this trip was supposed to be for our family. I had told Devon about it in conversation and that was it."

"Why is he here?" He folds his arms.

"Sara is divorcing him."

"So, what, he is coming here to take you from me is that what this is about? My mom isn't stupid Jordan, she told me things were happening and now I am not sure what to think?"

I can feel my skin turn pink and I so desperately want to raise my voice. I explain, "No Josh, see these tabloids are getting to you. Can't you see his world is falling apart, Devon didn't know where to go to get away. He had thought about visiting his brother in New York but his brother's wife is close with Sara so the next option was to come to us. He knew that you and I would be here and he needed a place to go that was removed from everything. That was all that it was. He made a snap fast decision and decided on us. Truth be told, I had breakfast with him once and aside from that he has been doing his own thing, a mini vacation, getaway, whatever you want to call it. Devon came to Fiji because he has the assurance of having us as friends close by."

Josh stands up and paces and returns back to the couch, "Okay" he pauses and I am not sure if I should say something but then he says, "I am sorry. You are right. These tabloids are getting to me."

I let out a sigh of relief, "It is okay." We sit there for a moment in our tropical hut. The warm breeze brings with it the scent of the ocean and of tropical flowers and gently makes the white window sheers ripple like flags in a gentle wind.

I say, "You know we had a really long day. You are tired and I am tired. It has been one of those days. Want to go to bed?"

"Sure"

Josh loves to cuddle, he will never admit it to his friends but he does love it and he is good at it and I love to fall asleep in his arms. He is always a nice warm body to snuggle up to and I am usually always cold so I make sure that he holds me close in his arms. I feel safe there.

He drifts off first and is asleep within minutes. I envy him. This has been a long day and I just can't get my mind to relax and I am left thinking what now? It is always that question and like some chime going off Desiree starts to cry.

Chapter 57
Restless Sleepers

I wake to a cool mist of the early morning. It rained gently in the night and the air smells crisp and clean. It is rare that I am awake before Josh but I decide to get up. My muscles are stiff from yesterday's climb. It's a good sort of pain, knowing that I pushed my body with a challenging workout.

The bathroom is clean. White towels hang from the rack and the shower is just inviting me in. I strip out or my t-shirt and panties and catch a glimpse of my body in the mirror. I smile, my body isn't yet quite there but it almost is. I am trimmer, fit and it's just a little swell in my belly that is left. Maybe I am imagining things but I look more defined since the climb.

The shower is wonderful. I set the water to a touch cooler as the air is warm and it wakes me up. The smell of the soap gliding over my skin feels wonderful and I give my hair a break for today and instead I just rinse it.

I step out and still the hut is quiet. I let my sweet husband sleep and instead wake my baby girl. I want to go for a walk and besides she wakes me up all of the time. I can get her back every now and then.

She smiles at me as I pick her up and get her changed into a cute little top and shorts.

I leave a note for Josh and put her in a carrier, strapped to my back and we go.

I guess I am not alone in my early hour excursion because when I arrive to the beach, there are others like me, perhaps restless sleepers who are strolling along the shore. Some are collecting shells, others are jogging, and some are solo, just out to stretch their legs.

I wonder if Devon is up. That's a stupid thought, I know him too well. He is up early. He always is and I am sure that he is working on his writing craft at this hour. I should work on some writing. I have just been so distracted with Desiree, keeping this affair secret and keeping myself at a calm mental state with the Steven Peach crap. Steven's letter and dealing with how he has gotten into my mother in laws head has been a major headache. I concentrate and look down, one foot in front of the other as I walk down the beach. The sand is moist and packed down from the waves.

Her mumblings make me peek back at her, "Hey baby girl you like this, just you and me?"

She sends me a smile. The nice thing with babies is they love unconditionally and I'm hoping when she is old enough one day, I hope to tell her everything. Explain to her how much I loved both her biological father and her surrogate father. I look into those bright eyes of hers. Even at this age I can see curiosity in them, trying to absorb all that she can. I hope that when Desiree is grown and knows the truth that I won't be judged by her the way that society judges.

I see flecks of brown. Her eyes are starting to change color and I know that it is Devon's brown eyes coming through and I believe Josh knows.

I continue to walk down the beach among the other few strangers out here. This letter, threat, it is like a warning or something. Is Steven Peach just giving me a scare to see if I can somehow come up on top and overcome this or is this some sort of promise?

I need to tell Josh. I need to come clean and tell him the truth before he figures it out. I can't, I am a coward. I am not going to lie about it but really Josh has done nothing to come clean to me either. Do I even bother? Do I want him to come clean to me? Is keeping one another in the dark a better approach? I know that he doesn't deserve to be lied to but I can argue do I deserve it? I am a coward but at the same time I can't stand to hurt him that way.

Chapter 58
It Wasn't

For however long my affair had been going on for it wasn't the sneaking around, the tabloids and media or the whispers of people's suspicion. It wasn't even Desiree's eyes changing to the same color of brown as Devon's. It was like Josh had ignored it all. Maybe a better term would be he saw the signs but waited for me to either decide who my heart wanted or to come clean with it. He actually never told me what it was that caused him to react. It was like he had just knew.

The last day in Fiji was not the memory that I wanted to leave with but we can't pick and choose the things that go on in our lives. You already know that halfway in the week Josh had made a flight out to join me and the family for the remainder of the holiday. I am not sure if it was the reception I gave? I remember showing him love but maybe it wasn't the same, I can't explain it?

It is late morning and soon approaching lunch when I come into our hut from having spent the morning at the beach with Hailey.

Josh is here and I am a little surprised that he isn't out enjoying the weather with his sister, Emma or socializing with his parents.

I close the door, smile and say, "Hey, what are you doing cooped up in here?"

He approaches me and asks, "Where is Desiree?"

"She is with my parents. Why what is up?"

"We need to talk."

"Okay, what's up?" I hate when people say those words. I always get goosebumps when I hear that sentence.

Josh admits, "I came here for you and we have hardly even done anything together here." My heart stops and I start to sense a shift.

I say, "I am sorry, it's just we brought a lot of people and"

He interrupts, "Don't blame it on the people we brought. If you wanted to be with me, you would. Do you even want me, want this, because I don't think that you do.'"?

"Josh you're my husband."

He asks, "Are you seeing someone else because if you are there is no sense in keeping us intact. If you no longer love me, cut me loose, that would be the nice thing to do and that way we could both be happy."

I wasn't ready for this and sit down in a chair near the bed and say, "Josh there is only you."

"Don't lie to me. Tell me the truth. Jordan you're always distracted with other things, and when I glance over your shoulder at your phone, you hide it. Couples don't do that."

"You know I do a lot of writing on my phone. I don't like people reading over my shoulder. It is a knee jerk reaction that is all."

"Then show me your phone."

"No"

"Why?"

"My work is on this phone."

"The people you talk to are on that phone. I don't think that you love me anymore because if you did you wouldn't be like this."

"Josh I"

He interrupts, "Let me talk. Jordan, I know that you are not happy and I can't go on living this lie that we have created. I knew what was happening, I could feel it, feel that your heart wasn't there. When we had our last talk about a divorce you said that you wanted me and I believed that you did and I wanted to win your love back but I know it's gone and there isn't anything I can do more. Jordan, I tried. I supported you this entire time, made the effort but I know that your heart is elsewhere."

A tear trickles down my face, "Don't say that."

He shakes his head saying, "Please, let me talk. Do you love me?"

"I do."

He shakes his head, "Is there another man?"

"No"

"Please, don't lie."

"Josh I'm not."

"I know you Jordan and can tell when you are lying, just be done with it."

"You're my husband." I can't let him go.

He lowers his voice to a whisper, "Jordan, please you can come clean and say it. I won't be mad. If we are over, we can settle this like decent human beings. The cruelty would be continuing to live a lie."

I say nothing and just stare at him and know that whatever I say next will change the course of the rest of my life.

He asks again, "Have you fallen in love with someone else?"

I look at my hands and then up into those blue eyes of his and answer.

Chapter 59
His Own Indiscretions

I whisper, "Yes" I burry my face into my hands and the tears flow. I love Josh, I really do. All of the years we have had together. The ups and downs and I always wanted to go back to loving him like before I had started to talk to Devon online but I just couldn't fall for Josh again. Devon had my heart from that point on.

I look up at him and see a changed man, sad, broken down, just as I remembered way back when we had first talked of a divorce, before I was pregnant with Desiree.

He is sad but has no tears. He was ready for it, the disappointment and I see it in his eyes, see the sadness and love for me that he has confirmed that I just can't return to him. I am such a shitty person and there are no more lies for me to use to cover up what has happened.

We sit there in the room, like two lost souls. What happened to us? Do I want this to happen? I don't know but it is done now and there is no back peddling.

He finally breaks the silence, "You know that I have always loved you, you knew that right?"

"Josh, I know what I did was wrong but why did you do it too?"

There is a flicker of recognition in those blue eyes of his and he knows that I know of his own affair. He doesn't deny it and shrugs, "Probably the same reasons as you. I needed to feel wanted and while you were out making your money, someone else gave me that. It was a slip and it only happened once and I knew after that, in my heart I loved you and couldn't pursue it."

I have a tear running down my cheek but I need to know, "Why did you continue to work? I mean I thought it was to see her?"

His eyes are a crystal blue and his responses come out with ease while I always struggled to be up front with these things. He explains, "In the beginning I don't know, I guess I didn't believe that what was happening with your sales and what not were real. It was like some dream that I was expecting to wake up from. Then when it sunk in, I don't know I just liked feeling appreciated and then she came into to the picture. I mean all of this is not important now."

I approach him and sit beside him on the bed resting my head on his shoulder and say, "I wasn't looking for another. It all sort of just happened and I tried to let go of him. I love you."

He puts his hand over mine, "But you love him too, I know Jordan. I have seen you struggle with it. I understand and really, I am okay with it. We should go our separate ways."

I love Josh, and I never thought that it would happen but things just do and life is out of our control. Lust, love, you can't change the things that your heart desires.

Chapter 60
Those Kinds of People

There is no point in dragging you through every last detail of what transpired in Fiji because Josh and I did what was best for us at the time. We were traveling with family and friends and the state that our marriage was in, we would not allow it to affect any of their vacations. Josh and I are not those kinds of people and the family wasn't told anything until weeks after they returned home.

We acted as a married couple for those last days in Fiji. It was haunting, hard to pretend to be happy when you are falling apart inside. We smiled for family photos together, took Desiree to the beach together and sat next to each other for each meal. It was a fake reality to not ruin the trip for everyone else.

Josh and I were good to each other and I couldn't leave him high and dry. I still love him even to this day. I gave him the home in Canada. It was already paid for and it was more suited to him. I ended up keeping the home in Texas and Desiree remained with me.

Josh loved her like a good father but he knew that she was Devon's. In Fiji her eyes were looking browner than blue and by the time the divorce was finalized her eyes were the same shade of brown as Devon. I didn't fight with Josh about parental rights and what not. I think once he knew that she was Devon's, seeing Desiree hurt him. He loved her but it hurt to know that she was the result of me loving another man.

I was gentle as could be to Josh and I told him that any time he wanted to visit and see Desiree or me or have pictures he could. I didn't want to hurt him more. Josh was good with that and for him he needed the space to regain himself, this I knew.

He never out right asked me if Desiree was Devon's he knew that she was, her looks and her brown eyes gave it away. In Fiji with some coaxing I came clean about everything, from how it happened, to the first encounter to the ongoing secret relationship that I just couldn't leave alone. Josh deserved to know. It was the little bit of respect that I could give him.

Josh offered to admit everything about his own extra relationship but I didn't want to know. Knowing that it happened and what he had admitted was enough for me. I didn't want to know who she was, for how long it was happening, none of that mattered at this point. I guess that is where Josh and I differ. He wanted to know as closure and I had enough, knowing more would only hurt more.

After everything was said and let go, I can't describe that moment. How do you let go of someone who you shared a life with, house, marriage, the good the bad, everything? I felt empty. I wanted to be with Devon so badly and now the opportunity was there to do so. I know ultimately separating would allow me the freedom to do that but I just didn't want to let go of the life I had made with Josh. Stupid right, well that is what I wanted, to have the best of both worlds.

Chapter 61
Two Something in the Morning

I am not sure when exactly I came to face Devon, following the end of my own marriage. Everything happened in one big haze. I was numb to everything in my world. Hell, I didn't even know what my world was anymore. My husband, our life together, crumbled. Devon's marriage, gone and thinking about these two men that both made me feel so happy at one point now, each brings tears to my eyes.

All I knew was that I could no longer be myself around Devon. The thought of him, everything, made me sad. Late one night, while tossing and turning alone in bed at my home in Canada. Josh is sleeping in a spare bedroom down the hall as I am in the process of packing the rest of my things to move to Texas. I finally get that braveness to do what I should have done before our worlds fell apart. I wrote him an email.

Hey,

I have been giving this a lot of thought and there are things in play that I can't ignore like how all of this makes me feel. We are the cause of this reality. Not me, not you but us. We did this and now it is like ground zero. I am not sure that you wanted this and neither am I and now that everything has happened, I wonder what now?

Our relationships have ended and now I am soon to be down there living in the United States full time, away from my family and friends. Yes, I get that this is my own choice. You sold me on this place and I did this for me but also with the encouragement from you. I wanted a home down here as a break from the winter but also to have my privacy and to be closer to you. I won't lie, you were a major factor in my choice to purchase a home down here because I care about you.

Now that the dust is starting to settle, I wonder if we have a chance at starting a relationship. I wonder if you and I can get passed the hurt that we remind each other of.

I have given you the space to work things out with Sara and I know you have been so gracious to do the same for Josh and me. Josh and I will soon have separated our lives and assets.

I want to have some sort of future with you but know in my heart that we remind each other of what has gone wrong in our lives. I want for us to get passed it but I can't be strung along and then ignored when things between us become more serious.

I just feel like something is off whenever we do have the chance to talk. I want us to love each other and grow as a couple but the reality is here, I am writing this email to you alone in my bed in the middle of the night because I can't sleep and I can't seem to work up the courage to talk to you in person about this.

I will soon be near you, just a short drive away and feel like we should have started in building something together by this point. If I was to be honest with my feelings, I feel like you have cold feet and doubts of us. I want you to know that I have come to accept that we will likely never be. If it was meant to be I wouldn't be writing you this in the middle of the night.

I want you to know that I have no hard feelings. I wish you all the best, and I believe that deep down, you want us to part ways, and that is okay. I should have realized it sooner when you had first raised your concerns.

Good luck with everything.

Goodbye friend

I sent that just after 2:00 am and it was very hard to click send. I remember just lying there in bed alone and thinking is this what I want? Do I expect him to fight for me? Do I want him to fight to win me back or are my words really what they are? Do I really want this to end? I take a few moments and think, will I be happier if this is off my chest once and for all? I close my eyes for a second to keep the tears from leaking out and with that click send. This is it, Jordan. This long ride, I just lay there thinking that I would have never guessed it to come to this but here I am two something in the morning and sealing my fate. The relationship with Josh is over and I have a sinking feeling that Devon feels the same sadness that I feel.

I finally close my eyes for the night and fall asleep.

Chapter 62
Okay Was All

The morning comes early. It is just before 7:00 am and my phone buzzes to the sound of a message on my bedside table. I roll onto my side and look over at my screen. It is Devon. I am surprised. It is so early for him to be messaging me. He writes:

Hey,

I got your email this morning and I completely agree. It is not fair to you or to me to keep this going. I feel guilt for everything that has happened to us and our marriages and it is not fair to either of us to continue if we both feel this way.

Out of respect for you I will honor your wish and we will part ways. I agree with everything you said and wish you all the best and continued success.

-Devon

I read it, and it is a confirmation of my gut instinct that this is what is supposed to be. I feel the loss of a companion but in another breath, I know deep down that I lost that friendship with him a long time ago. We were each other's demons. I wonder for a second do I leave it alone? We both need closure and I have the feeling that he is up and waiting for me to reach out to him one last time so that we can put this to a close.

I text to him, "Devon?"

Right away he responds, "Yes"

I am trying desperately to get my thoughts together, they are all over the place and as I try to write a text, he beats me to it and says, "Jordan, you don't need to explain. I get it and completely agree. We can't continue like this; we are constantly in this loop and that isn't good for anyone."

Finally, I dry the tears off my face and onto my pillow then type, "Is this a knee jerk reaction? Should we completely part ways and exit each other's lives' entirely; is this what you want?" My phone's screen is now dabbled with tears that were on my fingers from wiping my face.

He replies, "I think that this is for the best and I say this out of respect for one another. We will be able to both get passed all of this and I think we will both be happier in the end, okay?"

I simply type, "Okay"

Okay, was my last word to him, not good bye, not friends, it was just okay. Okay was all it could be. I was okay, all I had was myself and my baby girl. It will be okay. Won't it?

It was like a friend had died, that I lost my best friend in the entire world. I lay there for a moment in the home that is now only Josh's. Josh had taken some time off to help pack and send my things to the new home in Texas and those things that are going to be shipped from Canada still lay in boxes around this house waiting for the packers to load them in a transport truck. Josh and I didn't hate each other but seeing each other brought pain to the both of us and I couldn't confide in him and especially not for this.

I need to care for myself and be strong for Desiree. I roll out of bed and dab away more tears, determined that I won't cry for the rest of the day I go through the motions of taking a shower and getting dressed. I pack my things while I hear the mumblings of Desiree in the baby monitor. She is awake in her crib but not fussing, she seems content so I leave her while I can and pack some boxes with my things. The truck is coming today, ready to make the drive to Texas. I don't have much to bring as most of it is staying here. Josh and I have already agreed that he will continue to call this place home.

My books, laptop, clothes, awards and keepsakes are all stored away. Each box that I tape shut just solidifies that this is it and the motions of packing each box seems to get easier, at least that's what I tell myself.

Soon moving to Desiree's room where she is just rolling around in her bed mumbling many different sounds. She can't speak yet but I am sure soon enough I will hear her first words.

I pick her up and give her a long hug in my arms, she is so happy this morning and her joy brings tears to my eyes, she is perfect and I want to be happy like her.

Chapter 63
Say That It Was

These days that pass is dark, shaky and the future is unknown. I am going to be staying at my mom and dad's home tonight after the transport leaves for the United States. I just want to tie up some loose ends before I hit the road and head south.

My parents have me and Desiree in a guest room and again, the next morning, I am up early and feel so lost. I had my two men and now I have none.

My restlessness stems from the way that we left everything. Devon said that he would honor my wish to basically part ways but I didn't want that. I just thought that was what he wanted. I have struggled on that thought, wondering, do I reach out to him, should I reach out to him, am I being obsessive, clingy even. Maybe I am but I don't care I need to know and with that I send an email.

Devon,

I am not trying to confuse things or be disrespectful in any way, by the way, that is a strange way of asking someone to stop talking to them, but I guess that's a nice way of saying that you want nothing to do with me and that's fair, I guess. I know that I am reaching but if you don't like me or this friendship was out of pity or something, say that it was, please don't beat around the bush. I can count on one hand the people that have left my life for good because a friendship died and the other day what I said, it wasn't my wish to drop you as a friend. I didn't want that. Your words, "Honor your wish" that wasn't my wish. I just knew something was off and said what I felt. When you said that you felt guilt it made sense. I could understand the behavior, the hot and cold reactions I was feeling from you prior to Tuesday.

Maybe I am reaching into the past, but I remember saying we would be lifelong friends and I believed it and still do because for one thing I see that you have not dropped me entirely, you are still following me on twitter.

You are the only person that I have reached out for like this, in passed relationships I have always been the heartbreaker, and now I know what it feels like to be vulnerable. I am trying to do what is right but I'm not convinced that this outcome is what you want because it's not what I want. I want us to be able to joke and kid and have fun like friends do and we can cut out the "other" crap that gets us into trouble. I want a friendship that is clean and that I am not ashamed of.

If I am wrong, please be forward and just say it, say that you want nothing to do with me and I promise that I will never reach out to you like this again.

I click send without hesitation but know that I likely won't get the outcome that I hope for and the reality is that if he truly wants to part ways he may not even respond to my plea, not because he is an asshole but more because he likely doesn't want us to hurt one another more.

I don't care whether Devon responds or not. I will know and have my closure. I put my phone down. Desiree is still asleep so I just tip toe out of the room and head to my parents' kitchen.

"Hey Jordan" My dad says in a quiet but optimistic voice. "How are you doing kiddo?"

I shrug, "Oh you know just hanging in there. I never thought that any of this would happen Dad." I fight to keep my voice steady. Thinking about the divorce and all that has happened is hard and I am tired of breaking and I want today to be tear free.

He approaches and gives me a hug and says, "It is life sweetheart. None of us are perfect." My parents are not stupid. They can put the pieces together. They know that I strayed from my marriage and I am now paying for it emotionally but out of respect for me they don't ask.

In his arms I look up and ask, "Dad, why can't things be easier?"

He rubs my back with a hand and chuckles, "I don't know kiddo but I know you will get through it. Josh is a good man and the two of you will decide on something that is fair and things will get easier."

"You believe that?"

"I do."

My mom comes into the kitchen with Desiree in her arms. I am not sure if Mom woke her up or if Desiree woke on her own but I don't care to ask, it's not important.

We eat breakfast together and go through all of the paperwork and I had never really gotten the chance to do so before but I show them the photos of my new purchase near Austin, Texas.

It is funny how some things seem to work out the way that they do. I mean, I really didn't speak a word to anyone about this place other than Josh and Devon and I think that was a good thing because as far as anyone else is concerned, all they seem to think is that I will remain here in Canada and that is not what I need. I need to get away and that getaway needs to be a secret place, so I can find myself again and have a safe place for my daughter to grow.

My parents assure me that the choices I made can be worked out and that they agree that I need to make the trip, move to Austin and take a step back in order to find myself again.

My dad makes a tepee of two pieces of toast on his plate. He does this so that the toast cools off on his plate before taking a seat at the head of the kitchen table. I watch him from my seat beside him. He always does this when he has toast. It's cute but I never got why he didn't like his butter or peanut butter to melt. After his toast has cooled, he lays them flat on his plate and spreads peanut butter on each.

While he is doing this I say, "Dad I think I want to leave today, I can't stay here. I need a change now."

He scrapes the remaining peanut butter off the knife and fastens the lid to the peanut butter jar while saying, "Okay well, I think that you are good for now with taking all of the necessary steps for separation so far. Maybe give Josh a call to let him know that you want to leave today or if you want, I can call him?"

"I will call him." I know my dad is only offering to help and he and Mom have helped so much. I need to call Josh.

I pick up the cordless phone and leave the kitchen. I take a seat on the couch in the den for some privacy and dial our home phone and right away Josh answers, "Hello?"

"Hey, it's me."

"Hey me." Even at the darkest point in the death of our marriage he still finds it in him to joke.

I chuckle, "I am going to miss that the most I think." He is quiet. It is hard and I wonder if this is all a mistake while I talk to him. I say, "This isn't an easy decision but I just have to get away from everything that I know. I wanted to let you know first so that you know where you can reach me. I think that for now with this separation everything is done but I just wanted to talk to you and let you know."

"I appreciate that and that's okay I was expecting you to do exactly that."

I know that he is trying hard not to crack but my heart is breaking all over again. So much for not crying today. I blurt, "I will be going to Austin today, and am taking Desiree with me. If you want to come see her before we go, I can stop by the house with her before going to the airport."

He is trying to hold everything together and his voice quivers when he responds, "I appreciate that but Desiree isn't our daughter. She is yours and Devon's." His voice cracks on the phone, "I love her and I love you but let's face it, neither of you are mine and I am just trying to heal my wounds. Seeing you both will just open them up again, I'm sorry but I hope you understand."

Another tear runs down my face and my own voice quivers, "I know, Josh, I wanted her to be yours, well you know, ours with the IUI procedure but I guess that none of that matters now. I didn't mean to upset you I just wanted you to know where I'll be. If you need to talk, I will always be just a phone call or text away."

I listen on the line and hear his shallow breaths. He whispers, "Good bye Jordan."

"Bye Josh." I bring the cordless phone back to the kitchen and put it on the charger. My mom was listening in the entrance to the den and comes to give me a hug. I admit to her, "He didn't want to see us." The tears flow and I burry my face into her shoulder as she rubs my back.

Chapter 64
Fight Then Label

I didn't forget about the letter I had received from Steven. As far as I am concerned the damage is done and after everything it comes as some sort of relief that nothing more can go wrong. Everything that I feared has already happened and Steven no longer holds the power card in blackmailing me.

Yes, I am packing up my daughter and me and leaving my home and the rest of my family in Canada. I know it looks like I am running away with my tail in between my legs but really, I don't care. The people that matter will see us, all is not lost and I have a career that doesn't tie me down. I need to do this for mine and my daughter's wellbeing.

Steven can continue to feed the tabloids all he wants, it doesn't matter. Truth be told the negative attention still drives sales and if Steven and his little lackey, Miss Saito are making an extra buck, so be it. Tail Fin Books hasn't complained about the sales and I am able to provide for my family. Miss Saito and Steven Peach are bottom feeders and eventually I know the interest in the media will dry up. You can't keep talking about the same thing over and over again. People will eventually lose interest and move onto something else. As for Devon, my friends and family, the only control that I have to keep everyone safe from the tabloids is to leave and take a step back, and lead a more private life.

I likely have enough to go after Miss Saito and Steven Peach for harassing me and the people I care for but at this point I just don't want to put any more effort into it. I don't want to see Miss Saito or Steven Peach ever again. What I want is to just start over and focus my time and energy on my daughter and if this is considered to be losing or giving up in a fight then label me that. I just don't care anymore.

I am not sure what happened to Steven or Miss Saito after moving to Austin, Texas. I believe that Mrs. Saito still works in translation. I have gotten the impression that she is a motivated and driven woman and at the time when she was a pain in mine and Devon's side her motivation was just to please her employer. It was merely business and nothing personal in it.

For Steven Peach it was personal. He was like a dog after a bone. I don't think he published any books after it all because to this day I couldn't tell you a name of a title to any of his books. If he did publish anything it never went mainstream.

I think he got some work in the gossip columns for writing and that's about it. I know Devon had wanted to sue him for defamation but financially it didn't make sense. Devon's time is valuable and as much as he wanted to get justice for Steven dragging our names thru the mud even if he won, it just didn't make sense financially because Devon was making more money in writing and appearances and just like me the damage was already done. Wasting more time in the courtroom would have just been another win for Steven in costing Devon more loss in earnings.

In this life you win and lose and I'll call it a loss, lick my wounds and move on. Devon reluctantly did the same.

Chapter 65
Her Smiles

Mom and Dad help me and Desiree get to the airport. The rejection from Josh this morning and even with Devon, who never answered my email from earlier, it all hurts.

Desiree is the opposite today. My baby girl is all giggles this morning in her car seat beside me, while my dad drives and my mom sits shotgun. Desiree is a funny little baby and I am convinced that she likes to travel. Her smiles are like she is assuring me that we will get through it and I can't help but smile back to her and give her a kiss on those chubby little cheeks of hers. Desiree has no idea how much her smiles are helping me through this. She is my world and I can't help but feel that the roles are reversed. Desiree is the reason I can still smile.

My dad drives up to the airport drop off and says, "So this is it kiddo. Call us when you arrive. If you want your mom and I to come visit anytime don't be afraid to ask. We don't mind."

"Thank you."

We all step out of the car so that we can give one another a proper hug.

My mom asks, "If anyone calls for you, we will tell them to call your cell. I know that you didn't really say anything to anybody about your whereabouts with the exception of Josh."

"Yes, thanks, in time people will eventually find out that I am living near Austin, I guess. Well Hailey knows about the purchase but she doesn't know about my decision to go now but in time I'll let people know."

Dad says, "Think of this moment as a fresh start, okay?"

"Okay, I love you both." I give them each another hug goodbye and Desiree is all giggles for some reason which is contagious, I can't help but laugh, that beautiful brown eyed girl of mine.

I make my way thru the airport and within the hour take a seat in first class. Our plane is parked on the tarmac behind a short line of planes that are all waiting to take off. As we wait, my phone chimes with a message.

Hey,

I don't want to give up being friends and agree that the stuff that gets us in trouble has to be over with. I don't want our friendship to be built on the wrong reasons. Clean is the right way and it's the only way.

I'm guilty for that too and edged you on and I am so sorry. Please forgive me. I want to be your buddy and fellow author friend but the way it was before it can't be. I don't want to have any guilt just not right and fair. If you can accept me as a plain Jane honest friend, I would like that a lot. The last two days I felt like a friend had died and man I was bumming bad but wanted to honor your email. Same here, I don't want our friendship built of sexual stuff. I value you more than that. You are beautiful in and out and happy to know you and be your friend. I want you and Josh to be happy and in love just like my wish to be with Sara.

We have interests that are the same and that is what drew us in to begin. We let the other stuff take over and again please forgive me. It's ok but I did cry, sorry had to say but I did and likewise you are truly amazing and gifted. I hope you enjoy the life that you have, I mean that. This was a reality shock but it needed to happen.

I was at a fork in road and didn't have directions. My GPS was confused. Lol but yeah, I understand but you aren't that. It just needed to end with the sexual stuff. If we can do that our friendship will thrive because it's the right thing to do. It will. I am not supposed to know that about you. As that is sacred between you and your spouse and likewise. I broke that by insisting on it. I wrote many texts and ended up backspacing out.

Well, let me start over. Hello my name is Devon and I'm a fellow writer.

Chapter 66
No Spring Chicken

We circle above the airport in Austin and make our decent. Life has a way of working things out and I look at this as a new beginning. I actually don't bother to tell Devon that we are here. Devon doesn't know that I am going through a divorce and I don't think I am ready to share that information yet. I am still trying to get used to this reality. I'm just not ready. Besides we are just regaining our footing and we don't need to complicate it and to be honest. I need time, space, and I need to be with my little girl.

So much has happened in our lives and in such a short amount of time that we can't keep up with one another. I picked up in having read Devon's message the other day, that Sara and Devon are back together in some way, shape or form and I am happy for him. At least one of us was able to work things out.

I decide to rent a car from the airport. This new city, the spark, flare, whatever you want to name that energy is warm, exciting and it feels good. I have made the right choice to pick Austin. It holds promise.

My allergies make me sneeze a bit as I make my way to the outskirts and decide that I should probably stop and pick up some groceries. I pull into this small-town grocery store parking lot. There is the abundance of American flags that decorate the entrance way to the store. The late afternoon sun is warm, it makes for a strong heat and everything is just different from my home back in Canada. I scoop up Desiree and walk up to the store's entrance where the shopping carts are stored just outside. Desiree is a bit grumpy. It's been a long dull day of travel for this baby girl. She was a super star during the flight and I can't be upset for her fussing now. To be honest her mom feels the same. Desiree feels warm so I remove a top in hopes that it helps her calm down. The air conditioning in the store should also help too. I hope that's all it is.

It just dawns on me, I forgot to exchange my money. I sigh, well it's a good thing I have a credit card.

I pull into the produce isles and grab some bananas, apples, cucumber and roll on through to dairy and already a few shoppers are taking notice that I am a new face. I smile shyly and continue and start to think that I should have done this at a later hour. This is a small town and not the kind of town where there would be a lot of tourists making stops.

I politely continue and Desiree's fussing morphs into a cry.

"I hear you sweetie and feel the same way." Her sobs gain volume and heads are starting to turn. "Oh sweetie, you don't smell, I don't think it's a diaper change." Speaking of which I need to buy some diapers, wipes and cream.

I skip some isles and make my way to the baby section and load the cart and she just isn't having it and is turning beat red. What is with her? She is usually an easy-going baby and this is catching me off guard. I am stuck. I need to finish this but at the same time I want to run out of the store.

I coach myself to finish this grocery. It will be small and I'll have to do another one later when I have a happier baby. If Josh was with me at least one of us could take her and leave the store while the other finishes shopping but I don't have that luxury now.

I rush down the aisles and pick up some lunch meat, bread, eggs, butter, juice and milk and race to the check out. She has got to be hungry but the thing is I fed her on the plane so this is just odd.

In the checkout line there are a couple of people before me and one standing ahead of me is an older woman who takes notice of the crying but instead of a judging glance she says, "She has got some vocals on her. Maybe she will be a little singer that one."

I glance up and force a smile even though my baby is screaming bloody murder. I reply, "Yes maybe, she is normally such a good calm baby I am not sure what's wrong."

The lady takes a look at Desiree's red face, "She is what 3 or 4 months?"

"Yes"

"She probably has a tooth starting."

"No that can't be, she is all gums." I look down at my red-faced baby and wonder, could this woman be right?

The woman says, "It can take a few months for it to break through and if she is isn't dirty or hungry it's likely just her baby teeth. Just buy some teething toys to keep her happy. See watch."

She puts her finger to Desiree's mouth and Desiree chomps down on it and surprisingly the cries stop.

I smile, relieved, "How did you know?"

"Honey, I'm no spring chicken and have had my own babies. She is your first?"

"Yes." As I answer it's her turn to start putting things on the conveyor belt and she does so like a memorized routine and does so without paying any attention and still while speaking to me.

"You learn quickly with your first and she is just a little darling. Say are you from around here?"

"I just moved here."

"Well, welcome, this town doesn't see a lot of new faces. Where are you from?"

"Ottawa, Canada." She gives me a sideways glance and I explain, "It is about three hours north of the New York State boarder."

She recognizes New York and replies, "Well you my dear have come a long way. Why did you pick this little town?"

"I know someone nearby and this seemed like a good place to start fresh."

"Oh honey, don't get me started with divorce!" The cashier rings in her total. She acknowledges her, "Thank you dear" and reaches into her purse to pay with a debit card and continues to say to me, "It's hard to start fresh with a young one like your little sweetie but this is a good place, people are nice and I am sure that a pretty young thing like you won't take long to attract a man."

I blush, "That is good to know." Though I am not sure that I am ready to attract anyone. I have had my fill with Josh and Devon and have left each of them in some capacity and am still licking my wounds from both failed relationships.

She laughs, "Gosh you are a cute thing blushing like that." The cashier hands her the receipt and the woman says to me, "Well nice chatting with you and I am sure I will see you around."

I wave goodbye and realize that we never exchanged names after the fact but that is okay because I don't think I could have lied to her in such a small town. Secrets are eventually uncovered. Maybe she didn't ask because she knew or maybe she got the impression that I wanted to lay low. I am not sure.

The drive to my home is a moment that I will never forget. I have a soother for Desiree and it keeps her quiet for the time being. The familiar sound of the tires rolling over the gravel and the smell of the trees as I make my way down the road. I remember everything exactly as the day I visited with the real estate agent.

Come to think of it, this will be the first time that I see the home decorated to my own preferences. It was a fast transaction and in the closing sale the Realtor suggested a home designer to order furniture and I gave a few directions of what I liked and that was it. I wonder how the interpretation of it all worked out. Strangely enough I trust without knowing the designers work which is strange but ah well.

I pull up the driveway. The place is quiet with only whispers of the wind blowing lightly through the southern pines.

I look around at the property, the oversized garage just ahead and beyond is the barn and fields and to the right, the massive brick home with that welcoming wrap around porch. It looks like we are already here like the home was never left empty. I look back at Desiree and she smiles now that we are alone. I say, "Baby girl we are home."

Chapter 67
Josh Is Up

I'm up early. I always am and I don't know why really. I guess it is because I have trained myself to get up early for so long that my biological clock just knows it's time to wake.

It is still dark out and I'm not really sure that I want to leave the bed just yet. The house is quiet. There is no faint sound of static from a baby monitor on the nightstand table. That stuff has all been packed and sent to Jordan's new home near Austin. When they were both here, I longed for nights that were quiet like this. I love my daughter don't get me wrong but now that I do have the quiet, I know that I rather have the hum of a baby monitor nearby and the sense that I have my two girls near me.

I miss them. The woman sleeping here in my bed next to me isn't the same. She was the one that I confided in when Jordan was doing things that she should not have with Devon.

I glance over at her. A sheet covers her waist as her naked slender back and blond tasseled locks rest on the pillow and bed. She is hot, bubbly and fun. She has life in those topaz eyes of hers. She sounds perfect as I describe her and she is. She looks perfect lying here next to me but she isn't Jordan.

I wonder how long it will take to get over Jordan as I quietly get up and head to the washroom to take a leak. I shake and flush and as I return, I see that she is up.

She asks in that mousy, childlike voice of hers, "Are you coming back to bed?"

I stand in the entryway of my bathroom deciding what I want to do. I'm restless, normally I would get up and maybe shower or have breakfast but I'm not in the mood or hungry.

She is a smart woman and recognizes my wavering and convinces me with her hand tapping on the bed, gesturing me over. I settle back in bed by her side. She massages my back and makes me melt in her hands.

Jordan never paid this much attention to me and when I am so relaxed that I want to close my eyes and sleep is when she goes down on me, though I decide that I want to be in control of my release and flip her on her stomach and push in.

Chapter 68
This House

For my parents and brother and sister they understand the need for me to leave and start fresh, and as I get settled inside, I answer their texts and confirm that I made it okay. Hailey even strikes up a text conversation.

"Hey girl, missing you here. How is the new place?" My mom must have told her.

"It's nice, sorry I didn't tell you about it. The purchase was sort of made on a whim and well, it turns out I needed this more than I had ever imagined."

"Hey it is okay, you know that I am your friend first and I won't judge and when you are ready, we will see each other."

I send her a smiley face, "I would like that. I need time to regain myself and the moment I am ready you are coming to visit."

"Awesome!"

"Talk to you later."

"Yes, take care."

I take a tour of my new home after putting my groceries away. The designer didn't change the style of the home too much. It still has that relaxed, southern ranch flair to it. It's laid back, the home is equipped with comfortable furniture, beige corduroy couches, rustic wood tables, Mexican rugs, the decor on the walls is western, paintings of quarter horses in fields, there is the odd rusty horseshoe and there is even a bleached bovine scull on one of the walls.

I head up the stairs to Desiree's room first. It is decorated as a little girl's room. There are lots of pink and beiges and a plush rocking horse in a corner. Her window overlooks the driveway and off to the right of her view is the garage. Her crib is the traditional white with a carousel of horses.

Down the hall from Desiree's room is my master bedroom. It is gorgeous and has a four-poster bed with a canopy to conceal and area rugs line the room. I have my own master bath, walk in closet and a den. The designer even went to the extent of buying me electronics, a television is mounted on the wall. The rest of my personal things that I had packed won't arrive for a few days by truck.

I won't go through the entire house, but all I can say is this house is completely me and I know that Desiree and I will do well.

Chapter 69
Cute As Hell

It is the early hours of a Texas morning. It's still cool out at this time but from the porch, the pines in the yard are giving off that dewy fresh scent that is a reminder that I am home.

I sip my coffee with vanilla toffee cream that I picked up from the grocery store and look out at the yard. I walk around the side of the porch to see the driveway and the backyard. I let the horses graze out in the paddock overnight.

Everything is quiet and peaceful and I know as the sun rises in the sky that this will be a warm and sunny day. For one thing my parents are making the trip to see Desiree and me. She is now five and a half and a beautiful little girl. A busy girl, always running around outside, fearless, she loves the cats, dogs and horses and she is always asking questions like why do bees like to sting you, or how come sometimes we see the moon and sometimes we don't? She is always making me think. My mom said that I was like Desiree at that age but I don't know. Aside from all of her questions she is quite the independent little girl. She can keep herself entertained for hours, with coloring and I catch her with her dolls acting out stories and I wonder with her having the genes of two creative parents if she will take after us.

It's late August and come September my little munchkin will be back to school and oh I will miss her but realize that she needs to spend time with children her age. I missed her two weeks ago when I dropped her off at day camp but with that all wrapped up and her grandparents visiting, she is home today and it is just the two of us.

She calls for me from the kitchen, "Mom?"

"Yes sweetie." I go back into the home and find her where I left her.

"Mom you told me that when you were my age, you dipped your toast into the chocolate milk?" This morning while my coffee was brewing, I made her a piece of toast with butter and a glass of chocolate milk and I see that she took maybe one bite of her toast.

"That's right. See I used to take the piece of toast, dip it in the chocolate milk and eat it."

"Why?" Her face twists, partly in confusion and partly because I know she thinks it's weird.

I smile, "I liked the taste."

"What if I don't want to dip it?"

"It's up to you sweetie."

She stares at the toast in her hand for a moment.

I ask, "Do you like your toast?"

"Yes"

"Good, you know what, you are making Mommy hungry. I think I'll make myself a toast and chocolate milk too and join you at the table."

I pop a piece of bread down and after a few moments I am sitting at the table with her, having my own toast and chocolate milk. It has been a while since I have had this snack. The fun thing with her is it's neat to watch her firsts and she carefully dips a sliver of toast into the chocolate milk to see what it tastes like. I ask after she eats her first bite, "Do you like it?"

"Yes!" She eagerly dips the toast into the chocolate milk again.

"You know grandma and grandpa are visiting today. Do you remember?"

"I always remember." She winks. I am not sure where she picked that up but it's cute as hell because when she winks, she concentrates to make it.

"Silly girl." I giggle.

"I want to show them my kittens."

"Have you got names for them yet?"

"Only two have names. One is called Ball and the other is Tippy."

"Why did you name them that?"

She shrugs, "One's a ball of fur and one is always jumping on the others and then tipping over."

I chuckle, "Those are great names. How come you have not named the others?"

"Because the others are always eating or sleeping."

"I see, do you think you will name them today?"

She shrugs, "I don't know, maybe if they play today." We both are finished breakfast and she asks, "Can I watch cartoons?"

"Sure" I say. She hops off the chair and runs to the living room and leaps onto the couch.

She knows how to work the TV on her own and I leave her to it while I clear the table.

Devon is in my life. He is but isn't, well not the way you would think. I see him during the week. He comes over like clockwork and visits me and Desiree. Sometimes he even stays the night. We still need each other's friendship but it's not how I would have ever imagined it.

He loves me and Desiree but for him I think that I bring a combination of happiness and sadness wrapped into one. Before my divorce to Josh, before everything, he wanted to be the one to give me what I desired but wanted it to be for me and my own family, a gift. Hearts got in the way and well that didn't exactly play out the way that we had wanted.

It's a strange situation. Devon never introduced me to his grown-up son or his brother or any of his family for that matter and I have never asked him about it. My guess is because it is his way of keeping his relationship with Sara intact. Sara and Devon still live close to my home. Sara knows Devon's family and on that same thought she is his family and the rest of Devon's family knows Sara as his partner. Sara does know and acknowledge the fact that Desiree and I are now a part of his life and I know that Sara has given Devon consent to see Desiree. She knows Desiree is Devon's child and above the crap that Devon and I have put Sara through all of these years she can't bear to keep a father from his daughter.

Sara was close to her own father and even though Desiree is a reminder of Devon straying for Sara, she can't bear to put herself in the middle and prevent that bond between father and daughter. I know and respect Devon's wishes to keep Desiree and I separate from the rest of his life and I know that Sara could easily ask for Devon to stop seeing Desiree, so I don't push it. Sara is strong enough to put differences aside and let the relationship between father and daughter remain. Devon doesn't want to bring me or Desiree into the mix of introducing us to the rest of his family even though I am certain that his extended family all know about us with the press that we had received now years ago.

These days the press doesn't bother us which is perfect. I guess everyone got tired of us once things happened. Interest pretty well disappeared within a couple of months following Josh and my divorce. It is like as soon as the world learned that my marriage fell apart that was it, interest fizzled when the articles portrayed me as being miserable. I am thankful that at that low point in my life, my family and friends stayed quiet on my whereabouts and the paparazzi never caught wind of me and Desiree moving to Austin.

That was a pivotal moment in my life. That's when I was free from the paparazzi and today, I am free to write my books, publish and raise my little girl. I guess you were expecting more but that's just it, I didn't deserve the life I wanted. I wanted a family, relationship and love with a partner, a rewarding career and fortune. What I have learned is that life will never give you everything.

I peek over and see Desiree brushing one of her dolls hair while watching a cartoon.

My phone vibrates with a text from Devon, "Hey Jordan, sorry but I won't be able to visit while your parents are in town. Hope you are not mad. I wanted to be there. Well enjoy the time with them. Bye!"

Typical Devon, I know that he isn't mine, his heart is with Sara but I thought he would commit to visiting for Desiree. I don't think I will ever understand the reasons for his actions. It's like whenever there is the plan that includes anyone more than just Desiree and me, Devon removes himself from those plans. Just because he chooses to keep us separate from his own extended family doesn't mean that I feel the same way with mine. I want Devon to get to know my parents, Desiree's grandparents and just get to know everyone that is important in Desiree's life.

I text him back, "That is too bad, sorry to hear that you won't make it have a nice weekend." I send the text to him and don't bother with trying to wrap my head around his choice.

"Hey Desiree?"

"Yah Mommy?"

"I am going out to feed the animals soon. We should get dressed."

She jumps off the couch and runs back to the kitchen.

She looks up at me and explains, "Mom I wanted to wear my purple dress today for grandma and grandpa."

"That's a good choice sweetie but you don't want to get that dress dirty, do you?"

"I'll be careful." She glances down at her feet.

I chuckle, "Sweetie, we can put our dresses on later, right now mom is going to put her riding pants and boots on. Maybe we can take Champ and Molly out for a ride."

Desiree thinks about it for a moment, "They are not coming until later?"

"That's right, Grandma and Grandpa are coming later. We have time to do our choirs, go for a ride and then we can put that nice dress on for them." I have to convince her. Desiree is kind of like me in that sense in warming up to an idea. I say, "Come on, Champ and Molly will miss us if we don't go out and see them." I give her a reassuring nod and step towards the stairs, trusting that she will follow me and get changed into her riding clothes. I glance behind me to see if she is going to decide and she murmurs, "All right, I am doing it just for Molly."

The mist is starting to lift as the morning starts to grow warmer and the two of us head out to the barn. I have to admit that Desiree is the cutest little thing I have ever seen when she wears her chaps and riding boots and skips along the gravel path to the barn.

My home in Austin had some outdoor kennels when I had purchased it and I never did find out what type of dog breeders the previous owners were. I never got around to taking down the kennels and I am thankful that I didn't because just recently someone had left some kittens at the end of the driveway. I don't quite get why people do that, drop them off like that instead of leaving them at a shelter so now the kennels are being used to house these kittens.

She races ahead of me and peers in through the fencing as I walk up, I ask, "How are the kittens this morning?"

She hollers back at me, "They are hungry!"

"I bet, have you thought of names for Tippy and Ball's siblings?" My little five-year-old picked those names. I can't help but put the words together, Tippy Balls. When Devon hears these names, he's going to have a hard time keeping a straight face.

She looks back and says, "Hmm the black one we can call Darky?"

I assure, "That's a great name. You know when Mommy was around your age, she had a cat named Midnight? She was black like this one."

"What does that mean?"

"It's a time in the night."

She says, "I like Darky better."

In a covered bin on the side of the kennels is where the food is kept. I open the bin, reach in and hand Desiree a scoop of kitten food so that she can go into the pen and feed them while I refill their water. I say to her, "He looks like a Darky. I like Darky too. You have one more to name."

She sighs, "Its hard work naming them." She stands in the pen as she watches the kittens approach the food dish that she just filled with food.

"I hear you. Well, you can think about it more." I move their water dish so that it's backed into a nearby corner.

Champ is my quarter horse and Molly is her fat little pony. Devon was the one who purchased Molly as a gift for Desiree for her third birthday. I used to take Desiree out and walk Champ with Desiree on Champ's back until she was given her very own pony to ride.

Desiree does call Devon her daddy and he is very good to her. I have had to tell him to stop spoiling her so much. Up to this point Desiree hasn't asked many questions other than asking why her daddy has to be away so much. As she gets older, I know more questions will come but for now I am as honest with her as I can be and simply say that her daddy has to work a lot. I believe that Devon tries to spoil her so much to make up for all the time he is away.

We walk into the field where my horse and her pony are grazing not far from the gate. We both clip our lead ropes onto them and walk them back to the barn where we brush them off and saddle them up.

It is amazing how good of a rider she is. Kids are quick to learn and when it's something that they love they seem to become experts fairly quickly. Desiree has been riding since the age of three and at five it comes natural for her. Sometimes it takes some coaxing to get her to come out with me but if I tell her Molly will miss her, she seems to relate to it like her missing her daddy and I can always convince her to come with me. She loves her pony and Molly is the most well-behaved little pony I have ever seen. Devon did well with that gift even though I think he went overboard with giving her a pony.

We ride the perimeter of the property and up and down our long road before returning mid-morning for the arrival of my parents. We wash up after our ride. Desiree changes into that purple dress she wanted to wear and I put on a comfortable cotton dress and blow my hair dry.

By the early afternoon the crumpling noise of the tires rolling over the gravel driveway alerts me of my parents' arrival. They pull up in a rented SUV and Desiree runs out to meet them.

I follow her out and walk up to greet them. Dad is barely in park and Desiree is jumping up and down at the sight of her grandparents. They step out, Dad scoops her up into his arms, "Hi Sweetie. Did you miss me?"

She knows how to tease and makes a pinch gesture with her fingers and answers, "A little"

"Oh, you little bum." He tickles her making her kick and scream and he lets her down. My mom crouches down to give her a hug and asks, "Are you ready for school?"

"Yah, I guess. Grandma, look over there?"

"What am I looking at?" My mom tries to follow where Desiree is pointing.

"We got kittens!" Desiree's excitement is infectious and we all giggle.

My mom glances up at me, probably assuming that I have spoiled her. I give her an eye roll and say with a sigh, "We found them at the end of the driveway and thought that they needed a home."

She says, "I see." My mom stands back up as Desiree distracts herself with twirling around in her dress.

I ask, "So how was the trip? You know that we could have picked you up."

Dad says, "Don't be a goof. We figured it out and it's a nice drive in. Besides your dad likes to drive anyway." Dad gives me my hug that I realize in the moment that I have missed it while living down here.

I say, "Yes Dad, well at least let me help with your bags."

Desiree skips back over to us and asks me, "Is Grandpa your daddy?"

"Yes sweetie" I answer.

"Like Devon is my daddy?"

I flush, "Yes just like Devon is your daddy. Desiree, could you check to see that you dressed your dolly. I think you left her in the living room. You can put a purple dress on her to match."

She takes off to the house and my parent's give me a look. Not a disapproving look but more curiosity than anything. My mom asks, "So what exactly is your status?"

"Mom it's the same as the last time we talk. We are friends."

The three of us walk up the porch steps and through the front door, each rolling a luggage bag. When inside Dad asks, "Will he be stopping by during our visit?"

I sigh, "Not this time. Something came up." Dad gives me that look. That this situation doesn't seem right kind of look.

I glance down for a moment and look back up meeting his concerned eyes. I say, "I know. I suppose I can twist his arm and get him to visit for the next time. He is a busy guy but yes I should have insisted." Dad nods.

We get settled inside rolling the bags out of the way in the entrance and Desiree is eager to show them their room. She helped me the day before with picking out the sheets and she even drew them pictures and left them on the bedside tables. I make my parents coffee and soon we are having a late lunch while enjoying the warm afternoon weather from the porch.

It's hot here in Austin only a little drier than the summer heat we had back home in Canada. Things are good and I am already up to speed on what is going on back in Canada. My parents stopped asking years ago if I would ever get a cottage or a second home closer to them and I never did. Even though they are living in Canada and want me to spend more time up north, the memories still haunt me and I prefer living near Austin. The people are nice here, the pace is a little slower and people like to have fun in the south. I became an American citizen this year. I figured it has been five years and I was eligible so it's just another reason for me to stay. Besides, I feel home here and despite everything I have a sense of peace. Life is better here and if this is what the rest of my life is I am okay with that. I have learned to be happy with what I do have.

After clearing the table, I ask, "Do you two want to go out and walk the property? Maybe Desiree, you can show them those kittens?" Desiree perks up when hearing her name and jumps out of her seat eager to have her grandparents see the kittens.

We take the steps down the porch. The pine trees around the house produce shading and give the illusion of ripples on the ground as the sun creeps through the branches and creates a show for the eyes in my patchy grass. A light breeze gives sound to the trees and the odd snort from a horse or pony in the field can be heard. Desiree skips ahead of us to her kittens in the kennel. She is so eager to show her grandparents. My mind sort of wonders for the moment. Days like this make me happy. I watch my parents show interest by hanging onto her every word as Desiree speaks fondly of her kittens. I don't know exactly what they are saying but this moment in time, if I could just keep this feeling, this is where happiness has found me.

My mom interrupts my day dreaming, poking fun at me knowing full well I was somewhere else in that moment.

Desiree and I make sure to close the kennel door and then we continue on down the path passed the garage and barn onto the trails.

The conversation is all light hearted and about nothing in particular and by late afternoon we are having drinks on the front porch, chatting about the School I picked out for Desiree and the other moms that I have talked to in the area. I can tell that my mom finds this life I have made for Desiree and I intriguing. Without her saying it I know she would enjoy it here in Austin, only I know my dad would never move. Canada is home for him.

I hear the crumpling of the rocks on the gravel driveway as a car pulls up. Devon must have had a change of heart. I put my drink down and walk down the steps of the porch to the driveway to meet a white sedan pulling up. I don't recognize the car and wave to someone that I can't quite make out as the reflection on the windshield of the pine branches obstruct me from seeing who it is. I stand there a bit confused as the car pulls up beside my parents rented SUV and they put the car in park.

I walk over to the driver side. The door clicks open.

"Josh?"

He smiles shyly, "Hey!"

My old friend, I pull him into my arms not sure where to begin or what this is. I haven't seen him in years.

I dry a tear off my cheek with a finger and ask, "Did you talk to my parents, how did you?" I worked so hard to move on with my life after the divorce and now after all of these years, it is right back to square one. I have missed Josh and still regret letting myself stray and not fighting hard enough to make the relationship work.

Those blue eyes are twinkling. I think he is touched by my reaction. He smiles, "Something like that. It's just. I don't know, I needed to not have it end like it did. Maybe this is closure, maybe it's not. I just think that we didn't fight enough for it."

I smile. He looks the same as the last time I set my eyes on him years ago, only he has that look to him like we are on a first date all over again.

I realize I am still holding him in an embrace and quickly take my paws off him, step back, breathe in and out, then ask, "Do you want to come in for a coffee?

Chapter 70
Feelings & Egos

Josh was a good man and still is a good man. That day when he pulled into the driveway, feelings came flooding back for both of us. Despite all that had happened we still had a love for each other. Josh was right. We didn't fight hard enough to keep what we had.

One thing that I learned about time is it keeps on going. People learn to let go and move on. Josh and I were good at one point in each other's lives but everything that had happened, the lies, the affair the hurt feelings and egos, a divorce was the only option we saw in that moment years ago. Back then, I loved Josh but not the way a wife should love her husband. I did terrible things and to not try to confuse things, at the time I loved Josh like a treasured friend and that was the most that I could love because at the time I was taken by Devon.

I broke Josh's heart in betraying him. I know and have to live with that for the rest of my life. So enough of me rambling. I guess you can understand why we both thought that a divorce was the only option at the time.

Josh and I over the years had kept in touch. It was the least that we could do was to help each other. We worked together to make a plan for Josh to maintain the house that we had purchased back home in Canada. I knew that he loved that home and I felt awful enough as it was with going through with the divorce and it was the least that I could do to keep that sense of happiness in his life and with some coaxing and explaining that I had more money than I knew what to do with, he accepted the gift. The rational was that the house was paid for anyways and that I wanted to see him happy. In my heart I hoped that having that stress off his shoulders would be a way to allow him to move on.

The day that he followed my parents' journey to see me was the first time that he actually set foot on my property in Austin and he admitted to me that this place was one hundred percent me.

My parents knew the reason for his need to visit and retreated so that Josh and I could have time to talk.

While I stood at the counter and brewed him his favorite caffeinated drink, an iced cappuccino and brewed myself a coffee I knew that I didn't deserve his company. Yet I look up and glance over and there he is sitting at my kitchen table. He meets my eyes and smiles. I'm nervous, he's nervous yet here he is and somehow, I have been given this chance to have him back. Five years is a long time yet here I am filling a glass for him and my heart is doing flips because the last thing I want to do is screw this up. Five years and here we are, both still divorced. I approach with our drinks and take a seat at the kitchen table.

I ask, "So how are things?"

"Good, I mean really good." He takes a sip of his iced cappuccino.

"Are you still in the home?"

"Yes."

"How is work going?"

"Good, well I actually got a raise a few months back so I am lead in the department which is pretty nice. So, I am able to actually put things in motion without so much red tape."

I sip my coffee and say, "That's great. Wow, remember before all of this happened and you were working two jobs to get ahead. You and I have come a long way from those darker days."

"You are telling me." His eyes are just the brightest shade of blue. I know with once being his wife that when his eyes are really blue, it means he is happy and glancing into them and knowing this detail about Josh brings happiness to me in knowing that what he is expressing to me is true.

We stare at each other for a moment and both giggle at the same time and Josh says, "You know, you haven't changed in all of these years."

I turn my mug by the handle and chuckle, "Is that supposed to be a good thing or a bad thing?"

"Good!"

I sigh, "You were always such a charmer." I pause, looking into my half full cup of brew and look back at him and say, "You know something tells me that you are here for something more."

He smiles then sighs and explains, "I am and I will tell you."

He takes my hand into his and traces my fingers, seeing that I no longer wear my wedding rings. I think I detect a sliver of pain when he notices and finally, he explains, "You know, that you never quite get over the ones that you love and I will always care for you even after all of the cards were laid out on the table. I was hurt. It still hurts years later but to ask a man to stop loving his wife is something that is hard to do and I think you can say the same for me."

I nod, "Yes I can."

He takes a moment and explains, "We have had years apart from one another and life goes on. We pick ourselves up and move on."

"Yes." I say breathless.

He takes another breath. I know that he is nervous with whatever it is and give him the time that he needs to explain it. "Jordan, I came here because I felt that it was more important to be the one to tell you in person then to tell you over a text message or an email or even worse to find out through other people."

My heart starts to thump and I wonder, is he sick or something? He gently rubs my hand inside his and continues, "I met someone back home and she is great, she is good to me, caring, loving and her and I have a bond, a friendship." He takes another breath while my heart breaks all over again. He continues, "When I return home, I plan to propose to her."

He makes my heart stop. I want him to be happy but I thought Josh being here was because he wanted us to start over again. It is good news for him and I get why he is so happy. I can appreciate that he thought this news was important to tell me in person. A tear trickles down my face and he rubs it away with his thumb and cautiously asks, "Are you not happy for me?"

I giggle and more tears flow down my face, "No Josh, these are tears of joy. All of these years I have felt such a guilt for everything that had happened between you and I. I care deeply for you and I really want you to be happy." I don't want to burden Josh by admitting to being heartbroken over him.

He smiles shyly, "I didn't come down here for your approval. Well, maybe I did. I just wanted you to be the first to know. So, you approve?"

I get up and hug him, "Of course that I approve congratulations!" This may be one of our last hugs.

He hugs me back and of course makes another joke, "Well, I didn't ask her yet, so I am not sure if she will say yes."

"Oh, you are such a goof. A catch like you, of course she will say yes." I force my sadness down and try my best to be happy for him.

"Yes, you are right." I look into his eyes and can tell he is being silly and give him a playful shove in his chair.

I ask, "So, do I know her?"

"Nope, I did meet her through work. She was a contractor at the time but actually ended up settling down at another job so I no longer work with her but I did at one time. I guess that it is better that way."

"Yes, no conflict of interest."

We continue talking and eventually my parents returned and it was like old times all over again. Well sort of, it is a family dinner down south with my mom, dad, daughter and my old friend.

Josh stayed for a couple of days. His girlfriend back in Canada texted him once a day to catch up and see how his trip was going. I suspect that Josh left the part out that he was visiting his ex-wife out of the conversation, not because he is deceitful but merely because Josh didn't want her to worry. She didn't have to worry because I knew that his heart was now hers.

I showed Josh the sights along with my mom, dad and Desiree; we visited a spring just outside of Austin, the state capitol and even went to see some live music. The time with them passed quickly and before long it was time for my mom, dad and Josh to return home.

It wasn't the closure I was hoping for but I appreciated that he felt that it was important to see me. In case you are wondering Josh and I even joked about how I wasn't going to be invited to his wedding. We were both in agreement with that. I think no matter how close of friends that you are with your ex-wife or ex-husband that when one moves on and decides to marry again, out of respect for their new partner the ex should not attend. Besides, if the roles were reversed and it was me getting married, I wouldn't want Josh to be there out of respect for Josh and my husband to be. It is more than enough that he made this special trip down to tell me and that is over and above what I would have expected from him or anyone else for that matter. It was a kind gesture and in a way a peace offering that it is okay for us to fall in love again.

Chapter 71
Could with Her

That older woman that I had met in the grocery store that first evening in the lazy, Texas small town went on to becoming one of my close friends down here.

Funny thing is we always seemed to run into each other, at the grocery store, the posts office, the town park. Sue, she was great, funny and she was almost like a mother to me, always giving me parenting advice, giving me her family recipes, sharing the gossip of what was going on in and around town.

It wasn't long before I realized she was just a couple of concession roads over from me and it was the norm to meet up with one another for walks, or even drive to each other's homes to socialize.

Her kids were grown and lived out of the state, only visiting her a few times a year and her husband was a few years older than her, a nice man and seemed to admire all that Sue represented. She was there with me when I purchased my horse Champ and had him trailered in and she helped me get the barn prepared for his arrival.

She wasn't into horseback riding, she loved horses but whenever I suggested getting another one so that she could come out with me she would say that, she was just an old bag of bones and would just get sore and instead offer to watch my baby girl when I would ride.

It didn't take long for Sue to realize that I was a successful author and over the years I eventually opened up to her about all that happened. It was a confession to her that I never really admitted to my family or friends back home, even though most had guessed what it was. I just couldn't come clean and say it to them but I could with her.

When I admitted everything to Sue and my reason for initially picking to live near Austin, Texas, she didn't scowl like I thought she would. Sue can get caught up in the gossip going on in town and sometimes jump to conclusions quickly.

She said, "Sweetheart you did what was right for you. Everything that you did lead you to where you are today and you can't regret that."

"Sue, it's just no matter what I do, I feel like it is not enough or I did it all wrong."

"You can't beat yourself up for what has already happened. I mean look at the bigger picture. You said so yourself, you had always dreamed of having property and horses since you were a little girl and now you have it. Your husband was never the man to go ahead and give you that. You did it all yourself." She shrugs and continues, "Falling in love with someone else, it is wrong but you can't control what your heart desires and look what became of that union. He helped you launch your career as an author and you have the most beautiful little girl a mother could ever ask for." She pauses, for a moment we sit there on my back porch that overlooks my horses' vast field. She says, "Honey, nobody is perfect and I am not saying what you did in life was okay but you can't beat yourself up over it and as far as I am concerned you need to let Devon go."

I turn my gaze that was on the grassy field to her and say, "He is my daughter's father."

"I know he is dear and he blessed your life in giving you Desiree, but you know he made his choice. He has the opportunity to be yours fully and his actions speak louder than words. He cares for you deeply as the mother of his child and he loves his daughter but to him it just isn't right and you know it."

I look into those hazel eyes of hers, her skin warm and a little weathered with age and sun. Her thin hand touches mine, and I say, "I know, it's just hard to get passed when there are so many mixed signals."

She leans into me giving a gentle nudge with her elbow, "You don't have time for mixed signals, trust me you will kick yourself eventually for wasting so much time dwelling on it. You are young, beautiful and have so much to offer."

"Oh stop." I nudge back.

She chuckles, "Just accept my complements because there will come a day when you are old like me."

I roll my eyes and say, "Sue, you are beautiful beyond age."

She laughs, "Jordan, you make me feel young and thank you for the compliments."

Desiree comes racing up the porch steps in a cotton dress that has some new grass stains, paired with rubber boots, "Mommy can I take the kittens out of the kennel to play?"

She is just a cute busy little mess. Sue keeps her smile internal and so do I. My cute busy little mess needs to follow the rules. I explain, "No, they are still too young sweetheart. You can go into the kennel and give them some fresh water and play with them in there."

Desiree plants her feet on the porch, crosses her arms and wines, "But they are old enough to run around now."

"I know sweetie but what if one runs into the field and Champ ends up accidentally stepping on them? They are still a little too young for that and besides if someone comes to our home looking to adopt a kitten, we want all of the kittens to be in the kennel to show them."

She fusses, "What if I don't want anyone to adopt them?"

I lower my voice, "Desiree, you know that is not fair for the kittens or the people looking to adopt a kitten. What if there is another little girl, just like you who wants a kitten to love. Would it be fair to not let her parents adopt one for her?"

She looks up and sighs, "I don't know."

"Desiree, that's not how I raised you. Tell me is it fair to keep the kittens for yourself?"

"No Mommy."

I say, "You can play with them in the kennel but they need to stay in the kennel. Do you understand?"

"Yes"

I open my arms and say, "Come here." She stomps over and I give her a hug and whisper in her ear, "Go play with the kittens and tell them about the families they will belong to."

The breath from my whisper tickles her ear and she giggles and wiggles her little body out of my arms and races down the steps.

Sue says, "She loves those kittens."

I sigh, "Yes she does. I think this will be the first hard lesson she will learn in life, to let go of the things she loves."

We watch Desiree race off in the direction of the kennels. Sue says, "It's a good lesson for a five-year-old and a good lesson for her mother too."

Chapter 72
Falling For His Spell

It was still late August just days after my parents returned home and weeks before Desiree was to start school and Sue had been adamant on going to the town fair. I had said no to her but she didn't take it as a final answer. Truth is I was being stubborn and I gave her every excuse, like that I would be just an extra. I knew that Sue's husband was already going. I know that he is into watching the bull riding and stuff like that. Sue just wouldn't have it and just roll her eyes at me every time I made something up.

I don't know why I didn't want to go, I guess that I just got so used to my private life. These years that I have spent living near Austin had proved to be good for me. I was no longer hounded by the media the way that they used to do when I was still married to Josh and lived in Canada. I have published a few more books since living here and every book has done well. My readers are dedicated fans and I have learned that you can succeed without the drama of the media and this was good. My daughter's life was normal. My life was normal and my family is no longer haunted by whatever actions I do.

I guess I just thought this fair would risk that security but I am happy that Sue was more stubborn than me and pushed until she got her way. Sue convinces me of how fun it would be for Desiree to get to go on all the rides and be with other children her age.

It is late afternoon and Desiree and I are just riding back to the barn at a walk.

Desiree says, "Mommy, Sue said there is candy apple and cotton candy there."

"Yes." I answer, glancing down at Desiree and her pony, Molly. Molly's walk is a little faster to keep up with Champ, my horse.

Desiree asks, "What is that?"

"Candy apples are apples on sticks with a red candy coating on top. It kind of tastes like a lollipop."

She interrupts before I can explain what cotton candy is and she asks, "Can we try those?"

"Sure."

She asks, "So cotton candy looks like cotton balls?"

"Yes, well it looks like a giant cotton ball."

"How big?"

I rest Champ's reins on his shoulder as we continue at a walk and show her the size with my hands, explaining, "About this big."

I see more questions brewing in her. "So, it feels like cotton and tastes like candy?"

"Yes, sort of. I think it tastes more like fluffy sugar."

She scrunches her nose and blurts, "That is strange."

I laugh, "Des you are silly!" We are at the entrance to the barn and we both dismount. She is so good with her little pony. We walk them into the barn to remove their gear.

"Daddy tells me I am silly too."

"I know." She is a good girl and she has always known Devon to be her dad and there was never a time when Devon lived with us. He was always a visitor, a friend who did not live with us and she rarely questioned it. I do worry that she will one day ask more questions. So far, her questions have only been a few and I have managed to satisfy her curiosity with my responses. I know more questions will come and I will need to deal with it when that time comes.

We tend to my horse and her pony, brushing them down, picking their feet and take turns hosing them down before sending them out to pasture for the night. My cell phone buzzes in my pocket, a text from Sue, "Be ready for 4:30pm, we will be over to pick you two up."

I send a text back, "Okay sounds good, see you soon."

I say to Desiree, "It's time for us to get cleaned up."

Desiree and I head back to the house. It is routine for us to wash at the same time in the bathroom off my master bedroom. I run a bath for her and make sure the shampoo, conditioner and soap are all along the edge of the tub before I step into my stand-up shower that has a glass door. I can keep an eye on my daughter while she bathes and at the same time allowing me to wash up.

I turn off the shower and step out and she knows that it's time to pull the plug and allow for the water to drain from the tub. I pick up a fluffy towel and wrap her up before grabbing a second for myself.

When I get dressed a text from Devon comes in, "Are you going to the fair tonight?"

We live in the same area so it doesn't surprise me he may go.

I pick up my phone from the bedside table and text back, "Hey Devon, yes Desiree and I are just getting ready to head there soon."

He writes, "Nice, is it just the two of you going?"

I haven't put my phone back down and respond, "We are heading over with the neighbors."

"Well perhaps I can meet you there?"

I figure, why not and Desiree loves her daddy. She would be pleasantly surprised.

"Sure, I'll text you when we are at the ticket gate we should be there within the hour."

"Sounds good, See you soon."

Right on time, Sue and her husband arrive. Desiree and I are just waiting on the porch step as their car makes its appearance. I see it through the branches of the pine trees.

When we arrive at the fair grounds it is exactly as I had thought it would be. We had parked in a field where the grass has been disturbed by car tires and the traffic of many feet having flattened out the once standing grass. We walked through a sea of people who were also making their way to the entrance of the fair grounds. People of all ages are here in the evening sun to enjoy the fair. As we approach the air becomes thick with the smells of carnival food which is mostly the smell of sugar and deep-fried food. Young girls in cut-off jeans and tank tops, men in sporting cowboy hats, mothers pushing strollers, fathers with a kid on their shoulders are all here. There is also the odd person heading to their car with an oversized stuffed animal.

Sue is just all gab with her husband trailing behind, while holding Desiree's left hand and I hold her right. She says, "Oh look at the midway this year. Wow we got to go on that Ferris wheel."

Desiree looks up at Sue and asks, "What's a Ferris wheel?"

Sue explains it to her and points at it as we walk up to the ticket stand.

The fair grounds are a bustle of people with the loud sound of music along with the faint smells of the rodeo stand out more now that we are at the entrance. Her husband's goal for tonight is to check out the rodeo and watch the concert in the beer tent later this evening. For Sue and I, we are just sort of going with what feels right. I look down at Desiree and she is distracted by everything that is going on. Her bright brown eyes are hard at work as she glances up, down, left and right to take it all in.

Sue's husband explains that he is meeting an old friend in the arena to watch barrel racing and cattle roping.

Sue says, "Okay we will meet you in a bit." Sue then bends down to Desiree and asks, "How about we take a ride up?"

Desiree glances up at the Ferris wheel and says, "Yah."

A familiar voice says, "Hey, what are we saying yah to?"

"Daddy!" Desiree leaps into her father's arms and wraps her own arms around Devon's neck and you can't help but smile.

He gives her a kiss on the cheek and asks, "How is the beautiful Miss Desiree?"

"Daddy you are silly." She touches his cheeks with her hands.

He fills his cheeks with air then blows her bangs away from her eyes and replies, "Why because I called you beautiful? You are you know."

I see my shyness in her as she goes quiet, smiles and gives her daddy a hug, hiding her face on his chest. He continues to hold her, giving her a tickle so that she picks her head up. Devon says to everyone, "How are we all tonight?"

Sue and I say, "Good!"

It is times like this where life feels like it should. I feel like Devon is my husband and we are an intact family.

We all head over to the Ferris wheel and take a seat together. Desiree sitting close to her dad, holding his hand tight and I take a seat next to Sue. This is the only place where you can get a view of everything, the fairgrounds, the town and the hills beyond. The evening sky is changing colors. This is a first for Desiree to see a view like this and seeing her reaction is like experiencing a view like this the first time for yourself.

When we finish our ride, I ask Devon at a whisper, "So you never said what brings you to the town fair?"

"Oh, they asked me to announce the competitive division of steer wrestling."

I smile, "Is that why you are wearing a cowboy hat?"

He smirks at me, "Part of it. Why do I not look handsome?" He gives me that look with those brown eyes of his.

I chuckle, "You are just getting me to give you a complement and yes, you know that I think cowboys are yummy and you look good."

Sue rolls her eyes, "You two are just sickening!"

Devon and I just laugh, but I know there is a deeper truth to her words. Her talk the other day comes flooding back and I need to keep Devon at an arm's length. It's so hard to do because we click so well. It doesn't matter if we miss a couple of days or a couple of months of spending time with one another, every time we meet, we pick up like we were never apart.

Sue suggests, "My husband is already in the arena we should go meet up and watch the next event."

Devon says, "That sounds like a good idea."

As we approach the arena, we can see just outside some of the competitors practicing with their horses before they go in to compete, warming up and perfecting their final moves before their turn comes.

The benches are full of all sorts of people, young, old, city and country folk and all with one thing in common which is to see some great competition.

Over the years, with the help of Howard Stem from Tail Fin, I have been able to lead a more private life, releasing books, without having to really put myself out there while Devon on the other hand has chosen to embrace the celebrity side of having produced great books and as a result of walking into the arena he is welcomed and greeted by lots of people from the community.

He is a popular man and people tend to gravitate towards him. A few know of me as just a friend of Devon's. It is amazing how after a few years people forget the gossip columns and it is to my relief as this town was a fresh start for me.

Sue has been a great friend throughout these years down here and eventually I told her who I was but she sort of figured it out before but that's not the point. The point is she didn't make a fuss about it or let alone tell the community the truth to who I was. Today I am just another face in the crowed.

Sue spots her husband and we take our seats with him. The Ladies barrel racing is underway right now and those girls and their horses are fast.

Desiree nudges me, "Do you think me and Molly could do that?"

"Yes, with some practice."

"Maybe, tomorrow?" She asks me.

"Maybe, we will see sweetheart."

Those cowgirls are gorgeous and their horses are just something else and seeing the teams work together is like watching a dance. The horse just knows where to move and the girls urge them on making it all look easy.

Desiree is seated in between Devon and me and he asks Desiree, "How is that little pony of yours?"

"Molly is good. We went for a ride with Mommy and Champ today."

"Wow, good for you." He glances up at me with a smile and I smile back. It is hard to not give in to him. The way that he loves our daughter and the way that he looks at me, like I am the only person in this world for him. I think, Jordan you have got to get a grip on yourself, it always ends the same way. He decides that it is safe to give into his own heart and flirt, and I fall hard for it every time and we end up having the most amazing sex and then he feels guilt and puts space between us.

Sue gives me a glare. She doesn't hate Devon but she knows, she sees it, that I am falling for his spell.

Devon and Desiree are preoccupied with one another and Sue's husband is in conversation with his buddy. Sue says to me in only a level that I can hear. "You know the next event there is a man we know. He actually lives south of Austin and came tonight to compete. My other half says he has the skill that could win the event. Anyway, apparently he is something else."

I ask, "Have you seen him compete before?"

"No, well that's not true, when he was a boy, I have seen him compete at this Fair before but I haven't really seen him complete since. Actually, it is a bit of a surprise that he is at this event because usually he competes at the bigger events like the State Fairs. Tom says the reason that he is here today is apparently he needs to gain a certain number of points to be able to rank higher to compete at the level that he is used to and he is here tonight to gain some points to go on to the next level. I don't really understand how it all works. I guess it is based on winnings or something but whatever if Tom is excited to see him it means that he is really good."

"What's his name?"

"Rodney Strong"

"I can't wait to see this cowboy that you are talking about."

"You and I both my dear."

The Ladies barrel racing comes to an end and the winners, first second and third are awarded their metals and money and the cowgirls do a victory ride around the arena and then circle out.

Devon leans over to me, "This is my queue."

"Okay, good luck. Desiree, wish your daddy good luck."

"Good luck"

"He gives her one more hug and a kiss, "Ah thanks beautiful."

We watch Devon walk down to the announcer's bench. I know we have a bit of time while the crew set up the arena for the next event. I lean down to Desiree and say, "I need to go pee. Would you come with me and after the bathroom break, we can get some candy apples for everyone.'"?

She is good with that and we return with candy apples for the both of us, Devon and Sue. Sue's husband, Tom isn't really one for sweets. We are back just in time to hear Devon announce the next event.

As he sets foot onto the dirt of the arena, cheers erupt from the stands. The crowd waves their American flags. People whistle and others spin their noise makers for him. Devon is a household name here and everyone loves him. Desiree claps for him and so do I as he walks to the center of the arena with a cordless microphone in hand.

He waves and we hear his voice saying, "Thank you"

The cheers die down after a moment and he says, "Everyone is doing well tonight by the sounds of it." More cheers erupt and he continues, "That is good! Wow, I bet they can here y'all from the midway." Again, he gets a rise of the crowd. It amazes me how much charisma Devon has and he does it with such ease and a smile on his face.

"The next event is my favorite event of the night. The horses are strong and agile; while their riders are smart, quick and coordinated. It takes guts, brains, muscle and talent to be able to do this next event and I am happy to announce steer wrestling." The crowd erupts again with excitement as Devon remains quite for a moment until he can get his next words in. "With one of the biggest purses of the night the winner will ride home with $10,000. Good luck to all who are competing in this event, and let the games begin!" Music sounds from the speakers and the crowd goes nuts.

As Devon walks back to the announcers stand some young girls on horses circle the ring at a canter, one with the American flag, a second with the Lone Star Flag and a third with the Austin Flag. There is activity in the ring as you can see the steers are being lined up for the competition and the competitors on their horses are ready at the gate.

The first steer is released and the first horse and rider pair come out at full force from the gate and within a split second, horse and cowboy are galloping after. The horse and rider come up alongside the steer and the cowboy launches himself from his horse bringing the steer to the ground. His horse continues to gallop to the end of the arena. The timer stops and the announcer says, "That is one hell of a great starting time! That's some great work by our first competitor Robby Hill!"

The crowed is cheering on their cowboy stars and Desiree asks me, "Mommy did he hurt the baby cow?"

Oh, dear did I make a mistake in allowing her to watch? I say to her, "No sweetheart, they are just competing. See look, it's like playing a game of tag. See the cowboy let the baby cow go and he is just fine."

I think she is convinced and she then says, "I can't bite into my candy apple. Can you help me?"

I do as she asks and take a bite of her apple to help her get started and hand it back to her. I whisper to Sue, "Was it wrong of me to allow her to watch this?"

She whispers back, "I know that it's rough but you are fine. Just look at the audience there are other families here with young children."

I don't know how I feel. I mean what if a horse goes down and breaks a leg? I don't know if I want her to see that. I swore I would never be an overprotective mom but I don't feel comfortable now that Desiree is asking me if the baby cow was hurt.

"Sue, I think I am going to take her on some midway rides. If Devon comes back, would you give him his candy apple and just let him know that he can send me a text and I'll answer."

"Okay dear." She looks ahead and says, "Oh there he is!"

"Who, Devon?"

"No Jordan. Rodney!"

I look and see this cowboy racing after a steer on his dark horse. He is in dark denim jeans, a black shirt and black cowboy hat. I can see a whisper of dark shoulder length brown wavy hair blowing in the wind. He leaps and takes his steer down and the clock stops.

The announcer says, "Another great ride from Rodney!"

I turn to Sue, "Wow he is good. I'll see you later?"

"Sure" She gives me a quick kiss on the cheek. "I will meet up with you after the event.

"Okay"

I descend from the stands holding Desiree's hand as we exit the arena and back into the evening air. The sun has set and the midway is now a sea of sparkling-colored lights. Younger people are now out in full swing taking over the midway.

We walk by the practice rings where the competitors warm up and I catch a glimpse of Rodney just beyond the gate.

Desiree says, "Is that Sue's cowboy friend that we just saw?"

Her young little voice echoes in the night air and Rodney looks our way. We lock eyes. I feel my cheeks flush and hope that he doesn't see it. Desiree sort of stops me in my tracks wanting an answer, "Yes sweetie I think that is Sue and Tom's friend, Rodney."

He dismounts his horse and hands the animal off to a stable hand and casually walks over to the fence.

He says, "Hey, I couldn't help but over hear you."

I smile and say, "Oh we didn't mean to distract you. My little girl was just asking who you were."

He smiles and crouches down so that he is eye level to Desiree, "Well hello little lady. I have a boy about your age."

Desiree smiles and then hides her face behind my legs. I laugh, "She isn't normally shy like this." I swallow and pretend that I am not shy either and say, "So I am friends with Sue and Tom. They say they know you. They were in the stands and were there just to watch you."

He smiles and I catch a glimpse of his pearly white teeth in the moonlight, "Yes, we go way back." We have a moment of awkward silence and he says, "Wow, where are my manors." He removes his cowboy hat to reveal that wavy shoulder length brown hair. It is damp with sweat and I catch the faint smell of his pheromones and I have to remind myself to keep it together but I must say he smells good. He says, "I am Rodney, nice to meet you."

"Nice to meet you. I am Jordan and this little girl is Desiree."

"Well, it is nice to meet the both of you." His smile would make any woman melt. Wow what is it about cowboys?

He continues, "Well I better get back to my horse. Hope you two enjoy the fair and say hi to Sue and Tom for me?"

"I will and it was nice to meet you too."

Chapter 73
A Rodeo Star

It's a neat thing to watch your child get to experience things for the first time. It reminds you of your own youth. All of the rides are all the same as my own childhood. There is the giant blown up trampoline that she goes in, a giant slide, the spinning tea cups, an egg beater ride, a gravity defying ride where you stick to the side as the ride spins on the spot, a maze where it's all mirrors and you have to find your way through. There is also the bumper cars and I think it's Desiree's favorite the carousel.

She gets the experience that I wanted her to have and even got to interact with other children in the lines and on the rides. After all those rides it is getting late for a little girl.

I meet up with Sue who has a bag of cotton candy for Desiree. She says, "Tom is just headed over to the beer tent."

"Sounds like fun. Well, this little monkey needs to get to bed."

"I am not a monkey!" Desiree complains.

I pat her head and say to Sue, "It's time to go."

Sue nods, "I agree. I am tired too well are you tired?"

I give Sue a sideways glance, "What me? No, I am okay. Why?"

"Well, no reason." I see the look.

"What? Sue don't be like that. There is a reason."

She says into my ear, "I can take Desiree tonight and bring her home in the morning. You should stay here and enjoy the concert."

I glance at her. She is up to something and she wrinkles her forehead, raising her eyebrows.

I roll my eyes and say, "I don't know what you are up to but whatever it is, when I find out I am blaming you."

She laughs, "Okay dear well have a good night." She takes Desiree's hand. "Come on missy. How about you and I head home for the night and we can each have a handful of cotton candy?"

Desiree likes Sue a lot so it doesn't take much to convince her. I give Desiree a kiss on the forehead, "See you tomorrow sweetie."

I watch my friend and daughter disappear into the crowd and I wonder if Devon talked Sue into something. Well, that doesn't make sense. Sue is pretty adamant about how she feels about Devon.

I look in the direction of the beer grounds. The busy loud bustle of people having fun with their friends is almost overwhelming and I take a moment to look to see if I see Tom, then there is a gentle tap on my bare shoulder. I am wearing a black tube top. I jump, turning to come face to face with a cowboy who has his hands up like I am pointing a gun at him.

"Easy girl. Wow you startle like nothing."

"Rodney?"

He flashes those pearly whites at me, "That's me." He tips his hat.

I chuckle, "I am sorry. It's just I was looking for Tom."

"I ran into Tom and Sue after my event."

Now I know what this is about, and I play the game, "Sue just left with my little girl for the night."

"Yes, I saw that. Actually, I wanted to ask you, can I buy you a drink?"

His dark brown eyes, smooth tanned skin that is clean shaven is ruggedly flawless. He is gorgeous, tall, and lean but with muscle to him, how could I refuse. I answer, "I would like that."

He smiles, and says like a gentleman, "Well okay then, shall we?"

He gives me his arm and takes the lead to the grounds and orders a light beer for me and a regular brew for himself.

That feeling of nerves that you get around someone that you like, it's there and I know that I am crushing on him. I don't normally get to go out on dates well not without my daughter. To be honest, I don't remember the last time I was on a date and wonder if Tokyo with Devon was the last time I was on a date?

Well, whatever this is with Rodney is nice, really nice.

I find out in conversation that he won the competition and that was apparent because throughout the night he was greeted with plenty of cheers and congratulations. I find myself in the shadow of another star, a rodeo star and that is okay with me.

He keeps my drinks coming and soon enough we are dancing in the Texas night along with a few thousand others under the stars with the guitars playing and the beat of the drums and base. He leads in the dance. I rest my head on his chest, his hand resting on the small of my back and this feels nice. I can't be upset with Sue. How she managed this I have no idea but wow she just made my night.

Rodney is a gentleman and when the song ends, he says, "I'll be right back." He's going to get more drinks and I clap for the band that just played an amazing song.

I get another tap on my shoulder and turn. He says, "Hey I didn't think I would find you here?"

"Devon, hey yes well Sue ended up taking Desiree home and Tom is here somewhere with a friend. I'll probably get a ride home with his friend later on."

"I see, well you look stunning tonight."

Rodney approaches with our drinks, handing me mine and takes no notice of any sort of history that Devon and I have. Rodney says, "Well if it isn't for the man himself, Mister Devon Chambers. Gosh I have read all your books and today you announced my event I was completely blown away!"

Devon glances at me and smiles at Rodney, "Thank you and by the way congratulations, that was some amazing moves in the ring."

Rodney says, "Thank you." He pauses and looks at the both of us and asks, "If you don't mind me asking, how do you all know each other?"

My heart just sinks. If I tell him Devon is Desiree's dad whatever this is will either get weird or come to an abrupt end. I glance at Devon and it's like he knows what I am thinking he explains, "We go back a few years. We are old friends, both with writing in common."

He looks at me then at Devon, "No way, well that is amazing. Say, Devon it was sure nice to meet you outside the arena."

"My pleasure." The two men shake hands. I glance to Devon and he takes the initiative and extends his hand to me, "Have a good night, Jordan." I look into those brown eyes of his and search for signs of hurt, something? He doesn't let me see and gives me just a smile and a nod and disappears into the crowd.

Rodney says, "Let me introduce you to my friends."

"Wait Rodney, I forgot to tell Devon something would you excuse me?" He nods and I catch up to Devon.

This time I tap his shoulder and he turns to face me. I say over the beat of the next song that is starting to play over the speakers, "Look I am sorry."

"Jordan, you don't have to apologize."

I blurt, "Yes I do. Sue set this all up and at the last minute offered to take Desiree for the night. I didn't mean for Desiree to leave without saying goodnight to you and I didn't realize that Sue was arranging this blind date."

All he does is smile and say, "It is okay, I'll catch up with my daughter when she is awake. I know that it was getting late for her and besides Sue knows you well and he seems like a decent guy. Really, go have fun. I should get home to Sara."

The next morning, I find myself back at home after a late night. I drank but I didn't get wasted and I didn't do anything more with Rodney other than enjoy the night of music and beer with him. He drove me home and I gave him a goodnight kiss. There is potential with Rodney. It's not a burning fire but only a spark right now and sparks can turn into flames.

Desiree is still with Sue and I sit on the porch steps with a coffee in hand after bringing Champ and Molly into the barn for their morning grains.

I hear the crumpling noise of tires rolling over the gravel as an SUV pulls up. It's Sue and Desiree. I wave at them as I walk over and Sue puts the vehicle in park.

I open the passenger side door. Desiree is unclipping her seat belt and I say, "Hey sweetie, how was your sleep over?"

She looks well rested and is all smiles as she replies, "Good, Sue made pancakes this morning."

"Wow did you say thank you?"

"Thank you, Sue."

Sue gets out of the car and comes around to me. I say, "Thank you Sue."

"My pleasure and you know you have stuff to tell me." She gives me a nudge.

I roll my eyes and she continues, "Oh I saw that and you know that you do."

I know that I owe it to Sue to spill but before I forget I need to tell my daughter some news. "Desiree, we have a family coming to adopt a kitten today. Could you check in on them and maybe tell the kittens that one of them is about to go to a new family who will love them just as much as we do?"

"Okay" Desiree hands me her overnight bag and skips over to the kennels. I am a little worried about her reaction later today when the family visits and she will need to say goodbye to a kitten but so far, she seems to understand.

Sue and I walk up the steps and take a seat on the porch. Sue asks, "So?"

I shrug, "He was nice."

"Oh, come on." Sue rolls her eyes.

I smirk, "He is handsome, charming, and we have similar interests. I like him."

"So, what else?"

"Sue, I didn't sleep with him."

She crosses her arms and looks down her nose at me, "That's not what I am getting at. Do you think you will see him again?"

I smile, "Yes, the night ended with an exchange in numbers and a good night kiss. Say, enough of you asking me questions. I want to know how you arranged this."

She puts her hands up and argues, "I didn't arrange anything."

"Sue!"

"Honestly, Tom and I ran into him after the metals were handed out, we got to talking and he asked about you."

"Oh, come on. I wasn't born yesterday. A hot cowboy asking about me? No way."

She pats my back, "You my dear, don't realize how much of a catch you are. I swear on our friendship, he asked about you."

"How did he ask?"

She chuckles and says, "Oh I don't know. Tom and I were chatting with him about his win and at some point, Rodney said an attractive lady with a young girl had talked to him and mentioned us and I told Rodney that he must have run into you and Desiree."

Sue says it as though it is so and I am starting to believe her because unless she was watching from a far, I didn't have the chance to tell her that I ran into Rodney outside of the arena. I reply, "You know that is right. We met briefly before I took Desiree to the midway."

She laughs and replies, "Well there you go girl. You sure get your pick of men. That Rodney is one successful man. He makes a good living doing what he does and also has loads of endorsements and investments. That man is set for life just like you girl."

I blush, "Well we will have to see how the next date goes." I change topics and ask her, "You know I ran into Devon while the live music was on."

She sighs, "I figured as much. What happened?"

I explain to her the brief awkward moment and say, "Sue, I think he was trying to flirt and have my attention and well when Rodney came back with our drinks it kind of put things into perspective for him."

"Good! Devon needs to stop playing games."

"Yes, I guess so. I just don't know with Devon. Rodney didn't even notice the weirdness because he was too star struck by Devon. Rodney reads his books so that's good but Sue I worry about Devon."

"No dear, you are holding out for Devon is what you are doing. Girl you have a new opportunity to move on and you need to be open to that. Be Devon's friend and leave it at that."

She is so right. I hate her advice but it's true. I do hold out for Devon. Hell, he is handsome, the sex is amazing and he is a great friend and with him when we first met, it wasn't a spark, it was sun fire. The only down side to Devon is that he is a bit of a flake and Sue is right. I need a man who is fully committed and no matter how open I am to starting something with Devon, he can't commit because Sara is still his moon and stars.

At least with Rodney, it's early to really say how far it will go but he shows promise.

I admit, "I was going to send a text to Devon this morning to see if he was okay."

Sue fires off a sideways glance, "Jordan, his pride may have been a little hurt last night but he is a grown man and knows that you need to be loved. Don't message him. If he wants to talk about it, he will."

"You're right."

She smiles, "When am I wrong?"

Chapter 75
Close Friends

September brings the start of school. I could have easily paid to put her into a private school but let's face it, I know that I can be a little over protective and I think a private school would shelter her even more. She needs to experience life as I have. I went to a public school back in Canada and down here in Austin, I got to visit the district school and I know that this school will be good for her.

Normally the bus would pick her up in the morning but I received a letter from the school a week before the first day of class saying that pickup would commence on the second day.

That morning I packed Desiree into my truck and drove her in. I have to cherish days like this. She was a ball of excitement, with her new clothes, backpack with her lunch and all sorts of goodies, pencil crayons, ruler, sharpener and such. It's about a fifteen-minute drive to the school and as we pull into the drop off zone, it's just a bustle of parents dropping kids off at the school yard. I park the truck off to the side a little further down the street and walk her to the school yard.

She is leading me by the hand. If I let go of her hand she would run ahead to the yard. I say to her, "I want you to listen to your teacher. Say please and thank you and be yourself. Introduce yourself to the other kids."

"Yes Mommy. If I make friends, can I invite them to ride my pony?"

"Maybe at some point but let's just focus on today, okay?"

"Okay"

As we approach the yard it gets busier with people on the sidewalk. Children are running ahead, mothers calling out to their children, laughter, screaming and plenty of hugs. The atmosphere is lively and the excitement is strong. I look down at Desiree and sometimes I think she is just like me and other times I think that she takes after her dad. Today she is taking after her dad. I was a shy child and Desiree is more outgoing and ready to make friends.

"Mommy, can I go play with the kids over there on the swings?"

"Sure, but just give me a second, I want to take a couple of pictures."

Just as I take my phone out of my purse, I hear a familiar voice and look, it's Rodney, with his son. I am the first to spot him, "Rodney?"

"Oh, hey Jordan. How are things?"

"Things are great I was just going to take some photos of Desiree before she goes along into the yard. Would you like some pictures of Jack?"

He smiles, "Sure." He says to his son, "Jack this is my friend Jordan and this here is Jordan's daughter, Desiree."

The two glance at each other and smile. I say, "Okay you two, say cheese!"

"Cheese!" I capture a few photos and give Desiree the okay to head into the yard. Jack follows her lead and accompanies her. Rodney and I are two proud parents as we watch our kids run into the yard.

I say, "I think those two will become close friends."

He jumps in, "I think their parents will become close friends."

"Oh, you are cute, you know that!" I give him a playful shove and continue, "If that is the case why did you leave this girl hanging?"

He smiles, "It's a two-way street sweetheart."

"Sweetheart, so I am your sweetheart now?"

He proceeds, "No but I want you to be my sweetheart."

Oh, he is good and I can feel my cheeks flush. We have been messaging each other these past couple of weeks as he has been doing his circuit with competing. I knew that feelings were mutual but with busy schedules him and I took a back seat for the short term and the funny thing was that with the messaging that we both did, we hadn't even realized that our children would be attending the same school.

I change subject, "So, I take it that you are done with your competitions?"

"Yes mam."

I clear my throat and answer, "I would like to be your sweetheart but you owe me something?"

He leans in, "What do I owe the pretty little lady?"

"Do you have time to go out for a coffee?"

"Yes, I do."

I smile and he actually escorts me to his truck and we head to the nearest coffee shop. I'll pick my truck up later.

Chapter 76
Divided By Two

Rodney and I are a great match and I wonder how this world forgives, because I don't think I deserve this great a person. Rodney is handsome, no, drop dead gorgeous. He is charming, we have complimenting personalities, we both are single parents with young children and we are both leading above average lifestyles but in different areas where they don't overlap. Me, in writing and him in competing, endorsements and his investments. It gives us free time during the days to build a relationship.

I could go on and on about just how great we are together but I think that you get the point. Rodney came into my life when I least expected it and eventually, we made a life together. After everything fell to pieces, I was able to move passed it all and realized that when you think that's the end, truthfully you find out that the universe has something more for you.

Devon and Sara ended up splitting for good. Since knowing Devon, Sara had broken up and had gotten back together a few times. The last time that was it. It was long overdue. Sara and Devon were just too much of opposites and with the change in lifestyle and schedules, it just stacked up and eventually they both realized that going their separate ways was for the best.

Devon assured that Sara was doing well. Even though Sara and Devon had a tough falling out with ending a long relationship they still managed to talk to one another from time to time as they had the same circle of friends.

Sara was a tuff cookie. Even when the shit hit the fan, she stood her ground and took care of herself. I know looking back on everything that she must have known something was up for a while and catching Devon and I was the confirmation of her gut feeling. From what I gather she moved back to the New York area. Her kids lived up there and at this point in her life her kids were giving her grandchildren. In a quick comment, Devon had mentioned that Sara's brother had set Sara up with one of his friends. I never followed up with Devon on if that set up became something more. The truth was that it was confirmation that Sara had moved on and even though we were at one time sharing the affections of one man, I never hated her and it came as a relief that Sara's life was bringing her happiness once more.

Devon on the other hand, the final piece to this puzzle was an entire other story, a complicated one. We know that humans right down to the core need friendship, a soul mate and as adults we are always seeking that if it is not something that we already have. Some may argue this point with me but I believe my own statement. Sure, some could argue that they are not seeking it but I disagree. I think even at a subconscious level we are and even my own statements about how I met Rodney was a prime example of the subconscious forming a relationship.

Devon, Devon, Devon as I write this, I still love him deeply but know that however badly I desire him he does not feel the same. That night at the fair it was like reality sunk in for Devon. His world was turned on its side and it was that moment where he knew that he had to let me go in that sense. Give Desiree the chance to have a full-time father not that Devon was bad. Devon never left Desiree's life or mine he just couldn't commit full time because he was divided by two families.

My heart was attaching itself to Rodney and Rodney was everything a girl could want in a man, handsome, funny and a great father to my step son and his step daughter.

Devon was a bit of a lost soul after the night at the fair and as much as Sue said not to feel guilt for the way that Devon came to see me flirting with a new man. Again and again, she would say to let it go but I had a hard time with that. I would send Devon texts every so often, wishing him well and sending the odd picture of Desiree and her pony. Eventually he came out of the slump that he was feeling and the rocky road of our relationship would smooth out. It had to for our daughter's sake.

I enjoy the comforts and privacy of my home and as time progressed into the school year eventually Rodney and my relationship blossomed into a steady state. We kept our homes separate for the time being and spent the weekends at each other's homes or going out with the kids. Sometimes we would even trailer our horses to each other's homes so that we could all ride together.

Things were good and during the week one afternoon well passed the night of the fair and well into the school year Devon stops in at my place.

There is a tap at the door, it's a tap with a pause followed by two quick taps. That is Devon's knock and I walk over to the door.

His hair is cut short, just a little longer than a buzz cut with the front flecked up and he is clean shaven he smiles at me that same exact smile the day we had first met I can't help but forget about everything and love this man. He says, "Jordan, can I come in for a moment?"

I stutter and say, "Sure, Desiree is at school right now."

He admits, "I know, that is why I came at this time."

"Devon, we can't keep doing this to ourselves."

In a calming voice he says, "I know, I came because I wanted to talk."

Relieved I say, "Sure." He leaves his shoes at the door and we head to the kitchen table, where he takes a seat and I brew some coffee.

I ask, "How are things?"

"I can't complain." I give him a glance and he feels compelled to continue, "Jordan, I'm not going to lie, seeing that you are moving on it stings. I wanted that to be me."

I hand his coffee and take a seat with him, "Devon, I was here for you. I moved here for you, made myself available, everything. I put myself on the line for you. I couldn't have made it clearer. We have a beautiful girl now from our friendship and it could have easily been more than just friends. You knew that."

He takes my hand and shakes his head, "I know, everything as it happened, it has weighed on me these years."

"It is all a thing of the past. Devon, everyone that this affected has gotten passed it. Hell, Josh is engaged now and the last mention of Sara in moving back to New York she is now dating again. You can't beat yourself up or make the situation right for all of the wrongs that have happened and then to punish yourself, me and Desiree for it. That wasn't fair."

His glossy brown eyes peer into my blue eyes, "I know." It is all he can say.

"I wished you would be mine, wished that we could make a life together. Really, I wanted that."

"But you don't anymore." Devon asks.

I say, "My heart can only handle so much. It was time for me to let go of that hope. I still love you with all my heart. You have given me so much and I want us to stay friends. I want you to keep visiting as often as you do. Desiree adores you, but the games with us needs to stop."

"Agreed"

We take a breather from the conversation. It is hard for the both of us. He looks drained and I probably look the same and eventually I say something to change subjects.

"How is your son?"

"He is good. This is his last year of University." He pauses for a moment, then says, "Jordan, I love you and I should have showed it."

"I know, and I love you too." That is what makes this hard. I squeeze his hand.

He says, "I should go."

"No, don't. Please stay a little longer." I take my hand from his and explain, "It's just that it doesn't feel right to leave it like this. Please, you came here to talk, so let's talk as good friends."

That afternoon we caught up on all sorts of things, like we were starting our friendship over again, minus the hot and heavy stuff. We talked about our writing and our publisher. Devon explained that Howard Stem had managed recently to get the major gossip columns to stop prying into his Author's personal lives. It was years too late for Devon and I but at least in moving forward that wouldn't be a problem and it completely stopped the Steven Peach's and Miss Saito's out there from causing conflict.

Devon was working on a new crime series that was set well into the future. For me I have sort of let my writing take a back seat for the moment and explained that to him and he always made me feel that I wasn't wasting my time and when an idea would come to fruition then make sure that I get those thoughts typed out.

We eventually continue the conversation outside and take a walk along the property and get to talking about our futures. We used to do that a lot before we became successful authors. What is next for me? I don't know, I now just look at one day ahead of me and try to be the best mother I can be and give Desiree the best life I can give her. I explain this to him.

Devon says, "There is nothing wrong with that. You have a great life. Know that."

"I do, what about you; besides writing a new series?"

"What next? Well, I think I am going to actually go back and get my certifications to fly helicopters."

I kick a fallen pinecone out of the way and laugh; he asks, "What is so funny?"

"Remember in one of our very first conversations, way back before everything happened? I remember you telling me that you used to fly combat helicopters and I admitted to you my dream of owning my own tropical island?"

He throws his head back and chuckles, "Oh I remember. Things were so natural back then."

I smile admitting, "We had chemistry right from the start. It is good that we reached our goals but funny at the same time how I went from wanting a tropical island and helicopter to wanting my own ranch near Austin."

He playfully grabs me and messes my hair, "That is because you adored me."

"I do." I shrug, "It was an impractical dream, really. How would I get horses to an island or start a family? Where would Desiree go to school?"

He says, "Wow, Jordan you are one of the most immature people that I know but I think that is one of the most mature things that I have ever heard you say."

I shove him, "Don't be a turd!"

"Hey, no name calling. I am just saying that's all." He chuckles.

"It sounded like a back handed compliment." I admit.

"Maybe it was." He gives me a mischievous wink.

"Then you deserved to be shoved. So, tell me more about this training?"

I can see him start to really relax after we laid out our cards on the table earlier. He is always one to carry himself well but I can see the small hints of him becoming okay with this, us, and our relationship moving forward.

"Well, it isn't far from home. The training is at the local airport and apparently a lot of veterans like me attend. So, it will be neat to do and basically get into the social aspect of it all."

"Are you going to buy your own at some point?"

"Possibly, I have thought about it but I rather do the training first and then decide after. I am not sure if I am having a mid-life crisis or what?"

We walk past the barn and I say, "Devon don't be silly, we all need something more than just writing. I think it is a great idea and hey, if you end up not selling another book, it is a great back up career."

"You are just so silly sometimes. Well, I think it will be like riding a bike, it will all come back fast."

We loop back around the horse's field and then take a walk through the empty open barn. The barn has six large box stalls however I only have a horse and a pony, and the gentle breeze that wisps through carries the scent of Champ's oats and Molly's grains and molasses mix.

I catch the faint scent of Devon's cologne and I forget everything.

I take his arm and stop him from continuing and he sees what I want and I see it in him and go for it. One more kiss, just to feel him one more time and be taken up in his arms.

Our lips touch, his smell, the warmth of his skin just as I remembered. I get my taste before he pulls back.

He whispers, "Jordan I thought we went over this?"

I sigh, "I know, it's just hard to get used to."

"It has to be this way, if we are going to succeed." He holds my face in his hands and gently rubs my cheek with his thumb for a moment before taking my hands into his. I say nothing so he continues, "We can be best friends, right?"

"Yes, you know I struggle with this. You know the feelings that I have for you."

He pulls me into a hug and says, "I know Jordan but we will be better off this way I promise."

I look into those passionate eyes of his as he wills me to believe him. It is a hard thing to grasp in knowing that someone loves you that much to be able to let you go.

It's a hard truth and wow I wish this story ended like this, "and Devon and Jordan ended up together and lived happily ever after" but that is just a smoke mirror, nothing ever plays out like that. I just know that he is right and accept his gesture and respect the man that he is for me and my daughter.

It is late afternoon when we circle back to the home and Devon stays to meet Desiree's bus. The evening is nice, just the three of us and Desiree has chatted his ear off keeping him up to date on the things in her life, her pony, school, her teacher, and she talks about how her pony is faster than Jack's pony. He puts the pieces together that, Jack is Rodney's son.

I am just in the kitchen watching them in the living room and Rodney sends me a text, "Hey girl, how's your day been?"

I text back, "Hey boy, it's been nice. The weather was good, I walked my property earlier and Devon came over to meet the bus this evening and have dinner with us." One thing that I have learned with Rodney is that I want to be honest with him and make it clear that Devon is always welcomed into my home and will remain a part of my life.

Rodney texts back, "Glad to hear that your day was good."

I ask, "Did you have a good day?"

"Whenever I talk to you it is a good day."

"Wow, you are cheesy but thank you." I send a happy face to him.

Rodney explains, "I have business in Dallas that I need to go to this weekend. The business stuff should only take a few hours and was thinking that I could bring you, Jack and Desiree. Would that sound like fun?"

"Sounds awesome Rodney, Desiree would love that, she adores Jack. Count us in."

Chapter 77
His Lighthouse

This is what the motivation and the passion of writing has gotten me to. If anyone ever told me that this was what my life was going to be like, I would have thought that they were lying.

In the end things worked out not the way that I had hope but this was a good alternative. Rodney and I created a life together and our families became one and for Devon that helicopter training proved to be good and he ended up meeting his match there.

She was a couple years older than me but still younger than Devon. A successful woman with a strong personality, she sort of reminded me of a younger version of Sara in that sense. Devon has a type. This new woman in Devon's life had finesse in that she was feminine in a male dominated profession. She is a veteran just like Devon. She served in Afghanistan and had relatable experiences as Devon had when he had served in Desert Storm. She was beautiful, smart, witty, outgoing and strong both in body and spirit. She was good for Devon she was his lighthouse. She guided him on the best path and kept him motivated.

In getting to know her, I could say she was hands down a better match than I would have ever been. When I saw the two of them together, I could tell that Devon wanted to be her everything and strived to make her happy because she made him truly happy. At one time I would have died to have her spot but this is good. Devon is happy and he needed that strong personality type in his life, which I couldn't give him. I have a soft heart. I was a lamb and he needed a lioness.

Chapter 78
The Only Thing

As I look back on this and have told you my story and sort of said my peace, I am not sure how you feel about this now that all the cards have been dealt. I mean I used to be one of those people who would judge. I would judge the failing of others marriages, blame the cheaters for the tragedy that they had caused but now, years later and after experiencing it first-hand. Devon and I were not looking for any of this. We became friends quickly and fell hard for one another. The friendship the chemistry and attraction were too hard to ignore.

We helped each other with everything and that is how it happens, we were both missing something in our own relationships, friendship, companionship whatever you want to call it and with each other we were complete.

I don't blame Josh for causing me to find companionship in Devon. The fact of being hurt over and over again with the meaningless fights and long lonely nights where I was missing Josh, the heart gets lonely and when the little bit of time that I had with Josh was only fighting, love becomes questioned and lost even.

When I was in my darkest hour was when my friend Devon came into my life, lifted me up, and made me feel like the most important thing in his world. The relationship wasn't ideal but looking back I don't regret a moment of it. He taught me how to have fun, laugh again and push my boundaries. When things got messy, as a friend he urged me to fight for my relationship with Josh, make me dig deep and try to find the love that I once had for him.

Maybe you are rolling your eyes at me and I know affairs are not right but I ask you, is feeling numb to everything else right? It was like the wrong that we created forced me to fight for Josh and I did. I focused on Josh, tried to find things to smile about and for a while it worked but a while isn't forever and sometimes two hearts just grow apart and that is okay.

Our souls lead us down a not so easy path at times and trust me, you can think rationally with your brain. I knew what was right and wrong but explain it to your heart. The thing is you can't.

I allowed myself to love with my heart and soul and this ending is not a bad one, it is a reality.

I have learned to not judge others. I can say that I have allowed myself to follow my heart and sometimes the path your soul leads you on seems completely wrong but in the end, things work themselves out in their strange and twisted ways. My story that I have told, you have learned that some of my hopes and dreams have become my reality. I have a daughter and a family. I have the lifestyle and profession that I aspired for. I am an accomplished and successful writer. The people I cared for, the hurt that I had caused was overcome with being able to move on.

Josh, Devon, Sara and I we have found happiness. Maybe it was selfish of me to be guided by my heart, but I can't go back and change what I did. I guess that I owe it all to ignoring the ideals.

So, this is it, my story, this could be just another made up bullshit tale of love and romance and being swept off my feet from the hands of my lover. You are the reader and know that this story is like many others that were told a thousand times over. Take what you will with this one, judge if you need to, it really doesn't matter and it doesn't matter if my story is truth or bullshit. The only thing that matters is being able to know when to fight and when to move on and to know that love always finds its way.

About the Author

C.R. Misty, is an accomplished author who has been enchanting readers with her captivating romance novels. Misty finds solace in both the written word and the silver screen, where she delights in witnessing tales come alive. When she's not crafting extraordinary stories, Misty channels her creativity into the vibrant strokes of a paintbrush, nurturing beautiful blooms in her garden, and embarking on thrilling adventures in unexplored destinations. Sharing her life's journey with her ruggedly handsome husband and a devoted German Shepherd fur baby, she calls Ottawa, Canada, home. You can track her progress on book retailer sites and social media.

If you enjoyed this novel, please show your support for this book by writing a review online.